The Time-Travels of the Man
Who Sold Pickles and Sweets

The Time-Travels of the Man Who Sold Pickles and Sweets

Khairy Shalaby

Translated by
Michael Cooperson

hoopoe
AN IMPRINT OF AUC PRESS

This paperback edition published in 2016 by
Hoopoe
113 Sharia Kasr el Aini, Cairo, Egypt
420 Fifth Avenue, New York, 10018
www.hoopoefiction.com

Hoopoe is an imprint of the American University in Cairo Press
www.aucpress.com

First published in hardback by the American University in Cairo Press in 2010

Exclusive distribution outside Egypt and North America by I.B.Tauris & Co Ltd.,
6 Salem Road, London, W4 2BU

Dar el Kutub No. 26105/15
ISBN 978 977 416 792 8

Dar el Kutub Cataloging-in-Publication Data

Shalaby, Khairy
    The Time-Travels of the Man Who Sold Pickles and Sweets / Khairy
    Shalaby; translated by Michael Cooperson.—Cairo: The American University
    in Cairo Press, 2016.
        p.   cm.
        ISBN 978 977 416 792 8
        1. Arabic Fiction –Translation into English
        2. Arabic Fiction
        I. Title
        892.73

1 2 3 4 5   20 19 18 17 16

Designed by Adam el-Sehemy
Printed in the United States of America

A Narration Comprising
Events to Dazzle and Astound
Meditations to Divert and Confound
Histories to Edify
And Incidents to Horrify

By the Pen of God's Neediest Creature
The Knowing but Unlearned
The Tutored but Unwise
Ibn Shalaby, the Hanafi and Egyptian
The Seller of Pickles and Sweets
May God Guard Us from His Ignorance, Amen!

1

The Caliph's Invitation

THE FATIMID CALIPH MU'IZZ HAD sent me a personal invitation to break the Ramadan fast at his table—or his dining carpet, as the invitation put it. The occasion was the first celebration of the holy month of Ramadan in Cairo, or more exactly the first Ramadan to be celebrated in a city called Cairo. Before Mu'izz, no such place had existed. The capital of Egypt had been a town called Fustat, with various extensions built by successive invaders to break with the memory of old regimes and avoid rubbing shoulders with the lower orders. Before long, settlements with names like "the Cantonments" and "the Allotments" had become towns. The towns then merged into the great city of Cairo, which before becoming the capital was simply the district where the ruling Fatimid family had settled.

I had met Mu'izz before. One of my teachers, Ibn Khallikan, had taken me to North Africa. There, in the town of Qayrawan, we visited the Islamic kingdom where Mu'izz was the caliph. I was overwhelmed by the unabashed luxury and ostentation. The mosques were full of marble pillars, and even the people seemed to have something of the marble pillar about them. A few centuries later, I happened to be in modern Cairo—the Cairo of the French and the British—and was introduced to a man named Stanley Lane-Poole, who loved the city and had written a history of the place. He looked at me searchingly and said, "We've met before, haven't we?" I was racking my brains trying to remember him when he suddenly exclaimed (in Foreignish, naturally), "Got it! It was in North Africa, at Mu'izz's court in Qayrawan."

"How about that!" I exclaimed. We embraced and set off through the old streets and alleys, stopping at the cafés to drink green tea and ginger and smoke a water pipe, and talking all the while of Mu'izz.

Lane-Poole was a wily foreign gentleman who knew all there was to know about everything. He explained to me—and if you don't agree, blame him—that the Shi'i movement had three great achievements to its credit. First, the Shi'i Qarmatian sect had taken control of the Arabian Peninsula, central Iraq, and Syria in the ninth and tenth centuries. Then the Fatimid caliphate had expanded into North Africa and Egypt. Finally, the doctrines of the Ismailis had penetrated Persia and Lebanon. The Fatimid caliphate, named after Fatima, the wife of Ali ibn Abi Talib and the daughter of the Prophet Muhammad, was the most vigorous offshoot of the Shi'i movement. In the fertile soil of the Berber regions, it had flourished. In the year AD 910, in Qayrawan, the capital of the country now called Tunisia, Fatimid missionaries found, in the person of Ubaydallah, the Mahdi or "rightly guided leader," a worthy successor to the line of Ali and Fatima. The wily foreign gentleman added that it had taken the Mahdi only two campaigns to bring all of North Africa, from Fez and Marrakesh to the borders of Egypt, under his sway. Our Mu'izz was the fourth of the Fatimid caliphs descended from the Mahdi. It was he who had conquered Egypt. He was an able, honest, and intelligent man, and a consummately clever politician.

As we sat at a café in Husayn Square eating blancmange—or milk pudding, as you might call it today—the wily foreign gentleman abruptly vanished, doubtless to avoid paying the check. I decided to track him down and chew him out: not because he'd stuck me with the check, but because he'd left without explaining how Cairo was built. When the waiter looked the other way, I popped into the alley, taking care to look like someone who was *not* skipping out on the check but only going to buy something and come back. But I was barely out of my seat before I found myself surrounded by uniformed North African soldiers.

"Strange creature!" they said. "Where do think you're going?"

"What's it to you?" I replied. "I'm walking down the alley next to the mosque to buy some cigarettes. Then I'm coming back to pay my bill at the café."

"Café?" they said. "Bill? The only thing you'll be paying is the penalty for trespassing on a building site."

I looked up. To my astonishment, we were standing on a tract of open ground enclosed by a boundary wall. Around us, other walls of solid stone formed squares, rectangles, and circles on the ground. I looked around in dismay.

"My God, where on earth am I?"

A man came forward. He was a Moroccan who looked like a wise old soothsayer. "Son," he said, "you're in the same place you were before."

Dazed, I asked, "What are those mountains, then?"

"That's Muqattam."

"What's that town over there?"

"That's Fustat and the settlements around it. And those huts over there are the village of Umm Dunayn."

"If that's Muqattam," I asked, "where's the Salah Salim Freeway? Where's the City of the Dead? Where's Darrasa? The Mosque of Husayn? Where *am* I?"

He smiled and patted me kindly on the shoulder. "Come along with me."

I followed him across what in my mind was still an alleyway. A short distance away we passed the foundation of a building, then another and another. We were approaching what looked like a camp. It extended from the slopes of the Muqattam Hills down to the area that a short time ago had been occupied by al-Azhar Mosque. The area now contained an enormous orchard with a foundation trench dug around it. Scattered all around were tents of elegant appearance, with soldiers and officials everywhere. We passed an old man with a long beard. He was carrying a reed pen, a calamus, an inkpot, and a sheaf of papers. Some of the soldiers were arguing with him, but he was standing his ground, smiling gently and pausing from time to time to write something down. I recognized him: it was Maqrizi, author of the still-famous *Topography*. Wanting to show my companion that I knew people in high places, I called out without breaking my stride, "Hey, Maqrizi! How are ya?"

He nodded to me as gently as a shining star. Despite my predicament, I had the effrontery to shout, "If you need anything, just let me know!"

He called back, "Now that you mention it, I do."

My knees went weak. What if he needed money? Or someone to take his side in the argument he was having?

But he said only, "If you have any information about this particular plot of land, dictate it to me. I've kept track of everyone who's set foot here going back as many years as I can count, but it never hurts to double-check."

I stood there smiling at him like an imbecile and let the Moroccan soothsayer drag me away.

We walked along a path lined with potted plants and armed soldiers who saluted us as we passed. It led us to a cavernous space that looked as if it were built of marble but was actually made of tent-cloth, with carpets on the ground. The Moroccan turned a corner and I followed anxiously behind him. Suddenly we were face to face with the supreme commander himself. No one had to tell us who he was; it was clear without his having to say a word. The Moroccan bowed and then pointed to me.

"On the first of Ramadan AH 358*, t his individual was apprehended sneaking onto palace grounds."

---

* See page 327 for date concordances

"Palace?" I squawked. "What palace? I swear to God there was no palace."

The supreme commander laughed, looked over at me, and sat back in his gilded chair. To my great relief he said, "I hereby issue a general amnesty and command my troops to cease and desist from any and all hostile activity, in deference to a request by the women of Egypt, who have petitioned me for mercy. So tell me, you there: what mischief have you gotten yourself into?" He smiled.

"So far so good," I thought to myself. Then, out loud, I said, "General Gohar, the Sicilian, am I right?"

He nodded. I knelt before him and said, "I beg you to forgive me if I've done anything wrong! I'm a vagabond wandering through time, and I come and go as I please."

He beckoned me to get up and then pointed me to a chair so large that I nearly disappeared into it. With a glance he dismissed the Moroccan soothsayer. He passed a hand across his short beard and rubbed his face. It was a big, round, ruddy face, resolute and proud. "In the name of God!" he pronounced. "There is no power or strength except in God, the High and Mighty One!" He fiddled with his worry beads. Then he seemed to recall my presence.

"Are you fasting?" he asked.

"Happy Ramadan!" I cried.

"If you're not a Muslim, don't be shy: ask for something to eat and drink."

"No, Mr. General," I said, as embarrassed as I could be. "I'm a monotheist and a Muslim."

"God be praised," he said in his awkward foreign accent.

A chamberlain, dragging the train of his best-grade baize gown, came in with several rolls of paper under his arm. He came up to Gohar and unrolled the papers, which turned out to be plans for palaces, minarets, gates, colonnades, and balconies. The two men promptly forgot all about me. Gohar looked over the papers, comparing the plans. Finally, he announced with a scowl, "The builders' drawings don't match the ones prepared by our master Mu'izz!"

"The differences are minor," the chamberlain replied. "These are construction plans and they need to be detailed."

In the pleading tone of someone caught outside of his sphere of professional competence, Gohar explained that he was committed to following the plans of their master Mu'izz, who had designed this city down to the last period and comma.

"We're committed, too," said the man. "The only modifications we've made are due to the nature of the site. They're only minor changes."

"With God's blessing, then!" said Gohar, taking the pen from the chamberlain and signing one of the papers. Then he spread it out, giving me a chance to take a closer look. Delighted, I exclaimed, "That's al-Azhar Mosque! It looks just like it!"

Ignoring me, he rolled it up and unrolled another, signed it, and spread it out. It was a plan for an extremely impressive and elaborate palace. Even more delighted, I cried out, "That must be the Great Eastern Palace!'

Gohar rolled up the plan and said to the chamberlain, "That will be the seat of the Fatimid caliphate." He made a gesture of thanks and the chamberlain departed, crossing paths with another chamberlain, who was not so splendidly dressed. Gohar gave him an uneasy glance.

"So, what's happened?"

With a bow, the less splendidly dressed chamberlain replied, "We've come up with a clever solution to the long-distance communication problem."

Leaning back imperiously in his seat, Gohar asked him what it was.

"The scientists and astrologers posted in the Muqattam Hills are working out the best time to start construction . . . ."

"That's what I want to know!" Gohar interrupted. "When does the work start? Have you settled on a time?"

The less splendidly dressed chamberlain continued in a thin, faltering voice, "My lord, the scientists and astronomers are still working on it."

"On what?"

"On choosing the time."

"Which will be when?"

"Whenever the astronomers determine that the ascendant is auspicious."

"And when will they do that?"

"When Constellation A gets close to Constellation B, or when Planet X enters the sign of Y: astrological mumbo-jumbo, as if I have a clue."

Gohar growled to himself, as if admitting that he had no idea either. Then he asked what the clever solution was.

The less splendidly dressed chamberlain said, "The problem is that the builders have to start building the moment the astronomers issue the order. Even a second's worth of delay might be fatal. But how to communicate the order quickly enough?"

"How?" I exclaimed, drowning out Gohar, who was asking the same question.

The less splendidly dressed chamberlain replied, "That's what we solved."

"How?"

"As you know, there are no buildings around us except the Monastery of the Bones and no vegetation except Kafur's Garden."

"Right."

Suddenly curious, I jumped up on the chair to look out the window. "No kidding! So that's Kafur's Garden, from here to Ataba . . . and it ends at the Caliph's Canal, which is Port Said Street now. So what you're calling Umm Dunayn is what I call Ezbekiya Pond!"

Gohar was now standing next to me looking out another one of the round windows. The less splendidly dressed chamberlain was pointing and explaining. "We laid stakes down in a square, twelve hundred yards on a side. Then we ran cords between the stakes and hung bells from the cords."

"Why bells?"

"When the ascendant is in the right place, the astronomers will pull the cord at their end. The bells will ring, and the workers will start working."

"What a clever idea," Gohar and I exclaimed in unison. He gestured at the window and sat down again. Breathless, I collapsed back into my seat. The less splendidly dressed chamberlain suddenly noticed me. Alarmed, he glanced around, as if searching for a broom to swat me with. I thought about jumping up to frighten him and then making a run for it, but then remembered I had a personal invitation from the caliph Mu'izz. My temper rising, I sat up in my seat, but Gohar was already saying to the chamberlain, "Don't worry about him; he's a perfectly harmless Egyptian."

"With an invitation from His Majesty the Caliph," I interrupted. "I'm breaking the Ramadan fast with him today at the palace." I started rummaging through my pockets for the invitation, but Gohar stopped me. "Calm down, calm down! The palace where you're going hasn't been built yet. You're at least four years early."

"But it's Ramadan now!"

"Break your fast with us if you want."

"No, thank you, sir," I replied. "Sorry to have been a nuisance. I'll be back in four years."

"Have it your way, then."

I was getting ready to leave when all at once the bells began rattling and ringing in a wave that spread to the horizon and rolled back like a monstrous ululation. Gohar jumped up joyfully and embraced the less splendidly dressed chamberlain. Everyone was hooting and hollering, and the sounds of hammering and digging and chanting filled the air.

"You fellow there," said Gohar to me. "You came at the time of the lucky star. By God, I'll see to it that you're well rewarded!" He invited me to sit next to him at the Ramadan meal, and to accept some gifts. I danced with delight, thrilled to have been present at the birth of my beloved city. Meanwhile, a crowd of distinguished-looking people were pouring into the forecourt and lining up to sign what must have been the guestbook. I recognized the historian Ibn Taghribirdi, the biographer Ibn Khallikan, the chronicler Ibn Abdel Hakam, Maqrizi, the historian Abdel Rahman Zaki, the Fatimid scholar Hasan Ibrahim Hasan, the architect Hassan Fathy, the novelist Naguib Mahfouz, the critic Husayn Fawzi, the architectural historian Suad Mahir, and many other friends and acquaintances, all of whom were doing their best not to look at me sitting next to Gohar the Sicilian, commander of the army of Mu'izz, at the moment the ground was broken to build the city of Cairo.

But the celebration was short-lived. All at once everyone was scowling and an angry clamor was heard outside. Hoofbeats approached and a man came in. "It's a disaster!" he cried. "A calamity! How could this happen?" He burst into tears. We stared at him, shocked at his disheveled finery.

"Chief Astrologer! What's the matter?"

"A catastrophe! The construction started at the worst possible moment!"

Gohar rose, gasping. "What?"

Sobbing, the astronomer explained that at the moment construction began, the ascendant was in a position that was not at all auspicious—quite unlucky, as a matter of fact.

"How?" said Gohar angrily.

"Mars the Conqueror was rising!"

Gohar stamped his foot. "The Conqueror? So why did you order them to start working?"

The astronomer stamped his foot too. "We didn't! We didn't lift a finger."

"So who did?"

"A crow! That's right, a stupid crow! It couldn't find anywhere in the whole world to land at that moment except on one of the stakes. Of course, he liked it there, and had to start hopping around, and set off all the bells!"

An indescribably mournful gloom settled over Gohar. His Herculean body collapsed on the throne, dead-eyed and lifeless. I started thinking about how best to sneak away. But then a delegation of scholars, somber and self-possessed, entered the room, dragging the trains of their long robes with a great show of dignity. They bowed before Gohar, who ignored them. Their leader came forward and, doing his best to play down the disaster, declared, "Whatever happened is by the will of God. Let it be! We can still be hopeful. Mars is rising, so let us call the new city Cairo, 'the victorious.'"

In a voice that sounded as if it were coming from the bottom of a well, Gohar said, "Cairo?"

"Yes. That way the bad omen might turn out to be a good one after all."

A chorus of voices rose in agreement.

"Not a bad idea!"

"A good omen after all!"

"God willing!"

Gohar asked if it wouldn't be better to stop work and wait for a better ascendant.

"That would be a bad omen in itself, my lord," the scholar explained. "The ascendant was unlucky, but tearing down what we just built wouldn't be auspicious either."

A spark of life reappeared in Gohar's eye. He gestured as if to say that he was willing to try. The sages turned back to the crowd outside, calling out to reassure them. The dignitaries pushed forward again to sign the guest book. There waiting his turn was Stanley Lane-Poole. Gohar was distracted, so I scrambled away and headed for the wily foreign gentleman.

"Caught you! Come here, you!"

I leapt into the crowd, seized Lane-Poole, and whispered in his ear, "I paid the café check!"

He smiled at me, evidently having no idea what I was talking about. Then he pulled me aside and we lost our bearings in the crowd. A moment later I came to my senses and found myself wandering around the Mosque of Husayn. It was after sunset, and I was alone. I realized I was standing amid the colonnades of the caliph's Great Eastern Palace.

2

Too Late for Everything
except the Demolition

I LOOKED AT MY WATCH and realized that my dinner with Mu'izz was one thousand and thirty-eight years away: ten and a half centuries, more or less. "No problem," I thought. "I'll take a stroll around al-Husayn and have some tea at Fishawi's." I wasn't thinking of the modern café by that name, which is nothing to write home about. To find a seat in the old version, in all its glory, all I have to do is squat against the wall. Buildings, you see, are more than buildings: they're made of layer upon age-old layer of indelible images. I, the Son of Shalaby, can choose any image and live inside it whenever I want—except, friend, when I tumble down the well of time. When that happens, only a passing vision can pull me out.

When my mint tea and water pipe arrived, I let my eyes wander along the wooden partition worked in tiny V-shaped figures. I was the only one seated in the alcove. The café was trying to sell a past that was frozen into remnants of decoration and some old chairs. I slid my chair to a spot next to the door with a good view to the outside. I could see half-naked tourists carrying maps and cameras; Nazira sitting on the ancient couch where she was telling a little girl's fortune from her coffee grounds, as she seemed to have been doing for a thousand years; men selling semolina rolls, paint, electric fans, and imports from America and Japan; and the Safiri beggars. The Safiris were named after their patriarch, Safar, who reportedly came here as a soldier in the armies of someone-or-other and settled down to father a passel of children who did not believe in putting themselves to the trouble of working. Their great-grandfather was supposedly the first to take up begging as a profession and make a living at it. Looking at them, it struck me that the ones offering their goods and services were beggars too. Meanwhile, my ears were under assault from three adjoining music stores. Each was playing a different tape and trying to attract customers by drowning the others out. Suddenly I didn't want to be in Fishawi's any more: I was tired of being harassed by people who wanted to beg from me or sell me something. Slouching past the shops full of gold bangles, souvenirs, and trinkets, I submerged myself in the flood of wide-eyed tourists, feeling that I was, if not a work of art, then certainly a piece of work; and that one of them might be tricked into buying me.

Suddenly the crowd grew thicker, pressing shoulder to shoulder and bearing me down. I shrieked like a woman but no one responded. Trampled mercilessly underfoot, I hit and bit at people's shins, clearing a space big enough to wiggle through to a less crowded spot where I managed to get to my feet and start moving again through the seething masses of people. I was stunned: when I had fallen down, no one had paid the slightest attention. Had things gotten that bad?

Then I noticed that everyone was dressed in the clothing of another age. Around me was a carnival of pantaloons, Mamluk turbans, Egyptian gallabiyas, and Moroccan abayas.

Pulled along by the throng, I stumbled into a vast courtyard between two palaces grander than any I had seen before. "This must be the famous square between the palaces," I thought. "The one I'm walking next to now is the Great Eastern Palace; and the Lesser Western Palace is the one on the other side of the square. But what are all these people doing here?"

Transformed into a marketplace, the square was swarming with commoners and vendors of all kinds, sitting in front of their displays of meat, pastries, and fruit. Though it was night, the torches and oil lamps made it seem broad daylight. To judge by the goods for sale, it was Ramadan. So much was clear, too, from the festive cheer, which lit up people's faces despite the choking crowds that threw men together with donkeys and grandees with muleteers. Spotting a circle walled off by bodies and chairs and benches, I made my way over and saw a poet playing a rebec and reciting the adventures of some hero: Antar, perhaps, or Abu Zayd. In another circle, young men performed acrobatic tricks to the laughter and applause of the spectators. I noticed that people were gawking at me because of my suit and tie and Samsonite briefcase. Seeing someone who looked as bewildered as I was, I stopped him and asked, "Brother, why are people lining up here? Is this a wedding or a funeral?"

"That's what I'd like to know, too."

"Who are you?"

"Muhibb al-Din Ahmad, son of the Chief Judge, Imad al-Din Ahmad al-Karaki, just arrived from Karak."

"What year is this?"

"792."

I had ended up in the wrong time. I walked away, wondering how to get back to where I had come from. But the crowd pulled me along, this time to a festive tent full of watermelons and a throng as big as any in late-twentieth-century Egypt. Sitting nearby was Maqrizi. I thought he might be waiting for a watermelon to take home to his family, but he turned out to be questioning a boy who looked like a vagrant. I asked what he wanted from him.

"He and one of his friends work in the stables," said Maqrizi. "On this blessed Ramadan night, they stole some twenty watermelons and approximately thirty wedges of cheese."

"Do the melons and cheese belong to you?"

"No, I'm only asking him how he did the deed, so I can write it down."

"You," I said, "are a truly great man."

He looked at me suspiciously. "Didn't I see you being arrested by Gohar's troops?"

I admitted it.

"So what do you want, exactly?"

"I have an invitation to break the fast with Mu'izz, the Fatimid caliph."

"On the occasion of what?"

"The first Ramadan to be celebrated in Cairo."

"Go back the way you came," he said. "At the moment, you're walking along a line between the two palaces. The Fatimid caliphate has fallen to the Ayyubids, and the square's been thrown open to the public, as you can see."

He must have realized that I was a person of some importance, especially after I balanced my Samsonite briefcase on my knee and opened it with an impressive click. I brandished the gold-engraved invitation card from Mu'izz, thinking that even if the visit didn't work and I found myself busted flat I could sell the gilt to a goldsmith. That's why I kept it at arm's length and why my hand trembled when Maqrizi reached for it, hoping to read it: the card itself was so splendid that I should be able to pawn it for cash if I had to.

Maqrizi smiled. "Where were you before you came here?"

"I was coming from the Mosque of Husayn, going through the gate on the other side past the souvenir shops toward Mu'izz Street. The next thing I knew, I was here."

"Good enough," he said. "See that big gate?"

"Yes."

"That's the Daylam Gate. It overlooks the courtyard called Bashtak Palace Square. If you walk through the courtyard, away from the Storehouse of Banners, you'll end up at Husayn. It's actually right behind you, but there are a good many years in between. From the Daylam Gate you can go through to the Saffron Cemetery Gate, which is the burial ground for the caliphs and their families. By the way, the

Saffron Cemetery is going to be the site of the Caravanserai of al-Khalili. Have you heard of it?"

"I've never seen the caravanserai, but in my time Khan al-Khalili is world-famous."

He nodded and then said as if it were only a day between, "All that's left is the name. One more for Egypt to remember!" He continued, "Anyway, between the Daylam Gate and the Saffron Cemetery Gate are the seven passages the Caliph uses on the bonfire nights to reach the observation tower on al-Azhar Mosque, where he and his family sit and watch the fires and the crowds. You can go through the Saffron Cemetery Gate to Reeky Gate."

"Where's that?" I exclaimed.

He pointed to a grand old gate and said, "That's it."

"The gateway's still there in my time, too! I'll stand in front of it and hold on—maybe it'll pull me from the bottom of time up to the surface. From there I can come back down the well the right way."

Smiling, Maqrizi asked if I was invited to break the fast. When I said I was, he asked me if I knew what "Reeky Gate" meant. I said I didn't.

"It means 'Kitchen Gate,'" he said. I looked toward it longingly. Maqrizi tugged at me gently and sat me down at his side. Then he pulled out a pocket-knife—not a switchblade, which would have been illegal—with a handle elegantly decorated with Quranic verses and radiant Islamic designs. He rolled one of the watermelons over, tapped on it like an expert, stuck the knife into it and cut twice, then drew out an enormous slice and offered it to me with the suggestion that it would cool me down. I buried my whole face in it, indifferent to the mess it would make of my suit, tie, and shirt collar. As he sedately carved out a piece for himself, Maqrizi asked, "Don't they have watermelon in your time?"

"No, by God," I said, "only something like it, that goes by the same name."

"May God rest the soul of Ibn Arabi, who wrote: 'When Jupiter enters Gemini, food becomes dear in Egypt. The rich become few and the poor many, and death takes from them its tithe.'"

"So when does Jupiter enter Gemini?" I asked.

"Every thirty solar years," he said. "It stays there about thirty months."

"Ibn Arabi was right about some things," I said, "but the more poor people there are, the more rich people too—and the higher their property values."

"In that case," said Maqrizi, "Cairo's sign of Ares must still be ascendant."

"It's almost time," I said, "for me to meet Mu'izz!"

"I happen to know that Mu'izz arrived here at his palace on the seventh of Ramadan, AH 362."

"Now I can get there with no trouble," I said, writing the date in my appointment book. "I'll just take the direct bus."

I bid him farewell. Embarrassed at the condition of my suit, I tried cleaning it off with a handkerchief, but discovered that all the dust in Cairo had come off my face onto the cloth. Laying it on my wrist, I folded it over to get the clean side up; but every time I did, I would start sweating again and have to wipe my face, which dirtied the handkerchief all over again. The prospect of facing Mu'izz's guards in that condition was a depressing one. I might even be arrested and interrogated by the police, with unpleasant consequences. Leaning against the Reeky Gate, I ran a hand over it. It stood firm and strong: not a relic yet. People were staring at me, some suspicious, others amused.

"He must be a Crusader," said a young donkey-driver.

"Fool!" said a tripe-seller pushing his cart. "He's a Turk."

A peddler girl joined in: "No, he's a Daylami!"

Poking at her with his staff, an old man launched into a rant: "Turks, Daylamis, Zuwayla, Franks, Persians: there's no way to know where anyone's from anymore!"

The peddler girl stopped in the middle of the crowd and turned to face the old man—and me, too. She was beautiful: a product of Turkish, French, Greek, Persian, Caucasian, or Ethiopian blood, or most likely of all of them together, and a descendant of one of the former palace slave women and an emir, perhaps. Looking me over, she pronounced with formidable authority, "Poor thing! He must have been captured by slave-traders centuries ago and wandered off on his own. Are you still lost, sweetie? Don't worry, someone here will give you a place to sleep and bread to eat. What a city: cruel and tender all at once! This jinx of an old man thinks I'm an ignorant girl or a common whore, but he should know that I'm a lady of the day, not only of the night; and I can read and write, too. All those kings and emperors started out as slaves, but they fought and plot and schemed until they came to power—and turned into bloodsuckers!"

The old man curled his lower lip in distaste, brandished his stick, and said, "Get away from me, you she-devil! Go back to your house in Dar al-Ratli, or wherever the hell you live."

With a sprightly bow, she said, "All of Cairo is my home. You spend the night in any one of a hundred open mosques, but I spend the night in the hundreds of eyes enchanted by my beauty and the hundreds of hearts moved by my plight. My plight is theirs and theirs is mine; and how pretty a plight I have!"

She turned, making the light sparkle on her costly frock, and disappeared into the crowd. The old man shook me, saying, "My name . . . my name is . . ." When he saw that I was paying no attention to him, he shook the stick in my face and walked away, muttering to himself. When he vanished, he seemed to have given the whole scene permission to vanish as well. For an instant, I could see nothing, though my head was filled with the echoes of sweet voices softly chanting songs of Spain.

When I opened my eyes, I found myself leaning against Reeky Gate, which was now a ruin. The map of the reality I knew was popping into being bit by bit in front of me. Soon enough I found the bend in the alley that led to the Mosque of Husayn, a few steps away.

Cursing my heavy briefcase, I staggered across the square. I bumped into Ibrahim Mansur, who, walking with his cane, was pointing out the sights to two foreign scholars, giving a commentary that itself required a commentary. I hoped to dodge him, afraid that he would ask me—right in front of the foreigners—to pay him back five pounds I didn't want to return because he had forced me to borrow it at a time when I didn't need it. Fortunately, I spotted Abdel Rahman al-Sharqawi—in shirt, trousers, and flip-flops—hurrying toward the mosque with his prayer beads. Nervous about the five pounds, I started after him, but Ibrahim hooked me with his cane and stopped me in my tracks. He then launched into a speech of significant length, accompanied by frenzied gestures, and sputtering in his earnest effort to convey the point that he had discovered the finest and most charming of authentic Egyptian coffee-houses, located "right here," as he put it, pointing in the direction of nothing in particular.

"Where is it, exactly?" I asked. "Just so I know how far it is."

He told me it was in Atuf, and I told him that was a fine place for it to be. Atuf was a district next to Gamaliya. Originally the home of the palace servants, it had been named after their chief.

"I know how to get into the palace through the servants' door," I said to Ibrahim.

"So you've found your rightful place after all!" he said, and then translated his witticism for the foreigners, who laughed. I did not, perhaps because the remark had struck too close to home. But I did decide to keep back a bit of news I had been meaning to share with him: that he had been named a biographer of Cairo from the moment he had begun working on a book about Naguib Mahfouz and set out to explore the places where the writer had grown up.

We plunged into the alleys of Atuf. It turned out that Ibrahim already knew the news I had decided to keep from him. It also turned out that the two foreigners knew more than the two of us put together. The new houses complemented the old ones wonderfully, even if the old ones looked like authentic originals and the new constructions like ivy climbing the sides of ancient trees.

We had just passed a narrow street leading to the Bayt al-Qadi district when Ibrahim suddenly fell behind. Catching up with us a moment later, he claimed to have been caught off guard by the sight of Naguib Mahfouz sitting at a café and smoking a water pipe amid a crowd of master poultry-sellers, butchers, and other dignitaries. The gathering would certainly be well supplied with good jokes and good tobacco. In any case, said Ibrahim, he should certainly excuse himself long enough to greet him because it would be rude to pretend not to have seen him. He vanished down the narrow street, tapping with his cane like an errant warrior. I was left alone with the two foreigners, who looked at me, hoping in vain that I would say something. I was rescued by Ibn Abdel Zahir, the friend of an important Western historian who will be introduced to you later.

"Hello, Abdel Zahir!"

"Hello, Ibn Shalaby! How's it going?"

I told him I was fine, and he swore that wild horses couldn't stop him from treating me to a water pipe filled with cinnamon tobacco. I replied that since he had sworn an oath, I had better accept. Oh yes: would the foreigners like to come along? They declined politely, and so I made my escape.

I let Ibn Abdel Zahir lead the way, and suddenly we found ourselves in one of the most beautiful districts in Cairo. It was full of great mansions, bathhouses, markets, and mosques beyond counting. All of the locals were dark-complexioned and had something grand and proud about them; even the people in the street seemed to exude a quiet self-satisfaction. Ibn Abdel Zahir explained that all of them were relatives of Atuf.

"Who exactly is this Atuf?" I asked.

"A palace servant, and the attendant of Tawila, called Sitt al-Mulk, the sister of the caliph Hakim, the grandson of Mu'izz."

Ibn Abdel Zahir gestured for me to look up. Spilling out of a particularly distinguished-looking passageway into the street was a great procession of guards and attendants. Like a cat digging its claws into a wall, I climbed to the top of a lovely mashrabiya window. From there I could see a short, dark-skinned man who must have been a pasha, or something even higher, dressed in a brocade gown that scattered points of lim-pid light, preceded by a cloud of perfumed air, and walking with great deliberation. A crowd of relatives and passers-by smiled at him proudly, some even turning their heads and bowing as he passed. Following a signal from Ibn Abdel Zahir, I climbed down and we set off in the wake of the black pasha.

"That's Atuf," he said. "He's heading for the palace."

We stayed close behind him. I felt a surge of other eras close to our own, and was astonished to find that the present aura of old age was distinct even in the shadow of that far greater antiquity. We passed through an enormous gateway and I asked Ibn Abdel Zahir what it was called.

"The Gate of the Roofed Passage," he intoned. "On the Days of Immolation and the Festival of Ghadir Khumm, it is the custom to slaughter animals here and distribute the meat to the poor. In the year 516, the caliph Amer slaugh-tered 1,746 animals here and at the Manhar in just three days. Through this gate, twelve she-camels, eighteen head of cattle, fifteen water buffaloes, and one thousand and eight rams are taken in to feed the palace, the vizierate, the officials, and the attendants, and every day the offal of the camels and goats is given away in charity."

I told Abdel Zahir that the stench of the time that clung to me, or that I had brought with me, was coming to the sur-face; I could already catch the smell of Khurunfish. He told me that the Western Palace extended to where Khurunfish would be. Then he looked at a compass he had taken out of the palm-leaf basket he carried on his back. I asked him what time it was.

"It's Sunday evening, the eleventh of Safar, 401."

At that moment we crossed a passage paved in good-quality genuine marble, lined with banana trees, henna, and other plants I couldn't name. Alabaster walls, some high, some low, were half-submerged in flowering branches suffused by sunbeams and a silvery glow. The trees stretched as far as the eye could see, their numberless branches concealing palaces, some close together, others set apart.

"What is this place?" I asked. "Paradise?"

"Have you forgotten," he answered, his voice sounding far away, "that the Lesser Western Palace includes Kafur's Garden?"

"But I'm trying to get to the Great Eastern Palace," I said. "I'm invited to break the fast with the Fatimid caliph!"

Ibn Abdel Zahir promised he would take me there after we visited Sitt al-Mulk on a piece of important business. This palace, he said, had been built by Nizar, that is, the caliph Aziz, the father of Hakim, for his daughter Sitt al-Mulk, Hakim's oldest sister.

Suddenly Ibn Abdel Zahir's voice disappeared. I looked around, but he was gone. Afraid to call to him and draw attention to myself, I began flailing blindly around the palace garden, or the garden palace. From out of nowhere came a burst of laughter and I shuddered in terror. Then I realized that I was passing a balcony that overlooked a fountain. In the fountain were marble figures of animals shooting jets of water into a vast basin of colored alabaster. Peering down from the balcony was a bouquet of pretty faces, standing like roses piled together, stems out of sight. One of them suddenly appeared in front of me and asked with a gentle smile, "Are you a qasri like us?"

"What's a qasri?" I asked.

"A palace servant."

"Yes," I said. "I'm the new eunuch."

She laughed, as did her companions on the balcony.

"Who are all of you?" I asked.

"We're the slaves of Sitt al-Mulk. There are eight thousand of us!"

I gasped. Then she did too, before bolting in terror, crying, "It's Hakim . . . he's here!"

I dropped to the ground and started crawling like a snake flushed out of hiding. Picking a spot on the basin wall that would camouflage me, I hid in the shadows and then looked around for Hakim. He was coming out of a doorway that matched the design of the rest of the place but looked like the mouth of a cavern. I committed its location and its appearance to memory. The Caliph had barely reached the entrance of the right wing of the palace when Atuf appeared, greeting him with a majestic bow. Hakim raised his finger in an equally majestic gesture of dismissal. Atuf stepped aside but then set off after him. Hakim stopped abruptly, turned around, and looked at him, with a forced smile that looked like another gesture of dismissal. Atuf made an exaggerated gesture of deference to the Caliph's orders, but then, with a glum expression on his face, continued to march along behind him. Again Hakim stopped, stamping his foot in exasperation. This time Atuf backed off.

I, meanwhile, had seized the opportunity to jump up on the wall that ran alongside the Caliph's path, flitting along like a phantom from the future. I followed the wall until I reached a set of marble steps that led up to a part of the grounds where the twittering of sparrows and the strains of languid music wafted through the air. The walls were concealed by velvet drapes and the figures of guardsmen were visible between the drapes and along the sides of the court.

Hakim walked up to an enclosure in the center and cleared his throat. A blinding light appeared in the doorway and with it Sitt al-Mulk, who stepped toward us with the grace of a gazelle and a great air of nobility. She greeted Hakim with a smile as bright as the world and he nodded to her in a majestic gesture of esteem. I realized that he was performing a daily ritual and that he and Sitt al-Mulk enjoyed a relationship of particular affection. When he turned to leave, I was able to get a good look at him. He had piercing blue eyes and a long, sharp-featured face that bore an expression of cruelty. He walked on and then disappeared into a secret door I could not see clearly.

Going back the way I had come, I found myself in the anteroom of the palace, face to face with the servant—that is, the black pasha, Atuf. He was walking toward Kafur's Garden when men armed with swords emerged from the crowds of qasriya—that is, the ranks of palace servants. They surrounded him and raised their weapons, stopping him in his tracks. Then one of them stepped forward and beheaded him. Another picked up the head and wrapped it in a black cloth. Two others lifted the corpse and carried it out of sight. Then the whole group disappeared.

Breathless, I ran alongside the walls like a shaft of light from a closing window. The garden was filling up with thousands of stars that shone only there. Using them as a guide, I found my way back to the doorway that looked like the mouth of a cavern. From the outside it looked dark, but when I went through it I found the interior lit by dozens of chandeliers and the walls adorned with flowerpots. Beyond the door was a long, crowded passageway, supplied with fresh air that made it feel as breezy as the seaside in Alexandria. This, I realized, was the tunnel that connected the two palaces. Here the caliph would walk or ride whenever he felt like visiting the Caliph's Canal—which, in our time, is Port Said Street.

The tunnel felt so safe and enchanting that I didn't want it to end, but, like all good things, it did, and there I was, deep inside the Great Eastern Palace. As soon as I stuck my head through the doorway an alarm bell rang and the sound of boots filled the air. But the tunnel had infused me with a force of character that enabled me to face the soldiers with majestic equanimity. I pointed at the one who seemed to be in charge and ordered him to clear his men from my path. Then, in a tone that implied I already know the answer, I asked him what was going on.

"Sir, we've got an emergency situation here. We've got all the palaces under control, and now we're making an inventory of everything: furniture, clothing, money, jewels, precious objects, and slaves, male and female."

Annoyed, I thought to myself: "O Lord! Here I meant to attend the opening of the palace, and instead I'm here for the demolition!"

In a tone as disapproving as I could make it, I asked the officer, "Who are all of you?"

Dubiously he replied, "We serve our master, the Sultan Saladin. His orders are to confiscate everything in the palaces and evict the Fatimid family."

"Hmm, yes, Saladin," I said, nodding. "So I wasn't so far off: this is the coming of the Ayyubid dynasty!"

He nodded back. I smiled at him, saying, "It's the Ayyubids I want, so make way!"

He stepped back smartly but asked, "Who might you be, sir?"

Turning back slightly, I said, "I'm with the inventory team."

He bowed almost to the ground, then caught up with me, whispering as if we were old friends, "If it's not too much trouble, sir, could you save me something, even just a ring with a gemstone in it, as a souvenir?"

"Sure, no problem," I told him. "Anything you like. I'll do my best!"

3

Dying of Hunger at the Golden Gate

I HAD IMAGINED THAT THE palace consisted of one palace but it turned out to consist of several, and so I found myself in a giant maze. The friends who called it "the luminous palace complex of Mu'izz" had not been exaggerating. I passed a slouching Ayyubid soldier who gave a deferential bow when he saw me coming and called out, "This way, sir!"

I nearly turned on him to ask who had told him to call me "sir," but in the end simply went the way he was pointing. Ahead of me was a gate still visible only from the side. When the path curved around, I realized that it was big enough to be the Gate of the Sun, or the Gates of Hell, or perhaps only a gate built of golden spikes of grain melted all together. At first it looked only a stone's throw away, but I soon realized that an airplane's throw was more like it. With all the walking I was doing, I should have been getting closer all the time, but no new details came into view to confirm that I was making progress. Clearly, the earth was stretching under me as I walked. The road was as long as eternity, and it was filled— like all Egyptian roads—with potholes, bumps, manholes, and sewers, not to mention dust, animal droppings, and the like. Even on your way to the luminous palaces of Mu'izz, where the ground is covered with a verdant carpet of grass and rare plant species, the flower gardens along the path of time (or times past) tend to transform themselves—not that it's anything to boast about—into an Egyptian roadway full of holes.

Strange indeed were the potholes in that road of time. I stumbled slightly, and the distant gate seemed to drop noticeably against the horizon. At the same moment there emerged a laughing head, one I recognized as belonging to my friend Ibn Abdel Zahir. "Hey there, big guy!" he said. "Think you can get away from me so easily?"

"Unbelievable!" I said. "Is that really you?"

"The judge, scholar, and secretary Muhyi al-Din Abd Allah ibn Abdel Zahir Rawhi at your service."

Relieved, I asked him why he had run off and left me in the Lesser Western Palace.

"I didn't go anywhere," he said. "You're in such a hurry that when you try to walk you go flying off. Don't you see that it was you who ran from me? Time, my friend, is like space. It's full of colonnades and gates and windows and enormous gaps—and gaps in time are much more frightening than the ones in space. A void in space may be big, but a void in time is pure nothingness—a vacuum, a drought, dead air—because nothing happens there and nothing's ever been built."

I couldn't tell if he was rising up out of the path or if the path was bringing me down to him, but he was becoming more visible by the moment. The gate still dyed the air with the color of late afternoon. Pointing at it, I asked Abdel Zahir if it was the Gate of the Sun or the Gate of Grain. Smiling, he replied that the one came from the other, but that this was the Golden Gate, leading to the Greater Eastern Palace, the seat of the Fatimid caliphate: "It's the main entrance of the palace, the one used by soldiers and officials." Then he set off limping, leaning on his stick, and coughing into a large and elegant handkerchief. Apologetically, he explained that the smell of smoke was making him choke. As I couldn't smell anything except the cigarette smoke that clung to my own chest and lungs, I asked him what he was talking about. "It's the smoke from a period of time not too far off," he said, "a place like a little town, where the Egyptian habit of smoking different herbs and spices first began."

"Let's move away, then."

I pulled him back a little, but then, quickly as a ghost, he vanished.

When I reached the portal they called the Golden Gate, it turned out to be nothing more than a gate, but an elegant one, with the handiwork of the craftsmen and painters still clearly visible on the façade. A caravan of camels loaded down with handmills was coming from Umm Dunayn through Kafur's Gardens toward the Great Palace. Columns of North African soldiers stretched as far as the eye could see. There at the head of his legion I could make out Gohar the Sicilian. He was kissing the ground before a man who seemed to have appeared out of nowhere. Whether the man was on foot or on horseback I could not tell, but he was surrounded by a ring of white flags and wrapped in an aura of awe-inspiring dignity. I saw him smile gratefully and say something I couldn't make out. Accosting two soldiers who were coming toward me hand in hand, I put on a friendly face and asked what was going on. They waved me off rudely but I understood enough to realize that the Fatimid caliph Mu'izz had just arrived in Egypt and was seeing, for the first time, the palace that his general Gohar had built for him.

"This is my chance," I thought. "I've finally come at the right time. The Caliph is here and I can go say hello to him and introduce myself. No doubt he'll be thrilled."

I started looking for a way to slip through the columns of soldiers but their ranks were so tight that I could hardly stop myself from being pushed off the stage altogether. All the while, Mu'izz kept gazing at al-Azhar Mosque, which, freed of its scaffolding only moments before, glowed in the sunlight like a great murex—even if Ibn Shalaby has never seen a murex, and isn't sure exactly what it might be.

After taking a good long look at al-Azhar, Mu'izz gestured toward the caravan. There were almost five hundred camels laden with querns and he ordered them all to kneel.

Boys scrambled up, untied the ropes that held the querns, and pulled them open, releasing a stream of some golden substance that flowed like a liquid.

"What," I exclaimed in a frenzy, "in the name of God and the family of the Prophet, is that?"

A Moroccan soldier leaned back and surveyed me over his shoulder. "It's gold. Never heard of it before?"

"Holy cow! They pour gold out on the threshold like cement?"

The Moroccan grinned at me again and made a menacing gesture to warn me off before the guards got a hold of me. But instead of leaving, I tried to get closer to the great gate and catch up with Mu'izz and his retinue. Just then I noticed that the gate had grown two golden pillars, a floor, a threshold, and a gold-trimmed ceiling. The appearance of it attracted me powerfully. Everything else disappeared from the scene. I wanted to gaze at it and gorge myself on the sight. I picked up my pace, first loping, then running toward it, as if drawn irresistibly toward its splendor. But the closer I thought I was getting, the more details I noticed that made it look as distant as ever.

As I pressed forward, the square between the palaces grew clearer. There were people shambling and shuffling along. I saw men of respectable appearance sniffing at the ground, bending over to pick something up, tossing whatever it was into their mouths, and chewing at it, looking weary and disgusted. I saw women hugging small children to their breasts, and a boy scraping away at a piece of clay.

"Lord," I thought, "what's this?" Then I looked at my watch and realized that I had entered the time of the caliph Mustansir. This was a discouraging development, but I summoned the strength to face it. Evidently, I was going to witness the hard times of his reign with my own eyes.

"Now what?" Darkness was spreading and from all directions came a stream of phantoms. Swarming into the palace precincts, they stopped in front of the Golden Gate, and there they set upon one another grabbing whatever they could steal. One would pounce savagely on another only to be set upon in turn. Body after naked body fell to the ground, some moaning and others mute. Some of the figures were using metal files to cut away pieces from the threshold or one of the columns. All were armed in the manner of the Caliph's troops; they must have been palace guardsmen.

Then the darkness receded slightly and the column of light grew stronger. The phantoms, now clearly wearing guardsmen's uniforms, were placing the dead men under arrest and taking them away for questioning. From the minaret of al-Azhar Mosque came the call to dawn prayer, which rang out and then died away into embarrassed silence like a borrowed voice. The light dimmed, then grew stronger as it slipped the stranglehold of night. A mournful Mustansir, surrounded by guards and preceded by cries of "in the name of God!" came forward and stopped by the gate. Turning to someone who was standing directly behind him, he said, "They're fighting the guards to reach the gate! Let them file off whatever they want—but only a small piece, so there's enough to go around."

The chief of the guards bowed and the Caliph marched on. His party vanished. Bright sunlight flooded the square, which was now filling up with people carrying rasps and files of all sizes. Throwing themselves at the Golden Gate, they set to filing and chopping. Behind them came others carrying bigger, sturdier tools. Shoving their way to the front, they climbed over each other's shoulders and scrambled like acrobats to the top of the pillar to hack away at the gold. Then a third wave charged the gate like demons. For tools, this group had brought anything with a blade, and instead of attacking the gate they slashed at the people in front of them. A frenzied roaring and shrieking filled the air, and the color of blood mixed with the color of the gold glowing in the sun. The façade of the gateway was beginning to look like the face of a bride whose tears have ruined her makeup. Then an alarm sounded and troops of guards swarmed in from all directions. A voice calling out in the name of the Caliph proclaimed that "enough was enough already" and ordered the rest of the gold carried into the palace. The scene began to fade.

I pressed forward again, impelled this time by pity. Straight ahead of me before, the gate was now off to one side, but I had no problem turning to face it. To my surprise, an enormous crowd of respectable-looking people, now evidently fallen on hard times, had appeared in front of me. Surrounded by guardsmen, they stood beaten and cowed, but with a certain dull indifference in their eyes, like hardened criminals in the dock. I crept up close enough to see the tears on their faces and the silent pain in their eyes. Chewing on my lip, I tried to guess what atrocity they had committed. As I circled around them, I conceived the idea that they were a group of tourists from some distant continent who were standing there waiting for their tour bus. Going up to one, I whispered in his ear: "Got any baksheesh?"

He looked at me and smiled. Going up to another, I noticed that for no apparent reason they were divided into two groups, with the women on one side and the men on the other. I approached a lady whose features occupied the midpoint between refinement and vulgarity, with the refinement making her seem vulgar and therefore more attractive. I asked her, "Got any baksheesh?"

She stared me down with a look whose vulgarity encouraged me to continue even as its refinement warned me not to. I tried another woman, this time making an effort to look serious. This one was half old and half young. The moment she saw me coming toward her, she opened an expensive leather wallet studded with gold and diamonds, took out a golden piaster coin, and pressed it into my hand. Seeing a chance to make a killing, I shouted at her, "Peasant dresses! Silver! Khan al-Khalili! Palace Walk! Mosque of Qalawun! Azhar! Expert tour guide at your service!"

The old woman kept smiling at me sweetly, and asked with genuine interest what I was talking about. I declared again that I was a tour guide and I could take the group to see Khan al-Khalili and Ghuriya and all the rest. "What does 'Khan al-Khalili' mean?" she asked.

"Three or floor stories up in time," I said, "is a neighborhood called the Khan of Khalili, which was originally an inn built by a man called Khalili. Next to it is Ghuriya, on top of this spot here."

The old lady shook her head in despair and heaved a sigh. Then she began to show signs of a creeping panic. Meanwhile, I had been counting the people in the group. There were one hundred and thirty-five of them, plus seventy-five children. "What are all of you *doing* here?" I wondered.

The panic spread through the crowd. In the distance, where a tent had been hastily pitched, I saw a man wearing a military uniform festooned with countless medals and decorations. He was tall, fat, and big-shouldered, but his face was lean and stern and stretched as tight as the skin on a drum. Behind him were troops of soldiers marching in descending order of rank.

An older child, trembling in terror, whispered, "The yew-nick!"

The panic spread to the other children, who began trembling and weeping, their faces twisted in pain and their eyes filling with tears. I approached the weeping child. He looked like a little emir who thought he was still an emir. "Why are you crying, little guy?" I asked him. "Just stop, okay? What's the matter?"

With a pretty finger, he pointed up, "The eunuch is going to kill us."

"Eunuch who?"

"Don't you know who the eunuch is? Baha al-Din Qaraqush. Haven't you heard of him?"

Trying to stop my knees from knocking, I whimpered, "Qaraqush, you say?"

"Yes, that's him. Haven't you ever seen him before?"

Gaping, I asked, "*That's* Qaraqush?"

"What do you mean?" asked the boy. "You've *never* seen him before?"

"Just once."

"Where?"

"At the Rihani Theater," I said.

The boy looked at me in puzzlement, but I cut him off with a question, "But who are you all, exactly?"

With innocent self-assurance, he replied that they were members of the family of Adid and that the eunuch was carrying out the orders of Saladin.

"Don't worry, son!" I said. "The eunuch is a good guy, really, with a good heart."

I looked at my watch. I had traveled to Ashura, 567.

With rising indignation, I wondered how Qaraqush could be cruel enough to force these people to live in a tent city, like rabble.

Feeling only half courageous, I pushed my way into the palace. All at once I found myself face to face with none other than Qaraqush himself. Marching along with a crisp regimental gait, he spotted me and assumed an expression of arrogant contempt, as if all he needed to do to crush me was to thrust out a foot. So I put on my own expression of arrogant contempt—the one I had picked up from the pictures of American politicians I saw in the papers every day. With my left hand in my pocket and my right brandishing the Samsonite briefcase, I addressed him as if he were nobody and I the celebrity. "Excuse me! Where can I find the eunuch Baha al-Din Qaraqush?"

He stopped with a jolt. To be honest, I thought he was going to fall over. Something about the way I sounded or the way I looked must have frightened him. Whatever the reason, he answered in a deferential tone. "That's me, sir."

Switching the briefcase to my left hand, I stuck out my right and said in a friendly bellow, "Hi there, eunuch! How's it going? Long time no see! It seems like forever since I saw them play you at the Rihani Theater."

His hand trembled so hard in mine that I thought his whole body would start shaking too. I released his hand and asked him sharply, "How can you treat those people that way, eunuch?"

"They're Shi'a!" he replied. "They brought it on themselves."

"But why separate the men from the women?"

"So they can't reproduce. That way they'll die out more quickly!"

"Marvelous," I said. "The genius of the exterminator!"

"So where is my lord from?" he asked.

"Your lord is from a time that will see you without understanding you—a time that loves to hate you and greets you in the hope of wiping you out!"

"You're speaking in riddles, you—that is, my lord," he said, catching himself.

"In the time I come from," I told him, "people will see you as a strong man and a force for justice, even if it's a dimwitted sort of justice. But they won't remember you the way you dream of being remembered. They'll love you for the charming way you have of crushing and smashing everything in your path, which at least kept the country quiet long enough for Saladin to liberate Jerusalem from the Crusaders, for which he honored you in his inimitable manner. They'll make you a character in books and plays and movies just to make sure no one tries to follow your example."

Hearing this little speech, the eunuch looked as if he were going to faint. Then he said, "Follow me, your Excellency, if you please."

"I don't please! Where are you trying to take me?"

"Is your lordship angry for some reason?"

That's what the eunuch Baha al-Din Qaraqush said to me as he came up alongside me and followed me hesitantly. With him next to me, I could suddenly see the beast that lived inside him, and smell its power and ferocity. But then I remembered who he was, after all, and how the logic of history works. He didn't give me the chance to philosophize any further, though. Sensing my sudden fear, he snarled and stamped his foot, dismissing the soldiers and officers who followed in his wake. He turned to me as if to put an end to our little moment together, but then he softened. "But what is it that Your Excellency doesn't like about us?"

"Listen, eunuch," I told him. "Can you tell me who's supposed to live in the palace after you finish tossing the current residents out into the street? Can you tell me that?"

Only now did the eunuch tremble in earnest. But he answered defiantly, "The people responsible for law and order in the city."

Furious, I said, "No, what I'm asking is, who's going to live inside the palace?"

Nodding gently, he said, "That's what I'm telling you: there are people who've been ordered to move into the palace instead of those foul and filthy Shi'a bastards!"

"Eunuch," I said to him, "you're a liar!"

This remark left him speechless. Then I delivered the knockout blow.

"No offense, eunuch," I said, "but you've evicted the Caliph, his children, and his grandchildren from their ancestral home, and put your own cousins in there instead!"

The eunuch laughed and gave me a low five as if we had been friends for a thousand years. As my hand slipped away from his massive paw, I found that something had stuck to it— my little hand, that is—something that felt suspiciously like paper bills and a gemstone. I stiffened in embarrassment and my smile froze on my face. "Shame on you, eunuch! Do I look like a man who takes bribes?"

He gave me a friendly shake on the shoulder. "It's not a bribe or any such nonsense. It's a gift we give all our visitors. Everything we do here, we do in the open. If we kill you, we kill you in the open. If we impale you, we impale you in the open. It's all for the good of the Land of Egypt. The people that your lordship is calling my cousins aren't settling in the palace. I'm keeping them confined in the main building just until the Citadel is finished."

Sticking the gift in my pocket, I said, "Fair enough. I won't argue the point. But let me inside the palace."

With a bow, he stood aside. "Be my guest! But I still don't know who I have the honor of addressing."

"I'm a member of the inventory committee," I said.

I walked past him into the building. All around me were men in Ayyubid uniforms: guardsmen, viziers, emirs, and hangers-on. My watch read 13, Rabi' II, 567, which meant that Saladin had already taken over the palace, including the storerooms, the government offices, and all the property and treasures. As I came in, an inspector was presenting the first part of the inventory to Saladin's clerk. The list ran as follows: "The palace houses eighteen thousand souls: ten thousand noblemen and women, and eight thousand slaves, attendants, serving women, midwives, and nurses. The only able-bodied males are the Caliph and the men of his family." I had already learned from the eunuch that the heir apparent, Dawud son of Adid, called Hamid Billah, as well as the emir Abu Amana Gibril, Abul Futuh and his sons Abul Qasim and Abdel Zahir, Sulayman ibn Dawud, the Caliph's sons Abdel Zahir Haydara and Ismail, his grandson Abdel Wahhab ibn Ibrahim, Ibn Abi al-Tahir ibn Gibril, and other members of the family had been arrested and were being held at the house of Afdal in Birgawan Alley. I also knew that there were a number of world-famous treasuries that I had to see. There were storerooms full of books, of banners and weapons and shields and saddles, of carpets, draperies, and kipskin and cabretta—please don't ask me what "kipskin and cabretta" are, because I have no idea—wine cellars, spice pantries, and stores of tents, as well as the greenhouse, the pantries, the bakeries, the library, and the treasure room full of jewels and aromatics. Each was a building by itself. And each had a cushioned bench for the Caliph to sit on, and a servant, paid by the month, who moved from one treasury to another, cleaning them all in the course of a year.

A deputy was assigned to accompany me as I carried out the inventory. He held the rank of judge and was ultimately responsible for seeing that the operation was carried out according to all the legal rules and regulations. We greeted each other coldly. He took me for someone sent by his superiors to keep an eye on him, and I could tell he resented me, so there was no love lost between us.

Our first stop was the library. I was surprised to find it well organized. There were shelves divided into sections by partitions that moved on hinges and could be closed with a lock. I looked up two hundred thousand books and found them all there: jurisprudence, grammar, lexicography, hadith, history, royal biography, astrology, religion, and alchemy, with the volumes that were later to disappear still in their places, all listed on a card stuck to the door of each unit.

Then we went to the room of aromatics and gemstones. My companion wanted to pass it by, but I stopped and insisted on going in.

At that moment a figure suddenly ran up from behind me, calling out, "Follow me! Saladin awaits you in the Golden Hall!"

4

History on the Auction Block

So Saladin was waiting for me in the Golden Hall. How that
happened, I wasn't sure. But there was nothing wrong with
having him wait for me in a hall, or even in a coffeehouse. He
wasn't an uptight sort of guy, and he wouldn't mind standing
around on a street corner for a few minutes.

"Listen, kid," I said to the deputy. "Tell Sal I'm on my way.
And hey—tell him to have a cup of tea or coffee, my treat.
Make sure he doesn't pay for it himself!"

With an obedient bow of the head, the deputy
disappeared.

Suddenly feeling sorry for Saladin, I almost started back
the way I had come. But then I told myself with a smirk that
for generations, we had been waiting our whole lives for our
leaders. Why shouldn't *they* wait a minute or two for *us*? If
they had waited, for more than a few seconds—even once or
twice—then the whole course of history would have been different, that's for sure.

But why was he waiting for me in the Golden Hall in the
first place? The Hall was a shambles: it contained a throne
upholstered in pure silk, a raised seating platform with the
gold curtains, and a threshold with a groove worn into it by
tens of thousands of foreheads prostrated in obeisance to
the Fatimid caliph. I had a sneaking suspicion that there was
some sort of plot to get me away—for whatever reason—from
where they were doing the inventory.

Quickly I caught myself and called the little deputy back. He was already on his way to the Golden Hall, and when I called him he turned around with a smoldering look of suppressed disgust. I went up to him and suddenly realized that he was none other than the eunuch Qaraqush.

"Good heavens! Who's that I see?"

"I'm the deputy, sir," he said in his rascally way. "Have you changed your mind about meeting Saladin?"

"You're Qaraqush, dressed up like a deputy."

He let out a laugh like a spurt of water from a fire hose that fizzled against the satanic smoldering in his eyes. "Sir, I'm no Qaraqush; I'm not worth one of his toenails. But if you say I look like him, I'll take it as a good omen." The fire in his eyes died into embers, giving off a noxious dampness. "I take it you want to meet my master."

"No need to wait around," I said, cursing him under my breath. "Go back and tell your master that I've been assigned a task that requires me to stay here."

Waving him off, I retraced my steps. I passed the Storehouse of Regalia, which occupied a building of its own. From it wafted the scent of perfumes and of new and precious fabrics mixed with the reek of fresh sweat. Streams of people were coming and going and passing in and out, all of them decked out in Fatimid finery: gowns of Dabiqi fabric and turbans embroidered in gold, five hundred-dinar gilded turbans, collars, cuffs, ornamented swords like the ones given as gifts to high commanders, and the jeweled necklaces given to viziers in place of collars. I didn't understand: I was still awake and hanging on tightly to the period I was in. So why was this part of the palace totally Fatimid even though the rest was Ayyubid? These people *must* be Fatimids, I thought. I looked around for a treasurer, but found no one. Instead, I saw someone dressed up like the Caliph coming toward me.

Torn between contempt for people who wore clothes above their station and the fear that he might actually be the Caliph,

I approached him and said knowingly, "You look just like the Caliph." With a vulgar laugh like the roar of a bull, he slapped his hand into mine the way my colleague Muhammad Barakat does at the office. I almost said, "So you're not the Caliph, then." But he was spreading his arms and legs, turning in a circle, and looking with imbecilic delight at his royal outfit with its gilded cuffs, like a mischievous child in his holiday clothes.

"Are you a Fatimid, brother, or an Ayyubid?" I asked him. He told me that he was an Ayyubid; then that he was a Fatimid by origin; and finally that he wasn't one or the other, and didn't know where he was from, since he was taken by slavers in infancy and sold to one owner and then to another and another. Now he was the property of someone else, but couldn't say exactly who; though his master took orders from someone who took orders from someone who took them from someone else; and he himself had been sent to collect all the items of ceremonial dress and drapery and make a pen-and-paper inventory of them.

"I'll bet each of you comes out of it with a nice suit or two," I remarked.

He stared at me with fierce disapproval. "No, the clothes I have on got tossed out the window—or were supposed to get tossed out the window once the Caliph and his people got tired of wearing them."

"So where's Abda, then?" I asked. He stared at me dumbfounded, not knowing who I meant. "I want to see everything down to the last nickel!"

My shouting was drawing a crowd. One of the newcomers, who despite his Fatimid dress presented himself as the record-keeper in charge of counting up the items in the storehouse, motioned for me to come with him. Dazed, I complied, but as I stepped past him I spotted the historian Ibn Tuwayr. On his way out, he gave me a long-distance wave. Normally, since we had never been introduced and neither one of us wanted to be the first to introduce himself to the other, he would avoid me and I would ignore him whenever we met. He was clearly surprised to see me there, and I rudely pretended not to recognize him. Then I took the rudeness a step further by calling him over and asking him if he worked there. Polite and composed, he replied that he was doubtless unworthy of such an honor, since "working in the Storehouse of Regalia was a highly ranked position."

Thinking the better of my bad manners, I said, "Don't we know each other?"

He nodded and said curtly, "Indeed we do. You're the famous Ibn Shalaby."

"So begging you by the honor of your father Tuwayr, what can you tell me about this storehouse?"

"It's actually two storehouses," he said. "The first one, the External, is run by the Caliph's senior attendant—an ustaz or the like—and his men. There you'll find plenty of evidence for God's generosity to those He favors: fine linen, Dabiqi regalia in different colors for men and women, painted brocade, and silk stuffs of Saqlatun. All the best official stitchery of Tinnis, Dumyat, and Alexandria ends up there. It's also where the Master of the Scissors and his tailors ply their trade, making clothes to order as needed. But everything meant for the Caliph to wear is stored in the second storehouse, the Internal."

"Thank you, thank you, Ibn Tuwayr," I said. "Thanks so much!" I stumbled toward the entrance but had gotten only a few steps past the door when a terrifying shriek stopped me in my tracks. In front of me was a lady whose bearing gave the impression of beauty joined with self-possession and of audacity tempered by modesty. I examined her carefully as she stood there gasping with one hand on her bosom. Meanwhile, thirty ladies, even more lovely and alluring than the first, were converging on us, all staring at me in utter astonishment. To the senior lady I said, "Sorry, ma'am!"

Clasping her bosom again she said: "Who's 'Ma'am'? My name is Ornament of the Treasurers Forever!"

"And who might you be exactly, Ornament of the Treasurers Forever?"

"I'm Ornament of the Treasurers," she said, "and all these slaves work under me. Everyone knows what I do here. Who are you to burst in pretending you don't?"

"I swear to you, Ornament of the Treasurers, that I have no idea at all."

"In my presence—and in my presence alone—the Caliph changes his raiment, and everything he wears comes from this treasury."

I looked absentmindedly out of the window and noticed a garden overlooking the waterway.

"That garden," she said, "is an annex of the treasury."

"What does that mean?"

"It's set aside for growing wild rose and jasmine," she said. "Every day, summer and winter, we have the flowers brought in for our clothes and our storage crates."

I apologized to Ornament of the Treasurers, drawing out the proceedings as long as possible while sneaking peeks at her slave women despite my claim to good manners. Meanwhile, I was thinking to myself that Ibn Tuwayr had played a nasty trick on me by letting me wander into restricted areas where I would get my comeuppance.

Leaving before it came time for the Caliph to change, I managed to find my way back to the fellow who was writing up the inventory. He invited me to sit, pulling out a chair that looked as if it was only there for decoration. Pretending not to notice, I sat down immediately.

"Look, buddy," I asked him, "why are you wearing clothes that don't belong to you if you're going to end up listing them on the inventory anyway?"

"Perhaps a sultan is merely a person wearing the sultan's clothes," he replied, "while many a true sultan dresses like an ordinary man!"

"You win, smarty-pants. Show me that ledger of yours."

43

"There's nothing to show," he smirked. "Our master Qaraqush went through the inventory himself. The contents of the dress and drapery storehouse came to one hundred boxes of precious necklaces and sumptuous garments, some embroidered and some studded with gems."

He offered me a big silver cup filled with a drink that turned out to be first-rate lemonade. I would have chugged it down in one shot but I didn't want to embarrass myself. It was a good thing I didn't: the record-keeper had produced a large bundle, which he placed beside me. Examining it out of the corner of my eye, I realized that it was a bundle of clothes.

"A little souvenir," he whispered in my ear, "for your collection." Then he shouted for a boy to show me out.

I protested that I didn't accept gifts. "Unless," I added, "it's something really valuable. In that case, I'll take it if you let me pay for it."

"No one should have to pay for the same article twice," he said with a melancholy smile. "Every Muslim in Egypt has already paid through the nose for this finery."

It seemed to me that he was right, so I accepted the gift without further ado. Deciding I would drop by Sal's office to say goodbye, I left, with a boy following in my wake to carry the precious bundle of clothes.

The boy was a typical Egyptian harfush, not too proud to carry the bundle on his head as a woman would do. Then he took to switching it from one hand to the other. Running to keep up with me, he smiled as if wanting to tell me something he thought I should know. I stopped, beckoned him over, put a brotherly hand on his shoulder and asked him if he had something to say. Pointing to a nearby building that I had been too flustered to notice, he said that I should drop in on that treasury in particular. If I managed to take something out, I could give him the price of a nice dinner. I took a liking to him, impudent advice and all. I asked him which treasury it was, and he told me it was a storehouse for gemstones, perfumes, and rarities. I thanked the little harfush heartily, told him to wait for me, and went in.

The sound of my footfalls on the marble floor was pleasant, echoing from the silent rooms on either side. From a nearby chamber streamed a colored shaft of daylight broken by the silhouette of a figure pacing diplomatically back and forth. I was on the verge of greeting what I took to be the living, breathing shapes before me, but then, looking closely, I saw that they were male, female, and animal figures of every shape and size, made of gold, marble, camphor, and sandalwood, and smelling strongly of aristocracy. To one side, sitting on a low round table embroidered with Fatimid designs, was a model garden with a base made of silver interlaced with gold, ambergris for soil, and trees of molded and gilded silver. I was wondering to myself how much it weighed when I heard the harfush, who was suddenly standing not too close but not too far away, say that it weighed three hundred and thirty pounds.

"That's amazing!"

"And this," he said, "is a watermelon made of camphor. It weighs sixteen thousand mithqals.

"Meaning no disrespect," the harfush went on, "you look like a decent guy. So do the right thing. Otherwise you'll leave no better off than you were when you came in. You're an Egyptian, aren't you? In other words, you've got nothing: you work and they take what you make. So if you want anything for yourself," he said with a wink and a grin, "you have to look sharp. 'Yes sir, no sir, at your service, right away, sir!' Now that's the real inventory, meaning no disrespect. You're going in there to do an inventory. In other words, hand over the ledgers and all that stuff, unless you want to go back empty-handed. The ledgers will come back to you double-checked down to the last dime. But, son of Shalaby, don't get screwed! I'll just wait for you right here. Take your time; no rush at all."

I walked toward the room that was open to the daylight. When I spun around to face the door, I saw that the room was enormously long: beyond the velvet drapes at the far end were the waters of the Nile. It was hard to say whether it was really the Nile and not a private lake, or a replica of the Nile made of marble, sapphires, and pearls, for the reflections of its surface rippled all along the walls. All around were statues and treasures beyond counting.

When a slender, imposing figure dressed in gold-embroidered Fatimid regalia came forward to welcome me, I wondered for a moment whether he was a man of flesh and blood, thinking that he might be another gold or marble or sapphire or pearl or emerald statue. When I put my small hand into his smaller one, I felt no real pulse there. He withdrew his hand and it slipped out of mine like as smoothly as a chunk of leaded glass. Then he offered me a chair and I stood there staring at it bedazzled, shaking my head in stupefaction and making faces to express my astonishment. I must have said "Wow!" twenty times, and "My God!" a thousand times, and "Unbelievable!" a million more, until the man grew annoyed and said, with extreme politeness, "I offered you a chair so you could sit on it, not gape at it."

Afraid to commit myself, I looked at him and at the chair and back again and finally sat down gingerly on the edge. Looking quite full of himself, he sat down facing me, crossing his legs, and offered me a crystal goblet full of something that smelled like oranges. No sooner did I touch it to my lips than I handed it back empty, my mouth, my nose, and my entire body suffused with its invigorating scent. He was just touching his own cup to his lips when I surprised him by dropping mine with a clatter onto a nearby tray—which was made of gold and rested on legs of sandalwood and camphor. With a reproachful smile, which I ignored, he offered me his cup, and I chugged it down, burning as I was with the heat of ages past. He responded by assuming a disdainfully lazy posture in his chair, saying, "Well, then." So I assumed my own disdainfully lazy posture, saying, "Well, then."

Chewing on something that he had put into his mouth without my noticing, he said, "Your trip seems to have been tiring for you. But I told Fakhr al-Din that the matter wasn't so very urgent."

Having no idea what he was talking about, I said, "True enough, it isn't so very urgent, but . . ."

"What's your name, sir?"

"Son of Shalaby, the Hanafi, the Egyptian, seller of pickles and sweets."

He chuckled and said politely, "How is it, then, that you know about gemstones and pickles both?"

"God save you, sir; I may seem like a strange bird to you, but when I put my mind to a problem, why—with the help of God and with blessings on the Prophet—I bust it wide open."

"What does 'bust it wide open' mean?"

"It means I clean its clock."

"What does 'clean its clock' mean?"

"It means I make it comprehensible and clear."

"Why didn't you say so right away?"

"The Arabic language, may God preserve and enrich it," I replied, "contains expressions of every kind and species. It can take a single sensation and turn it into many, or a single pang and redouble it; it can change riches into famine, and tigers into butterflies."

Laughing, the man of imposing appearance said appreciatively, "All that matters to me is that you be truly expert in gemstones, as Fakhr al-Din claims."

"I am an expert in gemstones, actually; but I don't know who Fakhr

al-Din is."

"Then you must not know me either."

"I haven't had the pleasure," I admitted. "Who might you be, sir?"

"Abu Said Nahawandi, chief courtier. I had asked Fakhr al-Din to send me an expert in gemstones from Tripoli,

Morocco, France, or Spain. When you came in, I thought you must be the one."

Lounging in a self-important manner, I said, "I *am* the one. That is, I'm the expert you need, brought here in your hour of need by an inscrutable Providence. So what's on your mind, Ibn al-Nahawandi? If it's a matter of property, I'll put my neck on the line for it; and if it's action you need . . ."

"What does 'put my neck on the line for it' mean?" he interrupted.

Sensing that he would disapprove of any swaggering on my part, I explained that problems, in my opinion, were like bottles of rubbing alcohol, and if I didn't use my neck to stop them up, the contents would evaporate. Evidently I managed to win him over, for he sat up straight and said, "Since you're an expert, Ibn Shalaby, there's something I need to talk to you about."

I sat up straight too, and lit a cigarette, which startled him. "Right," I said. "Let's get down to brass tacks. Don't hold back!"

"The problem, Ibn Shalaby, is that times are tough right now in the Land of Egypt, to the point that the palace itself is suffering."

"There's no shame in that, friend. It's the sort of thing known to happen even in the very best of families."

"Be that as it may," he said, "we called in Egypt's biggest jewelers to purchase items from the treasury. They asked what the items are worth. We expected *them* to tell *us*, since it was their trade. But they can only estimate the value of an article based on the value of similar articles. Unfortunately, though, our items are unique. Now if *you* have a basis of comparison, Ibn Shalaby, then you really are an expert."

"No worries!" I said.

"What?"

"Show me what you've got on you."

"I don't have anything on me."

"I mean, show me the items in your possession."

He rose and led me along an aisle that brought us to an anteroom full of wooden crates.

"What's all this?" I asked.

"Here we have vessels that look like beer mugs, made of pure crystal, carved and plain."

"What else?"

He stopped in front of an enclosure full of gilt and enameled chinaware.

"What are all those thousands of boxes?" I asked.

"The ones here are full of gilded and silver-plated knives, with handles inlaid with precious stones. The ones there are full of pen-cases made of gold, silver, sandalwood and aloeswood, African ebony, ivory, and other materials, ornamented with gold, silver, and jewels. And over there are gold and silver drinking vessels of different sizes embellished in niello."

He opened a door and we went in. Pointing to the piles of bundles, he said, "This is the estate of Rashidah, the daughter of Mu'izz: thirty gowns of cut silk, twelve thousand fabrics in single colors, and a hundred bottles full of Sumatran camphor. The whole lot is supposed to be worth 1.7 million dinars at the very least."

We passed into another room, which he told me was the treasury of Abda, another daughter of Mu'izz. It was full. Suffice it to say that it contained four hundred reed baskets; thirteen hundred pieces of enameled niello silver plate, each one weighing ten thousand dirhams; four hundred swords inlaid with gold; thirty thousand Sicilian head-cloths; and an emerald that weighed 154 pounds.

Next we walked down another long aisle where I saw a mat of woven gold. The man told me that it weighed eighteen pounds and was the mat where Buran, the daughter of Hasan ibn Sahl, had been presented to the caliph Ma'mun on their wedding day. Next to the mat I saw twenty-eight enamelware trays inlaid with golden cubes and crates full of innumerable porcelain and metal or enameled mirrors, all decorated with gold filigree and some crowned with precious stones. I also saw a good many parasols with gold and silver handles, and more chess and backgammon sets made of gemstones, gold, silver, and ebony, with boards of silk and gold, than I could count.

Then we went into the treasure room, where I saw thirty-six thousand pieces of fine crystal and leaded glass, twenty-four thousand ambergris figurines, and innumerable statues of the Caliph.

At that point we were so tired we had to stop. I offered the fellow a cigarette, which he turned down in horror. I leaned back against one of the golden sunshades and said, "How much for the lot?"

Instead of listening to me, he was busy looking through a sort of porthole or periscope built into the wall. Looking through it too, I saw a distant street crowded with urchins and ragamuffins who were dragging their exhausted bodies along, yawning with boredom, and every so often lifting an imploring cry to the heavens. I saw peddlers steering clear of the palace wall and crying their wares in voices worn thin by hunger and fatigue. Their cries were the strangest I had ever heard: "Live dogs for seventy-five dinars! Dead ones for fifty!"

Turning back to the man of imposing appearance, I asked, "Live dogs I can understand, but why would anyone be selling a dead dog?"

The man of imposing appearance shuddered and pressed his hands to his ears. "I implore you to be quiet. What goes on in the street is none of your business."

"What goes on in the street," I said, "can't be separated from what's going on in here."

"Yes it can," he said imperiously. "Those people are scum."

"And all of you are tyrants!"

"But all of us," he said, genuinely pained, "will have to eat the same corpses."

"Know then, sir," I said, "that I have seen your baubles and your precious stones, and in my expert opinion they have no value whatsoever."

In a truculent tone, he asked me what standard I had used to make my assessment. Pointing to the people walking past the window, I said, "That standard right there."

"Those people are destitute," he said. "What value do they have?"

"You've trained them not to store up their possessions," I said, "but you've locked away everything in sight. Now you've got treasuries filled with tons of cold steel while they have hearts full of human sympathy."

"Now you're meddling with people's sources of income," he scowled. "That's atheism!"

"If you'll excuse me," I said, and set off down one path and then another, entering compartments that led to further corridors and finally to the main passageway, with Nahawandi on my heels the whole way. Hearing a tremendous racket above my head, I turned to him and said, "If you're unhappy with me, directly overhead by about a thousand years more or less there's a whole neighborhood called the Goldsmiths' Quarter. Just send for one of them."

I found my way outside, into a courtyard surrounded by a single row of buildings and gardens. I stopped to look around for the Golden Hall where Saladin was waiting for me. And where was the boy who was carrying my gift? I spun around blindly and hit my head.

"Why don't you look where you're going, you moron!"

I came to my senses, clutching my head in a panic. In front of me was a man clutching his own head. Around me were thousands of people and rows of shops. I rubbed my eyes. I was on Muski Street!

Disgusted and irritated, I walked away, fighting the crowds and trying not to break into a sweat. Even the trash heaps had been rented out for thousands of pounds and made into stalls selling American, Japanese, and European goods. The poor Sons of Shalaby, who actually live here, should have their products put on display too, even if they have to put a foreign sticker on them first.

On some of the storefronts were signs announcing that someone or other was putting on a celebration of the passage—I mean the beginning—of the year AH 1400. "What do they mean, a celebration?" I wondered. "Like with dancing and singing and storytelling?"

A man who had evidently read the sign at the same time and guessed what I was thinking spoke up, "What we really need," he said, "is some kind of dinner, even if it's slim pickings."

"Or big chickens!"

"I wish!" he said. He gave me a friendly smile, as if I had proven my good character. Then he vanished into the crowd. A moment later, though, he was back. I took a good look at him and it seemed to me that, though dressed differently, he was the ragged harfush who had walked behind me carrying the bundle of clothes an eternity ago.

"Looking for anything special, sir?" he asked hesitantly.

"Yes," I said. Then I thought the better of it and said, "No. Why do you ask?"

"Just trying to be helpful. Got any foreign?"

"Foreign what?"

"Hard currency. Dollars. I'll give you a good rate." Offhandedly he pulled a wad of red ten-pound notes—the ones with the minarets on them—out of his pocket, lined up the edges, and stuck the bills back in his pants.

Pushing past him, I headed off in the direction of Hamzawi and Ghuriya and started climbing the steps up to the pedestrian overpass built by the armed forces between Ghuriya and Mu'izz Street. But I was tired and I had to slow down. As I climbed, I cursed the people who insist on cutting between the barricades and crossing the street on ground level. I also double-cursed the soldiers who argued with them for a good long while but then let them sneak through.

Suddenly a truculent voice boomed out at me: "Stop! One more step and I'll cut you down!"

I looked up and found myself climbing steps up to a great high gate. From a distance, the gate looked like the jaw of some mythical sea monster, and I looked like an ant scurrying between its teeth. In front of me was a guardsman holding a sword.

5

Emigrating to Work in Distant Ages

WAVING THE END OF HIS sword at me like a man swatting a fly, the Persian guardsman gestured for me to stop. I stared back at him defiantly. He gave his head a quizzical wiggle. I heaved my Samsonite briefcase into his range of vision. That brief-case, as far as I'm concerned, is worth its weight in gold. If I wave it at taxi drivers, they always stop. If I snap it open and shut, salesmen and petty brokers treat me with respect. But the Persian guardsman, far from deferring to my briefcase, regarded it with contemptuous disdain. Surprised that American industry had lost its magic touch, I made a mental note to report the incident to the Arab opposition papers so they could use it as an example of the disappointing performance of foreign imports.

"Happy now?" I said to the guard. "You've done your part to undermine U.S. interests." Impudently I continued, "Out of my way!" and tried to duck around the sword.

"What do you want in the Golden Hall?" he asked.

I told him that Saladin, son of Joseph son of Job, was wait-ing for me there and that it wasn't a question of what I wanted from the hall but what it wanted from me.

"Job, eh?" he said. "There's no one as patient as he was any more, not since he went to rest among the prophets."

"Not that Job," I said smiling. "Not every Job is a prophet, nor is every patient man a Job."

"But every Job is an Egyptian," he finished.

"So you understand how this country works."

"Up to a point."

Sensing diffidence in his tone, I made bold to say, "Patience isn't the only virtue we have in Egypt. It's not just the ability to endure pain and suffering, it's the ability to endure the remedy. Our leeches can hold out even longer than we can. Our wounds keep opening but they keep treating them. It's amazing what they put up with. They keep fighting us until we lose our minds."

The guardsman nodded like an imbecile. Then he wiggled his chin and thrust it out straight a few times in succession to make way for a belch. When it came, it drove me back a good distance. I grimaced at the smell of roast lamb, and had the sudden impression that the whole animal was still alive and kicking in the guardsman's belly.

"Get away from me, you leech," I said, flapping my hand at him. He lashed out with the sword and I leapt out of the way like an acrobat.

"Who are you calling a leech, you insect?"

"You claim to know how things work here," I said. "So you must realize that you're one of the leeches. Our history is covered with chronic pustules and abscesses, and every country that invades us leaves a massive ulcer behind. If not for Nile water, our wounds would all have festered."

He began cursing me savagely, calling me an insect, a commoner, an ignoramus, a runaway slave, and so on to the end of the usual monarchist calumnies. Like any Egyptian, I responded by slipping in all the mollifying remarks I could think of: "I'm sorry you feel that way. . . . Maybe you can think of something nice to say, too. . . . I think of you as a little brother, really." But he only became more abusive, so I protested, "Hey, you're the one making personal remarks, not me."

At that point, I have to say in all fairness, he did calm down. Regaining his composure, he turned around to call someone on the inside, ignoring me completely. Seeing my chance, I slapped him quick as lightning on the back of the neck and then bolted, leaving him stumbling in confusion behind me.

I ran blind, tripping over bushes, bumping into pillars of gold, and jumping over railings of platinum and marble. All of the doors I passed were closed; only the windows and balconies were open. When I sensed that I had outdistanced any pursuers, I climbed a staircase that I happened to see in front of me. It led me to a long corridor paved in alabaster, decorated with golden figures, and lined with conical columns. Between the columns were canes of red roses spreading in profusion over the paving stones. Buoyed by the splendor and the roses, my steps took on an effortless, regal rhythm. From the grand salons on either side, the echo of my footfalls doubled and redoubled. Then I sat down at the top of a nearby tower. Below me was a big square room full of silver cabinets packed with vessels of odd shapes and sizes.

Suddenly a door opened as if out of nowhere and out came a black slave wearing striped regalia and a Fatimid turban. I stood up trembling as he approached. Stopping some distance away, he shouted, "You're already slacking off, you rodent? Do you think they sent you here to sit? We asked them to send us boys to prepare the dinner service, not to sit there like that!"

"Dinner service?"

He pointed back to the door he had come through. "Go on, you ugly slave, and report to the chief of the dinner service."

"Yes, sir!"

I jumped up, hurried toward the door, and raced through it. On each side was a row of facing doors, all of which I was too shy to open; so I kept walking down this new corridor, which was carpeted and lined with gold and silver planters. Carried along by my own momentum, I followed the corridor into a long hall of imposing proportions. Everything there was terrifyingly bigger than usual. The carpets on the ground were so thick that my foot sank into them and then sprang lightly back. There was a window as wide as a movie screen, and a couch or throne of pure gold stretched out in front of it. I walked along a wall decorated with designs that seemed to be made of wood or ironwork, covered with silken drapes of impressive grandeur. The floor was carpeted with matching gold-threaded rugs from Tiberias and Tabaristan, the likes of which I had never seen. On the throne was a cushion arranged for formal audiences. I might well have continued walking through that enormous space all the way to the end, except that off in the distance I noticed a series of gateways, through the last of which I could see the Persian guardsman, still rubbing the back of his neck and huffing and puffing in a fury. So I started back the way I had come.

Suddenly I felt a hand poking at me. Trembling, I looked around and saw a group of black dignitaries dressed in gala outfits and carrying something that turned out to be a dining table made of silver. The one who had poked me said, "Move it, you clod! Where do the slavers get you people from, anyway?"

Another chimed in, "It's luck of the draw: sometimes you get a prince and sometimes you get a lowlife."

They laughed heartily, but without making a sound. A third added, "Slave dealers aren't all the same, either. Some of them have a line in snatching children from princes and noble families, and they've got gangs working for them everywhere. Then you have the ones who lurk in alleyways luring children with sweets. So which kind of slaver sold you, kid?"

"Do you mean, which kind bought me?"

"Whose slave are you?" he asked. "Fine, then tell me: did the slave trader buy you or sell you?"

"It amounts to the same thing in the end," I said, "and it's the same slave trader either way. If someone is selling me, then someone must be buying me."

They exchanged uneasy glances full of sardonic misery. The one who had poked me said, "You're lucky that everyone who makes it in here is intended as a gift for the Caliph. Otherwise you'd be in deep trouble, you filthy loudmouth. Now toss that box you're carrying and led a hand. What's in the box, anyway?"

"It's a briefcase," I said. "I've got my credentials in there, and some personal items."

The leader gave a command and the briefcase was deftly pulled from my grasp. He then ordered me to join the group of workers. As it turned out, though, almost everything had already been prepared. The silver dining table had been placed in front of the bench—I mean, the throne. So I joined them in running back and forth between the kitchen and the hall until we had set more than five hundred plates on the table. All were of gold, silver, or porcelain, and the food itself was aromatic and appetizing: vegetables and plump chickens prepared with wholesome herbs and spices. The dinner service had been set up along the length of the room between the throne and the door opposite, on structures like wooden benches, with vessels piled up to make a dining table ten cubits wide. On top of the plates we strewed flowers and along the edges we laid out loaves of semolina bread. Each loaf was three pounds of pure flour sprinkled with water as it rose to give it an attractively shiny crust. On the inner part of the table we laid out twenty-one trays. On each tray were twenty-one grilled sheep and three hundred and fifty chickens, pullets, and baby pigeons, stacked as high as a standing man. All around, we piled slices of halva, including colored pieces for decoration. The empty spaces were filled with ceramic plates each carrying seven chickens stuffed with melted sweets. The smell of good food was everywhere.

Looking at a figurine made of ebony and gold standing on a marble shelf, someone called out that the Caliph and his vizier would soon be back from the mosque. Peeking at my special watch, I saw that the date was Ramadan 380—that is, the fifteenth year of the reign of the caliph Aziz, the son of Mu'izz. From the air of merriment in the palace I realized that Aziz had captured Hims, Hama, and Aleppo, been acclaimed in Mosul and Yemen, and had his name inscribed on the issue—on coins, that is—and banners.

Finally the Caliph made his entrance. He was dark-skinned, with reddish hair, big dark eyes, and broad shoulders. The vizier, who had reached the door first, saluted him and began removing his regalia, including the turban with his insignia, and replacing each item with other garments specially prepared for the occasion. When this was done, the Caliph came forward and sat on the throne in front of his round dining table. Flanking him were four of his most experienced high officials and four of his attendants. He summoned the vizier to come up to the throne and sit on his right. Next, he invited the commanders with their ceremonial collars, followed by those below them in rank, to sit at the dining tables.

At that moment the slave who had poked me appeared and hauled me away, telling me that there was another meal being served outdoors for the lower orders. Then he shoved me through a door I had not noticed at all. I came right out onto the square between the palaces. Spread out there was a well-arranged dining cloth decorated with raised figures painted in gold and seemingly molded one by one.

I set off at a run, hoping to find a place amid the hordes of my fellow citizens who were thronging to the feast, eating, and stuffing whatever they could into their sleeves. Then I heard people shouting. A man, it turned out, had shoved another and knocked him into a little girl, who had screamed. The man who had fallen then got up and punched the first man. A group of people rushed in to separate them, trapping me in the middle. When the two finally stopped cursing each other, everyone tried to pick up where they had left off.

But me, I was suddenly looking for a seat at a table on the street in front of a cheap restaurant in Ghuriya. Everyone was sitting and waiting for the cannon shot that signals the end of the fast, but the little dishes in front of us looked like leftovers unlikely to make a dent in anyone's appetite. Furious, I decided to find my way back to the Fatimid feast, even if I was too late for anything but leftovers. No doubt about it: even the leftovers from Fatimid times are better than the main courses we have today. But even though there were people waiting for me to leave so they could take my place, I was reluctant to be seen getting up and leaving food behind. So I made a show of getting up to rummage through the bread bin, and then snuck off in the direction of the toilet.

Trying to go back the way I had come, I ended up going off to the right, in the direction of Gudariya Alley. But I was afraid that the alley would carry me too far back in time—not to mention that it would drop me in the middle of a barracks. So I retraced my steps to Ghuriya Street and set off, keeping the quarter of Khurunfish behind me. Along the way I spotted Naguib Mahfouz, disguised as a tomato vendor, pushing a cart but laughing out loud instead of hawking his wares. I saw Muhammad Qandil, the singer, shopping for toys for his children. I also saw several artists whom I know but who don't know me, or know other people altogether. All around me, barreling along in opposite directions, or across traffic, were pushcarts, bicycles, and motorcycles, pickup trucks owned by importers, and Mercedes-Benzes driven by drug dealers, body-shop owners, and pushy businessmen. Somehow, though, the Sons of Shalaby, bowing to the blaring horns and the cursing passengers, were making room for them all on the narrow street. Should a vehicle box itself in or get stuck blocking traffic, they would pitch in to give it a push or guide the driver.

In the middle of all this I saw a tall, cruel-featured man who was doing his best to pretend he hadn't seen me. So I went up to him and extended my hand in a friendly greeting. "How are you, old fellow?"

"Hello," he responded curtly.

Somewhat at a loss, I asked, "You are Murtada Abu Muhammad Abdel Salam, right?"

"Yes," he said, as coldly as before.

"Son of Muhammad, son of Abdel Salam, son of Tuwayr?"

He nodded.

"Of Cairo and Caesarea, scribe in Egypt?"

"Yes," he said, exasperated.

"Do you remember the day you got me in trouble by sending me in to see the Ornament of the Treasurers?"

He smiled. "But you handled yourself, didn't you?"

"How can you show up in my day and age and walk around in the streets as if you were still alive?"

"The same way you show up in our times," he said. "You'll find me everywhere on earth."

"Ibn Tuwayr," I told him, "I'm sick and tired of living here."

Suddenly he smiled. "What if I got you a contract to work outside the period?"

"I'd be eternally grateful!" I said. "What would really work for me is a position with competitive benefits: housing paid for, and hiring at a level commensurate with rank in my own time."

"And what rank is that?"

"I work as an editor at a newspaper," I said. "I own a famous pickling plant and a confectionary, too. And I'm thinking of opening a broad-based literary agency."

"What's a 'literary agency'?"

"I'd bring in writers, editors, and artists from around the world and sponsor them to work in different countries, all in return for a hefty commission from both parties. I'd also collect essays, short stories, and investigative pieces written by people who don't like to travel. I'd sell them to more than one paper, and use the proceeds to expand the pickling plant and the confectionary. If the authors insist on being paid, I would claim that the piece never sold and give them ten pounds to keep them from bothering me. No one would ever find out because I would only sell to newspapers, magazines, and journals that aren't distributed here."

"I don't know what you mean by 'magazines' and 'newspapers,'" he said, "but I think you're qualified to work in the chancery."

"What period is that in? Keep in mind that I'm allergic to hot weather."

"Don't worry," he said. "They have air conditioning, and everything's fine."

"Is it central air conditioning, or just fans?"

"Whatever you like."

"Great," I said. "I'd really appreciate anything you can do for me."

He lowered his palm-leaf basket off his shoulder. It was a beautiful basket, much nicer than the ones that the tourists walk around with. He took out a card, a quill, and a decorated pen case. He opened the case, dipped the quill in the inkwell, and wrote a letter in lovely ruq'a script to the head of the Fatimid chancery, asking him to give me all assistance possible. I put the card away carefully in my briefcase. He slung his basket onto his shoulder and started off. But then I noticed that we were standing in front of Gad's Pastries—the one next to the Caravanserai of Ghuri and the Ghuri Cultural Center—and I called him back and asked Gad for two plates of basbusa. When I pointed out the cultural center to Ibn Tuwayr, he asked if it was anything like the literary agency I was planning to open.

"Not at all," I said.

"And are these sweets yours, or does the center make them?"

"Neither," I said. "It's just that Egyptians can find a commercial use for any building."

At that moment a stream of pedestrians came between us and I lost sight of Ibn Tuwayr for a good while. Then, seeing no trace of him or the basbusa, I set off through the narrow streets and alleys to look for him.

Noticing a ruined gateway, I stopped short, charmed by the precision of the craftsmanship. When I walked through it, everything went dark for a moment. Then the light rushed back stronger than before, the way it does after a momentary blackout. I was worried that the bulbs in my brain might have burned out, but then the bright new light showed me where I was: a wide courtyard lined with doors and balconies. Scores of people were coming in and out, greeting one another and exchanging salutations.

I took a few hesitant steps forward. Sitting by a doorway was a ragged harfush, doubtless one of the errand boys. I greeted him and he rose to return the greeting. I asked him where we were.

"The government offices."

"Great," I said. "So what's the office you're sitting in front of?"

"Shh!" he said, raising a finger to his lips in alarm. "It's the Central Bureau. But what have you done to yourself?" he asked, pointing at my foreign clothes.

"It's my formal wear," I said.

"Are you planning to wear it inside?"

"Why shouldn't I?"

"This is the Central Bureau," he said. "It's the bureau that controls the rest. Everything the regime knows is stored in here. Each of the scribes has his own audience room. The head of the bureau has the last word on land grants." Then he whispered in my ear, in a portentous tone: "He has the right to a seatcushion, a backpillow, a pen case, and a chamberlain. He's invested with a robe of honor and has charge of the archives."

"So it's like the Central Admin in my time," I said.

"I don't know what you mean," he said, "but here we have a payments office run by a veteran ustaz, with authority over covert emoluments; periodic disbursements; yearly honoraria; sacrificial animals; clothing for children, relatives, and dependents; and so on."

"Okay, that's enough," I said. "I get the picture. Excuse me, will you?"

He stepped aside and in I went.

I turned right and asked another harfush which office this was. "The Inspection Bureau," he said. "It oversees the other departments, dismisses and appoints officeholders, and presents documents at regular intervals to the Caliph or the vizier. The head reserves the right of incarceration in any premises served by a state appointee, and has the right to a seatcushion, a backpillow, a pen case, and a chamberlain of the rank of emir."

"Lovely, thanks," I said, heading off in another direction, as if I were in the Central Admin Building in Liberation Square. I asked a third harfush which office we were in. "The Accounting Office," he said. "It audits the other offices. The director is always an expert secretary, reserving the right to confer robes of honor, to use the seat-cushion and the chamberlain . . ."

I thanked him and made for a hall that seemed to have opened up beside me. I was stopped by a fourth harfush, who asked me what I was looking for.

"The chancery," I said.

"What?"

I opened my briefcase and showed him the note Ibn Tuwayr had written.

"Who's it to?" he asked.

"The head of the chancery."

"You mean His Illustrious Excellency."

"That's what you call him?"

"That," he said, "and Secretary to the Noble Seat. What do you want with him?"

"To ask for a position."

"The position of His Illustrious Excellency," he said, "is restricted to the most accomplished rhetoricians. He receives sealed communications and presents them to the Caliph, and he's the one who orders the scribes to sign them and reply to them. He has direct access to the caliph at all times, and the Caliph consults him about nearly everything."

"How much does he make?"

"A hundred and twenty dinars a month, and he's first in line for land grants, clothing, salaries, and other payouts."

"Please," I begged, "let me see him right away."

He waved his hand dismissively. "There's no way to see him in his office at the palace, and only high officials can meet with his staff."

"Where's his chamberlain? I'll talk to him instead."

"His chamberlain is an emir and a senior official, with couriers, a *very* big seatcushion, backpillow, and pen case."

"I absolutely must see him. Take this card and tell his chamberlain to give it to him."

The harfush refused to take it, and we stood there arguing until we saw a man of imposing appearance coming toward us. The harfush whispered, "That's the chamberlain."

"What's going on?" asked the chamberlain, coming up to us.

I offered him the card. He stared at it fixedly for a few moments, then called out, "Guards! Seize this wretch and lock him up until we look into his case."

From out of nowhere came a troop of guardsmen, who surrounded me and then took hold of me. The chamberlain, meanwhile, had somehow disappeared. My wristwatch read AH 501.

6

Not a Banner Year:
Detained in the Storehouse of Banners

SURROUNDED BY GUARDS AND THREATENED from all sides, I wondered how a few simple words, spoken by a man who afterward flitted away unfazed, could get me in so much trouble. To be honest, I was feeling faint. On the basis of things I had read and the testimonies of people imprisoned under Nasser, the mere sound of the word "prison" was enough to give me goose bumps. If I knew a way to avoid using the letters P, R, I, S, O, and N, except in some other order or with lots of other letters in between, I would adopt it. But in proportion to my terror there existed deep in my innards a covert desire to see what a prison was really like—on condition that I go there for an extremely good reason. And now here I was, about to be thrown in jail for no reason whatsoever. Hoping to prevent my children from being orphaned over nothing, I tried to pull myself out of the time period, but found that I couldn't. All I could do was curse all the dictators who keep people in line using prisons and whips and swords.

Looking at my watch again, I realized that I had lost track of time: the hands had leapt ahead to 512, the seventeenth year of the reign of Caliph Amer. His proper name was Mansur, his patronymic Abu Ali, and his full title al-Amir bi-Ahkam Allah, The One Who Enforces Divine Judgment, son of Musta'li, son of Mustansir, son of Zahir, son of Hakim, son of Aziz, son of Mu'izz, son of Mansur, son of Qa'im, son of Mahdi the Fatimid. Amer was the tenth of the Ubaydi line of North African caliphs, and the seventh of them to rule Egypt. I had met him a long time ago, when my friend Ibn Taghribirdi showed up at my house one day with a five-year-old boy whom he introduced as the country's new ruler. Since then I had kept track of him and his activities, which were astoundingly wild and irresponsible. He killed Afdal Shah-anshah, the power behind the throne, replacing him with a new vizier named Bata'ihi. No sooner did Bata'ihi begin mistreating people and accepting bribes than Amer arrested him, confiscated his wealth, executed him, and had him crucified, killing five of his brothers for good measure.

Whenever in the course of my career I ran into the Caliph at a social gathering, I would make a point of snubbing him. Once, when I was invited to dine at the salon of the French emperor Napoleon Bonaparte and found the Caliph among the guests, I made it clear that I was uncomfortable and left early. On another occasion, when I was invited to attend the opening of the Aqmar Mosque, which he—Amer—had founded, I stood as far back as I could to avoid shaking his hand, but the TV and movie cameras insisted on shooting my face to show the viewers the depth of my aversion. But I had good reason to hate him. He was a dissolute, bloodthirsty, and rapacious sinner; he suffered delusions of grandeur, loved vain display, and neglected the jihad. During his reign the Franks captured Acre, Tripoli, Edessa, Baniyas, Tyre, Beirut, and Sidon without his lifting a finger to stop them, to the point that Baldwin the Frank attacked Egypt itself, occupying the town of Farama and burning down all the mosques. (Farama was a fortified town that guarded the frontiers of ancient Egypt; it stood on the east side of Lake Manzalah, where Port Said is today.) Amer remained in power for twenty-nine years and nine months, during which time I never spoke to him or sent him regards of any kind. So matters remained until 524, when, crossing the bridge to Roda Island, he was ambushed by a group of men who hacked him to death with swords. Who could have imagined that one day I would find myself at his mercy? As it happens, though, I was less terrified by the prison than I was furious at Ibn Tuwayr for humiliating me again.

The guards tried in vain to stand me on my feet. Someone was rubbing my chest and lifting my arms, and someone else was saying something about me I couldn't catch. Then—what a fragrance! It was an eau de cologne I had never smelled before, and it was redolent of all the flowers in the world. That was what made me open my eyes. I let myself slump onto the shoulders of two powerful guardsmen. Thick walls rose up around me; men popped up out of nowhere to stand at attention; people were yelling and looking around and blowing on trumpets.

A man came out toward us, walking as if the earth had been created for his feet only. He moved with an unhurried, lordly, awe-inspiring gravity, with red reflections glimmering darkly around him like cigarette smoke. Looked at him closely, I recognized him as the man who had ordered my arrest. Slipping away from the guards, I ran toward him shouting, "Please, sir, I'm here by mistake, and I've got a family to feed! I don't know anything about Statecraft or the Imamate or the Secretarial Art or the Office of the Chamberlain! All I do, if you'll allow me to mention it, is sell pickles and sweets; and it's Ibn Tuwayr who tricked me and gave me that piece of paper."

The man stood there holding himself stiffly upright and looking at me in disgust as the guardsmen's truncheons rained down on my rear and my shoulders. As I jumped up and down calling them infidels, filthy Shi'a, and sinners, he raised an eyebrow in astonishment and cast me a meaning look I couldn't interpret. Then he exclaimed, "He could be working for the Franks! How did he get inside the palace?"

The guards, led by the sipahsalar—that is, the military chief—came forward, marveling that I should be there at all. The sipahsalar said, "Don't worry, sir, you'll have answers soon enough." Then, turning to his troops, he shouted, "Put him in the common prison!"

They shoved me forward, abusing me with foot, hand, and tongue; the vizier disappeared. Then the sipahsalar said, "Put him in the Storehouse of Banners!"

All at once the guards were patting me on the shoulder with a kindness that almost made up for the way they had been treating me. We had barely left the great hall and entered the corridor when a kind old man (endowed, nevertheless, with a grip like a vise) took charge of me. "Who was that vizier?" I asked him.

He looked at me indulgently. "If you had asked me that question on the way to the common prison, I would have let you have it with the point of my shoe. But since you're asking on the way to the Storehouse of Banners, I can answer, no problem." He began staring at my hands with a pleading look, so I pulled out a hundred-millieme note and handed it to him. He clasped my hand. When I pulled it back, I noticed that my silver pinkie ring was gone, but I didn't dare ask what had happened to it.

With a twitch of the mustache, the old man said, "Here's the way it is, sir. That was Bata'ihi, vizier to Amer. When he ordered them to take you to the common prison, he was insulting you, since the only people who go there are criminals, vagrants, and fugitives. But then for him to order you dragged to the Storehouse of Banners means that he respects you. That's where they put high officers, government officials, and other prominent people."

I laughed. "So you know how to treat me based on the kind of prison they put me in?" I added, "Name your prison, and I'll tell you what kind of man you are!"

"Who are you, anyway?" asked the old soldier.

"Ibn Shalaby, a Hanafi, an Egyptian, a seller of pickles and sweets, and a writer."

He raised his eyebrows in surprise and said, "Hmm."

We went through the Festival Gate and into the Palace of Thorns, which adjoins the Great Palace. We could look down onto the Storehouse of Banners, which the caliph Zahir had built alongside the Great Palace. Sitting in front of it was a dullard of a soldier who, directed by the man who was with me, stood up, opened the gate, and invited me in. Tears sprang to my eyes as I groped my way forward though a mountain of darkness.

For a good long while I stumbled around in the dark. At first I could sense only earth under my feet, but soon I was running up against a mass of bundles and bales. Then I remembered that I was carrying a cigarette lighter. I took it out and lit it. I saw a fine display of what they call standards, meaning battle flags, banners, and the like; more than a thousand leather shields; as many gold and silver vessels; endless numbers of lances; cockades and insignia; ceremonial regalia, plate armor, and chain mail; and saddles and bridles, along with a hundred thousand jeweled swords, give or take. All these items were kept in display windows, glass cases, or cabinets along the walls.

My flame went out but the glow remained. Suddenly I was afraid to keep the lighter out. I put it back in my pocket, shuddering at the thought of what would happen if anything caught on fire, especially since there were sacks of linen and all sorts of furnishings only steps away from me.

Suddenly my heart leapt into my throat as I noticed a number of attendants coming out of another door with candlesticks in their hands. As they set about trying to find a place to put them down, another group entered, led by a man who had an air of rectitude about him. I thought about hiding somewhere but then I decided to bluff my way through like a Cossack laying about with a whip. "Who's there?" I shouted.

Calmly one of them spoke, "May God protect us! Are there spirits living among the banners?"

"I'm no spirit, just a man," I said. "Why are all of you rushing in here?"

"Who might you be, sir?" asked the attendant who had spoken before.

"That's none of your business. You tell me who *you* are, or I'll shoot to kill."

All of them laughed. Pointing to the man with the air of rectitude, he said, "This is Saad al-Dawla, known as 'Peace Be Upon You.'"

"Hi there," I said. "Welcome, Mr. Peace Be Upon You."

"You do know who he is, right?" said the attendant.

"I haven't had the honor of meeting him."

Saad al-Dawla, known as 'Peace Be Upon You,' then spoke up: "My master, the caliph Muntasir, gave me everything in this storehouse as a gift."

Looking at my watch, I saw that it was Safar, 401. I looked up at the attendants, who were starting to pick things up, organize them, and carry them out. I had the feeling I had seen this fellow Saad before in the company of Maqrizi. But Maqrizi had never told me exactly who he was, making me resent the both of them. Now he came up to me, greeted me, and said that he would be honored to know my name. I sort of lost it—meaning that I was stuck and didn't know what to say—but then fate intervened to save me.

One of the attendants dropped his candlestick and a great clamor went up. All around us were hides full of naphtha, and in an instant they burst into flames that leapt up, attacking the walls, the inventory, and the cabinets, and consuming everything in a conflagration like the fires of Hell. Saad al-Dawla was whisked away by many hands. As for me, I had witnessed so many wars that I had become immune to fire. Finding a pole made of gold, I climbed it and hid in a distant corner. Torrents of water crashed over me and poured into the room from every direction. The uproar was tremendous: tens of thousands of hides and skins full of naphtha were bursting and feeding the fire. Within minutes, the place was a charred ruin. Then troops of soldiers, attendants, and laborers poured in, lifting away the debris in the hope of recovering what was left of the swords, gold, and gemstones. Among the items rescued, the number of jeweled swords alone came to something like fifteen thousand.

One day, then another, and possibly even several months went by, with me standing in the same spot witnessing the sad fate of the Storehouse of Banners. I watched the workers come in and clean the place, leaving it empty.

Lighting a cigarette, I lapsed into a meditation on the authors and novelists I had read, both Western and Eastern. I was trying to capture a thought that kept flitting away, to the effect that the history of Egypt poses a real challenge to the talents of her citizens. One of those citizens, admittedly, was the artist hardly bigger than his own chisel who carved out the statue of Ramses, not to mention tens of thousands of other colossal images. But would the country ever produce a novelist whose imagination could grapple with a history that overwhelmed all powers of perspective, creativity, and organization? It's a good thing that the novelists who've already made a name for themselves have never read any Egyptian history. If they did, they would be mortified by their amateurish attempts to depict it.

With a nerve-wracking squeal, the door opened and through it came flying a man who began groping in the darkness and cursing with elaborate futility. He shrieked when he saw the glow of the cigarette in my hand. I shouted out to him not to be afraid and—like any jailbird—ordered him to come closer. He did, then plopped down fearfully to the ground beside me, asking if I had paper, an inkpot, and a calamus. I handed him a piece of paper and a pen.

"Have you a lamp?" he asked.

"Right here," I said, taking out the lighter and lighting it.

"By your leave," he said, and started writing, frequently crossing things out, and admiring the pen.

"What nonsense are you scribbling?"

"I'm writing a letter to Kamil ibn Shawir."

Then he wrote, reciting as he did so:

O masters of Storehouse Prison
Let the breeze blow soft on me
Ask the dawn that breaks there:
Is it the last I ever see?
Despair not of God's mercy,
And let Kamil set me free!

"Well done," I said. "But who on earth are you?"

He looked at me in disbelief. "Do you truly not recognize me? I am chief judge of the Shafii legal school, Ibn al-Zubayr, now confined in this place." He went back to his writing until the lighter grew hot in my hand and I dropped it. I went down on the ground to grope for it, but it had disappeared, as had the judge. Trembling, I called out to him, but all I heard was my own voice echoing off walls and distant corners.

The wall of darkness was suddenly split by a column of white light approaching from some distance away like the beam of a searchlight. I quickly realized that the storehouse door that was located directly across from me, about two hundred feet away (or so it seemed), had opened. A booming voice followed the beam of light: "Where is the one called the Pickle-and-Sweet Vendor?"

After the echo had died away, the voice tried again, "Where is the agent of Baldwin the Frank?"

"There's no one here," I shouted back.

"Why did you say nothing until after I told you what you're accused of?"

"All you interrogators are the same," I answered. "You put us in a delicate situation and then you trap us. What do you want from Ibn Shalaby?"

"Write down exactly what you just said and hand it to me."

"Write?" I shrieked in alarm. "You've got to be kidding. So forced confession dates back to you guys? Anyway, I don't know how to write."

To my astonishment, I heard him laugh. "No, I want you to file a grievance. Don't you have grounds for complaint? Write it up, then, and we'll pass it on to the Court of Redress."

Overjoyed, I agreed. The ray of light withdrew and nearly disappeared, though I still see it in my head, where it lasted long enough for me to realize that in the dark I had forgotten what a vast space I had to move around in. I began walking forward cautiously.

As my eyes adjusted to the dark, I saw a light spreading through the emptiness. It soon took the form of a group of men dressed in brocade and carrying a couch and other furniture, which they arranged on the ground. I was surprised to see such luxurious items brought into a prison. No sooner had the men finished than they vanished like genies. Then another group, this one made up of high-ranking officers in uniform, came in guarding a man of some importance. They led him forward gently and directed him to the couch and the other items, shaking their heads as if to apologize. He gazed at the furniture in disappointment, smiled sadly, and finally nodded as if in resignation. Then he dismissed them and sat on the couch, head bowed, the picture of abjection.

A few moments later, another high-ranking guardsman entered, bowed before him, and then summoned a boy who had been standing behind him. The boy came forward with a low round table. On it was a silver tray full of dishes whose outlines were visible under a clean cloth. The prisoner thanked him and the guard withdrew. A moment later I came forward, bowed respectfully before the man as the others had, and then without further ado made a grab for his pot and the cup. Filling the cup with whatever was in the pot, I drank it down. It was a drink I didn't recognize, but whatever it was, the cup wasn't going to help me get enough of it. I lifted the pot with the thought of drinking right from it, but then I put it back, nodded my thanks, and began examining the tray. The man was watching me dumbfounded, half frightened and half angry. But then I saw him make a gesture of invitation. I raised the cloth, looked under it, and, seeing a variety of food and drink, put the cloth back, saying, "Better save it. Who knows how long we'll be in here?"

The man looked at me and asked what sort of spirit I was.

"No spirit," I said, "just a man."

"What sort of devil, then?"

"The only devils are the ones that lead man to perdition," I answered.

"Are you a genie, then?"

"It would serve you right if the genies carried you off!"

"Sit down, please."

I sat down beside him. Looking at me kindly, he said, "You do me a disservice to take me for a tyrant. If you knew who I was, you would respect me; and if you knew how much I've suffered, you would forgive me."

"Who are you, sir?" I asked.

"Ibn Anbari, vizier to the caliph Mustansir."

"So who put you in here, vizier to the caliph?"

"The new vizier," he answered. "Ibn Fallahi."

"Such is the way of the world!" I exclaimed. "There is no power nor might save in God the Almighty. But isn't being sacked punishment enough? Why did he imprison you in the Storehouse of Banners?"

"It's a long story. Would you like to hear it?"

"I certainly would," said I.

Ibn Anbari crossed his legs and began his tale. "Ever since the days of the Caliph Hakim, the palace has worked with two Jewish brothers, Abu Saad Ibrahim and Abu Nasr Harun, sons of Sahl of Tustar, one a trader and the other a moneychanger, both famous for being able to import things no one else could find. When Caliph Zahir, son of Hakim, came to power, he hired Abu Saad to procure various sorts of goods for him. Abu Saad went far in his favor. He sold the Caliph a black slave woman who won him over completely and bore him a son, Mustansir. The Caliph remained grateful to Abu Saad for that. When in due course Mustansir became Caliph, his mother showed favor to Abu Saad and employed him exclusively in her service."

"Where do you come in, then, Ibn Anbari?"

"When Gargarai the vizier died," he said, "I sought his position, and they gave it to me. Abu Nasr, the brother of Abu Saad, came to pay me a visit and ask a favor, and I let one of my pages send him away empty-handed. Abu Nasr resented me for it and spoke against me to his brother, who passed the word on to his mistress, who spoke to her son, the Caliph Mustansir, who dismissed me from my post. Abu Saad, again working through the Caliph's mother, managed to get Ibn Fallahi appointed in my place, at least officially. But it's Abu Saad who really runs the vizierate now."

"So far everything sounds like business as usual," I remarked. "Happens in every period. But what brings you here?"

"Ibn Fallahi made it his business," he replied, "to stir people up against me and saddle me with debts and destroy my reputation with the regime. In the end he got his way, and so they arrested me."

"On what charge?"

"Embezzling large sums of money from the treasuries that I used to run. Someone whispered to me a few minutes ago that they've confiscated all my property."

With a sigh, he bowed his head. Then, making an effort to distract himself, he asked me how long I had been in for.

"I've been imprisoned in this country for thousands of years," I told him.

His eyes widened in surprise. "On what charge?"

"Ask yourself!"

He looked even more surprised. "What do I have to do with your being here?"

"What I mean is, ask anybody who sits like you on a sultan's throne, or hangs onto it for dear life."

I had barely finished speaking when a little committee consisting of three men and an executioner entered the jail. The oldest stepped forward toward Ibn Anbari. I could tell that as far as he was concerned I was not in the picture at all.

"Ibn Anbari," he said, "I've come to carry out your sentence. It's been proven that you have abused state funds, attempted to deceive the government by forgery, and traduced its principles. I beg you to accept this explanation for what I am about to do."

He bowed reverently and then glanced at the executioner, who drew his sword from its sheath and brought it down on Ibn Anbari's neck, sending the head flying and spattering our faces with warm blood. Then they wrapped his corpse up in a piece of cloth. A shallow grave had already been dug at the spot where the head had landed. They buried Ibn Anbari and his head in the grave, flung earth over them, and left as if nothing had occurred. I stood there paralyzed. My watch said it was Monday, the fifth of Muharram, AH 440.

The beam of white light passed in front of me again and I realized that the door had opened. The voice came back along the beam of light, saying, "Good news, Pickle-and-Sweet Seller! The Court of Redress has received your petition and will meet in the near future to review it. Have no fear!"

I told the beam of light that no one anywhere in Egypt had any reason to worry, since the country was haunted by spirits, all of them with a history; and there was no way to avoid having them appear before you and add to the list of awful and terrifying stories, keeping you entertained and placating you to the point that you became too circumspect to think of taking part in any kind of revolt. In a regretful tone, the beam of light explained that imprisonment had affected my mind, and then retreated until it had faded out altogether. So there I was, without a couch or anything else to sit on in the storeroom except emptiness and gloom.

In the fading light I had marked the spot where Ibn Anbari the vizier had been buried. Being the sort of person who likes company, I was moved to pay a visit to the place and read the opening verse of the Quran over his head. But no sooner did I begin making my way over than a light from some invisible source began streaming forth from the very spot. Eventually it grew bright enough to reveal a group of uniformed officers guarding yet another prisoner who looked like a member of the elite. They left him there and were gone. The man began babbling, smacking his palms together, and repeating in a frenzied voice, "That was my one mistake! I granted a safe conduct to people who didn't deserve it. But no! I have to set things right. They *must* listen to me! This is unfair, and I don't deserve to be treated this way."

"Yo, pal, give me a break," I shouted at him. "You're making my head hurt!"

He shouted back, "Silence, you beast, you rabble! Do you know who I am? You can't talk to me in that disgusting tone of voice!" He went on. "Not to mention that the Storehouse of Banners is a prison for people of standing. How did they let someone like *you* in here?"

I got close enough to him so he could see me and asked, "And who might you be, sir?"

"I hardly believe you don't recognize me," he said, "but I'm Ibn Fallahi, the vizier."

"The one who was just a front for the Jew?"

"You've been sent to trap me," he responded weakly.

I laughed. "Who, me?"

No sooner had I finished laughing than the same committee, equipped with executioner and gravediggers, made its appearance. The leader said, "Ibn Fallahi, I've come to carry out your sentence. It's been proven that you have abused state funds, attempted to deceive the government by forgery, and traduced its principles. I beg you to accept this explanation for what I am about to do."

He gestured to the executioner. But the gravediggers had stopped in astonishment. All of us looked into the scrape.

"That's the head of Ibn Anbari," cried Ibn Fallahi. "I killed him and buried him right there! 'Many a grave-shaft has been filled and refilled / Laughing all the while as rivals press in, side by side!'"

Then the sword came down and his head flew into the pit, landing next to the head of Ibn Anbari. The gravediggers covered both of them with earth.

At that moment the beam of white light passed in front of me again and the voice spoke saying, "Good news, Pickle-and-Sweet Seller! Your petition has been reviewed and signed with the Lesser Pen."

"So you're letting me out?"

"No! Now the petition has to be signed by the Greater Pen."

He disappeared without explaining what difference there was between the two.

7

Locking Out the Doorkeepers

I REMAINED SITTING ALONE IN the Storehouse of Banners awaiting any news of my petition, which, as I learned, had finally
been honored with the signature of the Lesser Pen prepara-
tory to being honored by the signature of the Greater Pen.
What with one incident following hard on another, the place
was beginning to wear on my nerves. Here no head was so high
that the sword couldn't reach it. Even if you were tall, so long
as you kept your head down, the sword would take no notice of
you. But hold that head of yours too high and the sword would
leap up with a magisterial flash and send it spinning to the
ground. My only reason for hope was that my head had not yet
ascended to a point where it might be of interest.

Looking up, I focused my gaze as if calling on a higher
power. The ceiling of time looked like layer upon layer of
clouds; the ceiling of the storehouse itself was no longer visible. From my brain came rays that played against the ashen
clouds as if trying to dispel them. Spectral figures passed back
and forth, but all I could see was their feet. This was a game
I enjoyed. I thought of a story I had read by someone whose
name I couldn't remember. The hero works in a cellar; the
only part of people's bodies he can see is their feet passing
back and forth. Eventually he acquires the ability to recognize
people by their feet. I must have acquired the same ability
in a very short time: as thousands of millions of feet passed
above the ceiling of time, I recognized those of several people

I knew. I took to tickling them with pieces of straw and window-hooks and watching them stumble, clutch one another in fear, and resume their walk.

Then, as the portico of time grew thinner and more transparent, I could see entire figures rushing from one far-off place to another. Vehicles crawled along endlessly. There was Shaykh Shaarawi, walking past in his simple gallabiya and his white cap, with TV trucks following in his wake. I kept my eye on him until he disappeared into a mosque. The trucks stopped and the TV crews began setting up. I realized that the square in front of the Mosque of Husayn was directly above the Storehouse of Banners. Rising, I walked toward the rear of the storehouse in the direction of the Festival Gate and stopped right under Fishawi's. There I took in a marvelous spectacle: wave after wave of Egyptian celebrities, writers, politicians, and artists descending on the café and disappearing again in the time it takes to turn the page of a book—all disappearing, that is, except for Abdel Fattah Barudi, whose pronouncements on the drama continued to echo even here.

When I looked back at the ground, a curtain seemed to close over the scene. Sitting next to me all of a sudden was Maqrizi, with an invisible barrier of glass standing between us. "Where have you been all this time?" I exclaimed.

He peered this way and that, astonished. When he saw me, he asked, "Is that you?"

"It's me. So what brings *you* here?"

"I'm not in the Storehouse of Banners at the moment," he said. "I'm actually sitting in a friend's house."

"How's that?"

"The house I'm sitting in now," he said, "is partly in the Saqifa quarter and partly in the Banner Storehouse quarter. As you can see, it's located between Salami Street, as you leave Festival Gate Square, and the Storehouse of Banners. By the way, the part of the house I'm sitting in is where petitioners would present their cases to the caliph."

"You must be sitting in Jabarti's house."

"Who's that?" he asked.

"An Egyptian historian from the reign of Muhammad Ali Pasha the Albanian and his viceregal family. His house was here, in Cratemakers' Alley."

"What matters now," he said, "is how you ended up in here."

"Just my luck, I guess."

"Your luck is actually quite good. You're a member of the elite now," he laughed. "Which means that you're in danger of losing your head."

Shuddering, I explained to him that I had filed a grievance with the Court of Redress, and that it had been signed by the Lesser Pen and would soon be soon be signed by the Greater Pen.

"Which period are you in?" he asked.

"The reign of the Fatimid caliph Amer."

"And who told you that your appeal had been signed by the Lesser Pen?"

"A voice belonging to the jailor."

"Don't believe it," he said. "The Greater Pen signs during the same session as the Lesser Pen."

"So who signs with the Lesser Pen?"

"The Illustrious Elder, Head of the Chancery and Scribe to the Royal Seat," he intoned. "The Caliph by necessity has in attendance someone who can supply him with whatever Quranic quotations and calligraphy he might need, and recite tales of prophets and kings. They meet most days, along with a veteran ustaz in possession of the requisite qualification, our ustaz making up the third of the party. He reads the Caliph a summary of the Prophet's life, repeating for his benefit any passages that mention exemplary traits of character. He brings along an ornamented pencase, and has charge of the writing-stand for signatures, and a seatcushion and a backpillow and an attendant to hand him the documents that need signing. He enjoys the privileges granted to representatives of the Bureau of Correspondence with respect to protocol, robes of honor, and the like."

"So that damned jailor lied to me?"

Maqrizi laughed and rebuked me for being so trusting, adding that the guards were taking advantage of my confinement in the Storehouse of Banners to practice their abilities to lie, trick, and deceive, and that what I should do is ask to see the Caliph and present my petition to him myself, which was it my right to do.

At that moment someone called Maqrizi in to lunch, so he excused himself and disappeared. The storehouse was again plunged into darkness and silence.

I looked for something to do to pass the time, but found nothing. Then I remembered that I had with me a small cassette player about the size of my hand. Joyfully I took it out, turned it on, and turned up the volume all the way. Out came the voice of Umm Kulthum singing songs composed for her by Muhammad Abdel Wahhab. Within minutes, every door to the storehouse had opened and soldiers were converging on me, looking at the device in amazement. When I shut it off and put it in my pocket their astonishment turned into something like fear.

"Are you a sorcerer?" asked their chief.

"Yes," I said, "and that's one of my inventions. I want to present it as a gift to the Caliph."

"Give it to me, then, and I'll see that he gets it."

"No," I said. "I want to hand it to him myself."

Trembling, the chief gathered his men and left, barring the doors behind him. A few minutes later, one of the doors opened to admit a man wearing a suit of gold brocade adorned with medals and decorations. Behind him came a group of men who looked like commanders or something of the sort. The man approached me, bowed slightly, and asked, "Are you the illustrious pickle-and-sweet vendor?"

"That's me," I said.

"Splendid! Where is your gift for the Caliph?"

"Who are you?"

Smiling like an embarrassed celebrity forced to divulge his identity, he glanced around and one of the others came forward to introduce him, "This is His Excellency, Master of the Door. We, on the other hand, are men of the sword—commanders. As for me, call me Vice-Guardian of the Door."

"What's your name?"

"Guide to the Door."

"That's your name?"

"It's what I'm always called," he said.

"And what's your job, Mr. Guide to the Door?"

"I receive ambassadors from abroad," he replied modestly. "The gatekeepers work for me. I keep the envoys safe and settle them in their quarters, and then I lead them in to greet the Caliph and his vizier. The Master of the Door stands on the right and I stand on the left. It's my job to keep an eye on the envoys, see to their comfort, and prevent anyone from ill-treating them, or forbidding people to see them, or learning about the reasons for their visit; and I make sure that they can receive messages."

Crossing my legs, I said, "I'm really impressed! I never thought I would meet anyone so popular outside the age of the Sons of Shalaby, where I come from."

The Master of the Door asked me kindly, "What exactly are you carrying with you, my lord?"

"To begin with," I replied, "I'm not your lord; I'm not even my own master, and don't you forget it! What I am, if you don't mind my saying so, is a guy like you. I work in palaces too. Of course, the palaces you've got here really exist. The ones we've got are in the clouds: you know, the kind of make-believe Egyptians are good at. If you could see our movies and TV shows, you'd see how much we've done to get the word out about our glorious ancestors. Thanks to the media, even children from distant villages know that we Egyptians are the cleverest people on earth. We're the ones who drilled a hole through the first penny, not to mention being the inventors of sliced bread. Did you know that we can also spray-paint the wind and fit an elephant into a handkerchief? Anyway, Master of the Door, let's cut to the chase. Tell me what you really do around here so I can fill you in on my invention."

With icy politeness, the Master of the Door adroitly replied that if I did not yet grasp the true nature of his role then he would gladly undertake to inspire in me a desire for better understanding. "In that case, my lord, you'd have a glimpse of my true nature."

The fellow was beginning to irritate me. "So is that why you're standing there like you want to arrest me? What do you want from me, anyway?"

They exchanged a glance of diplomatic amusement. The Master of the Door stepped forward and, pointing to the man next to him, said: "Allow me to present the sipahsalar."

"What does sipahsalar mean?" I demanded, even though I knew. "Are you threatening me?"

"My apologies," he said with a smile. "The sipahsalar is the one who supervises all the overseers and commands all our troops."

"You *are* threatening me. If you mention troops, then you're threatening me."

"I was merely noting," he smiled, "that he's next in rank after me."

"A pleasure to meet you," I said, with all the hostility I could manage.

Ignoring my tone, the Master of the Door continued the introductions. "Next after the sipahsalar comes the Bearer of the Caliph's Sword and the Orphan Diamond on procession days. Then—lemme see—there's the collar-bearers who serve the elite corps of the Amiriya and the Hafiziya. Then come the ones with the gold brocade and the standards—meaning the flags—then the various detachments, followed by the nominees for high office."

"Great!" I said, clapping my hands. "Keep going: you could talk a dog off a meat wagon!"

They all laughed. "Look, buddy," said the sipahsalar, "you seem like a smart guy. You sure you can't see your way to helping us out here?"

I unbent and extended my hand for him to shake, which he did with an alacrity that gave me the sense that somewhere inside him was a little boy who had wandered through streets and derelict buildings, slept in sewer pipes, and befriended the night watchmen at the public piss-troughs.

"Why don't all of you gentlemen have a seat?" I asked.

Out of nowhere came a troop of palace attendants who flitted ghostlike across the scene like stagehands during a play, setting out a number of sumptuous chairs upholstered in gold fabric. Everyone sat down except for me. I was left sitting on a wooden bench that would never have passed muster in the shabbiest Egyptian police station. Apropos of nothing, the Master of the Door commented that the state offered positions such as theirs only to the toughest and most resourceful men.

"Of course," I said, as if in agreement. "No doubt. Which is why those jobs are all in the hands of Armenians, Greeks, and God knows who else."

"What're you getting at?" said the sipahsalar, with a spark of anger in his eye that was visible a thousand miles off.

Trying to master the fear I still felt, I explained that it wasn't me but Maqrizi who had said so. "And that's not all he said, either. He also said everything that you and I have been saying ever since you came in. You've been repeating him word for word, maybe because he was just repeating *you*. But only God knows for sure!"

Like the veteran master of ceremonies he was, the Master of the Door remarked that we were all getting along very well. "My lord should have no doubt," he continued, "that our only interest is in his welfare and safety. Furthermore, as he is doubtless aware, we find ourselves at present bearing the brunt of Frankish hostility. We fear that they may have come up with some new device to deprive the Caliph of life."

"Of course," I said, exhaling cigarette smoke. "You're trying to protect him from dirty tricks on the part of the Franks. But he's going to be assassinated by cowards while crossing the Roda Island bridge."

"We make it a policy to eliminate all hostile Frankish interlopers," said the sipahsalar. "And it seems likely that Baldwin is involved here."

"Why should you care?" I laughed. "Baldwin invaded Egypt and occupied Farama, but the people rose up and destroyed him and liberated the place for themselves. The place they call 'Lake Baldwin' is a tribute to the true Egyptian spirit."

"You're a wiseass," said the sipahsalar with undisguised contempt, "and we don't intend to waste any more time on you. So talk!"

I pressed my knees together to prevent them from shaking and gave the Master of the Door a disapproving glare—or a beseeching glance, I can't recall which. The Master made a pulling-down gesture with his fingertips in the air in front of the sipahsalar, urging him to calm down. I did the same, and between the two of us we nearly poked the fellow in the face. Then, with a dramatic flourish, I exclaimed, "Now listen to this!"

Putting my hand into my pocket, I rewound the cassette tape, startling them with the hissing noise of the machine. Then I pushed another button to play the recording I had made. Out came our voices, repeating every word and exclamation that had passed between us. Flabbergasted, then terrified, they burst into hysterical laughter. The Master of the Door leapt up and said, "Please do come, my lord, and see the Caliph at once!" I rose immediately. He stepped aside to let me pass, and I jauntily took the lead.

I had only gone a few steps before I found myself bitterly regretting my promise. The cassette player wasn't fully paid for. I had asked a friend who was traveling to Port Said to buy it for me, thinking that it wouldn't cost more than the extra ten days of salary that the government gives out at the beginning of the school year. But my friend, bless his heart, couldn't get me an exemption from the customs duties and I still owed him a tidy sum, which I had promised to pay in two monthly installments. I hadn't even enjoyed the cassette player yet! How could I be so cavalier about giving it away as a gift, even if it was to Caliph al-Amir bi-Ahkam Allah, the Commander of the Faithful?

But then I decided that the Caliph would certainly reward me handsomely for the gift. As a result of the climate I had been living in for the past several years, I found myself using the same logic that I was exposed to every day. I would ask after a friend, only to hear that he had gone abroad to work as chief editor of a magazine in Wadi al-Naml, or that he was running a bank in Sahl al-Ashram and had just built his seventh housing complex, or that an acquaintance known for his charm and his unimpeachable character had gone off to found an establishment for the promotion of one thing or another. So it was that I had seen all of the people I cared about go away to run this, found that, and eat, drink, and be merry beyond my wildest dreams. I did occasionally run into one or another of them, and we would sit and talk, but I still felt that they were lost to me.

Fine! Whoever wants to go abroad can go. I had chosen to travel through time instead, and it looked as if my approach was about to pay off. I would make a big entrance and impress the Caliph—there was no reason he should treat me less respectfully than he would anyone else. I would negotiate a contract for radio and TV broadcasting and—if things worked out—a combination movie theater and meat market. It would be best to corner the market from the get-go and work out a deal with the Caliph personally to set up a satellite network—and a light saddle fretwork, too, while I was at it. Then I could go back to my own Cairo, gather the many talented but unemployed Sons of Shalaby, and make them offers they couldn't refuse. It's true that I'd be paying them about half of what they deserved so I could make more money myself, but any hard-luck Son of Shalaby will take any work that's offered at any rate of pay. I would choose only the most talented; that is, the most adept at domestic service, the quickest on their feet, the best at playing with my children and taking them to school, the handiest at serving coffee to my foreign guests, the ones best able to recall the conversations they overheard and repeat them back to me, the most responsive to my wishes, the likeliest to agree with all my opinions, the ones who got along best with my wife, and the ones least able to drive a hard bargain. How, in fact, could they bargain, anyway? I would know where they came from and would remind them of it if they talked back to me. Sellers of newspapers, soft drinks, and beans, even if they make money and earn respect, would still have to kiss my feet top and bottom.

I awoke from this daydream to find the Master of the Door touching my shoulder gently, pointing to a chair, and asking me to sit and wait for a moment. We were in an eastward-facing room that was impressive despite its small size. In different corners were doors of heavy sandalwood decorated with carvings depicting the martyrdom of Husayn, each leaf in the form of a book page framed with Islamic motifs. The Master disappeared behind one of the doors and reappeared looking pleased. I rose to meet him and he placed a hand on my shoulder, whispering excitedly that they had conveyed to the Caliph exactly what they had seen and that I would be given the post of vizier immediately if my magic proved of benefit to the people and the dynasty.

"Now you're talking," I said. "It'll benefit everyone, that's for sure."

"By the way, I told His Highness that you're a good honest fellow, quick on the uptake, and a man of learning."

"Well done!" I said. "I owe you one."

"At the moment, he's presiding over the Court of Redress, and he's given you permission to enter. Fortunately for us," he added, "the petitioners left early."

He opened the door for me and in I went, gaping at the enormous, high-walled audience room. In front was the golden throne and behind it a window topped by a dome. Caliph Amir was sitting on the throne, surrounded by figures I cleverly guessed must be his chief officers. I knew there were ceremonies I was supposed to observe, but I decided to overlook them without worrying too much about it, so I called out a hearty greeting that left them dumbfounded. Sensing that I had gotten off to a bad start, I put my hand in my pocket, took out the cassette player, flipped it over a few times, and put it back in my pocket. Their eyes never left it, and a combination of fury, resentment, brute contempt, and fanatical self-defensiveness was clearly visible on their faces.

Amir himself was a stocky fellow of a russet complexion (by the way, I have no idea what "russet" means, but it sounds nice) and bulging eyes, with a confrontational look about him. He was a young man in the prime of life, dressed in layer upon layer of costly gowns, with chunks of emerald and gold glinting on his chest, sleeves, hands, and throat like sightless magic eyes. He raised his head to look at me and, speaking across the great distance between us, said, "Come here, you."

I took a few steps forward but, suddenly sensing my own insignificance, stopped. Smiling, the Caliph said, "If what I've heard is true, the dynasty can make use of you to confer great benefits upon the lands of Egypt and of the Arabs."

"It is true, Your Highness."

"So that metal hand you have in your pocket can collect voices and remember them and make them speak again?"

"Yes, Your Highness."

"Can it spy on enemies of the Caliph?"

"Yes," I said with a condescending smile. "Yes, it can."

"Can we make thousands of them out of gold and silver and rubies and sandalwood?"

"Absolutely, Your Highness."

"Can it keep the Caliph from growing bored, and banish any sort of thoughts and worries from the minds of his subjects?"

"No question at all, Your Highness."

"If that's true," he said, "I will make you my vizier."

"Your Highness," I said, "will now hear everything he just said."

Everyone stirred uneasily and looked at me with fear, expectancy, and delight.

"Then I make you my vizier," he said. He sat up straight as if expecting me to do something. Unaccountably confused about what to do next, I bowed several times. The Master of the Door caught me on one of my ascents, stopped me from bowing again, and whispered, "Go over to your master, greet him, and kiss the ground before him."

"My pleasure!"

I had once before seen someone kneel before the Caliph and kiss the ground as passionately as one might kiss a lover's lips. I did the same, kneeling on the ground and bussing the top of my hand in a well-staged display of fervor. When I rose to my feet, the Caliph extended his hand, which I shook warmly and then kissed. Then he extended his foot. I stood there bewildered. Exchanging awkward glances, his officers gestured for me to kiss the Caliph's foot, as they did. I knew they all did, and that doing so was a condition of working for him, but I stood rooted to the spot, trembling. The Caliph ordered me to kiss his foot.

"Do I have to, sir?"

"Kiss the Caliph's foot!" he shouted.

I screwed up my face like a stubborn child and got ready to start crying and screaming. As if sensing that I really would, the Caliph forced a smile and pulled his foot back onto the throne. "In light of your circumstances I exempt you. Sit!"

I sat.

"Show me what you have there."

I took out the cassette player and turned it on but nothing happened. Alarmed, I looked at it and began shaking it and pressing all the buttons to no avail. The courtiers were looking at me raptly, as still as if they were carrying pitchers full of water on their heads. Breaking into a sweat, I croaked, "I don't have a plug here with me!"

Everyone exchanged scathing looks. "A palace like this," I exclaimed, "and you can't find room for an outlet or two?" Then I realized. "Oh . . . I forgot that you don't have electricity."

"What's a 'plug'?" shouted the Caliph. "And an 'outlet'? And what's 'electricity'? Why didn't it talk?"

"The battery's dead," I told him.

"Show me."

I gave it to him. He turned it over and over, gingerly pushing the buttons. Then he flung it away as hard as he could. Someone instantly popped up to catch it as I looked on in dismay.

"An impostor!" the Caliph was shouting. "Throw this pickle seller back in the storehouse."

Hands landed on my shoulders like a horde of bats and held me fast.

8

When Prison Becomes Home

I NEVER IMAGINED BEING UNLUCKY enough to have my fate hang on the crankiness of that complicated little device. I should have mastered it and learned all its ins and outs before trying to use it as way to make it to the top. The Third World (may you be spared its fate!) imagines that importing industrial products is the civilized—or civilizing—thing to do. But we fail to grasp that even if you learn how something works, and even when you own the raw materials needed to manufacture the thing in the first place, all you are is a consumer. This is a problem bigger than all the Sons of Shalaby in all their branches throughout the region can imagine.

I tried my best to placate the caliph but the soldiers had already surrounded me. They seemed diffident, as if they had never before had to confront anyone who had been sitting with the sovereign. Perhaps they were unused to seeing riff-raff like myself spoiling that rarefied atmosphere. To protect the Caliph's reputation—my reputation of course being of no concern—the sipahsalar stopped the soldiers from manhandling me. I felt as if everyone at court, from the senior courtiers down to the lowliest guardsmen, resented me for working my way up gradually to the biggest gaffe of all: refusing to kiss the Caliph's foot, which heads far greater than mine had bent to smooch. For that reason alone, I shuddered to think what would happen to me after we left the Caliph's audience. By the time we left, though, I had come up with a plan.

With the sipahsalar walking ahead of me, and the soldiers behind, we left the audience chamber, went down the steps, and headed back down the corridor we had come from. Moments later we had left the grounds and were walking along the side of the palace. In front of us was the Storehouse of Banners, and I was able to see what the place really looked like. It was enormous: the space it occupied was enough to accommodate several giant skyscrapers (even if the sky, in those days, was too high for anyone to scrape). Hoping to get back into the sipahsalar's good graces, I said, "I know some foreign firms that could take that lot and fill it with skyscrapers."

"We have no plans to scrape the sky," he replied scornfully. "Why would we?"

"You'd solve the housing crisis!"

"The only crisis we're facing at the moment is what to do with you."

He walked on ahead, and between us for a moment fell the shadow of a tree. Suddenly I felt as if layer upon layer of time was crashing down on my head and that I had to struggle to the surface. By dint of some extraordinary effort I was able to glimpse, at the topmost level, the housing units that Princess Shweikar had built above the shops in Khan al-Khalili. I saw Sanusi's Creamery and, behind it, the café where I always sit whenever I visit the Husayn district; in the back was another creamery, Maliki's. I had managed to climb almost all the way up when an angry shout from the sipahsalar brought me crashing back to earth. There we were, at the gate of the Storehouse of Banners, but the gatekeeper was nowhere to be seen.

Yelling into empty space, piling on curses and imprecations, and denouncing the lack of organization that had brought us to the edge of collapse, the sipahsalar dashed around in search of the unfortunate fellow. The guardsmen followed suit, peering here and there in consternation. "This is my chance," I thought. Joining the search, I added my voice to the chorus of complaints about "that filthy doorkeeper," suggesting that they fire him—or hang him, "as we would do in my time." All the while, I was inching closer to an open gate, with nothing but blackness on the other side.

Then, suddenly, I was in an obscure spot behind the storehouse. There was no one near the building. I sat down on a ledge at the bottom of the wall and felt the dampness suffuse my joints. In the distance I saw a troop of soldiers wearing an assortment of uniforms marching toward me with military precision. "The country must be under foreign occupation," I thought, noticing how confidently they moved and wondering whether Egyptians as well as foreigners could seem so self-assured. Though I couldn't be certain, the faces I scrutinized seemed familiar and the style of clothing was one I felt sure I had seen here many times before. To my surprise, they disappeared without paying me the slightest attention.

I plucked up the courage to stand and look at the wall of the storehouse from the outside. It looked washed-out and bloated. Even more daringly, I climbed up the ledge and put my fingers through the metal railing, parts of which had rusted away and sprung free of the wall, leaving an opening big enough for me to put my fist through and reach a round metal door that looked like a porthole. When I pushed it, it opened. Peering into the storehouse, I saw a small room overlooking a long passageway. Both were utterly deserted. I couldn't believe that *this* was the Storehouse of Banners where they had imprisoned me, and that *this* was the place I had tried so hard to escape from.

I climbed down from the rail and sat. I could see enormous crowds of people, of more kinds and colors than I could count. Some of the faces were long and red, and others were round and brown; some were as radiant as the moon, and others as battered as a ball made of rags. They betrayed no shared ancestry and resembled one another in no particular feature. The one thing they had in common was their language—Arabic pronounced with an Egyptian accent—which they were using to raise a terrifying chant: "Qalawun, you're our friend! We'll fight for you till the end!"

We Egyptians are like water: we'll let any tide sweep us along. Although I had no idea what was happening, a wave of enthusiasm carried me to the center of the crowd. There I spotted all of my important friends: Ibn Abdel Hakam, Ibn Abdel Barr, Ibn Abdel Zahir, Ibn Taghribirdi, Ibn Iyas, Ibn So-and-So, Ibn Whoever, and Ibn What's-His-Face, marching along and looking as if they were shouting slogans too, even though you discovered as you got closer to them that they were doing nothing of the kind.

Ibn Taghribirdi pulled me aside and whispered, "What were you doing next to the Storehouse of Banners?"

With some pride, I told them that I had been imprisoned there. He seemed distinctly unimpressed. I was taken aback by his indifference, and he was surprised that I was surprised.

"In my time," I told him, "people used to brag constantly about being in prison. Anyone who came out of it was treated like a hero with medals tattooed onto his body. Go figure!"

Then I changed the subject. "So what's going on? What's happening now?"

Ibn Taghribirdi told me that the people were coming out to welcome Nasir ibn Qalawun, who was making his triumphal return from Karak. Ibn Qalawun, he added, was the seventh Turkish king to rule Egypt.

"Is he still fighting the Mongols?" I asked.

"No, the Mongol presence is an established fact. No one launches wars against them any more, if you don't count the constant wrangling and skirmishing that goes on. The Mongols have won a few and lost a few, but they're here to stay."

"How did that happen?" I asked.

"I'm sure you know the painful truth."

"Tell me."

"Given our enormous population," he said, "anyone who invades this country or tries to colonize it can always find soldiers to replenish his ranks. All he has to do is start out strong. As long as he wins the first battles, even if his troops retreat or succumb to the plague, he can replace them with Egyptian volunteers."

"That's going too far, Ibn Birdi," I said. "You've accused our people of the worst possible crime."

"The way I see it," he said, "our people are caught in the middle of all this mess. It doesn't take long for the invaders and colonizers to blend in. Once they do, the abuses continue, but now in the name of the nation."

"True enough, Ibn Taghri," I said. "But the hardest thing to take is that the invaders and colonizers and butchers all recruited Egyptians to fight for them. How many heroes have fallen in vain! How many champions have been slain by cowards! How many clashes have been joined on the heights, only to tumble to the bottom of the hill!"

Packing his nose with snuff, Ibn Taghribirdi said, "It's a question of justice and injustice. It's the cruelty of tyrants that makes the world an unjust place, and it's injustice that turns brother against brother and eventually turns people against themselves. That's how this nation will destroy itself: one person has his way with everyone else, and soon enough no one is safe from anyone."

A moment later he added, "This is the third time that Ibn Qalawun's been installed as sultan. He's come back from Karak and he's ready to rule in Cairo. The last time, it was two of his father's Mamluks who were plotting against him: Baybars the Taster, called the Victorious; and Salar. After fighting the Mongols in Syria, Ibn Qalawun was sick of war; but he came home to find that those two had seized the reins of power. It should also be noted that Salar was a double-dealer who betrayed the Sultan, who was the son of his master, to the Taster, and later betrayed the Taster to the Sultan. And there he is, sitting in the Citadel waiting for him, after issuing declarations to incriminate the Taster and freeing whichever of the Sultan's Mamluk slaves he had detained."

Vexed, I blew out a breath. "Be quiet, Ibn Taghri! There's no need to air anyone's dirty laundry." My watch was pointing to Tuesday, the 23rd of Shawwal, 698. "But how is it," I asked, "that the Sultan managed to defeat his father's Mamluks after they stripped him of all authority, which he let them do out of disgust?"

"When a dog tastes blood," said the historian, "it becomes enraged. The same thing happens when men struggle for power. It wasn't enough for the Mamluk slave to depose his master's son. He wanted to kill him, too, to rest his own behind more comfortably on the throne. But Syria, Iraq, and Egypt were full of Burgi Mamluks loyal to Ibn Qalawun, who showered money on them, taught them chivalry, and looked after them. If one went bad, there were others to take his place. So Ibn Qalawun left his exile in Karak and entered Cairo guarded by the Mamluk rulers of Damascus, Aleppo, Hims, and Hama, along with their troops."

He abruptly fell silent, distracted by the extraordinary events that were now taking place. On both sides of the road leading from the Citadel down through Palace Gate, great masses of people were quarreling and chaffering. "I'll take fifty dirhams!" one would shout. "I'll take seventy!" said another. "Take a hundred!" cried a third.

"What's going on?" I asked.

Smiling, Ibn Taghribirdi replied that the people standing at their doors were the owners of the houses.

"Why are they bargaining?" I asked.

"The Sultan will pass down this road," he replied.

"So?"

"For anywhere from fifty to a hundred dinars, you can go up into one of the houses and look out of the window or the lattice or the balcony as he goes by."

"No kidding!"

Wriggling through the crowd, I made my way closer to the Sultan's cavalcade, which had reached the Victory Gate.

There the emirs all dismounted. The first on the ground was Badr al-Din Buknash Fakhri, the Grand Master of Armor, who carried the Sultan's weapons. The Sultan ordered Badr al-Din, who was an old man, to mount; but he refused and continued on foot. The rest followed in order of rank. They had set up little arches, called "citadels," in the streets, and each had spread headcloths on the ground between his citadel and the one provided by the next emir. As soon as the Sultan passed one citadel, the cloths would be spread on the path to the next one, allowing him to ride comfortably and with fitting dignity in the presence of the emirs. The royal party would stop to inspect each citadel and admire its contents, thereby winning over the one who had built it. Then—but wait! What was happening with the cavalcade?

Catching up with me before I lost my mind, Ibn Taghri-birdi said, "Keep looking, but stay calm."

I looked and saw emirs in fetters with other people's severed heads strung around their necks.

"Those are the Mongol commanders," he said, "and those are the heads of the fighters killed in battle."

There were a thousand more heads mounted on spears. Behind the commanders were the prisoners, all sixteen hundred of them, each with a severed head around his neck. In front of them were their drums, now punctured. I asked Ibn Taghribirdi if this were Ibn Qalawun's second triumphal return or his third.

"This is the second, after the battle."

"Why did you say that this was the third?"

"I had ducked out for a moment during his third return, but on my way back I got lost and ended up at the second. The problem is that all these processions look the same, except for the captives."

Meanwhile I was enjoying the spectacle of the "citadels." They were decorations mounted on wooded structures and hung with lamps, something like a parade float today. There was the citadel of Nasir al-Din ibn Shaykhi, the military governor of Cairo, at the Victory Gate. Next was the citadel of Emir Mughaltai, Supervisor of Physicians; and after it the citadels of Ibn Aytmay Saadi; Sunqur Gawuli; Tughril Ighani; Bahadur Yusufi; Sudi; Bilik Khatiri (who, by the way, has a mosque in Bulaq named after him); Burlughi; Mubariz al-Din, Master of the Hunt; Aybak the Treasurer; Sunqur the Left-Handed; Baybars, the Master of the Inkwell; Sunqur Kamili; Musa ibn al-Malik al-Salih; Aal Malik; Alam al-Din Sawabi; Gamal al-Din Tashlaqi; Sayf al-Din Adam; Salar the Deputy; Baybars the Taster; Baknash Master of Weapons; the eunuch Murshid the Treasurer; Baktamur, the Liason to the Emirs; and Aybak of Baghdad, the Deputy in Absence. Then I lost track of the citadels and the names of all the many emirs who had stripped the flesh from Egypt's bones century after century.

The crowd grew denser. We had arrived at the Mansuri Hospital on the square between the palaces. There the Sultan dismounted and went inside to visit the grave of his father Qalawun. The Quran readers began reciting before him. The crowd moved again, pushing me forward blindly. Everyone I recognized from the procession, including the Sultan and his entourage, disappeared from view, leaving only the chained commanders and prisoners of war with the heads strung around their necks.

Then blows began to rain down on us, driving us forward to—no, it couldn't be, but it was: the Storehouse of Banners! Not again, I thought to myself: what have I done, good sirs, to deserve such a fate? I'm not a prisoner. In fact, I'm not even from this period! But there was no one to appeal to. We tumbled forward into the Storehouse, which felt like a tomb too small to breathe in.

There the real unpleasantness began. People were shrieking and wailing in languages that Ibn Shalaby did not understand and had never even heard before, striking their faces in lamentation, rending their garments, and fetching up cries that seemed loud enough to split the walls and rip through outer space, or else making a sound that was either laughing or weeping, or perhaps hysterical weeping that had turned into laughter, if not a belly laugh that had turned into a sob. The severed heads dangling from the prisoners' necks were knocking into each other in the crowd, splattering our faces with dried blood and tiny pieces of torn human flesh.

All at once, to my great astonishment, the whole storehouse fell silent, as if the clamor of a moment before had never been. The light came on in my head. Now, the ground before me was covered with thousands of bodies piled one on another. The severed heads were piled together in various places, in some cases keeping the bodies apart and in others pushing them together. The storehouse had expanded into a great space divided into numerous rooms. Dwarfed by the heaps of bodies and the contents of the storehouse, I set off across the mass of living flesh, creeping like an ant. But I soon found that the enclosures inside the building were crammed so full of people that even an ant couldn't get in. I clambered up to one of the windows and looked out. The guard was fast asleep with his head on his chest, snoring. When I pinched his ear, he leapt up with a cry of alarm.

"Why are you keeping us here, you tyrants?" I asked him.

He turned to me with a cry of pain like the one you hear often enough in the voices of Egyptians in our own day. "Not *again*! We told you: it's not a prison! We told you a hundred times that you're not in prison. Sultan Ibn Qalawun—may God preserve him—abolished the prison in the Storehouse of Banners and gave you the place to live in, God bless his good heart. You should pray for him!"

"What do you mean by 'you'?"

"You know, the prisoners of war: the sons of the Greeks and the Mongols and the Tatars."

"First time I've seen prisoners of war treated like guests," I remarked.

"What you don't know," said the guard, keeping up a steady winking and twitching of the mustache, "is that Sultan Ibn Qalawun is different from other sultans. He makes peace with the Frankish kings—no offense to you—and wins their loyalty. He's the sort of man who doesn't go looking for trouble, especially the kind that comes from abroad. It's true that he beat the Mongols and the Tatars more than once, but he isn't a professional warrior. What I mean is, he doesn't live to fight. That's why people like him. You wouldn't happen to have a bit of snuff on you, by any chance?"

"No," I told him, "but I've got codeine and Ritalin, and I can give you a noseful that'll knock you flat and send your head into orbit."

"Is that like snuff?"

"It's a hell of a lot stronger," I told him. "It's a drug invented by the Franks and sold by pharmacists, but drug dealers have made tons of money on the stuff by getting people of all ages hooked on it. I know a guy who sniffs twenty pounds' worth every day even though he doesn't have a job and has to steal to live."

"Now that's something!" he said. Then he said, "I ate some hashish around sundown but the effect wore off after dinner. Let me try some of what you've got."

"If I give you what's left," I asked, "will you open the door?"

"The door will open all by itself in the morning so you can go in and out and buy what you need."

"Will the guards be around?" I asked.

"They'll take off later," he said. "Don't worry about it."

At that moment, one of the bodies lying right under the window stirred and a voice said in broken Arabic, "Everything the guard wants, I've got right here."

I jumped down immediately and asked to see what the fellow meant. Opening a sack like a reed basket made of waxed linen and festooned with cords, he took out a wad of hashish.

He waited. Then he took out a tin full of snuff, and paused again. Next he took out another container, this one full of opium, showed it to me, and waited. Finally he pulled out a large bottle that smelled of arrack and fermented raisins.

"That's pretty impressive," I said. "What's all this you're carrying around?"

"This was my trade in Syria after I came from Byzantium," he said. "I saw there was a lot of demand for these items, so I started supplying, and I charged an arm and a leg for it, too."

I took a little of everything and told him to put the rest back. Then another body moved, this one belonging to a giant. He turned over and stretched, striking his neighbors, who moaned and shouted. The severed head dangling around his neck struck one of them on the nose. The fellow shuddered in disgust, even though he was doing the same to the person next to him. The giant's chest was exposed, and I could see a big tattoo that told me he was a cannibal. I shuddered. "What does that damned guard want?" asked the cannibal.

"Nothing, nothing," I said. "No need to get excited!"

"I thought he might be causing trouble. If he is, I'll eat him, seeing as I'm hungry anyway."

"If you're a cannibal and you're hungry," I asked, "why not eat that head hanging around your neck?"

"It's not fresh," he said serenely.

Jumping away from him, I bumped into a more-or-less beautiful woman, dusty-faced and dressed in rags. She was choking and trying to get the cord off her neck. In the course of her journey, the cord had twisted and tightened. When she slept, she had turned over and pulled on the head, which made the noose even tighter. I cut the cord, helped her get the rope off, and set the severed head in the window. She brightened and promised to reward me. Opening a reed basket, she took out a set of bottles. I could see that there was something big still sitting in the basket and I asked her what it was.

"A press," she said. "For wine."

"You got captured with a wine press?" I asked.

"We were at work in the market when the soldiers came."

I asked her what the tattooed cannibal had been doing when he was captured.

"He was fighting," she said. "He's a mercenary who'd been living in the area for years, fighting for Hulagu, among others. A lot of others like him were captured too, and they're all here."

She poured out a little of what was in one of the bottles, mixed it with something from a second bottle and something else from a third, and offered it to me. The taste was so delightful that my head "was kindled into whiteness," as the Quran says. She gave me a whole bottle, telling me to give it to the guard and she would be my friend.

"Everything will work out for everyone, hopefully," I told her.

Getting to my feet I saw a cowed, hunched-over, slippery-looking fellow beckoning to me. I gave him my attention and he whispered in my ear: "Are you a friend of the guard's?"

I told him I was.

"Get him to sneak me out, and I'll give you something really great."

"What would that be?"

"I've got a group of beautiful slave women," he said, "and I'll give you one for free."

"Where do you get slave women?"

"It's my profession," he said. "I'm a slave trader. I shop around for them all over the world, and then I buy them and resell them. There they are; pick any one you like." He pointed to a group of women, all extremely beautiful, lying in a stupor. Something told me to be careful. I also felt a little angry. I wished him luck and moved away.

Now someone else was beckoning to me. It was a well-dressed young man clutching to his chest a valise like a big box. He had forgotten about his severed head, which had migrated up to his shoulder, where it sat as if attached to him. Stepping over bodies, I made my way over to him. He asked if I could pass on a bribe to the guard so we could get out.

"No, but a gift might work. What have you got?"

"Rare gems," he whispered in my ear. "Here they are."

He tapped the box and the gold inside it rattled.

"Wonderful," I said. "Are you a jeweler?"

"No," came the honest reply. "I'm apprenticed to a jeweler in Iraq. I was on my way to Syria to deliver these items to one of my master's clients. When fate appeared in the form of the Muslim army, they took all of us, without distinction. I'm prepared to give away all this jewelry if they let me out and let me go back to my master."

"Let me have what you want to give the guard."

Opening the box, he took out an anklet of pure gold. I stuffed it into my pocket, reassured the young man, and turned away, feeling important.

In my path was a polite, dignified man who stopped me, saying, "I have nothing to give, but I do have this," and pointed to his head.

"What's your line?"

"I'm a thinker," he replied. "I offer advice on planning battles and escaping them, and dealing with crises. It's a mistake and an outrage that I was taken prisoner."

"We'll avail ourselves of your services when the time comes," I told him.

I tuned away, only to be accosted by a thin fellow wearing a cross around his neck. "What about me?" he asked. "Don't you need me?"

"What do you do?"

"I'm a doctor. Wealth of experience."

"You, too," I told him. "We'll avail ourselves when the time comes."

I walked away, with offers of all sorts coming at me from the bodies I was trampling underfoot: carpenters, blacksmiths, tailors, poets, and so on and so forth.

Suddenly I was brought up short by something that looked like a restricted area. It was guarded by prisoners fitted out with special insignia in addition to the usual severed heads.

"Who are you?" I asked.

"We're the Emir's men," one of them answered.

"What Emir?"

"He's a Tatar. We broke his fetters off and now he's sleeping in here. He was an emir before he was captured, and we were his right-hand men. He'll be an emir here, too, and we'll be his men just like before."

I looked into the room and saw that it had been emptied of bodies. Having appropriated the space for himself, the Emir had fallen dead asleep and was now snoring loudly.

Turning to go, I noticed that there were quite a few restricted areas. I could tell that there was no lack of emirs and that, immediately after being taken prisoner, they had resumed being emirs. I asked the men in front of me how an emir in prison could still be an emir.

"Each one takes his treasury and his treasurer with him," one of them answered. "They don't just wander around like ordinary people."

"That is certainly unusual," I remarked. Sitting down on whoever was under me, I thought about which restricted area I should join. "There's a lot more strangeness waiting for you in here," said a voice in my head.

9

The Imprisoned Cannibals
Found a Powerful State

As a genuine Son of Shalaby, I've earned the equivalent of several degrees from the school of life in figuring out who is going to come out ahead in any given situation. I admit I'm an opportunist. But God knows that the only thing I'm after is peace of mind, unlike some of those other Sons of Shalaby who keep a lookout for new leaders in the hopes of turning a profit. Those are the ones you see "building bridges of friendship" with people they don't like and never will. In such cases, though, both the parties are very skillfully constructing imaginary bridges so they can size each other up and learn where to strike when the wheel of fortune turns. As a Son of Shalaby, I've learned to side with the strong against the weak, knowing that there's no such thing as justice except among the strong—and even then, only when one of the strong slips up for a moment.

So it was I had a feeling that this Tatar emir was going to end up controlling the Storehouse of Banners. I could tell from the way he had set himself up, occupying the cleanest and most prominent spot in the storehouse: the corner where the officials sat, keeping track of the stock and monitoring shipments and deliveries as they passed in and out. It was a big raised platform like a veranda, with four elegant steps of real marble, lined with a railing of real brass mounted on marble posts. Also, the number of his lieutenants—that is, the people he had put in positions of authority before they were all taken prisoner—was considerable. There were at least ten of them, and all were unusual in their movements and gestures. They sat in a circle around him, unfazed by the wretched conditions inside the prison. As for his guard, there were easily thirty or forty of them, including five or six or seven of the cannibals, all of them large and powerful. Other emirs were scattered about in the enormous crowd, but this group stood at attention in front of that beautiful platform. Above our emir was an awning like the pavilions of patterned cloth that the Sufi brotherhoods set up at the festival of Husayn and the like. Meanwhile, one of the other emirs had occupied the room where swords were kept, posting guards on either side of the door. Another had seized the room where the decorations and insignia were stored. A third had taken the armory, and a fourth had staked a claim to the salon where, in the storehouse's days of glory, distinguished visitors who had come to order supplies would be received.

Everywhere else, bodies were piled up one on another, issuing sounds that were endlessly frightening: moans, but so many that it felt as if some horrific earthquake were taking place. The severed heads, now removed from around the prisoners' necks, posed the biggest problem that the prisoners could imagine: since all of them were strangers, there was no way of knowing who had fought on which side. Among the prisoners were mercenaries, Greek citizens, Mongol citizens, Tatar citizens, and others, not to mention a number of Egyptians who had worked as merchants in Damascus and Baghdad before bad luck put them at the mercy of captors who knew no mercy and had no interest in listening to explanations.

From the direction of the brass platform came precisely four of the tattooed cannibals, each preceded by a potbelly as big as the dome of the Citadel Mosque. The leader had facial tattoos that identified him as a member of a clan of savage predators. The four fanned out, stood in silence for a moment, and then burst into thunderous laughter. The prisoners' seismic muttering stopped completely as walls echoed with the rumbles of brute hilarity. Then cannibals began collecting the severed heads. Each head was securely attached to a cord, and the cannibals managed to loop at least ten cords around each finger. The four Herculean figures, each carrying at least fifty heads in his powerful arms, set off for the storehouse door. The leader gave the door a kick that made the walls tremble. The guard was forced to open the door. With another kick, the cannibal sent the guard flying past Bashtak Palace, leaving the others paralyzed and speechless.

Signaling to the other cannibals to open the door all the way, the leader began flinging the severed heads into the street outside: first the one he had been wearing, and then the heads passed forward by his comrades, until the four of them were operating like a line of laborers, passing the bundles of heads ten at a time up to the front, where the leader would heave them into the street. The little piles of heads soon had traffic completely blocked. On both sides of the street, and from the latticed windows overhead, people gathered to watch in silent astonishment—silent, that is, except for the sardonic braying laughter of some harafish overcome by shock and distress.

For those of us inside the storehouse, the street looked quite wonderful as it proceeded broadly and elegantly to divide the palace from the Atuf quarter whose extremity it formed. But all eyes had turned to a latticed window not far from the storehouse, a window attached to a house that looked much more luxurious than the houses of Atuf. Emerging from the window was the head of a man of dignified bearing who seemed to have nothing but seas of pain, vexation, and shame running through his veins. When the crowd of people reached the window, they began begging for his help and addressing panic-stricken speeches to him from the street. He responded with a menacing shake of the head that seemed suffused with pent-up anger.

We prisoners, meanwhile, had emerged from the store-house to breathe the fresh air, which we did only skittishly for fear of mixing with the passersby and suffering some misfortune. We asked one of the guards who the man in the window was. "The Emir Polo Master, the pilgrim," he said affectionately and without cringing. Some of us trembled and others paid no attention.

All the while, the guards continued to toss heads into the street. People were fleeing in all directions and windows were slamming shut to keep out the flying particles of dry and putrid flesh. Then the tattooed leader, like a mischievous child, spread his legs, put his fingers to his lips, and emitted a whistle like the blast of an air horn. All of us turned to look. He gestured at us as if to say, "Time to go home."

Everyone, including him, trooped inside, and he shut the door behind us as if he did that sort of thing every day of the week. Inside there were exclamations of delight: the store-house seemed to have expanded, and now there was room to walk around. Certain of the cannibals had taken on the job of clearing paths between the bodies to connect up the places where the emirs had settled. I found myself gravitating toward the emir in charge of the brass-and-marble platform.

The rumbling noise had moved from the storehouse to the street, where we could hear people clearing away the rubbish. Suddenly overcome by exhaustion, I lowered myself into a spot next to the enclosure and stretched out half-asleep. But at the very moment I began to drop off, I was awakened by an outbreak of stifled sobs that had begun among the people nearby and then spread through the storehouse. Muttering, I turned over and bumped into a lady with a Roman nose, thick eyebrows, and big, deep-set eyes. I apologized but she ignored me and continued to weep. "Why are you crying, gentle lady?" I asked.

"For the same reason they are," she said.

"And what reason is that?"

"Because we've thrown the heads away and now they're gone forever!"

"Would you rather have kept them?" I asked, surprised.

"No, but I was hoping to find my father's head. Almost everyone here was looking for someone's head: a brother, a son, or some other relative killed in the battle." She began weeping again.

"Don't take it so hard," I said. "These things are fated and crying doesn't help."

She sat up as if realizing that she had found someone to console her. She offered me a small piece of dried date, which tasted wonderful. Her head dropped to my shoulder, whether spontaneously or by design, and I let her fall asleep. I dropped off soon afterward myself, though it can hardly be said that captivity in Storehouse of Banners provided a restful environment.

After a short nap, I awoke to find that the lady, who was of Roman origin but spoke Arabic, had attached herself to me. "Are you mine?" I asked her.

"Yes," she said, adding in broken Arabic, "According to the practice mandated by God and His Prophet," making it clear that she had lived among Arabs since childhood.

"I'm yours too," I said. "According to the practice mandated by God and His Prophet."

A moment later a loud voice rang out: "Are there any women left who haven't found a husband?"

Even my new sort-of wife looked surprised and embarrassed, and I felt the same way. The guards who served the different emirs, following different paths through the bodies, were coming toward the brass enclosure, some with women in tow, and others carrying things I couldn't make out. I asked my new sort-of wife what was going on. She explained that the other emirs in the prison had taken the initiative of sending gifts to the Emir Khazaal. I asked if she knew him.

"I got to know all of them during the journey," she said. "They're all emirs and their story is stranger than you can imagine."

"How's that, gentle lady?"

"Khazaal became an emir in return for fighting in the campaign against Baghdad and the Arab lands. Outside those places he had no authority, since all of his commanders and the people with him had fallen in battle and he was the only one left alive."

Then she whispered in my ear, in breathy accents that might have been Greek as easily as Arabic, "Khazaal was planning to escape from his own detachment, flee to the Arab side, and ask their rulers for asylum on the grounds that he'd become a Muslim. But then he was captured."

"Maybe he really had become a Muslim," I suggested, "and had a change of heart that made him abandon his fellow invaders."

"You are *such* an Egyptian," she said, smiling. "You're a big idiot."

"And a Son of Shalaby, too!"

"You are so stupid," she said, "that you help your enemies and treat them respect because you consider them guests in your country. You've played host to your enemies for a long, long time, Ibn Shalaby."

"Anyway, back to Khazaal," I said.

"He was responsible for supplying the detachment and keeping track of plunder and spoils during the campaign."

"So how did he end up a prisoner of war?"

"That was another bit of stupidity on your part," she said. "Ibn Qalawun, being a cousin of the Mongols, fought like a Turk. It's true that he drinks blood like a Mongol, but he learned enough of Islam and the Arabs to make him into an honorable warrior. When he learned that there were Frankish, Mongol, and Tatar emirs among the prisoners, he let them keep their loot, in case there were negotiations and he had to decide who owned what. So the only people who were stripped of their property were the paupers like us."

"What about the other emirs?"

"It's every man for himself," she said, "and none of them are accountable to anyone. They're brutes like nothing you Arabs have seen before. They bury their loot in Syria or Baghdad or on the borders and then, a few days later, send someone to bring it here."

"How do they manage that?"

"Did you think these emirs were total strangers here?" she replied, the outline of her Roman nose bobbing against the wall. I made an effort to get my mind around what she was saying. She continued, "They had already begun their invasion years ago by coming into the area and making friends with the merchants and petty princes. Some of them even joined the armies of Muslim kings and governors and fought against their own brothers. The only reason they're prisoners now is bad luck, bad faith, or bad friends."

"I don't think I can stand to hear any more," I said. "You've turned my brain into an elephant and you're asking it to fly with the wings of a gnat."

She laughed. Feeling wretched, I wept silently.

The door of the storehouse suddenly flew wide open and the sipahsalar himself peered in. A moment later, surrounded by soldiers on all sides, he marched into the prison. Though armed with swords and daggers, his men were doing their best to look harmless. He and the men were directed to come forward to the brass-and-marble enclosure near us. We figured out that he had agreed to open talks with Khazaal and his imprisoned emirs. As he led his men into the enclosure, I followed them in. He pronounced a salam alaykum and the emirs responded likewise, but with a conspicuous lack of courtesy. He had evidently been expecting something of the kind and sat down unfazed in the spot Khazaal pointed out to him. When he turned to signal his men to stand back, he found no sign of them.

"Where are my forces?" asked the sipahsalar, jumping back up.

"Your forces are safe with us," said one of the cannibals. "You can have them back when you leave."

The sipahsalar sat down, looking like a mouse pretending to be a cat.

Khazaal had a head like a piece of petrified wood and an enormously broad chest full of gashes, as patched and pitted as a Cairo street. He was chugging arrack from a bottle in front of him. He offered a clay cupful to the sipahsalar, who pushed it away, embarrassed.

"I don't drink, and I'm here on business. You know that the Sultan, may God magnify him, has treated you well and graciously provided you with a comfortable place to live. If we wanted, we could treat you as prisoners, but we're not in any hurry to do so. All we ask is that you refrain from stirring up trouble. Otherwise . . . ."

He paused. Khazaal looked at his men and asked for something to eat. As if out of thin air came a man carrying an entire, untouched leg of beef on his shoulder, telling Khazaal he'd have it grilled for him right away.

"Where did you get that meat from?" asked the sipahsalar. "And how did you get it inside? That's a violation right there!"

"Anything we want, we get," said Khazaal, "even if you lock it up in a tower somewhere." Then he gave a shout, "Hey, Khawarnaq!"

The most enormous of the tattooed cannibals came in and stood there grinning like a sperm whale.

"The sipahsalar says we aren't supposed to bring meat in here," said Khazaal.

"What kind does he object to? The livestock, the carcasses, or the carrion?"

Ignoring the implications of this, the sipahsalar said, "We're the ones who say what kind of meat comes in or doesn't come in."

The cannibal laughed so loudly that the brass columns rattled and the sipahsalar shuddered. "Don't eat any of my lunch, then, until you get a new set of orders."

At his summons, a boy emerged from one of the inner rooms dragging an enormous, piteously bleating sheep.

"Where did you get that?" cried the infuriated sipahsalar, rising to his feet. "I couldn't find one for myself outside the storehouse if I tried!"

"If you need anything and you can't find it anywhere in the country, let us know and we'll be happy to get it for you. Hey kid!" he shouted. "Where's that knife?"

The knife appeared, and he thrust it into the sheep's neck and then tossed it away. A crowd of people pounced on the knife and began fighting over it. Within seconds, he had skinned the sheep. Sitting down cross-legged in front of it, he began tearing off strips of flesh and eating them with relish as the sipahsalar looked on, fearful and disgusted.

"Help yourself," said Khazaal, "and we'll follow your orders."

Thanking him, the sipahsalar jumped up and went out to rejoin his men outside the storehouse.

That night, the door stayed half open. We stayed up late to celebrate. In fact, we may have spent months or even years in celebration. During that time, we would stop the festivities just long enough to find something to eat. Some of us would go out into the streets of Cairo to shop, beg, pillage, kidnap, or steal things for ourselves or for the Emir, without anyone saying a word. We also used to listen to the emissaries sent by the emir they called the Polo Master to negotiate with us regarding proper neighborly conduct. The emissaries were always surprised to find that we were people like themselves, that some of us spoke their language, and that some of us—the Egyptians who had been taken prisoner by Egyptians though no fault of their own, but only because they happened to have been trading in markets near the battlefield—knew them by name, and knew the names of their fathers and mothers as well. These Egyptians would sit by Khazaal during the negotiations and help him outwit the envoys by explaining the verbal tricks they were trying to play on him. At first I was surprised, but then I reminded myself that they were citizens with families living in the alleys of Cairo and I forgave them, telling myself that nothing in the world has so powerful an effect as oppression. Most surprising of all, these captive Egyptians were allowed to come and go as they pleased, accountable to no one, wandering through the streets and meeting up with their families and their childhood friends. But they would still come back to the storehouse at night, bearing little delicacies, like fathers coming home to their children after a long day. All of us knew that their businesses had started up again and were thriving as well as ever, and that their property was stashed in safe places outside; but we didn't hold any of that against them as long as they continued to profess loyalty to the storehouse and refuse to spend the night anywhere else.

One night, Khazaal, the emir of the prison, summoned me. "She-of-the-Roman-Nose" insisted on coming with me to support me during whatever ordeal was to follow. When we reached the enclosure with the elegant brass railing, I looked for a spot far from the shadow of the Emir, but failed to find one: his shadow extended into every corner of the storehouse, as if it were the night itself, covering even the secret heart of things. I offered all the mandatory greetings in various styles, which astounded him. Thinking I must be a person of great importance among my people, he asked me about my nationality and my religion. Cautiously, I replied that my style of address might have misled him into thinking I was someone important, but that I had actually learned to speak from reading books.

"Then you must be one of the elite of the elite," he said confidently.

I was astounded to hear him speak in such civilized tones, which seemed a world apart from his person and his circumstances. Nodding respectfully in my direction, he asked if I were a scholar, a man of letters, an astronomer, or a philosopher.

"I'm only your humble servant, Khayri son of Shalaby, a Hanafi, an Egyptian, a seller of pickles and sweets, and a writer."

Emir Khazaal rose to his feet and extended his hand. I shook it enthusiastically. She-of-the-Roman-Nose crossed her legs and struck an aristocratic pose. Resuming his seat, the Emir said, "We need to find something for you to do here. Listen: take charge of getting the word out about the wines we produce here in the storehouse. We have dozens and dozens of old vintages that our merchants sell wholesale in the countryside, but we need to promote them more inside Cairo itself; that'll be your job. Near the storehouse is an emir called the Polo Master who harasses us every day with messengers who threaten to inform Sultan Ibn Qalawun of what we're doing here. We're not worried on that count, since our informants inside the palace tell us that the sultan has no intention of interfering with us and is planning to make a truce with the Franks. Our envoy has personally seen the Sultan ignoring the Polo Master when he tries to turn him against us. But our relationship with the Polo Master needs to be discussed and formalized, if nothing else to impress upon the Sultan that we have our own way of doing things that has to be respected if we're to reach an understanding. As you may have noticed, the storehouse is now the only bright spot in the region. What you have to tell them on our behalf is: Look! Every day the storehouse takes in new people who come to us because of how badly this country treats them. We have no choice but to accept everyone who knocks on our door asking for protection. Everyone needs to be aware of this, and it's your job to make them aware. I know this is a demanding assignment, but I'll open a chancery to handle your correspondence."

"To hear is to obey, great Emir," I said, bowing.

"Get to work, then!"

Full of enthusiasm and polluted air, I jumped to my feet, asking for an office facing the door, a private room, air conditioning, and fancy chairs. He agreed, but for now, he said, I was to use the grated window that looked out over Kiman al-Darrasa as a workplace, with the storehouse entrance reserved for the residents to come in and out and the window for carrying out any discussions that needed to be carried out.

Life was good. Acting in my name, She-of-the-Roman-Nose launched a career as a swindler and rip-off artist inside the storehouse, creating new business, attracting followers, and bringing in heaps of cash. Gifts and money, accompanied by cards and inside information on merchants outside the storehouse, began pouring in. Within a few months, the soldiers disappeared completely, leaving the shadows of the cannibals as the only guards of the storehouse—that, and the stories that made their way outside. As for me, I carried out my duties to the letter. Give a Shalaby of peasant stock a job to do and he'll do his best, even if it means working for his enemies against his own interests; he has no idea that doing a good job is an ingrained part of his character. He toils without caring who it is he's toiling for, for one reason: among his people, anyone who doesn't work is a despicable slacker who doesn't deserve to live. On that basis, I did an excellent job. The only thing that gave me sleepless nights was something I gave permission for without thinking.

One day, a group of respectable-looking visitors showed up unexpectedly in front of the storehouse and stood there looking downcast as the most grizzled of them came forward, saying, "If you'd be so kind! We beg you, give us Abdel Al!"

"Who's he?" I asked.

"A great felon: he's murdered ten men. The police hunted him down, but he dodged them by coming to the storehouse to ask for asylum. Hand him over to us, and God will reward you in this world and the next!"

I sent a request for clarification and received the following memo, which I read aloud, "Hear ye! You are hard-hearted and cruel, and Abdel Al is a victim sorely used by you and your generation! It is you who made a criminal of him! He is blameless and innocent, and the storehouse will not give him up now that he has sought sanctuary!" I cut off their protests by locking and bolting the door. When they tried again, this time bringing the police, the cannibals met them halfway, ate the arm of one and the neck of another, and sent them back the way they came.

Another time, an old woman made me the indirect offer of a bribe. I mocked her and brought people to over to join me, telling her that the right way to offer a bribe was to do it right up front; otherwise it lost its resonance. She told me that her daughter, who had been supporting her and her family, had fled and taken refuge in the storehouse. I made an inquiry and was told that the girl deserved leniency because she had been raised in a broken home and had come on her own initiative to the storehouse to have a taste of freedom. The old woman went away and never came back.

On a third occasion, a man of some importance came looking for his wife, who had run away and come to the storehouse. I told him that she was free of him and his authority and the best thing for him to do was to forget all about her.

On a fourth occasion, a troop of policemen tried to show off in front of us, putting on a pathetic display of force that only revealed how weak they were. When it was over they asked us to hand over a major smuggler—I mean, a spy who was smuggling intelligence to the enemy. I told them that the man in question may well have been the most patriotic of us all, as evidenced by his plea for asylum from the storehouse, and that the aspersions they had cast on his patriotism made them liable to prosecution. When they refused to stop wrangling, a team of cannibals came out and began playing a pickup soccer game with them, but dribbling and shooting *them* instead of the ball.

The same sort of thing happened on a fifth, sixth, tenth, and thousandth occasion, until vast numbers of Cairenes had taken refuge at the storehouse and every night held the prospect of some novel incident or new personality to stay up late for: a grocer running from the quota office, a thief running from the police, a murderer sick of the taste of blood, an emir threatened with punishment by the Sultan, and—another emir threatened with punishment by the Sultan. The storehouse became a state within a state and a force to be reckoned with.

One night we learned that the Sultan had lost his temper with the Polo Master for continuing to complain about us. "Why," said the Sultan, "don't *you* just move away from *them*?"

So the Polo Master moved out of the house he had been living in near our Storehouse of Banners. Having renovated his house in Husayniya, along with the stable, the mosque named after his family, the bathhouse, and the inn, he moved there.

What a night it was! We toasted our victory, and one of the cannibals, transported by joy, took a chunk out of one of the young ladies who had taken refuge with us.

10

Oppression Does Wonders
for Oppression

WE SPENT MANY A NIGHT joking about what happened to the Polo Master and repeating what the Sultan had said to him— "Why don't *you* just move away from *them*?"—in tones of voice ranging from the gloating and pitying to the smirking and nasty. Whenever a boy from the storehouse came across an aristocrat who looked like an emir walking in the street, he would make faces, stick his tongue out, and say, "Why don't *you* just move away from *them*?" The fellow who looked like an emir—or like the Polo Master himself—would rouse himself and shout, "Out of my way, you ruffian!" In my capacity as the official in charge of the window, I heard that sentence tens of thousands of times at different distances and in different accents and intonations. "Out of my way, you ruffian!" One man might say it as if to spare the feelings of the Emir who—he imagined—would hear about the incident. Another would say it fearfully, as if the Emir had already heard it. A third would say it in alarm, as if *he* were the one making fun of the Emir. A fourth might say it as if venting his anger against the Emir and the Sultan, and a fifth might use it to flatter the storehouse by implying that he could not believe that a place so refined could produce ruffians.

All of this made the storehouse, which was already powerful and respected, even more influential. I copied out new declarations that overrode not only my own reason but that of mankind in general and sent them through the window grate. They proclaimed that peace would reign between the storehouse and murderers, thieves, and other enemies of humanity; and that the storehouse would strive to spread the spirit of peace in the region in honor of the Sultan who had won them over and taken their side against one of his most powerful emirs. We had to train the cannibals to treat the public in a manner consistent with these ringing declarations, Khazaal having agreed—after I caught him in a good mood— that the people of Egypt would not put up with ill-treatment and public displays of lewdness and that it was important to keep them on our side. I laid special stress on the blessed and wretched Sons of Shalaby, who—I told him—may well be the only people in the world who immortalize their conquerors and oppressors.

Khazaal was delighted to hear this, and sat back arrogantly on his throne. "That's right! That's what I want to be immortalized for."

"No, great Emir, that's not what I mean. It's not enough to be immortal: it matters *why*. They'll immortalize you as you are, including virtues and—no offense meant—vices too."

"What's that mean?" he said with a dismissive gesture.

"What it means is, treat the people right and we'll love you."

"Okay," he said, "but only because you asked."

He then called a meeting for the whole staff, semi-emirs and cannibals alike. In my capacity as head of the prospective chancery division, I sat next to Khazaal. Behind me I placed dozens of pageboys carrying briefcases and files and bottles of arrack, on orders to pour me a drink whenever my throat went dry. I drank and smoked as I waited for the meeting to come to order. Khazaal introduced me to his men by saying that the Storehouse of Banners—long may it stand—was proud to offer asylum to refugees from every time and place. It was particularly proud of having sheltered me, despite my being from a very distant time, and having offered me not only protection but also a position of influence. He wrapped up his introduction by saying that I wanted to revamp our code of public conduct toward our enemies and he would be obliged if I would explain why I had made this request.

Nodding politely to those present, I said that the issue was in reality quite simple and hardly worth discussing. What it came down to was a request for humane treatment and self-restraint toward everyone in the region, including people who wore the uniform of our enemies. Then, as usual, I went on for at least ten hours, clarifying this one simple point with digressions and asides and emphasizing the importance of my request by telling anecdotes and stories with no apparent connection to the topic or to each other. The cannibals began fidgeting. Suddenly one of the more articulate of them burst out with, "Just tell us exactly what you want from us!" He went on, "We cannibals don't understand wishy-washy rhetoric; give us some rigorous scientific method. What does 'humane treatment' mean? And what about 'self-restraint'? First of all, we have no idea what 'mercy' is or what it means. This is the first time we've heard of it. How are we supposed to agree to something we don't understand? Tell us what we're supposed to do and we'll do it!"

I laughed until I cried, smacked the table in disgust, and said, "How can it be 'wishy-washy rhetoric' when it's perfectly clear? How could it possibly be any more obvious?"

Khazaal signaled at me to stop talking and calm down. "We're sorry to say, Mr. Seller-of-Pickles-and-Sweets, that your presentation was not entirely successful. I myself didn't understand a word of it. But let me try to convey your point to the cannibals in language they'll understand."

Turning to them, he shouted, "Cannibals! I'm ordering you to treat people as follows: Instead of snapping boys' necks and drinking their blood, dislocate their arms. Instead of killing traders who are making a profit, take what they have and leave them alone. Instead of gouging out both of a ruffian's eyes, gouge out one. Instead of grabbing a sheep from a butcher shop and eating it on the spot, take it and eat it somewhere where no one can see you. Got it?" During this speech he kept looking at me as if teaching me how to communicate with the cannibals.

With a shudder, I realized how dismal the lot of Egypt was, as if it were condemned to misery by some unchanging law of nature. "God help the people bear it!" I thought to myself.

Looking around, I could see the many Egyptians who had joined the storehouse. They listened to the speeches I disseminated from the window and applauded every word, passing them on and even inventing their own speeches to encourage the butchers to butcher, the murders to murder, and the thieves to thieve even more. I would make a point of glaring at those Sons of Shalaby, and they took special pleasure in ignoring me. But I didn't let their crassness bother me because I knew that it didn't represent the real character of the Sons of Shalaby. Not only that: this particular sample didn't represent all of Egypt. The members of this group were simply thieves, petty brokers, and opportunists of the kind that crop up in every period and at every court, bringing good families into disrepute. After the meeting broke up I took them aside. "Sons of Shalaby, why are you loyal to people who feel no loyalty to you? Why do you love people who don't deserve it? Why do you look at people who torment you and drink the blood of your brothers and encourage them to keep doing it?"

One of them, fighting mad, said, "Because we know that everything is going to stay the same whether we like it or not. No one's ever asked us if we wanted to be mistreated or killed, but we are. So we might as well act as if we like the way things are. Death is free, right?"

Another spoke up, as if trying to make up for the rudeness of the first. "Look, sir, we don't have a horse in this race. We buy off the ruler with flattery—or at least we manage to keep him off our backs."

Upset, I went out to get some fresh air. The storehouse itself no longer felt like a prison. The feeling of being locked up had disappeared long ago. In fact, the residents of the store-house probably felt safer than people living outside in their own homes in Egypt. We enjoyed more freedom than they did. Their freedom may even have been a burden to them, but ours meant liberty for us. I asked myself why this should be so. I really didn't know, but I suspected that it was because the rest of Egypt was governed by a sultan and an administration and a set of laws. We, on the other hand, weren't governed by anything. For us, freedom was a matter of having the ruler deliver things we wanted, deal with our problems, grant us titles, and give us people to entertain us. As for the ruler himself, he was respon-sible to no one at all. I tried to figure out what it was about the storehouse that allowed it to occupy this position but I could find no good explanation. Then again, I can't explain why the Sons of Shalaby behave as they do—and I'm one of them—so I could hardly claim to be any good at explaining things.

Following my nose, I had wandered absentmindedly into the square between the palaces. I walked back the way I had come, strolling through Atuf, coming out at Kiman al-Darrasa, walking around the storehouse and crossing back toward al-Azhar. Of all the people I saw, the residents of the storehouse were the most conspicuous. They were also the most powerful. They no longer needed to wander around selling bottles of wine on the sly. Instead, they hauled their stills around with them and set up shop on any corner they liked, like juice vendors in the fourteenth century after the hijra. I enjoyed watching knots of people gather in different parts of the square between the palaces, and even Victory Gate and off toward Khurunfish, standing around the still and displaying the same kind of awkward self-righteousness that you see in people who pretend to be fasting during Ramadan. Whenever they passed a group gathered around a still, any dignified old men, high-ranking emirs, or persons of virtuous demeanor would curl their lips in revulsion, look thoroughly disgusted, and mutter curses and imprecations. Deep down, I felt as if I shared their anger, though it came from motives more powerful than their tradition-mindedness and needed to be expressed differently. How I wished I could stay outside the storehouse forever! We were free to wander the streets of Cairo, but in the end we still had to go back to the storehouse. We could run, but the volunteer militia would catch us and we'd be right back where we started.

I collided with a girl wrapped in the sort of high-quality Dabiqi silk favored by the well-to-do. From the way she had run into me, I had thought she might be a lunatic, but when I looked at her she wrapped her arms around my neck and, weeping, cried out, "I'm at your mercy, good Frank!" She was clearly panicked.

"I'm no Frank, young lady, but what's wrong?"

She looked around fearfully. "Where'd they go?"

"Where did who go?"

"They're sons of emirs and wealthy merchants," she said. "We know each other, and they're after me. If they catch me they'll kill me."

Surprised, I asked her why. I examined her face for signs that she was lying, but I saw nothing but panic, misery, and sorrow—all genuine—and a flood of hot tears. She was six-teen, and looked like a houri from Paradise, except that terror had turned her into a panic-stricken victim looking high and low for someone to defend her.

"One of the emirs has a son, by the grace of God, whose real father must be a demon or a wild animal," she said. "No one in Egypt knows. Maybe he's ill, or maybe not, but he's got something wrong with him than no one can explain. May God protect us!"

"Tell me: what's wrong with him?" I asked, shaking in my boots and looking around for a cannibal to come over and lend a hand.

"Every day he needs to slice up a girl with a sharp knife and drink her blood. Then he leaves her and goes off to practice decapitation on thirty small boys."

Forcing myself to move, I struggled to find my voice. "L-l-listen, young lady, are you a character from *The Arabian Nights*?"

"Never heard of it!" she said.

"Are you a genie from a fairy tale?"

"I swear I'm from right here in Egypt, and my father and my grandfather too! We have a mausoleum where we read the Quran over ten generations of ancestors, or maybe more."

"But what you're saying sounds like a fairy tale or a nature show."

In a panic, she pulled at me, shrieking, "Look!"

I looked. A group of young men was dragging along a lovely young girl, who was screaming, digging her heels into the ground, and wriggling out of her clothes. Finally one of them picked her up and slung her under his arm like a sack. An old man standing nearby asked them sadly, "Is she your daughter?"

"None of your business!" said the one doing the carrying.

"Out of the way, man!" said another.

"She's a delinquent," said a third. "She was planning to run away from home, and since she's from a big family, they were going to stone her to death."

"That's what they always say!" said the girl who was with me. "They kidnap good Egyptian girls to satisfy some crazy bestial urge. Her only 'delinquency' is that she went outside and happened to fall into their hands. And now they're going to take her away and kill her."

"Are they the ones after you?" I asked, shuddering.

"Those are the scouts."

"They have scouts?"

"They send refined young men to follow girls and flirt with them," she said. "When the girl slows down to listen, they pour on the compliments and the smiles and the sweet talk, but then the gang appears and carries all of them off. Then they send the boys away and grab the girl."

The blood went to my head. The gang had nearly vanished into the Atuf quarter when I saw one of our tattooed cannibals nibbling at a sheep's head some distance away. I shouted for him and he hurried over, shaking the earth at every step. I pointed him toward the hooligans and told him to catch up with them and save the girl. Reaching them in two or three great bounds, he instantly took control of the situation. I grabbed my girl and went over to see.

The cannibal crushed two of the young men to his chest and let them drop to the ground. Then he stuck out a foot and tripped three others, who fell in a heap. He pulled the girl from under the arm of the hooligan who was carrying her and gave him a kick to the belly that killed him on the spot. By the time I got there, the girl was struggling in his grip. Extricating her, I told him, "Deal with the rest of them."

From the ground came the voice of one of the young men warning us of the grave consequences of what we were doing and telling us that he and his comrades belonged to the entourage of one of the emirs and that we should leave the girl to them instead of stirring up trouble between the storehouse and the emirs. Laughing, the cannibal replied, "I'm going to kill everyone except for you, and that's so you can go back to your emir and tell him what happened so he can come and show me what he's made of."

Then, pouncing like a wild beast, he ripped open the belly of one young man, yanked off the head of a second, squashed the body of a third, and crushed a skull of a fourth, leaving only the one with the big mouth, who was looking like a heap of rags. The cannibal picked him up and set him on his feet, telling him to go and find his emir. But the fellow, who had already died, collapsed onto the ground. I glared at the cannibal. "They wanted to eat the girl," he said quietly. "As if! We're the ones who do the eating around here."

To reassure the two girls, I told him that there wasn't going to be any eating or any drinking either. "We've made a clear statement on behalf of the storehouse by saving the girls from a dire fate. It's a noble message, all right, but you've created another problem that we didn't need."

"You mean killing them?"

"No, it's the bodies," I said. "What are we going to do about them?"

"No problem," said the cannibal. "I'll drag them over to Kiman al-Darrasa. If it were the old days, I would drag them back to the storehouse to eat, but now there's no shortage of meat any more. Leave it to me; go on and don't worry."

He wrapped the bodies together using their clothes and the bundles they had been carrying with them. Then he dragged them all away, with the ground wobbling under him as if the bull that carries the earth on one of its horns had chosen that moment to switch to the other horn. Looking at my watch, I saw that the year was AH 741.

I walked off with the two girls. The world seemed an utterly dismal place. No one seemed to acknowledge anyone else and I saw nothing to suggest that the people of Cairo even knew one another. No one stopped to greet a friend, or even to see if he recognized a seeming stranger. No one waved from a distance and no one smiled. A smile, in fact, was the rarest of commodities at the time. People moved nothing but their eyes, shooting covert glances at people and objects and then flickering sadly away, like shifty characters who knew too much but were afraid to confess. The bearded merchants uttered their cries of "In the name of God!" and "There is no might or power save in God!" and drove their jaded bargains, swearing up and down that such-and-such a price was utterly absurd, and then agreeing to it.

Suddenly the air, which until a moment ago had been filled with clouds of dust, grew clear. I saw that people were closing their shops and making their way in groups toward al-Azhar

Mosque. I realized that it was Friday, and time for the public prayer. I felt a sudden urge to pray with other people around me, and in al-Azhar. I headed over to the storehouse, handed the two girls over to one of Khazaal's retinue, and hustled back to al-Azhar in time to catch the prayer.

The façade of the mosque was clean and the towering minarets seemed to be pushing their way through to the sun. The courtyard was packed but I managed to get in anyway. The sight of thousands of worshippers standing shoulder to shoulder, their heads reverently bowed, cheered me up enormously. Oddly enough, I saw a few of the tattooed cannibals ambling stupidly through the crowd like lost sheep, some dripping water and others filth. Carried away by enthusiasm, the preacher was firing off Quranic verses and Prophetic Hadith one after another, and the courtyard was ringing with the names of Umar, Uthman, Ali, and the righteous members of the Prophet's house. I could see that the worshippers were giving the cannibals embarrassed looks but, like the preacher, were too afraid of them to shush them or tell them to behave properly, as they would have with anyone else.

Seeing my opportunity, I gestured to each of the cannibals to sit down because we were about to meet the One and Only God. Out of respect for me, each of them sat down wherever he happened to be, on top of those who were already seated. They made room for me too, and I squeezed myself in and then turned my attention to what the preacher was saying.

I realized that he was shouting "That's right, Uuumar! That's the trrruth . . . . So how can you say that, Uuumar?" stretching out the words and waving his arms like any trash-talking housewife from Clot Bey or Muhammad Ali Street. I couldn't stop myself from laughing.

"What's so funny?" said the man next to me.

"Who's the preacher trashing?"

"What's 'trashing' mean?"

"In my time," I told him, "in the fourteenth century after the hijra, there are women who've trained themselves to win slanging matches. They open their wraps and flap them at each other, and then they clap and wave their arms and say 'What do you say, Uuumar?'"

"So this heretical style of preaching is destined to catch on?"

"Who's the Uuumar the preacher keeps talking about?" I asked.

"Our master, Umar ibn al-Khattab," he said. You call it 'trashing,' but the preacher's stretching out his name like that and making a song out of it to mock him because he's such a fervent Shi'i."

"The preacher's a Shi'i?"

"He's left over from the Fatimids."

"But how do they let him . . . ?"

"Everything is topsy-turvy these days, old boy," he said. "Nothing is pure the way it used to be. Everything's mixed up with something else, even prayer and worship. More than half the Muslims perform newfangled rituals and ceremonies they don't even understand! If you saw someone praying like that, you would think he was a dyed-in-the-wool Shi'i, but if you asked him you would find out that he wasn't, or that he didn't know the difference between Shi'a and Sunnis in the first place. No one knows anything about religion any more. Everybody just prays any way they want to, making it up on the basis of all the heretical innovations they pick up from one or another sect. On top of that, the scholars are government employees now, and nobody pays attention to what anyone else is doing. All you can do is ignore them and keep your thoughts on God and God alone."

"There is no god but God!" I exclaimed. "And no might or power save in God."

I noticed that the people around us were looking increasingly annoyed. Some of the older worshippers were signaling to the preacher to wrap up the sermon and let them get back to their business. But every time he seemed to be coming close to the end, he would set off on a new tangent, working himself into a fury and pounding his sword on the floor of the pulpit. The man next to me laughed.

"What are *you* laughing at?"

"At how excited he's getting," he replied. "If he keeps that up he'll knock a hole through the pulpit."

"What's he excited about?" I asked.

"He wants to stop. He's already repeated himself several times over. Soon he'll have to start weeping, unless some miracle comes to save him."

"I can't make heads or tails of this," I said. "Why does he need a miracle to save him?"

"He's going to keep on preaching," the man whispered back, "until a deputy comes from the palace to tell him what to do about the benediction."

"What benediction are you talking about?" I said, losing my patience.

"At the end of the service," the man said serenely, "the custom is that the preacher prays for our master, Sultan Muhammad ibn Qalawun."

"Fine," I said. "But does the palace have to tell him the words of the prayer every single week?"

"No," said the man. "But Sultan ibn Qalawun has been on the verge of death for days now. The emir's men have told the preacher to hold off on the benediction because if the Sultan dies, then the new sultan, Mansur, son of the present sultan, can use the Friday prayers to announce his accession."

"By God," I said, "this is a repellent mix of things that shouldn't be mixed. I'm not letting *this* preacher lead *my* prayer!" I got up, finished my devotions alone, and went out.

It was a good thing that I left before the rest of the worshippers. The streets were filling up with people running away from the storehouse. Some were dragging broken legs, others had broken arms or cracked skulls, but all were laughing, though painfully. When I reached the storehouse, I saw a detachment of soldiers, defeated, disarmed, and demoralized, beating a retreat.

Spotting one of the storehouse crowd, I asked him what had happened. He said that the emir with the perverted son had come to prove that he was not to be trifled with, but had been trounced and would have been taken prisoner if one of the girls had not intervened on his behalf.

"That's the Egyptian spirit of forgiveness for you," I said. "Those two must really be Egyptians born and bred."

I had barely made it to the storehouse gate when I heard the voice of the town crier ringing out. "Long life to the bereaved! Sultan Nasir Muhammad ibn Qalawun is dead! Long live his son and heir Mansur!"

"God help us," I said on my way inside.

11

A Sultan Undone by the Sultanate

THE STOREHOUSE CONVENED THE LARGEST meeting it had ever held. It went on all day and all night, receiving a stream of storehousers returning from missions inside the city or further afield. Some had cut short business trips; others had heard the news in a village somewhere and ridden back posthaste, as if the storehouse had become our homeland and needed us to rally round her in her hour of need. Each newcomer, discovering to his surprise that the matter hardly demanded the serious face he had put on for the occasion, soon relaxed, and began laughing, joking, and staying up late to tell stories, like the prison emirs. Even so, something about the scene made me uneasy. Here we were in the middle of a crisis, wasting time with fun and games. Our greatest ally had died and abandoned us to the wolves but no one seemed concerned. Emir Khazaal was so indifferent to the tragedy that (as I feared) he asked me to open the window to the drummers and revelers in the courtyard. When I opened the grate, a crowd of drummers, pipers, percussionists, horn blowers, and hautboy players poured into the storehouse, filling the air with their racket. I watched them with a feeling of anxious discomfort. Khazaal gave me a jolly smack on the knee and knocked me to the ground. Propping me back up with his foot, he said with a laugh, "We'd be honored if Mr. Pickle-Seller would join the fun."

"I'm having no end of fun, really."

"No doubt."

He tossed a silk scarf over me and said, "Get up."

"Why?"

"Show us how much fun you're having."

"How?"

"Put that on and dance!"

"What?"

"Go on! 'If you don't dance, life's not worth living!'"

He made a sign to the drummers, who started laying down a beat. My body began swaying of its own accord. "How are we supposed to dance, Emir, when we don't even have a plan for what happens tonight, now that our ally's dead?"

"I can't see why you're so worried," said Khazaal. "You're Egyptian, so you know how this country is governed."

"Right! That's why I want us to think about how to deal with this crisis."

"Idiot!" he said. "You can be sure that no one is thinking about us at all at the moment. Know why? Here in the Land of Egypt, kingship is something you have to fight to get, and the sultans and emirs have no ambitions besides wealth and power. They think of no one but themselves. Tomorrow it's *us* who might be kings, since people are always calling on us for support. Until the people show up, though, let's dance—unless you're afraid of losing your reputation as a sober seller of pickles."

"That's it exactly," I said. "A pickle seller like me isn't supposed to tie a scarf around his hips and dance, even if he's happy."

"Suit yourself, then."

He pulled the scarf away, tied it around his waist, and danced every dance there was, including dabka, quarterstaff fencing, and baladi. As soon as he hit the floor, the whole storehouse joined in, forming a seething mass like water at a rolling boil. Then, leaving the rest to dance, the Emir slipped away, his smile fading, took a seat among his officers, and asked for the latest news. One of them reported seeing the

Sultan's troops dragging certain emirs off to Shamayil's Storehouse in the middle of the night.

Clapping his hands in delight, the Emir, with a meaningful glance at me, said, "You see, Pickle Man? The massacre has already started. Emirs are getting thrown into Shamayil, which is the worst prison in Cairo, right?"

"Yes, I've heard about it from my friend Maqrizi. You mean the one next to the Zuwayla Gate, on the left if you're coming in, along the city wall? It's named after Emir Alam al-Din Shamayil, governor of Cairo under the Ayyubid sultan Kamil. It's a horrifying, nasty-looking place. It's where they put people condemned to death or amputation, including robbers, highwaymen, Mamluks the Sultan wants to do away with, and major felons."

"We don't need a history lesson," said Khazaal. "All I'm doing is reminding you that we have more freedom than the emirs who were in power not too long ago."

I was impressed. Khazaal understood more about life—high and low—in the Land of Egypt than the Egyptians themselves. With a bitter laugh, I realized that a good many Sons of Shalaby knew nothing of life, let alone politics.

I asked Khazaal how he came by his insights. He told me that there was no easy way for Egyptians to understand their own country. Not only was there no need for them to understand: their life was set up to prevent it. Once, he explained, the Egyptians had been divided into pyramid builders on the one hand and serfs on the other. To hide the light of knowledge and civilization from the serfs, the builders preserved it in a language that only they knew, like pharaohs who believed with passionate intensity in maintaining their dynasty. When the builders died, they were buried in magnificent tombs. For their part, the serfs were buried under monumental ignorance; and from the caverns of ignorance their children have come marching in long lines, like rats, and spread throughout the Fertile Crescent. Civilization, he went on, has vanished, along with everything else except the genius of the land itself. Given the ignorance of the serfs, the genius of the land requires that someone come and rule it. Egypt is destined to be the property of its rulers, and its people are doomed to be subjects with no horse of their own in the race. From this it follows that seizing the sultanate is like herding cats. "The sultanate," he said, "has no honor or shame. It gives itself to the strongest."

By then I was itching to give him a piece of my mind. Admittedly, I still had no idea how I was going to rebut him, but I had learned from my journalism days that you had to say something, no matter what. Meanwhile, he was already waving a reproachful finger at me, saying that he had expected me to do something big to help the storehouse.

"What am I supposed to do if everyone's dancing?"

"You could help them dance," he said. "Any kind of help is better than none."

Biting my tongue, I said, "So the Emir wants me to spend my time performing this sort of function?"

"In general," he said, "it's wise to jump on whatever bandwagon you see coming down the road."

"But what about my integrity as an individual?"

He laughed. "What's with these strange new ideas you've been repeating? Have you joined a sect, or what? My advice to you is to avoid partisanship, no matter what the cause. Otherwise you'd best look for another country to live in. Remember how the late Sultan tossed out the Polo Master just to keep us happy? People liked him because he was a genuinely good person who lived by his principles and called on people to be upright and honorable. But what good did it do him?"

"He did what he thought was his duty."

Khazaal laughed. "He might actually have won if his real aim had been to help others. The late Sultan could have put an end to our so-called excesses. But the Polo Master's real reason for attacking us was to protect himself and his family from our occasional high spirits. When the Sultan refused to help, the Polo Master moved away and left the neighborhood to us. You see, when you're fighting for yourself, and you keep getting beaten, you give up. But when you're fighting for a common cause, you never give up, no matter how many times you lose, because you draw strength from the cause and from the ones fighting for it with you."

"You're a wise man, great Emir," I said. "You're right: that's how the emirs are, one way or the other. But tell me: do you think of yourself as fighting for yourself or for a cause?"

"I'm not fighting at all," he said simply. "I used to be a fighter, but now I'm a defender, standing up for anyone who's gotten the short end of the stick. Some of the oppressors may be Egyptians, but only because they themselves are being trampled by a corrupt system. If you step on a snake, it bites whatever's in front of it!" After a pause, he said, "So, how would you feel about doing some spying for the storehouse?"

"Where?"

"At the Citadel. There's going to be a bloody fight over the throne and I want to hear about it."

"But why do we need to spy, great Emir?" I asked. "We have a window we use to deal with the public. We could send envoys everywhere to represent us and do their jobs in the open without anyone feeling sensitive about it. That's how the super-powers collect their information: thoroughly but discreetly."

He waved a hand. "Organize it any way you want, but you need to go to the Citadel in person and then report back to me. The storehouse will look out for you from behind the scenes."

"I want a travel allowance in hard currency."

"Agreed."

"And my own transportation."

"You got it."

"And one secretary," I said, "to carry my briefcase and another to interrupt me during meetings and whisper in my ear all the time."

"What is he supposed to whisper about?"

"Nothing," I said. "Why do you ask?"

"So why do it, then?"

"I'm not sure, exactly, but it's one of those things you need to have if you want to make an impression and feel important."

"You Egyptians are obsessed with having servants," he said. "But I'll grant your requests."

Borne on the back of a stallion and ringed by an honor guard, I set off at once to the Citadel, and caught up with the Sultan as he was mounting the throne.

The new sultan's full name was Malik Mansur Sayf al-Din Abu Bakr, son of Sultan Nasir son of Qalawun. He was to assume his seat in the portico of the Citadel as designated successor to his father. To get in, I needed someone to vouch for me. Fortunately, I spotted Ibn Taghribirdi on his way in to meet the Sultan. I greeted him and followed him inside. On the way, he told me that this Mansur was the thirteenth of the Turkish kings of Egypt and the first descendant of Ibn Qalawun.

In no time we had reached the Citadel portico, where the Sultan's formal public audience was already underway. Sultan Mansur was sitting on a throne facing the hall. He was a good-looking young man, graceful and slender, about twenty years old, big and healthy-looking. I greeted him and kissed the ground before him. Someone in the group made room for me and I sat down, as did Ibn Taghri, who began introducing me around.

"This is Emir Tuquzdamur of Aleppo, the Sultan's father-in-law; given his rank and his tie to the Sultan, he's second-in-command in Cairo. That's Emir Qawsun Nasiri, chief administrator and first adviser; and that's his fellow counselor, Emir Bashtak."

"Hey, great to meet you guys," I said.

Paying no attention to me, they nodded and said, "Likewise."

Then I got up close to the Sultan and whispered in his ear that I wanted to talk to him about the Sons of Shalaby of the current epoch who had made me promise to lay their complaints before him.

"Gladly," he said. "First, though, I have to go to the Citadel. The judges are meeting to discuss whether the caliph Hakim should return to the throne."

"Take your time," I reassured him. "The caliphate certainly takes precedence over the Sons of Shalaby."

Nodding, he said that his errand at the Citadel would not take long. He would be coming back to the audience room and would be honored if I would attend him—or more exactly, remain until he returned. To be honest, he was so nice about it that I was embarrassed. Worried that he might think I was putting on airs, I agreed to wait for him to come back.

As I sat waiting, I was presented with cups of silver and cups of gold. I drained them all and handed them back. When I finished, I found a plate of sweets. I gobbled it down and handed it back, only to be presented with a napkin for my face and hands.

I glanced over at Tuquzdamur, a pale, sharp-jawed, purse-lipped fellow who made me uncomfortable. I looked at Qawsun Nasiri, who looked exactly like a watermelon with the rind removed. Resentfully, I occupied myself by looking at the decorations, which were expertly made and beautifully symmetrical. Between one thing and another, I managed to distract myself for what seemed forever.

When I came to I found myself alone. Tuquzdamur, Qawsun, Ibn Taghri, and the young sultan were all gone, leaving only the servants, who were still looking after me tirelessly. I asked one of them where everyone had gone but he didn't know.

Then the Sultan appeared, greeting me and apologizing for having fallen asleep and forgotten our appointment. Ordering those with him to come in, he introduced them to me.

"Emir Yalbugha Yahyawi, who's closer than a friend. Emir Maliktamur Higazi, my closest boon companion. Emir Taqar Dawadar. Emir Qataliga Hamawi."

"What about the others?" I asked, pointing to a small group of men who had come in with them.

"They're part of the guard," he said, smiling.

"Nice to meet you," I said.

"The pleasure's ours," they replied.

Maliktamur then rose and began moving smoothly around the room, calling out to one subordinate, whispering into the ear of a second, issuing a reminder to a third, and joking with a fourth. Presently the servants reappeared with bottles and glasses and laid them before us. Clapping delightedly, I exclaimed that we had hit the jackpot and had a fine evening ahead of us.

Smiling at the company, Maliktamur began pouring. Then Tajar spoke up. "Whatever happened to Bashtak Nasiri? He had his heart set on being governor of Damascus."

"He's in prison in Alexandria," said the young sultan. "Qawsun Nasiri wouldn't let him alone. He kept after me until he convinced me to put him in prison."

"But, Master, you were already angry with him," said Qataliga.

"That's true."

"Because the late sultan named him governor of Damascus before he died?" asked Yalbugha.

"No. If he had been a little less eager, he would have gotten the job. But when I told him that he'd have it soon enough, he began acting as if he were already the governor. That's what made me so furious at him."

The company roared with laughter.

"The thing that made me even angrier," the Sultan continued, "was his reckless gift-giving. He gave away huge tracts of land, camels, horses, gold embroidery, and robes of honor to people of all kinds, including Mamluks."

"He gave me more gold and gems and pearls than I dreamed of getting from the Sultan himself," said Maliktamur.

"He gave me two beautiful slave women," said Altunbugha.

"He gave extravagant gifts to all the emirs," said the Sultan furiously.

"So why, Master," asked Maliktamur, "would you arrest a good-hearted, generous fellow like that?"

"If we hadn't," said the Sultan, drumming with his fingers on his cheek, "he would have made a grab for power."

"But he's incredibly rich," said Yalbugha. "Just think, Master: he gave out more than nine hundred tons of grain from his own silo to the emirs, and he gave trousseaus of cloth and brocade to eight girls and married them off at his own expense."

"Let's drop the whole subject of Bashtak," said the Sultan. "Damn him!"

"But, Master," said Maliktamur with a sort of disingenuous impudence, "I want to know. Is it true that he's dead?"

The young sultan seemed shocked, though his distress looked staged to me. "Where did you hear that?" he asked.

"I heard that the governor in Alexandria had him killed for some reason or other."

Looking preoccupied, the Sultan replied that the report might be true.

"And they say that Qawsun the Nasiri is the one who put the governor up to it."

"Could be," replied the Sultan, and began drinking. He kept on drinking until he was drunk. Then he got up, went over to the window, and shouting as loudly as a marketplace tout, called twice for Emir Aydughmish. From the base of the wall outside, an embarrassed voice called back: "Master? Is that you yelling like that? I mean—is everything all right, Master?"

"Send me Qutqut!"

"There's no horse of that name here, sir!"

"High equerry!" shouted the exasperated Sultan, "Qutqut is a singer and you know who she is! Have someone call her right away!"

He returned to his seat as if this sort of thing happened every day. I looked at him and said, "You are totally awesome!"

Everyone laughed.

But then, from somewhere far away, I could hear the beating of drums. One by one, a number of terrified-looking officials entered the room and whispered in the ears of the emirs.

"What's going on?" said the Sultan, slurring his words.

"There's some kind of plot afoot," said one of the officials.

"Tajar!" said the Sultan. "Go and find Tuquzdamur. Ask him what's going on and bring him back here." Tajar left and I followed.

We found the governor of the Citadel with Jankali ibn Baba, the vizier, and a number of the Citadel emirs. Tajar told Tuquzdamur to report to the Sultan.

"I'm not going," said Tuquzdamur. "I'm staying with the emirs until we know where this is heading. It's all your lot's fault: you're the deadbeats who corrupted the Sultan. Tell him to gather his Mamluks, and his father's Mamluks, around him."

Tajar and I went back to the Sultan and told him what had happened. The Sultan went out, summoned the Mamluks, and sent them to the Citadel gate. In moments they had returned to say that the gate was shut. The Sultan was trapped.

I had the feeling that something unpleasant was likely to happen in the not-too-distant future. Scrambling up to one of the window ledges, I looked for a pipe to climb down, but saw nothing. If I were the "Runaway Mamluk," I could have thrown myself off the rampart. Fortunately, I had a mount even better than his: my imagination. So I put it to work, and pulled myself out of the portico like a hair being pulled out of a bowl of dough.

Stopping some distance away, I looked back to see the Sultan standing at the same window calling for Aydughmish to strike the cymbals and saddle the horses for combat. Aydugh-mish replied that there were no grooms or pages left to saddle the horses.

"Send me the governor of the Citadel," cried the Sultan.

"He refuses to come!" came the cry.

Then Emir Barsbugha and his men charged the Citadel, stormed the portico, and seized the Sultan. Binding his wrists behind his back, they handed him to some of their comrades. The raiders went into the Sultan's quarters and reappeared with seven figures in tow. I looked closely and recognized them as the Sultan's brothers. Each was acompanied by a young Mamluk, a servant, a horse, and a bundle of clothes. As they walked defeated through the Citadel gate, they were a dismal sight. Spotting Ibn Taghribirdi among them, I joined them in the hope of witnessing "an admonition and a lesson to the wise." On the bank of the Nile, they made the brothers dismount and board a skiff that would carry them to the town of Qus, far to the south of the capital. Ibn Taghri said that it was Qawsun who had led the coup d'état against Sultan Man-sur and that he had left none of the Sultan's brothers in the Citadel except Kuchuk. Recovering from my consternation at this turn of events, I suddenly thought of the storehouse. In a transport of joy, I raced back, eager to share my eyewitness report of the historic event.

Inside the storehouse, the dancing was still going strong, and the drums and pipes still booming and squealing. Khazaal was sitting in his usual place, gulping arrack and eating raw meat sprinkled with pepper. Coming up to him, I asked if he had heard the latest.

"Have you?" he asked mockingly.

"They've packed the Sultan off to Qus."

"That's old news, Pickle-Man," he snickered. "I've just gotten a report from the middle of the Nile, where the skiff is traveling!"

"How?" I asked. "You don't have wireless yet!"

"We're stronger than the wireless," he said, chewing. "We've got the non-wireless!" He gave me a playful jab with his elbow and knocked me to the floor, where I fell into a deep sleep.

By the time I woke up, entire days had passed. The dancing was still going on, but it was no longer anything that we would understand as dancing: it was barbaric, meaningless motion. Khazaal was still in the same spot. To my surprise, though, Ibn Taghri was sitting next to him, staring at him in fascination. I shook myself awake and went to say hello.

"You're exhausted," said Ibn Taghri with a smile.

"From seeing so much," I said.

"You haven't seen anything yet," he said, "just the tail end of one of my chapters. Just imagine seeing a whole chapter, or several!"

"Please don't show me," I begged. "I couldn't handle it."

"Did you see Mansur going off into exile?" he asked.

"What a sorry sight!"

"His fall from power and his exile are a lesson to those who draw admonition from history," he intoned. "His father, Nasir son of Qalawun, sent the Caliph Muktafi and his children and entourage to Qus in exile and disgrace, and now his descendants have suffered the same fate: Qawsun, his son-in-law and highest ranking Mamluk, has expelled his master's sons."

"A admonition and a lesson to the wise!"

Ibn Taghri rose to go. I went with him intending to accompany him to the door, but I got caught up in the conversation and was soon walking with him through the crowded streets of Cairo. We could see that something was wrong: people were weeping, shrieking, and wailing, or trudging gloomily past. I asked a passerby what had happened, but he said nothing and walked on, weeping.

"Something really important must have happened," I said to Ibn Taghri.

"Such as?"

"As an Egyptian and a Son of Shalaby, I can tell you that this kind of mass mourning happens only here, and only for a good reason, like the death of a major political figure."

"That's the Egyptian spirit all right," he said. "Egyptians really get upset when a leader dies."

"So did one die?"

"Let's ask."

We did, and we learned that Sultan Mansur had been killed by one Abdel Mu'min, the military governor of Qus, and that his head had secretly been delivered to Qawsun.

"But how can the nation mourn a sultan who had never been tested, and ruled for only a few days?" I asked.

"He was a generous ruler," answered the chronicler, "and he was young."

Night fell and the streets of Cairo filled with girls dressed in black and carrying drums, wailing rhythmically in mourning, with a crowd echoing them like a chorus.

"What a place!" said Ibn Taghri. "The country of sorrows."

12

No Way around Impalement,
Even for the Innocent

WHEN EMIR KHAZAAL TOLD ME that he had a way of knowing
what was happening the very instant that it happened, I was
embarrassed. Coming as I did from the age of telephones,
radios, and satellites, I had always thought that ours was the
most advanced of all periods when it came to espionage,
eavesdropping, communications, and the like, but here was
Khazaal outdoing us without using technology. Even though
I had witnessed an historical event, there were many things I
had failed to see and write down. As a result, I failed to grasp
the significance of many other things that happened later.
How then had Khazaal understood all of it without leaving
his seat in the Storehouse of Banners?

Sensing what was going through my head, which was in
any case obvious enough, he asked with a grin if I wanted to
know how he got his information.

"For God's sake, yes!" I exclaimed. "And tell me the whole
truth."

With an unselfconscious fart, Khazaal sat up straight.
"The whole Sons-of-Shalaby clan," he said in a philosophic
manner, "are my eyes and ears. News travels as fast as you can
fill an Egyptian street with victims of abuse. As you know, the
storehouse has extended protection to a good many asylum-
seekers. The ones still out on the street need our protection
even more, but for some reason or other haven't asked for it.
And yet they do what they can to help us survive. They never

know when they might need a protector, and they want to be sure that we—as terrible as we are—will always be around. That's why they volunteer to defend us against the regime.

"Your clan includes another set, too: the ones who don't want protection and don't expect much from the storehouse in particular, but have religious reasons for hating the way the government treats the people. They want to make sure that someone in Egypt will always be able to stand up and fight back. So, without our having to ask, they volunteer to defend us. There are times when I'll be walking down the street without a thought in my head and suddenly someone bumps into me, pulls me aside, and whispers in my ear, warning me of a danger I hadn't even thought to worry about, or giving me a tip that turns out to be incredibly helpful. And so on."

Distressingly, he was right about us, up to a point. "All God's creatures, from all over the world," I thought to myself, "visit other countries and stay for a while, but in the end they have to go back home. The one place that's different is Egypt. People of every creed and color come here, dig their heels in, and refuse to budge. They become natives—and sometimes end up running the place."

Hoping to unwind, I asked Khazaal's permission to go out for a walk. Looking me over, he told me to keep an eye out for any sudden changes of policy on the part of the Sultan. I pointed out that the new Sultan was not yet five years old and as far as anyone knew had yet to adopt any sudden changes of policy. He asked if I was thinking of Nasir's son Kuchuk, who had taken on the trappings of kingship and assumed the title of Sultan Ashraf.

"Right, Nasir's second son, the fourteenth Turkish king of Egypt."

"Wrong again!" he said. "Ashraf's the ruler in name only. The real sultan is Emir Qawsun. He's the Sultan's deputy, as you may know; but he prefers to live alone in the his palace without going to the governor's residence outside the Gate of the Keep of the Citadel. He's the one who overthrew Emir

Bashtak, who started with an advantage. He also deposed the last sultan, and he's powerful enough to depose a whole family of sultans. Watch out for him!"

"Don't worry about me, Emir Khazaal. I know how to take care of myself."

"Whatever you say," he said with a smile. "I've done my duty and warned you."

Reminding him that all we could do was trust in God, I went out.

As I made my way toward the Citadel, I saw that candles had been placed in the shops and along the streets and hoped it was a good sign. Then I heard loud noises and drumbeats approaching from a distance, and hoped this, too, was a good sign. A crowd appeared. My watch read Saturday, 26 Jumada II, 742. Leading the marchers were dignified youths and wizened old men animated by a strangely malicious joy, behind which seemed still to lurk some battered vestige of human feeling. I asked one of the young men what was going on.

"A public shaming—what else?"

"What's that mean?" I asked.

"Join the procession and you'll see," said an old man.

"But how can I join if I don't know what it's for and where it's going?"

"Join us and find out!" said another old man.

"Or join us," said a third, "and don't find out!"

"He's already joined whether he knows it or not," said a fourth.

"That's how these processions go," said a fifth. "Every other occasion is either happy or sad, but with processions you get both at once."

"That's why we can't help joining them," said a young man, philosophically.

"We can't help laughing, either," said a second young man, more philosophically.

"What do you mean by that?" said the first, flaring up.

"He meant," said a third in a soothing tone, "that we laugh despite ourselves."

Evidently, people's brains here in the land of Egypt had reached the stage of short circuits and blown fuses centuries before our modern brains had.

Walking on, I found that I had somehow joined the procession. True, I was still clinging to the illusion that mine was an individual consciousness playing the role of detached observer. But like it or not, I was now a part of the mob, and its emotions became my own. Moving at its own pace, it carried me along like a wave. I had no will of my own or any impulses to control: who could wish for anything in the midst of that senseless, mindless torrent? Forced from the vanguard to the center, I let myself savor the sensation of being pushed backward through the crowd.

Then, amid a knot of cheerful drummers, I spotted a big camel. It marched along with enormous dignity, craning its neck right and left and smiling a smile so profoundly mocking that only a very great philosopher could have produced it. On its back was a wooden structure consisting—I suddenly saw— of a rectangular scaffold and, inside it, a cross. This, I thought, was the first time I had ever seen a cross put into a scaffold to protect it and block it from view. But this cross was throbbing with almost invisible pulse-beats and shedding pools of blood. It also had a head that hung down on a bent neck and two arms that were nailed to the wood. The legs and buttocks had been nailed up as well. I noticed that the arms needed only two five-centimeter nails, while the rest needed large blacksmith's nails. Whoever was crucifying people on behalf of the government, I thought, was a master craftsman capable of inventing a first-rate nut-and-bolt system, drilling through human limbs, filling and smoothing the surface after driving the nails through, and finishing it off with an attractive paint job.

Finding me drifting like a feather on the current, one of the men who was marching alongside the camel jabbed me with his elbow. I shot him an angry look. He wiggled his hand next to his ear as if to ask, "What's the matter with you?" Matching his pace and pointing to the crucified figure, I asked him sadly who the poor wretch was.

"Poor wretch?" he exclaimed angrily.

"I mean, the accursed fellow."

Equanimity restored, he gestured with his chin at the victim. "Don't you know him? It's Wali al-Dawla Abul Farag Ibn Khatir, brother-in-law of Nashw. It's Qawsun who nailed him up like that."

"Why?"

"He had used the good offices of his master Maliktamur to appeal directly to Sultan Mansur," he whispered.

"So what?"

"He did a few things," said the man evasively, "to make Qawsun angry."

"You mean he complained about him, or plotted against him?"

"God knows!" said the man, clearly trying to put an end to the conversation.

"So why are you so happy?" I asked.

"We belong to Qawsun's guard. Why shouldn't we rejoice if one of our enemies falls?"

"But all these other people are just Egyptians and Cairenes. Why should they care about the battles all of you fight among yourselves? What's in it for them?"

"Egyptians and Cairenes," replied the man, "love to see an arrogant oppressor meet his end, especially when he was one of Nashw's entourage and in-laws."

I looked back at the victim as he swayed slowly and monotonously in time with the camel's gait, which was nothing like the pace of the procession. "My God!" I exclaimed, finding the whole scene revolting. "What *is* this place?"

"What's that you're saying?" the man shouted at me in a fury.

"You've been had."

Eyes blazing, hand reaching for his sword, he cried, "What did you say, you coward?"

As if I had not heard him, I went on in the same disgusted tone, "That fellow there is no craftsman, if you want my opinion."

The man's hand stopped. "What fellow where?"

"The one who did the nailing up there. Nothing professional about it at all. Anyone could have done it. How much did you pay him? Nothing, I hope. I'm a master carpenter and I know what I'm talking about. Your guy doesn't know a thing about crucifying people. I mean: do you call that a nail? You've got blood coming out all around the hole. And what about that one? The nail goes crooked into the thigh so he leaves it in and bends the end? What kind of workmanship is that? Doesn't he have a pair of pliers to yank out the bent one and drive a new nail? What a shoddy job! In my time we'd have thrown him out of the union."

The man's hand had slipped off the sword and his demeanor returned to normal. Smiling, he tried to humor me. "Now that you mention it, I think you're right."

Other people were smiling at me too. An imposing figure came forward and introduced himself: "Gamal al-Din Ibrahim Mi'mar, man of letters."

"Nice to meet you, bro," I said.

Approaching even closer, he launched into a stagy declamation of the following verses:

The upstarts left a man behind
Who did his best to rob us blind;
But now we've caught him, as you see,
And nailed him nicely to a tree.

"That was apparently poetry," I said.

"I certainly hope so!" he retorted. Gifted as he was with an acute literary sensibility, he had noticed my deficient appreciation of his verses. After reciting only those lines, he turned away and vanished into the crowd. Then the procession itself began to fade away slowly, until it was gone.

I found myself sitting in the Court of Justice, directly beside the throne. On the throne was five-year-old cutie-pie Kuchuk, now Sultan Ashraf. In his specially tailored pint-size royal outfit, he looked like a doll for sale on a street stall piled high with merchandise. I wasn't sure exactly why I had appeared at this particular session at this particular moment, but I supposed that my presence had something to do with my being a representative of the storehouse or a colleague of Ibn Taghribirdi. I passed the time watching the people who were there, especially the gigantic emirs who came forward to kiss the ground before the boy sultan. Each emir was given robes of honor. There were so many emirs and so many robes—twelve hundred in all—that just watching them strained my envious eyes. At one point I found myself sitting next to Qawsun. I remembered Khazaal warning me in no uncertain terms to steer clear of him, and I was surprised that I had been lulled into sitting beside him. Perhaps I had made a point of seeing him up close because I was afraid of him. I also told myself that there wasn't much hope of avoiding him at the court of Sultan Ashraf since he was the Sultan's viceroy and brother-in-law.

Without my noticing, the robes-of-honor session had ended and some new ceremony was taking place. I saw someone come up to Qawsun and listen to something he was saying. I gathered that Maliktamur Sarguwani, the governor of Karak, had been driven to despair over the rebellion of the Sultan's older brother, Emir Ahmad of Karak, who had renounced obedience to the governor. Ahmad was also enamored of the young men of Karak and addicted to drink. He was refusing to obey Qawsun's request that he come to Egypt except on the following conditions: that the leading emirs go to him in Karak and swear loyalty, that the brothers exiled to Upper Egypt be sent to him, and that he be brought to Cairo and sworn in as sultan. Because of all my bouncing around in history, I tended to confuse one period with another, and so it took me a while to realize that this session had been convened by the emirs to discuss what to do about Ahmad and that they had decided to send troops to capture him.

When the meeting ended and the emirs rose to go I got up too, but I found my path blocked by a jovial, handsome, worthy-looking man, who would have frightened me but for his appearance. I looked around, but we were the only two in the hall. The fellow was beckoning to me and smiling sarcastically, as if to say, "Yes, I mean you, smart-ass." I approached him nervously and asked him who he was.

"Don't you recognize me, you rascal? I'm head of the Sultan's Mamluks."

"Hey there!" I said. "How's the Sultan? And what are the Mamluks up to these days?"

Taking hold of my shoulder, he pulled me along. "None of the Sultan's Mamluks is supposed to go anywhere," he said. "In fact, none of them wants to. So why did you think you could escape?"

"You think I'm one of the Sultan's Mamluks?"

He jabbed me with his elbow. "Of course you are! Emir Qawsun has asked for you by name."

"But . . . this is all wrong! Emir Qawsun asked after me? This is a disaster!"

The head Mamluk never paused. Pulling me along gently, he pointed toward a splendidly appointed part of the building and ordered me to go inside. I found myself looking at a vast number of halls and rooms where men as beautiful as women, or more so, were coming and going. One room was marked COHORT. One of the men came forward to receive me. "So it's you," he said, apparently making fun of me. "Come on!"

When I reached him, he scrutinized me and then ordered me to turn in a circle like a fashion model. "Do you belong to the Sultan or to Qawsun?" he asked.

"I don't belong to anybody," I told him angrily. A hand like a thunderbolt struck me in the temple and knocked me silly. "A smart-ass from day one, eh?" he said, furious. "An infiltrator and impudent to boot! Go into that room over there."

I went. It was partially furnished and partially elegant, and was redolent of some feminine perfume that gave me goose bumps and nausea. Heartsick, I sat on the bed and began plotting some means of escape.

I was too miserable to notice the passage of time, so I don't know how long it was before I heard the commotion coming from the other rooms. People were rushing in and out and voices were being raised. I went out to see what was going on. My watch read Saturday, 16 Rabi I, AH 742. I saw the head of the Sultan's Mamluks standing with his hand on the shoulder of a good-looking pageboy and a large number of the Cohort Mamluks blocking their path.

"Emir Qawsun has asked for a good-looking pageboy," said the headman. "This is the one we want."

"He's not leaving," said one of the Cohort.

"He's doesn't belong to Qawsun, so how can he leave?" said another.

"This one—and the others too—are under our protection," said a third.

"If that boy leaves you'll have hell to pay," said a fourth.

"We won't let him out!" cried a fifth.

"Men of the Cohort!" said the headman in a calm and reasonable manner. "Show a little patience. Why the insubordination? All of us were pages, and we're still pages. They're the Sultan's Mamluks and you're the Cohort, and you take orders from the Sultan. You know the Emir Qawsun's in charge now: same as if he were Sultan, but more powerful. Or would you rather have a boy king who doesn't know anything about Mamluks and pages and can't appreciate all the hard work you're doing? Maybe you don't like it but why resist when it won't get you anywhere?"

One of the Cohort threw his hands up in disgust and walked out. A second muttered something about having nothing to do with either side. A third shouted something in a language I didn't understand and ran off. Soon they had all disappeared, leaving the head Mamluk, who was roaring with laughter, to drag the pageboy off.

With the Cohort humiliated and scattered, we spent the night waiting for the pageboy to return, which he did only at daybreak. With him was the headman, who let him go to his room and then sat down and beckoned some of the Cohort to join him. A good number of them gathered around, anger clearly written on their faces. "The Viceroy has a new request," he began.

"New or old makes no difference," said one of the Cohort angrily. "What's happened is more than enough. Didn't the boy spend a night with him?"

"The Viceroy's requests cannot be postponed, let alone refused."

"What's his highness want now?" cried several voices.

"He wants the following Mamluks of the cohort to spend the evening with him," said the headman. "Shikhun, Sirtamnims, and Itmins Abdel Ghani."

A babble of voices shouted back at him and from out of nowhere came many more Mamluks. The Cohort was obviously no longer interested in reaching a compromise. As one, they were shouting that they didn't belong to the Sultan or to Qawsun either. When they pushed the headman to the ground and began trampling him, he jumped to his feet and took off running.

With him out of the way, the Cohort began to plan its next move. After some discussion they decided that they had no choice but to go out and join Emir Baybars Ahmadi.

At some point Emir Barsbugha, the Sultan's chamberlain, along with his secretary Severus, entered the room along with a group of Mamluks belonging to Qawsun. "I could have taken those men from you by force," Barsbugha began, "but . . . ."

The men of the Cohort gave him a shove and he backed away, ordering his men not to fight back.

Finally all of us went out to look for Baybars. On the way we were told that he was out riding, so we headed for the house of Emir Jankali ibn Baba in Hawd Marsud. When we ran into him on the road, he stopped in surprise to ask us what was wrong.

"It was the Sultan Nasir's money that bought us," said one of the Cohort, "and we belong to him."

"How can we abandon our master's son Ashraf," asked another, "and serve a Mamluk, same as us?"

The clamor and the shouting grew louder as scores of Mamluks began speaking at once. Jankali urged them to calm down. They responded with obscenities, insults, and imprecations.

"Listen to me," he said. "Stop this nonsense at once!"

"No, by God," they shouted. "We'll never back down!"

"Only yesterday you were singing a different tune," snarled Jankali. "When you rebelled then, Tuquzdamur the Viceroy told you to go back and serve your master's son. But you said you had no master but Qawsun. So now you don't want him either?"

The senior man in the Cohort then suggested that we go to Mankali Fakhri, so we did. At his house we found Barsbugha, who had been sent there by Qawsun. The Cohort clamored for his head but Fakhri declared him under his protection and the clamor died away. Then the Cohort departed without explaining to me exactly what they had agreed to do next.

Hearing that Qawsun had summoned his Mamluks, I decided to obey the summons, thinking I might pick up some news for the storehouse. Qawsun himself saw me arriving and seemed surprised, but I had the feeling that he would let me attend his council since I had, after all, been declared his property. When the commanders had gathered, he began speaking to them of plots and conspiracies, telling them that if they did not act, the Sultan's Mamluks would lose respect for them, run amok, and perhaps even gain indirect control of the throne, especially since the Sultan was a boy and could do nothing to restrain them. At that the commanders muttered and looked furious.

Seizing his chance, Qawsun called for his chamberlain, Emir Mas'ud, and asked him, on behalf of all the commanders, to go and fetch the Sultan's Mamluks, whom he had asked to spend the evening with him. Mas'ud left and was gone for a long time. Seething, we passed the time in pointless chatter until he returned to report that more and more Mamluks were gathering around the Sultan and no one had paid any attention to him.

Flying into a rage, Qawsun ordered Altunbugha and Qutlubugha, two of his most powerful emirs, to go and fetch the Mamluks in question. The two left. After a considerable delay, they returned with the men Qawsun had asked for. The three came forward and kissed his hand. He rose, kissed them on the head, reassured them that all was well, and let them go.

Tired of sitting and eating and drinking, I asked Qawsun for permission to leave. He glared at me and said he needed me to stay to give him my opinion on a few matters. He explained that he had spent the previous night tossing and turning because he had heard that the Mamluks loyal to Sultan Nasir had sworn to assassinate him. Glancing at my watch, I saw that it was Monday, 18 Rabi' II.

Qawsun then ordered his horse to be saddled. The emirs and I mounted as well, and we rode out in the shadow of the Citadel. Calling for Aydughmish, the High Equerry, Qawsun began reproaching the emirs for various reasons. Then Emir Baybars caught up with us and whispered in his ear that the Sultan's Mamluks had decided to kill him.

Qawsun and the emirs headed off in the direction of the Victory Dome to find the Citadel in an uproar. After barring the gates, the Sultan's Mamluks had taken up weapons and broken into the armory. Meanwhile, the people had swarmed into Rumayla Square—called Saladin Square today—and begun shouting "Men of Nasir, we're with you!" Voices from the Citadel called down to them to attack Qawsun's house. The mob raced off in the direction of the house. Whirling around, Qawsun set off after them, leaving me by myself on a horse that was free to wander at will.

After dropping in at the storehouse to show off my royal mount, I went out again to find Cairo in a sorry state. Groups of people were running in all directions and the wounded were everywhere. I learned that Qawsun had defeated and captured the Mamluks and had begun making an example of them. Passing Zuwayla Gate, I noticed with a shudder that someone had been cut in two and then hung from the gate. Nearby, Qawsun's men were taking the captives and crucifying them on the gate using big nails and a hammer. "So that's what a real nailing looks like," I thought. I overheard someone say that one of the new Mamluks had escaped and that Qawsun was going to cut him in half if he found him. Realizing that he meant me, I gave the horse a kick and raced off like the wind.

13

The Dregs of Madness

LIKE AN EXPERT RIDER, I gave the horse a kick, and it flew across the square as if it owned the place. I admit I had never ridden a horse before, or even stroked one: the closest I had come was admiring how they went through their paces to the sound of a reed pipe. But now that I was mounted like a knight I became a knight—or maybe it was just that the horse did such a good job of keeping me balanced that I was free to think about escaping from Qawsun, who was reportedly hot on my tail.

I thought of slipping out of the time I was in. Unfortunately, the prison of time turned out to be harder to break out of than prisons in space. When I thought about the future, I could make the different periods of history shimmer before my eyes. But every time I saw ahead clearly enough to jump beyond the time where I was imprisoned, I trembled at the thought that I might be sinning against God. Though I could see the future with my own eyes, I surprised myself by recoiling from it, afraid of whatever punishment one gets for being a fortune-teller. So I decided to let time have its way with me and left the future in the hands of the Almighty.

But where to fly from Qawsun, who with all his power was bound to catch up with me? No sooner had the question formed itself in my mind than I roared with laughter. Of course: I enjoyed diplomatic immunity by virtue of my affiliation with the Storehouse of Banners—the prison for foreigners who were originally prisoners of war but now ruled a state of their own. All I had to do now was make it to the gate and I'd be out of danger. Going back would also be a chance to show off my horsemanship, not to mention all the information I had gathered, which was so recent and detailed that even Khazaal would be impressed.

"How is it," I asked myself, "that you forgot about the storehouse, Son of Shalaby?"

"That's how people are," I said, answering my own question. "Including me. I happened to be riding a noble steed and so I forgot about the storehouse. It's hard not to get distracted when you're riding a purebred stallion that obeys your every whim."

The Son of Shalaby who had asked the question said that the Son of Shalaby who had answered it was harebrained and shortsighted. But the Son of Shalaby who was both of them—that is, me—laughed at them both, dug in with his heels, and sent the horse flying. But then he noticed that they would have to slow down: the crowded streets that surrounded the storehouse were straight ahead.

The horse stumbled and Ibn Shalaby was nearly hurled to the ground. He was nearly knocked out (out of what, though?), a circumstance that provoked the Ibn Shalaby who had asked the question to stick his tongue out at the one who had answered it. In any event, it was only thanks to the skill of the horse that Ibn Shalaby was spared a fall.

Honor intact, he crossed the threshold of the storehouse. There he was welcomed by a crowd of whooping children, some of whom followed him in at a run. Led by Khazaal, a group of men, including some of the emirs, appeared in the doorway, laughing, cheering, and clapping sarcastically as I rode toward them at a stately pace like a cowboy in a movie. All I needed to complete the thrilling scene was a torrential rainstorm.

I dismounted with an athletic leap that stirred the envy of most of the onlookers. Looping the reins around the brass door handle like a proper swashbuckler, I stepped forward to greet Khazaal and the other emirs. I condescended to nod to some of the lower orders, and, condescending even more, smiled at the attractive women who were present. Then I followed Khazaal toward his enclosure. Something about the way the emirs carried themselves gave me the feeling that they had something up their sleeve and were waiting to see what I would do. "By God," I thought, "I'll surprise you with the news I've gathered and the things I've seen."

We sat down. Arrack was served. All of a sudden I was knocked flat by a stabbing pain in the stomach and a wave of nausea and dizziness, along with a Technicolor rainbow of calamities that left me vomiting, coughing, scratching, and carrying out such operations as cannot have been pleasant to behold. All of this happened, mind you, before I had even had a drink. I realized that the few days I had spent with the boy Sultan and the villainous Qawsun amid heavenly scents, rich foods, and fine wines had made me a stranger to the storehouse. Now, awash in the smell of bodies and arrack and cannibals and decrepitude, I felt as if I were swimming in a sea of carrion. Miserable as all that was, though, the real misery hit when they tried to revive me, beginning with the crushing of an onion on my nose and ending with the dislocation of my joints as a result of forceful pulling, bending, and suchlike operations. Their brutal ministrations would doubtless have done the trick eventually, but I only came to my senses good and proper after Khazaal, laughing wildly, his eyes glinting like a madman's, clapped his hands in demented glee. Nodding to me, he said, "First, we owe you a big thank-you for bringing such a fine appetizer. This is going to be a splendid night, with only the finest meats served."

I looked up and saw the horse—my horse—being dragged into the storehouse like a sack, with its throat cut and hot blood everywhere. Thunderstruck, I stood up; crushed, I sat down again. I looked from one person to another hoping to find some explanation for this madness. When they slaughtered my purebred stallion, they had slaughtered me as well. It seemed to have been some kind of insult, one that would supply fodder for jokes for the rest of the night. I asked Khazaal how they could do something so low and nasty. "It was my horse," I said. "It deserves the same respect as I do. How could you slaughter it without asking my permission?"

Khazaal burst into laughter and the earth shook. The others opened their mouths in a token gesture: his laugh was loud enough to do for everyone. Taking a gulp of arrack, he asked, "Did you think it was yours? You fool! It belongs to us, just as whatever dignity you have, you have because of us."

"True enough," I said, "but the man gave me the horse as a gift. You'd think it would be my property."

Everyone laughed. "Would you really be happy owning a horse while we starve for lack of something to nibble on?" he asked.

"Never!" I said. "You win, Emir. I now see how deficient I am in civic responsibility. Let's have a glass of arrack and toast my defeat—I mean, my recognition of the right way of seeing things."

With his own hand, Khazaal offered me a glass. Then he stood up and disappeared behind a thick curtain, telling me to follow him. I realized that he wanted me to report on what I had seen.

Sitting back in a self-important manner, I launched into the story of Qawsun, trying as best as I could to spice it up. But the emirs grew restless, and I could guess from the looks on their faces that they wanted me to drop the story and move on. Then Khazaal spoke up, "Everything you're telling us about what happened to Qawsun we know already. We had up-to-the-minute reports coming in the whole time. In fact, they're still coming in now. What we want to hear about is your experience with the Sultan's Mamluks." The eyes of the emirs glittered wickedly.

So I told them the whole story as faithfully and honestly as I could. They were nodding as I spoke, but there was something wrong. Their tone made it clear that they didn't quite believe what I was telling them. Evidently, they felt that I was hiding some critical point about what had happened to me in the Cohort's quarters. I realized that there were certain experiences that leave a mark on people that can never be expunged. With the arrack going to my head, I got excited and treated them to a harangue that verged on abuse, as if defending myself against some shameful accusation.

Khazaal then took pity on me and explained what the conspiracy was about. To make a long story short, he had gotten in touch with Qawsun and said to him jokingly that he would present him with a Mamluk of rare distinction. In this period, people gave away Mamluks the way we give away cigarettes: men of all ranks and stations would accept them without objection, even if the gift was really more of a bribe. Qawsun accepted the offer immediately. Before sending me, though, Khazaal gave him reason to believe—on the basis of a third-party report—that I suffered from a particular vice. The point was to create a misunderstanding between us that would lead to a scandal of historic proportions—one that Khazaal could use against Qawsun. In short, it was a dirty trick. Even dirtier, though, was the fact that the man behind it was explaining it as dispassionately as if he were writing an autobiography. Realizing that I could have died in the course of the prank, I wondered how these people could put me at risk for the sake of a few laughs, even though I was working for them. But then I answered my own question: "Anyone who works for tattooed cannibals really shouldn't expect too much affection on their part. No matter how much you do for them, sooner or later they're going to eat you too, even if they don't mean anything by it." I shuddered, and took some consolation in the fact that I still had a body to shudder with. Concealing my disgust, I remarked that Qawsun was a real devil.

"Don't you know his real story?" asked Khazaal.

"Certainly not."

"Did you know that he and Baktamur started out as Sultan Nasir's cupbearers and became his greatest Mamluks?"

"I had no idea!" Suddenly the penny dropped, and I gaped like a rustic idiot. "So that's why they have titles like Qawsun the Cupbearer, Baktamur the Cupbearer, and so on. Go figure!"

"There's nothing unusual about it," he said. "It's a fact of life and everyone is aware of it, except maybe ragamuffins and bandits who've been living under a rock."

"Instead of coming up with new ways to put me down, His Royal Highness might instead tell the story of that devil Qawsun who stops at nothing."

"In the year seven-hundred-something," said Khazaal, "Qawsun, who wasn't a Mamluk slave at the time, arrived from the land of the Turks with the retinue of Khund, the daughter of Uzbek Khan, who was later married off to Sultan Nasir. It so happened that Qawsun went up to the Citadel with a merchant he was working for. Sultan Nasir saw him and liked him. He offered to buy him, but the merchant told him that Qawsun was not a slave. But the Sultan refused to take no for an answer. He weighed out eight thousand dirhams and sent them to Qawsun's brother Sawsun in the land of the Qaymaq, where they came from. Make sense so far?"

"Yup."

"So Nasir took Qawsun under his wing and made him cupbearer. Later he promoted him to the command of a hundred and then a thousand. Qawsun rose so high that the Sultan married one of his daughters off to him—that being the second time he'd married one of his daughters off to a Mamluk. That was in 727."

"You know the date, too, Emir? You're as good as any historian!"

"Did you really think that with all the time we spent here, we never knew anything about the place?" asked Khazaal.

"Not a chance! We've been at the heart of the region for years and years, and we would get news from Egypt instantly—news that the Egyptians themselves might not hear for years. You poor people who live here need to learn that this country will never amount to anything until you keep up with whatever the rulers are doing offstage, even when news is hard to come by."

"Can we get back to Qawsun?"

He laughed. "So Nasir threw a big wedding party for him, and the emirs chipped in with a gift of fifty thousand dinars."

"Wow! When it rains, it pours."

"That's why, every time Qawsun and Baktamur the Cup-bearer would get into an argument about something, Qawsun would boast that he hadn't worked his way up from the stables. Instead, the Sultan had bought him and made him an intimate all at one go."

Those words sounded familiar and I said so.

"Everyone knows the story of Qawsun," said Khazaal.

I told him that I heard the same story word for word from my friend Ibn Taghribirdi.

"What age is this Ibn Birdi from?" he asked.

"He's after your time," I replied.

"Then he got the story from us." He poured some arrack for both of us and we sat for a time in peaceful silence.

While we were still sitting and drinking, news arrived from Qeta, an Egyptian town on the road from Cairo to al-Arish, that Qawsun had captured a messenger sent by the governor of Aleppo, Emir Tashtamur the Cupbearer, called Green Garbanzo and put him in prison. The messenger had been carrying letters addressed to the Egyptian emirs, including Qawsun, reproaching them for exiling the children of their master, the late Sultan Nasir, to Upper Egypt and sending an army to attack Nasir's son Ahmad in Karak. Soon afterward, we learned that Aydughmish, the high equerry, and his men were planning to attack Qawsun. After fortifying his position, Aydughmish addressed Qawsun rudely and began locking his cavalcade out of the Sultan's stables and stationing a troop of Grooms to keep him out. They were later reconciled, but rumor had it that Aydughmish still bore a grudge.

Then the news came that the troops that Qawsun had sent with Emir Qutlubugha had descended on Karak. The citizens had refused to admit them and fortified themselves in the town, raining curses and imprecations on them.

Next came news from Damascus to the effect that Tamr Musawi had arrived from Aleppo and persuaded a number of emirs to join Tashtamur, a.k.a. Green Garbanzo, the governor of Aleppo. Qawsun had ordered his arrest and sent a formal delegation to Green Garbanzo, who spurned it rudely.

Next came a report from Shatt, the Emir of the Arabs, that Qutlubugha and his associates had plotted against Qawsun and sworn loyalty to Ahmad, declaring him Sultan. Lost to Qawsun with Qutlubugha's change of heart were forty thousand dinars, not to mention horses, fabrics, and gifts. Qawsun had then written to Emir Altunbugha, governor of Syria, ordering him to take the governors of Hims, Safad, and Tripoli (all of whom received money from Qawsun for expenses) and engage Green Garbanzo. The latter, with the support of Delfesar and his Mamluks, marched out to meet Qawsun's forces. Dereliction, chastisements, and flogging had ensued. Qutlubugha had then come from Karak calling on people to join the new sultan. He had occupied Damascus, confiscated endowments and private fortunes, distributed the plunder to the troops, and rewarded the Turcomans and the soldiers who had distinguished themselves with gifts of cloth and weapons. Everyone swore allegiance to the new Sultan Ahmad, and the uniforms of the royal and caliphal guards, as well as the stables, saddles, saddlecloths, parasols, and other paraphernalia were given his insignia.

From the one side, then, news was coming thick and fast. As for Qawsun, we sent people to find out why our information was being delayed, and then sent other people to find out why the first set of people were taking so long, and so on, until we were fuming. Finally, we learned that he had assembled the emirs for consultation and decided to dispatch Barsbugha the chamberlain and Ala al-Din Ali ibn Tughril Bey with troops to Gaza.

More news soon followed. Seizing control of the situation, Qutlubugha had written to Qawsun rebuking him for exiling his master's children to Qus and killing Sultan Mansur. He had also announced that the emirs had agreed to support Ahmad as sultan. Finally, he instructed Qawsun to choose a village and stay there until the new sultan decided what to do with him.

The next thing we learned was that Qawsun had assembled the emirs, who decided to dispatch troops again, but this time to meet the victorious emirs rather than fight them. It was then reported that he had opened up the Sultan's reserves and had begun plying his allies with emoluments to the tune of six hundred thousand dinars. This tactic alarmed Aydughmish, who feared that Qawsun might thereby snatch the sultanate. Accordingly, he had summoned the senior emirs and all agreed to travel to Karak, meet up with Sultan Ahmad, and offer allegiance to him.

Khazaal and I were following the news so eagerly that we completely lost track of how many hours—or days—we had been sitting there. But then, as I scratched an itch on my hand, I looked at my watch and noticed that it was Tuesday night, 29 Ragab, AH 742. What with the fumes and the potency of the arrack, we were in a sorry state; so we decided to go out and take a walk through the streets.

Five of the cannibals marched in front. Behind them came three armed emirs and behind them Khazaal with his entourage, which included me. Bringing up the rear was a large company of paramilitaries trained to fight with knives and daggers and leap over walls. As Cairo's eternal silence drew us ever forward, Khazaal suggested that we keep walking as far as the Citadel. Everyone agreed, and on we went.

We arrived at evening prayer time to find that the senior emirs, led by Aydughmish, had ridden against Qawsun, who was now besieged on the Citadel mount. They were supposed to go to Karak, and for that reason had gathered at the horse market at the foot of the hill: Altunbugha, Yalbugha, Bahadur, the Polo Master, Juquli, Qumari, Artbugha, and Aqsunqur. The Mamluks belonging to all these emirs had dressed themselves in all their finery and brought out their children. Then Aydughmish, with his Mamluks and Grooms, came out and all of us stood waiting for Qawsun to show himself.

The sun rose but still there was no sign of Qawsun. Then one of his Mamluks came out of the Citadel to let us know that his side had dressed and prepared themselves to ride out, and had asked him to come down and save his stable. But Aydughmish quickly ordered the Grooms to go up to the Sultan's tablakhana, take out the small drums, and strike up a war beat. Then he called out, "Soldiers of the auxiliary corps! Mamluks of the Sultan! Idle men at arms! Come forward! If you have no mount and no weapon, come and take a mount and a weapon! Ride with us to meet Qawsun!"

Soldiers, some in uniform, some on horseback, others on foot, and others again on donkeys, converged en masse. The ruffians and harafish crowded in as well. Hordes of commoners came pouring out of every crevice and hurled themselves forward with shocking ferocity. Aydughmish's voice continued to ring out: "Looters! Go to Qawsun's stable and sack it!"

Before he had finished speaking, the mob charged the stable, indifferent to the arrows that Qawsun's Mamluks were shooting at them from the windows of the Citadel. Yalbugha, whose house overlooked Qawsun's house on the Citadel, stepped in to provide air cover for the mob until the looting was over. He and his Mamluks climbed onto the roof of the house and overpowered Qawsun's men, wounding many of them. The rioters were able to plunder Qawsun's armories, warehouses, and property, and break down the door of his mansion with pickaxes. What a sight! It was the biggest opportunity the lower orders had ever seen. In the melee, we wriggled our way forward and joined the mob that was attacking the house, everyone grabbing whatever he could carry. Watching from his window in the citadel, Qawsun was calling out, "Muslims! Hands off: that's my property, or the Sultan's!"

"That's no way to thank the people!" Aydughmish shouted back. "You've got enough treasure up there for the Sultan anyway."

Qawsun, looking worried, called for an immediate sortie, but his Mamluks talked him out of it. "Tomorrow, master," said one, "we'll ride out and kill them all."

"Don't let Aydughmish worry you," said another maliciously. "He's just skirmishing with you."

"We'll beat them," said a third, "and teach them a lesson."

I could tell that his guards were plotting against him and were stringing him along just long enough to stab him in the back. All the while, people were coming and going, keeping up the looting with consummate ferocity, with Qawsun slapping his palms together in frustration and berating the emirs for letting his property be pillaged. Finally he turned away and sent a member of his retinue over with a message for Aydughmish declaring that this great heap of possessions belonged to the Muslim community and the Sultan and demanding to know how Aydughmish could call upon the people to pillage it. The Mamluk returned with Aydughmish's answer: "What we're after is *you*, and you we'll get, no matter how much property is lost."

By now it was past midday, and almost time for the call to afternoon prayers. The gates of the Citadel were still shut. Coming back to the window, Qawsun, seeing his Mamluks fighting off the rioters with the last of their arrows, and the rioters collecting the arrows and giving them to the besiegers, seemed utterly distraught. Finally he raised his hand in a gesture of surrender. Malik al-Gamdar and Maliktamur made their way inside. "Choose a place to stay," said Maliktamur, "until your master's son comes from Karak and deals with you as he sees fit."

Qawsun bent his head in submission. Then Jankali, Mas'ud the chamberlain, and Artbugha came forward, clapped him in chains, and carried him off to the great tower on the Citadel mount—the same tower in which he had imprisoned Bashtak.

As Qawsun marched along in chains, I ran up behind him and asked what he had lost in the looting.

"My life," he answered. Then, after a moment he said, "In my warehouses I had four hundred thousand gold coins in sacks, and more vessels and gold belts and embroidered bangles than I could count; and a hundred thousand dinars' worth of jewels and gemstones in three satin bags; a hundred and eighty pairs of carpets, some forty cubits long, and some thirty cubits long, from Byzantium and Amul and Shiraz; and four silk carpets too beautiful to stand on." His eyes shone with tears. Standing some distance away was Khazaal, who was glaring at Qawsun with savage satisfaction. "May you see better days, you dog!"

"I hope so," groaned Qawsun.

I got an arm around Khazaal and drew him away.

When Khazaal suggested that we pass by the goldsmiths' market to ask the price of gold, I could tell from his barely suppressed glee that he must have made off with a vast amount of loot. Since I had too, I agreed to go.

We found that the price of gold had dropped precipitously: from twenty dirhams to a dinar it had plunged to eleven. The quarter was jammed with visitors loaded down with such quantities of gold that it might have been dirt. Children and young men were playing with baubles as if they were toys, and the ignorant were trading precious stones with the more ignorant in exchange for a cucumber, some lunch, or a glass of juice.

Khazaal insisted on going into one of the shops to see what he could get in exchange for a small part of what he was carrying, figuring he would save the rest for later. The shop owner welcomed us, pulled out a wooden couch inlaid with mother-of-pearl for us to sit on, called for glasses of juice, then disappeared, only to return a short while later, looking apprehensive and doing his best to hide it. Within minutes, a troop of soldiers had converged on the shop and surrounded us. I asked them what was going on.

"You're under arrest."

"Why?"

"The jewelers are under orders from Aydughmish to turn in anyone who brings in gold."

I looked at the backstabbing jeweler in disgust. "So you ratted us out?"

"You must have had a hell of a time bargaining with him," said one of the soldiers. "These merchants have been exploiting the hell out of this whole situation. Either you sell to them at dirt-cheap prices or they report you. We know what's going on, but . . ."

He grabbed at us, but Khazaal gave him a kick that knocked him flat and snapped his neck. With a single blow, he knocked the others down as well. Then, grabbing the jeweler by the hair, he threw him down, laid a foot on his neck, and smashed his skull with a glass plate. Going over to the shop window, he stuffed his pockets with gems. Then he pulled me away and off we went as if nothing had happened.

Noticing my shudder, he said with a smile, "They're poisonous vermin, and the more of them you crush the better." He gave me a mocking look. "It was a good deed, right?"

I said nothing. When we reached the storehouse, we learned that Qawsun, escorted by a hundred horsemen, had been sent to Alexandria and imprisoned.

14

Tougher than Camels

I FOLLOWED EMIR KHAZAAL THROUGH the streets of Cairo, gold spilling out of our pockets. The people of the lower orders cared so little for it that they would call out whenever they saw us drop any of it. If one of us bent down to pick up a bracelet, a ring, or a necklace, ten more pieces would spill out; but the children and the commoners would help us gather them up, some even bringing us items that had rolled out of sight. But then we spotted soldiers and militiamen hauling away people caught selling gold. Glaring ferociously, Khazaal stuffed his loot into his side and front pockets, hung some of it around his neck and on his ears, and put the rest on his fingers, his ankles, and his wrists. Having made himself into a walking arsenal of gold, he raced after those arrested for selling the very same commodity. When I caught up with him, he was haranguing the suspects with staggering impudence, paying no attention to the soldiers. "Who wants to get off scot-free?" he asked.

The soldiers recoiled and the suspects looked at him half-disbelieving. "Don't worry," he said. "Hand over what you've got. I'll keep it for you and get you off the hook."

Without waiting for permission, he reached out and relieved one of the suspects of the gold he was carrying. One of the soldiers moved to stop him but Khazaal flipped him to the ground so quickly that no one saw him do it. He stripped a second prisoner, punched another soldier in the face hard enough to knock him off his feet, and stripped two more prisoners. He cocked his head at me and off we went, the gold jingling and rattling and clinking in our wake in the most irritating fashion possible.

We reached the storehouse to find an altogether unaccustomed sort of atmosphere peering at us through the gate. There were people who looked as if they had been beaten and others who looked humiliated. Raised voices could be heard coming from different directions. Khazaal stopped. "What happened?" he shouted. One of the storehouse emirs approached and told him that the Emir had discovered the existence of a gold market in the storehouse. All the residents had joined the mob in attacking Qawsun's mansion and stable and in looting, pillaging, and demolishing his estate. But no sooner had they set up a market than the Emir had shut it down, confiscating the vast quantities of gold he had found in the hands of the rabble. Though he suspected no treachery, Khazaal clearly disapproved; but suppressed his reaction as he looked over at the storehousers, saying that no harm had been done. "The one's who've been beaten up won't bother us; they can cry to themselves. The ones who've been humiliated will have to learn to live with it. What the Emir did was for your own good. We'll sell this gold and spend the proceeds on you."

He then took the storehouse commander by the shoulder and led him into the enclosure. A good while later, the emir reappeared, looking thrashed to the marrow. Khazaal, his gold put away and a glass of arrack in his hand, came out behind him. "So, you've become sultan, Ibn Bayad," he sighed. "Well, you deserve it. You seized it from Karak, and you escaped an octopus. Here's to you!"

"Who's Ibn Bayad?" I asked.

"Sultan Ahmad, son of Sultan Nasir."

"But who's the Bayad he's the son of?"

"She was a singer," he answered.

"A singer?"

"She was famous," he said. "Her name was Quma, and Bahadur manumitted her. People used to hold parties for her. She was a first-rate performer."

"Strange," I said. "How did she end up as the mother of Ahmad, the new sultan?"

"Sultan Nasir found out about her and tracked her down and made her his exclusive concubine. She gained his favor and gave birth to Ahmad in his bed. After that, Emir Maliktamur married her, while the Sultan was still alive."

"So that makes Ahmad a descendant of Qalawun."

"Right, and the fifteenth Turkish king to rule the Land of Egypt."

"And a lot of good that does us!" I said.

At that moment news arrived that Emir Aydughmish, who had done away with Qawsun and overthrown Sultan Ashraf five months and ten days after his accession, had sent Jankali, Baybars, Qumari, and Shikar to Ahmad in Karak with letters from the emirs informing him of what happened and inviting him to ascend the throne. He had then met with Altunbugha Maridani, Bahadur, and Yalbugha, and summoned the other emirs. When they had assembled, he ordered the arrest of Altunbugha, the viceroy of Syria, and Artuqay, the viceroy of Tripoli. Both were imprisoned in the Citadel. Later, twenty-five others had also been arrested. Meanwhile, Aydughmish had conferred the governorship of Cairo upon Gamal al-Din Yusuf, governor of Giza, who had reportedly arrived in the capital to study the situation in the streets. "There's no time to waste," I said. "I should get up and see what's going on."

"Good riddance!" said Khazaal.

I thanked him and left.

Cutting across the streets toward the Citadel, I saw the soldiers seizing some commoners and hauling them roughly away. A few minutes later, I was surprised to see some twenty donkeys, each bearing a rider who had been turned around to face in the direction opposite to the one he was riding in.

The riders had their faces covered in tar and indigo and were wearing dunce caps on their heads. Behind them marched the soldiers, who every so often smacked them with switches. I recognized this as a public shaming, ordered by Gamal al-Din, the new governor of Cairo. The roads were full of seemingly powerless onlookers. As individuals, they were indeed powerless, but if they were to join forces they would become a fairy-tale creature like a dinosaur, and almost impossible to resist.

"See that?" exclaimed one of the mob, as if he had known me for years.

"Unbelievable!" I shouted back.

"Can you believe this?" cried another.

"This is oppression!" cried a third.

"They're infidels!" added a fourth.

"They wouldn't do anything like that to emirs," said a fifth, "or rich people."

"The only people who suffer around here," said a sixth, "are the paupers and the harafish like us."

The cries and shouts piled one atop another, from six rabble-rousers to sixteen to six hundred or six thousand, pouring out of side streets, alleys, corners, and graveyards, and in the blink of an eye that maddened fairy-tale creature had come to life. Carried along by the mob, I didn't know where we were headed until we reached Rumayla Square and ran right up against the Citadel. Clamoring like a flock of crows, the protestors called for Aydughmish to come out immediately, protesting that the Emir, who was in charge until the Sultan arrived, could not simply ignore them. When I realized that the mob wanted to give Aydughmish an earful on the subject of their new governor, I thought that he would certainly inflict some dire punishment on them, if only to uphold the dignity of his office and that of the man he had appointed. So I was surprised to see him appear, plain as day, at a window of the Citadel, and call down in a solicitous tone, "Muslims! What trouble brings you here?"

"You've appointed an anarchist governor who won't leave us in peace!"

"What did he do?"

"He went into the streets," shouted the mob, "and arrested people and made a public mockery of them, and then put them in jail for looting, but they're as innocent as we are! Do we look like looters? Never! We're not the ones doing the robbing and pillaging around here!"

"Quite right," said Aydughmish. He turned around and gestured to someone in the room behind him. "I've sent the Grooms after him."

"May God reward you!" cried the rabble.

Moments later the Grooms emerged from the gates of the Citadel. I ran after them and the rabble followed suit. Some of them caught up with us, saying that Gamal al-Din was in Saliba, "the Cross," and was on his way to the Citadel. Ahead of us, the Grooms headed down a street just outside Zuwayla Gate in the direction of Saliba. There four streets—Saliba, Shaykhun, Rakbiya, and Suyufiya—met at a single point, forming a cross right next to the Mosque of Ibn Tulun: hence the name, I realized. And there, in fact, was Gamal al-Din with his cavalcade, making for the Citadel.

The rabble rushed forward, calling him an ally of Qawsun and an enemy of the Sultan, and pelting him with broken bricks. As soon as he realized that the mob was intent on stoning him to death, Gamal al-Din turned his cavalcade around and rode off at terrific speed along the south side of that patch of ground where, centuries later, the Mosque of Sultan Hasan would be built. The Citadel guards and the grooms tried to keep the rabble from following the governor's party, but to no avail. Rather, their attempts to stem the tide only inflamed the mob. Fighting broke out and blood flowed freely, forming muddy puddles where the guilty, the suspect, the innocent, and the clueless sloshed around together. One of the rioters shouted, "Know where Gamal al-Din's gone?"

"Where?"

"To Altunbugha Maridani's!"

All of us rushed off in the direction of Altunbugha Maridani's mansion. It was a beautiful, imposing building. As I stood in front of it, fuddled and exhausted, I saw it changing before my eyes and growing old; and I saw the workers and the engineers climb over it, demolish it, and erect in its place the Mosque of Sultan Hasan, which is still there today, in the fourteenth century after the hijra. I came back to my senses, and there were Altunbugha's Mamluks fighting us off with might and main, wielding whips, sticks, clubs, swords, daggers, and arrows; and there we were fighting back, with groups of us picking up Mamluks and flinging them bodily against their fellows, letting them slash each other's necks and noses with their own swords.

Suddenly a stentorian voice rang out, repeating a single cry: "People of Egypt! Commoners and harafish! Emir Aydughmish needs you now!"

Many obeyed the summons immediately, and the rest followed soon after. By the time I finally caught up with them, I found them swarming over Rumayla Square, climbing over every object in sight, like strange growths on the side of some fantastic mountain. Looking down, Aydughmish called out, "I've brought you here to ask you who should be your governor!"

A succession of voices rang out: "Nigm al-Din! The one was governor before Ibn Muhsini? Yes! We want Nigm al-Din!"

Cried Aydughmish, "Bring me Nigm al-Din!"

The mob let out shrieks of mad delight and began capering like clowns and cavorting like actors in our day and age. Then it was announced that Nigm al-Din had arrived and accepted the governorship of Cairo. He himself appeared at the window and saluted us with both hands. We all cheered and called out, "Long live the Sultan!" Aydughmish looked relieved and Nigm al-Din looked happy. Suddenly, and for no apparent reason, Nigm al-Din said, "Any requests?"

With one breath, the mob cried out, "Dismiss Ibn Rakhima the commander and his partner Hamas!"

"So be it," said Nigm al-Din. "I hereby dismiss them both."

"They deserve a good pillaging!" came the cry.

"You have my permission to pillage!"

In a flash the crowds had rushed off, borne by a tide of rage, toward Fishmarket Street, with me in tow. Crossing over to the Street of Abu Taqiya's caravansary, we reached the Court of Kukay at the end of the street, where the house of Ibn Rakhima stood next to that of Emir Kukay. By the time I got there the people had swarmed over the two mansions like an army of ants, leaving no standing room on the walls, the windows, or the roofs. Everyone was taking something, stripping off even the doors, the window grills, and the door handles. In the end, there was nothing left of the two houses but bare walls draped in emptiness and ruin.

Looking over my shoulder I found Khazaal looting and pillaging right along with the mob—or more exactly, supervising those who were looting on his behalf free of charge. Oddly enough, he would pause from time to time to shout at the rioters, rebuking them for what they were doing and calling it an offense to honor and conscience. The looters would pretend to believe him and then snicker behind his back.

When Khazaal was satisfied that all his loot was safe and nothing had slipped into the hands of an itinerant vendor, we left. We were walking along tranquilly when he abruptly broke the silence by shouting in my ear, "That man has no business sitting on the sultan's throne, or next to it either!"

"Who do you mean?"

"Aydughmish!"

"Why not?"

"How could he let himself be ordered around by a mob?"

"But he acted wisely," I said. "He put down a rebellion and prevented bloodshed."

"In the end, though, he consulted the lower orders and did what they asked. That sets a bad precedent. Soon enough you'll hear that something's happened to punish him for his crime."

"That's going a bit far, isn't it?"

"But that's the way things have always worked in Egypt," he said.

"God help us both!" I said.

"How much loot did you get away with this time around?" he asked.

"Nothing, I swear. But I'm guilty all the same."

"Enough philosophy!" he said. "How much did you get?"

"Nothing," I said. "Really!"

"Then you have no business living here with the rest of us!"

"How do mean, Emir?"

"If you're given permission to pillage and you don't, then you're naïve. If you're ordered to do it and you don't, then you're crazy!"

"What if I reject the whole idea of pillaging in the first place?"

"If you live in a society that doesn't believe in God," he said, "you'll never be accused of unbelief!"

"That doesn't make any sense," I said.

"Neither does what you said. Forget about principled rejection, and hypothetical premises, and all the other sophistries that you've got coming in from the West."

"Don't get angry, chief! I take back everything I said."

"Then don't expect me to respect this position you're calling 'principled rejection.' You go right ahead and reject all you want, and deceive yourself with 'principles.' But don't expect us to be grateful for your fine example. Got it?"

"Got it," I said.

Then he said meaningfully, "You know, anyone who doesn't generate revenue for the storehouse is a dependent."

"Dependent!" I said, catching his meaning. "So what? As if anyone were an adult in this day and age!"

He pinned me with an awful look and I trembled. "In *my* day and age, I mean."

He lapsed into a truculent silence. With a shudder I recalled that I had absolutely nothing to fall back on if I left the storehouse and had better do what I could to soft-pedal it (whatever that means!) to avoid the talons of the tattooed cannibals. When a situation escalates into a farce, I thought, the number of spectators naturally increases. It's a mistake and a delusion to think that you can keep your distance and watch something go down the drain: after all, doesn't "go down the drain" mean that everyone gets sucked in?

Khazaal, who had been walking several steps ahead, slowed down to walk beside me. Then, as if picking up an earlier train of thought, he said, "You said before that you hadn't plundered anything but you were still guilty. I'm sorry if I got it all wrong about you: what is it you're guilty of?"

"I got caught up in the spectacle," I said. "I was watching."

He slapped his palm in exasperation. "And you have to confess it too? You say you were watching. What nerve!"

I trembled for fear that the discussion might take a turn for the worse. "I'm grateful to you in any case," I said. "But tomorrow you'll see that being a spectator has its advantages. Numerous advantages!"

"Numerous," he repeated with distaste.

"Yes," I said, disgusted.

"Such as?" he asked, his eyes flashing.

"What I mean," I said fearfully, "is that you believe in a different philosophy than I do. You believe that a person should become a cog smart enough to fit into any machine that happens to be working. But I believe that a person can do more to benefit mankind by remaining an observer."

With a wave of the hand, he dismissed me as hopeless. Suddenly he sprang into motion and, limbs flying, dashed across

Ibn Tulun Street toward Duhdeyra, the place my teacher Yahya Hakki loved to describe. Following him, I saw a group of pages walking along carrying a bundle of staves with gold and ivory handles, and candlesticks made of gold, silver, and alabaster. The next moments were like an episode of "Animal World" on Cairo television. Like a predator of some unknown species, he pounced on the pages, who stood rooted to the spot at the mere sight of him. With the flick of a finger he sent the ear of one flying. The page screamed and tossed away the staves. Twisting the arm of another, ripping it free, and tossing it away, Khazaal snatched up the candlesticks. The third page, offering no resistance, silently put what he was carrying on the ground. But Khazaal grabbed him by the collar, tossed him up like a ball, and punted him, sending him flying through the air. He came down stone dead atop a handcart making its way from Saliba and his skull burst open, spattering us. The carter began shrieking and wailing at the misfortune that had befallen him. Picking up his load, Khazaal walked away. I ran after him, buffeted by indignation, resentment, and fear. "Wasn't what you did to the others enough?" I asked him. "The last one gave you what he had without a fight. Why pick on him?"

With a jab of his elbow, he sent me flying. "There was betrayal in his eyes," he answered. "Betrayal and resentment always appear if you look for them carefully."

"But why be violent when you can just intimidate?"

"Look, son," he said, in a tone that suggested he no longer had my best interests at heart, "you live in a society that allows looting and pillaging as long as the right procedure is followed. What that means is that everyone loots and pillages as best he can, and the strongest is the one who loots and pillages the most. Power is like sea monsters, or perfume: it rises to the surface sooner or later."

"We're all eternally grateful, I'm sure!"

"I'll see you tonight at the storehouse."

"God willing!"

Turning away, I went back to Saliba to see if anything more had happened, and found nothing there at all. Even the corpses that Khazaal had flung about had been carried off by the rabble and the harafish, who had gone looking for the people—not necessarily next of kin but masters—who needed to be notified.

I don't know how long I had been walking in Saliba, whether alone or with Khazaal, but when I saw a cavalcade of emirs coming from the direction of the Sahil quarter amid a great hurly-burly of rejoicing, I looked at my watch and saw that it was Wednesday, 7 Sha'ban, AH 742, and realized that emirs whom Qawsun had imprisoned in Alexandria had been freed by Aydughmish and had now returned. Among them were the emirs Maliktamur and Qataliga, along with fifty-four of the Sultan's Mamluks, parading along to the sound of drums and pipes. I looked for members of the lower orders and found a good many of them there. They allowed me to sneak into the procession and then work my way closer to the two returning emirs.

When we reached the Citadel, the emirs dismounted, and cool as a cucumber I followed them in as if I were a member of the entourage. Reaching the inner rooms, we were greeted by a troop of slave women playing tambourines and reed pipes. In the middle was a woman in every sense of the word. Solidly built, she filled the room with a dance that had stirred up the singer, who had fired up the musicians, who in turn were setting my heart ablaze. I asked who it was who was showing us how a belly dance is done. "That's Khund," I was told, "daughter of Sultan Nasir Muhammad son of Qalawun. She's celebrating the return of her husband, Maliktamur."

My informant was a palace pageboy dressed as a waiter. I asked him about the woman who was flitting about serving the company like a drowsy butterfly.

"That's Khund's sister," he said. "She's Bashtak's wife. She's helping her sister celebrate as revenge against Qawsun, who killed her husband."

Then I heard a bitter weeping and wailing and followed it. It thought it might be coming from the same room, but it turned out to be coming from the main hall, where a very lovely lady was slapping and tearing at her cheeks and wailing hard enough to spit out her soul.

"Who's that?" I asked the page.

"She's the third sister," he said. "She's another daughter of Sultan Nasir Muhammad, and the wife of Qawsun. That's who she's mourning for."

Feeling conflicting emotions, I said, "There is no might or power save in God!"

"Right," said the page. "That's the world for you: joy here and sorrow there!"

"But why are they being joyful and sorrowful right next to each other? Isn't it a little awkward?"

"Well, not too long ago it was the other way around. The joy was here," he said, pointing to the wailing lady, "and the sorrow back there," pointing to the dancer. A moment later he went on, "If you stay here longer, you'll have plenty more to see."

"How's that?"

The page explained that the three sisters dealt with one another using force and kindness at the same time. Each was both a sister and a spouse, which made for some extraordinary conversations.

"Are you in the entourage of one of the emirs?" he asked.

"No, son, I'm not."

He looked stricken, as if I had played some great trick on him.

"So what are you doing here then?" he asked. "And how could you let yourself drag all that information out of me?"

"Calm down," I told him. "I'm here because I'm lost. And I didn't drag anything out of anyone. Now if you'll excuse me . . ."

I bid him goodbye and left. Finding myself alone, I looked at my watch and saw that the hands were on the cusp of Ramadan. Astonished at how quickly time had passed, I asked myself where it had gone. Then I remembered that I had spent a good long time looking at the dancer's body. She had gone on dancing and dancing, just as her sister had gone on wailing and wailing.

In any event, I soon reached the foot of the Citadel. The sky was overcast. From the adjoining streets, long lines of people were pouring into the square and then stopping as if waiting for something. Surprised, I asked them what they were doing. "Yalbugha and Maliktamur got into an argument," they told me. "Now the emirs have split into two factions and they're getting ready to fight."

"So what does that have to do with you?"

"We're here to pillage the house of whoever loses."

I stood stock-still in astonishment.

15

A Pedigree More Servile than the Sultan's

PERHAPS BECAUSE I WAS TOO dazed to do anything else, perhaps because the place itself had made such an impression on me, I continued my walk through the Saliba quarter. There, where the four streets meet, was a flurry of motion and activity like nothing I had seen in my life. For a relatively small place, the intersection feels frighteningly big: how, you wonder, does it accommodate such a rush of activity? Soon enough, though, you realize that the motion never stops for a moment, and you let yourself enjoy the ebb and flow as the four great streams meet and whip one another into renewed activity. I also like the aristocratic feel of this particular spot: everyone—rich, poor, or utterly destitute—who passes through on his way to one of the great tributaries seems to acquire a sudden dignity and hold himself higher as he walks, like a nobleman of old. No doubt it was the nearby mansions, all of them flourishing houses inhabited by numberless Mamluks, that gave the neighborhood its character. I've always loved narrow little streets—I'm a pavement-pounder as much as I am a pickle-seller, a sweet-vendor, and a writer—and I've wandered down tens of thousands of streets and alleys and turnings and passages, but never found any quarter as fresh and lovely as the one called Saliba.

Out of nowhere came one of the tattooed cannibals, running along with a group of people intent on rushing into the intersection. "Where to?" I asked, motioning for him to stop.

With one finger he hooked my wrist and took off running, saying, "It's the children of Sultan Muhammad!"

"What about them?"

"They've arrived from Qus and we're going to meet them!"

"In what capacity?"

"Whatever capacity you want," he said. "The emirs are there already with horses for themselves and for the new arrivals. We're trying to catch up with them on the Giza shore."

I saw that it was Thursday, the seventh of Ramadan, same year as before. I did want to go with them, but the number of commoners seemed enormous, and I wasn't convinced that loyalty was their only motive. I do believe in the absolute loyalty of the lower orders, but I'm skeptical of any explanation for their attachment to down-and-out members of the ruling class.

At the corner of Nafis Street, I found a caravansary that catered to travelers looking for rosewater, juices, and other beverages. I took a seat overlooking the street, where the rabble was piling in thick and fast. Soon they were so tightly pressed together that none of them could budge. For a good long while, the great mass of bodies stood as still as a line of cars at a red light. I figured that some unexpected crisis had delayed the new arrivals or the people going to meet them. I grabbed a man coming in from the street and asked him what was going on.

"Nothing," he said. "Nasir Muhammad's children—the ones Qawsun exiled to Qus—just arrived in Cairo."

"I mean, what's with this crowd on the street?"

"They're escorting the visitors."

"Are they on their way," I asked, "or coming back?"

"Coming back," he said.

I stood up. No waiter stopped me to make sure I had paid the check, since there was no waiter in the first place. The owner, saying he was happy to see a new face, treated me to a cup of carob drink. I thanked him and left. Fighting my way through the crowd, I realized that all those bodies were working as a sort of human retaining wall. Down the middle of the street ran the stream they were containing: the rabble, the mob, the riff-raff, and the harafish, in the tens of thousands, marching behind the cavalcade of the emirs and the Sultan's children. At first I thought that the human barricade was the work of whatever security police they had at that period, but then I dismissed the thought and plunged into the torrent along with the crowd. From time to time I spotted a tattooed cannibal who had joined the mob and was shouting just as enthusiastically as they: "Welcome back!"

"We missed you!"

"We knew we'd see you again!"

"They couldn't get away with it!"

"It's their father's good name that brought them back!"

And so it went until we got as far as the Great Cemetery. A number of commoners had stopped in front of an elegant mausoleum and more and more were joining them. "This," shouted one, "is the tomb of Geraktamur!"

"He killed our master Mansur!"

I knew that Mansur's children had come to the cemetery to visit their dead. I wanted to go with them, but the sight of the common people had stirred me: there they were attacking the tomb and ripping it open with picks, pieces of metal, and bare hands. They pulled out everything in it, destroying it and leaving nothing but a pile of earth in its place. "Sons of Shalaby," I said to myself in surprise, "I had no idea you cared so much about your master, or yourselves! But is this really about revenge? Or were you just looking for something to sell to make ends meet?"

Turning away, I caught up with the party of emirs, who were walking along the base of the Citadel behind Ramadan, son of the former Sultan. Waiting to receive them was Gamal al-Din, the former governor of Cairo. He came up to Emir Ramadan, bent down, and kissed his knees. Ramadan gave him a kick and cursed him roundly. "You bastard! Remember when we were on the boat on the way to Qus? We asked you to bring us something to eat from Giza and you said, 'There's nothing to give you. Get the hell out!'"

By then the mob had gotten close enough to see what was happening. Seeing their chance, they pointed to Gamal al-Din and shouted, "He's with Qawsun! Let us pillage his house!" Ramadan gestured his assent.

The crowd stampeded away like souped-up racehorses, crushing one another without mercy. I took off after them and followed them as far as the Mosque of Zahir near Husayniya. Gamal al-Din's house stood on the west side of the square, between it and the canal—Port Said Street today. As we passed through Conquest Gate, we were attacked by a vast number of armed men whom we recognized as family and friends of Gamal al-Din. We pushed against them with our bodies and they struck back with weapons. For every one of them who fell, we lost ten. Every death and injury made both sides fight more fiercely, either for revenge or on the principle that once they had started they might as well go all the way.

Hours passed and still the battle raged between our lot and Gamal al-Din's. All at once masses of soldiers were falling upon us from all directions. Aydughmish, we realized, had sent them to rescue Gamal al-Din. A few minutes later, Nigm al-Din, the governor of Cairo, arrived with his troops and joined the fight, hacking at us left, right, and center, until we began dropping by the hundreds and they by the tens—but only from exhaustion. As the number of dead rose, we began to skitter away, singly or in groups. Anyone who fell into the hands of the soldiers was taken prisoner and held for trial.

I raced back to the storehouse before anyone dared catch me and hold me for questioning. Khazaal was gone and no one knew where he was. I was told that he might be taking part in the negotiations going on among the emirs. Aydughmish had summoned them to Rumayla or Saladin Square and presented them with a copy of an oath of fealty to the Sultan and after him to Qutlubugha, which is why they were unwilling to take it.

Figuring this was a scene I probably shouldn't miss, I went out hoping to catch it, but ran into Khazaal, who told me with a laugh that it had ended some time ago. Now, he said, they were all waiting for the Sultan to arrive from Karak. I asked him why he was laughing. He told me that the lot of them—meaning the emirs—had been climbing the walls trying to send messages to the Sultan and get on his good side while he (the Sultan) had strung them along until finally—and here he whispered in my ear: "Three of them, with Abu Bakr the Falconer in charge, came to announce the Sultan's arrival, saying that he would be coming to the Cemetery Gate at night and wanted them to open the secret door for him."

"Are you sure?" I asked.

"I may be the only one who knows that Aydughmish is sitting by that door right now with Altunbugha, waiting for the Sultan."

My watch was pointing to Thursday, 28 Ramadan, AH 742.

"If what you're saying is true," I said, "I'd like to see it."

"Come on, then!"

He pulled me along toward the Cemetery Gate, pushing people out of our way, until we reached the secret door of the Citadel. Sure enough, Aydughmish was sitting there with Altunbugha, looking as nervous as could be. When he saw Khazaal he reached for the hilt of his missing sword in a gesture I recognized as an attempt to camouflage his anxiety. In an aristocratic tone that soon slipped away like a treacherous urchin, leaving him speaking in a manner altogether too familiar, he said, "What do you want, Khazaal? And how'd you know to come here at this exact time? Well?" Turning away, he shouted, "Get this wretch out of here and throw him somewhere the sun never shines!" He was speaking with such utter seriousness that it was immediately clear that the speech was a put-on.

Khazaal, clearly acting too, controlled himself with an effort and said, "Master, I came here only because I had no choice. I don't mean any harm—honest!"

"So what do you want?" said Aydughmish, as if he had never seen him before. Stealing apprehensive glances at me, he seemed both fascinated and afraid of what he didn't understand. Khazaal leaned forward and whispered in his ear: "Don't get upset. I'm on a job like the one I do for you— or have done for you—all the time."

Aydughmish stormed at him and ordered both of us put under arrest. Attendants seized us and turned us over to the soldiers, who turned us over to the Cohort, who dragged us to a clean room and ordered us to throw ourselves inside. We did. The soft bedding was enormously restful. To my surprise, Khazaal was still laughing.

It was only a short time before Aydughmish came in, passing us on the way to another room, which we recognized as a lavatory as soon as he opened the door. He went in and closed the door behind him, then emerged a few minutes later and passed us again on the way back. He stopped for a moment, turned to us, and pointed furiously at Khazaal. When Khazaal leaned forward, he said, "You thick-headed ignorant bastard! What have you done? How can you talk about things like that so freely? Huh? Anyway, now you can tell me: what exactly do you really want?"

"Sultan Ahmad," said Khazaal, "will be here any minute."

"I know that, you idiot," said Aydughmish.

"But you didn't know it before. You've been sitting for hours without knowing a thing. If it weren't for my men, you would still be scrounging for news, searching for clues, and paying your dues!"

Aydughmish poked him rudely in the chest. If not for his awareness that he needed him, he would have yanked his soul out and stomped on it. It was then that I stepped forward and in all humility said, "Master, don't be upset with Emir Khazaal. He only wants the best for you."

Surprised, Aydughmish looked at me and asked, "Who's that?"

"That's my gift to you," said Khazaal.

Aydughmish gave me another looking-over. "Oh! A new Mamluk! He's more than welcome. What's he like? I mean, what are his fine points? I mean, how much trouble is he?"

"He's everything you've ever dreamed of," said Khazaal. "His education cost his weight in gold. His family sent him to the best schools and the state spent its last penny on him, but he's left them to fend for themselves. Here before you stands someone who's been to a town they call America, and washed dishes don't-ask-where, and so on and so forth." He pointed at me. "Not to mention that he's gone wandering through time here in Egypt—a guy who goes out of his way to make himself miserable, in other words—and fallen into our hands. Congratulations, old fellow—I'm sure you'll be *more* than satisfied with what you get out of him!"

Having stared at me for the duration of this speech as if I were some sort of marvel, Aydughmish gave Khazaal another jab and said, "Get out! Leave him to me, and get the hell out!" Khazaal set off through the Citadel, borrowing a junior member of the Cohort to let him out through the Cemetery Gate.

To test my coffee-serving skills, Aydughmish ordered me to the kitchen, where I made one cup of coffee, Turkish-style, then another, and returned to Aydughmish's station beside the secret door. I put the coffee in front of them and waited. But the wait was interrupted when a dozen men burst in on us. We looked up, expecting the worst.

"They're from Karak," said Altunbugha.

"The Sultan must be with them," said Aydughmish, "or right behind them."

All three of us stood up to greet the newcomers. One of them had veiled his face and was dressed in loose-fitting clothes. Aydughmish gave him a searching glance, smiled to himself, and after greeting the others singled him out for a second salute. But the veiled man paid no attention to anyone. Instead, with breathtaking arrogance, he gestured for his men to follow him and led them inside. As soon as the last one crossed the threshold, the door closed behind him, leaving Aydughmish and Altunbugha looking chagrined and slapping their palms in dismay. To add insult to injury, they noticed that several emirs who were passing by had witnessed at least some part of the incident. Aydughmish sat down where he was and the rest—without bothering to seat themselves properly—sat down as well. Everyone then began doing some serious thinking. Deciding that it would be safer to make myself scarce, I went in and asked the Cohort to show me where I was supposed to sleep. They showed me, and I slept without a toss or a turn until morning.

I awoke to a gentle prodding by one of the Cohort, who asked me to tell him the secret of my amazing new method of serving coffee to guests. Of course, I laughed: when I served the coffee, all I had done was imitate any waiter at any street café in the Land of Egypt in my own fourteenth century AH. What if I had imitated the waitresses at the Sheraton, the Hilton, or the Meridien? When the Cohorter, looking very earnest, insisted that I had come up with something entirely new, I laughed at him and told him the truth. Stunned, he said, "How strange, by God! I've known some of the toughest people around—people with *very* servile pedigrees—but I've never seen anyone serve coffee like you."

That ticked me off. "Shut up, you moron!" I shouted.

"That wasn't an insult," he said apologetically. "I was going out of my way to compliment you! The point of life here is to excel at being yourself. Being a dedicated worker—having a sense of honor—means being the best at what you are. If you're a slave, but a real one; or a con man, but a real one; or a coward, but a real one; or a murderer, but a real one—if you make the best of whatever category you belong to—then you command a certain respect in society!"

To tell you the truth, I needed some time to absorb this bit of wisdom, but he didn't give me any. Shaking me resolutely, he said, "Get up! Aydughmish has given you as a gift to Sultan Ahmad. So get up and make him some coffee—right away!"

The day had barely begun—the sun hadn't risen—and I hadn't slept enough to be perky, but I hauled myself out of bed and stood myself up. As the Cohorter looked on in dimwitted fear, I jumped around like a clown to get myself warmed up. Then I gave him a quick slap on the back of the neck. When he recovered from the sudden shock, he found me walking along beside him, hands innocently at my side. Afraid to accuse me, he picked up the pace, saying in alarm, "The Sultan must have brought spirits with him. What a bad omen!"

When I reached the kitchen, he vanished. I made the coffee and headed off with it, swinging the tray around like a waiter in a low-end café and humming "Crazy" by Ahmad Adawiya:

I'm crazy, crazy, crazy, so let me shout!
I went to her house but she was out!
I knocked on her door but they threw me out!

On the way in, I bumped into people I couldn't place—were they emirs, or guards, or people of no importance?—but all were residents or regular visitors at the Citadel. Meanwhile, I noticed that I could keep the tray balanced without dropping the cups. People spotted me and stopped to gawk. Suddenly I was a public spectacle. If the Sultan hadn't been waiting for his coffee, I would have shown my audience a trick or two.

Promising to come back soon, I popped through the door into the Sultan's audience hall. I marched in prancing, swaggering, high-stepping, and whatevering. When Sultan Ahmad and his people from Karak saw me, they smiled and laughed. I couldn't bear to deprive them, so I picked up the tray I had just put down and headed back to the door, then spun around and came back toward them, repeating everything I had done the first time. All of them burst out laughing. Buoyed up by a boundless sense of pleasure, I picked up the tray and replayed the scene. They watched me with enormous delight, roaring with laughter, this time standing up and exchanging high-fives.

Happy beyond all reckoning, and against my better judgment, I kept hamming it up. The Sultan and his retinue started making ribald gestures to express their enjoyment, of which the least obscene involved rubbing up against each other, snorting, and sticking their tongues out. I noticed that the fun for them included teasing me too, so I carried my tray into the crowd, bumping them with my rear end here and my shoulder there, or kicking them, or smacking them with my belt, or making clowning gestures even lewder than theirs. They, meanwhile, were afraid that the coffee or the water would fall on them, and so wriggled and hopped and shuddered like a bunch of good-for-nothings. Finally I put the tray down and started to leave, having remembered that I still had a number to perform for the audience I had left behind in the reception room.

But the veiled man—I mean, the one who had been veiled the day before, and who still dressed like a nomad even though he was now the Sultan—pulled at the corner of my robe and said magnanimously, "No, you belong here." He yanked me into a seat and I sat down amid a crush of friendly revelers, exchanging quick handshakes and making no attempt to conceal how pleasantly surprised I was to meet such a kind and merry ruler.

A man came in and the jolly Sultan stopped in mid-laugh to ask him what was going on. Leaning over to me, he whispered that this was Abu Bakr the Falconer, his private chamberlain. The Falconer, speaking as if he were simply the Sultan's friend, not his chamberlain, said, "The man you were asking for earlier today is here."

The jolly Sultan, his merriment draining away, made an exasperated gesture. "Phooey! I asked for him, but I didn't want to see him. I mean, I wanted to see him, but I didn't *want* to see him. Anyway, send him in."

"Who is he, boss?" I asked.

"The one they call Aydughmish," he said.

"Aydughmish? The one who saved the throne for you?"

With a thrust of the elbow he gave me to understand that he made a point of keeping people like Aydughmish in their place. A moment later, Aydughmish came in, knelt, and kissed the ground. Making nice, the Sultan said, "I never had any ambition to be sultan. I was settled where I was. But when you sent for me I had no choice but to comply with your request."

Aydughmish rose, kissed the ground again, and said, "With the permission of my lord the Sultan, I will write on his behalf to the Syrian emirs to let them know of his arrival in Egypt and to say that he is awaiting them."

The Sultan waved him away impatiently without saying anything one way or the other. Taking the silence as approval, Aydughmish rose to go.

No sooner had he left than we burst out laughing. The Sultan called for something to eat and drink and then asked me to entertain him while he was taking care of business. So I did impressions of Adel Imam and Abdel Min'im Madbuli and Amin Hineidi. Then I did a Nagah Salam song that turned into a medley of Farid al-Atrash, Shafiq Galal, and Kahlawi. Without quite getting to the point of the business the Sultan had in mind, I stopped suddenly to find him going off into a corner with one of the young men from Karak he had brought with him. Pretending not to notice, I kept on doing imitations and raising a ruckus for a good long time.

I'm not sure how long it was in terms of days or hours, but at a certain quiet hour of the morning, with the Sultan engaged in business with the young men from Karak, I was startled by the chamberlain, who was coming to announce that the festival was approaching.

"What festival is that?" said the Sultan, who was drinking arrack.

"The Festival of Sacrifice, of course," said the Falconer.

"Many happy returns!" said the Sultan. "We're just thrilled about the festival, but we're too busy to bother with it at the moment."

"The people are waiting for you at the Citadel Mosque."

"Why?"

"So you can perform the festival prayer," said the Falconer.

"Festival, shmestival," said the Sultan. "Do I look to you like a man with a lot of free time on his hands? Go on, get out! Scram!"

The Falconer went out. Then we heard a clamor approaching from somewhere far away. The Sultan clapped his hands and he came in again. The Sultan told him to fetch the chief Mamluk—the eunuch Anbar Saharti—and his deputy. The Falconer went out and soon afterward returned with the two of them in tow. They kissed the ground before the Sultan, who told that from then on they were to sit at the Citadel gate and turn away all callers.

"What about the emirs, Master?" asked the chief.

"To hell with 'em," said the Sultan. "I'm busy!"

"But they have to offer you their festival greetings," said the chief.

"I don't need any greetings," said the Sultan.

"What about the banquet? We can't just drop a tradition established by our forefathers."

"Let the emirs throw their banquets at home," said the Sultan, preening himself.

"As you command," said the chief. He departed with his deputy in tow.

A moment later, the Falconer came in to report that some-one named Hagg Ali was asking to see him regarding a matter of great importance.

"What Hagg Ali?" asked the Sultan. "Didn't I say that I didn't want to be disturbed?"

"It's Hagg Ali, the Stuart."

"I've never heard of anyone by that name."

"His name is Hagg Ali," said the Falconer with a smile. "Stuart is his title, which was originally 'Steward,' which is Persian for 'one who presents the laden table,' but the people in Egypt pronounce it 'Stuart,' so now he calls himself that too."

"So he's a waiter!" I said. Everyone ignored me.

"When this Hagg Ali Stuart comes with my food," said the Sultan, "take the table and bring it in. Then have him wait outside until I'm done so we can give him back the plates."

The Falconer left to pass on this instruction, and I set about inventing new games to give the merry Sultan as wild and crazy a time as I could manage.

16

The Joys of the Rabble and
the Mercy of the Emirs

I WAS AS CHARMED BY Sultan Ahmad's high spirits as he was
with my bizarre antics. The spark of lunacy that animated me
had joined with the one that animated him, and a flame had
leapt up to search for fuel. The Sultan never tired of fun and
games, and I never tired of ranting and raving and clowning
around. The more clowning I did, the more everyone called
me a genius, and the more they came to regard me with pro-
found admiration.

One day the Sultan, with one of the young men from
Karak sitting next to him and the rest standing around, sent
for a physician. The head physician, Gamal al-Din ibn al-
Maghribi, came in and listened to the Sultan's complaint. He
palpated the painful spots but found no symptoms of illness.
After a look at him and at the young men from Karak, he prescribed something appropriate and he and the Sultan laughed
loudly together. Then the doctor departed, leaving us chuckling at his keen eye and his enlightened prescription.

At that moment, we heard a clamor that grew louder and
louder. I got up and looked out the window. There at the base of
the Citadel I saw Emir Aydughmish, the Polo Master, Gawuli,
and Altunbugha receiving delegations that seemed to stretch to
the horizon. We recognized Qutlubugha, Tashtamur the Cupbearer (or Green Garbanzo), and all the emirs, judges, viziers,
and garrison commanders of Syria, pitching tents below the Citadel and settling down. Turning back from the window, I said to

the Sultan as seriously as I could, "I'll bet your Highness is going to take some of that medicine now and sleep a little, right?"

"What medicine?" he asked, having already forgotten about it.

"The one the chief physician prescribed for you," I said. "You need to keep taking it until your head feels better."

"Where are you going?"

"Down there," I said, "to look at all the guests we're having."

"Go," he said, "but don't stay away more than a few minutes."

"As you command," I said, and left.

Rumayla Square and the area around the base of the Citadel were jammed with tents like the ones put up by Sufi orders at religious festivals. Passing between them, I saw that from the inside many looked like traveling palaces, worthy of emirs like Aydughmish or the Syrian dignitaries. But something out of the ordinary was happening. Qutlubugha was moving from one tent to another with a pack of hangers-on following in his wake. Like a secret agent, I followed him, trying to find out what was going on. If Qutlubugha had been one of the regular customers at Café Riche or a member of any of our modern cultural associations, he would have suspected me immediately of being a government spy.

Aydughmish, looking extremely anxious, followed Qutlubugha into his tent. Behind them came an angry-looking Green Garbanzo, and behind him the rest of the emirs. Everyone took a seat.

"Listen, Qutlubugha," said Green Garbanzo. "Get the idea out of your head. Otherwise you'll get us all in trouble. I mean it!"

"We were all so glad when the Sultan arrived," said Aydughmish. "How can we stab him in the back now?"

"He's shown no respect for us," said Qutlubugha furiously, "or for anything sacred. And we're supposed to put up and shut up?"

One of the emirs I didn't know spoke up. "As far as he's concerned, we have no standing!"

"How can he come here disguised as a nomad," said Qutlubugha, "and then spend all his time fooling around with those young men from Karak, not seeing anyone else, and then make Abu Bakr the Falconer his chamberlain? He shouldn't be able to get away with it. Whatever respect we've earned as emirs is on the line—that is, if we haven't lost it already."

Aydughmish seemed to flush, then turned pale and trembled. He said, "What are you getting at? You're against everything the Sultan's been doing. We're with you on that. Actually, we disapprove of him more than you do. But what are you saying we should do about it?"

"We get together, depose him, and send him back where he came from."

"What are you saying, Qutlubugha?" said Green Garbanzo. "Depose the Sultan and send him back to Karak? How? By God, I won't allow it. Aydughmish, say something! Emirs, speak up!"

"I don't agree either," said Aydughmish.

"Nor I," ventured another emir.

"Nor I!" said another. Then they all jumped in.

"Nor I!"

"It's not right!"

"For shame!"

"The Sultan can do whatever he wants!"

"How can he be sultan without doing what he wants?"

"Go depose yourself!"

Furious, Qultubugha seemed as if he were waiting to say something, but as the clamor died away Green Garbanzo beat him to it: "See? None of the emirs share those extremist ideas of yours. Looks like you're on your own. But we're not letting it rest until you put the idea out of your head for good. What do you say?"

After a moment's thought, Qutlubugha replied, "Fine! You're free to do as you like. I was hoping you'd stand up to defend your honor, but if not . . ."

Green Garbanzo, impressing me with his forcefulness, interrupted him. "There's nothing wrong with our honor, Qutlubugha. Don't you start that again!"

Qutlubugha fell silent. At that moment all of us heard a commotion outside the tent. Aydughmish went out, leaving us to exchange anxious glances. Then one of the emirs pointed at me and asked, "Who's that?"

"I'm one of the Sultan's Mamluks," I shot back.

"Are you from Karak?" asked Qutlubugha ominously.

"Get outta here!" I said impudently.

"'Get outta here?'" he said indignantly. "What's that mean?"

"It means 'Get lost!'"

Green Garbanzo intervened. "It means that he reproaches you in the strongest terms for suspecting him of being from Karak."

Qutlubugha beamed. "And *that* means you're a friend of ours. Welcome!"

Aydughmish came back in. "The Caliph Hakim and the four judges of Cairo, plus the four judges of Damascus, are here. Let's go!"

Everyone jumped up, adjusted their outfits, freshened their appearance, and marched out, with Aydughmish and Green Garbanzo in the lead. We entered the Citadel and went up to where the Sultan was sitting with the young men of Karak, taking the medicine that the chief physician had prescribed. Mortified, Aydughmish stood still for a moment to give the Sultan a chance to throw his clothes back on. As best I can guess, the Sultan had forgotten that he was about to receive the oath of allegiance, without which he would not be sultan—or anything else, for that matter. Retrieving his silken gown, he threw it over his naked body and fastened it closed.

One of the young men of Karak helped him into a shoe, the other member of the pair having disappeared.

"Shouldn't he have gone to the audience hall," I wondered, "instead of bringing them into his private quarters? And couldn't he have drawn the curtains?"

Laughing at myself, I followed the last of the emirs inside. But when I got in, I was surprised to see that the room where I had seen the Sultan naked was not the room we had entered, and that none of the emirs had seen what I had. Clearly, the two rooms were connected by some sort of trick curtain that had been dropped over the Sultan without anyone noticing. Now Aydughmish, the emirs, and I were standing in another room, which looked to be the audience hall. I laughed at myself again. The audience hall lay right alongside the room where all sorts of obscene entertainment took place, with nothing separating them except a curtain. Wonders, clearly, had no intention of ceasing.

A moment later the place went utterly dark. There was a sound of bodies, voices, and objects, followed by an abrupt silence. Then, lo and behold, there was the Sultan seated on his throne and facing us as if he had been sitting there for years.

The Caliph Hakim—not the famous Hakim, by the way—came forward and offered him the oath of allegiance as sultan. As soon as he was finished, the emirs and judges came forward and kissed the ground before the Sultan, as was customary. Then he stood up and the emirs kissed his hand one by one in order of precedence. Finally the Caliph came forward again, followed by the chief judges: the first chief judge, the second chief judge, the third chief judge . . . and then a sudden silence as we waited for the fourth chief judge to grace us with his presence. But he did not come forward, nor indeed did he seem to be present in the audience hall at all.

It soon became clear that the missing judge was Husam al-Din Ghuri. Where was he? Had he even left his house? All in a rush, the judges and chief judges said that he had been with them earlier that day and come up with them for the gathering in the Citadel Mosque. As this information was conveyed to the Sultan, everyone began to look embarrassed to various degrees. All of them, not least the Sultan, were afraid that Judge Husam al-Din had stayed away as a form of protest. Aydughmish pulled himself together and rose, but I beat him to the door and reached the Citadel Mosque first. We Egyptians, especially the Sons of Shalaby, can't resist a spectacle. Oddly enough, this rubbernecking mania of ours doesn't extend—or so I've heard—to the theater. But that's because our life is already a venue for eclectic performances. All you need is a gory accident and you can get everyone behind it to stop their cars to get out and watch.

Its imposing appearance notwithstanding, the Citadel Mosque had turned into a hornet's nest. It was swarming with rabble, but rabble dressed in the uniform of the Citadel. A good old-fashioned Egyptian brawl, complete with shouting and yelling and wailing and hollering and lots of fuss, was in progress. Standing at the door of the mosque was Ibn Taghribirdi, who was explaining the situation to a bunch of my relations, including Naguib Mahfouz, Husayn Fawzi, Abdel Rahman al-Sharqawi, Hasan Ibrahim Hasan, Suad Mahir, and Stanley Lane-Poole—who, by the way, belongs to the Sons of Shalaby too, but on the foreign side. Anyhow, I joined them to hear about what was happening and to see it for myself.

The judges (we were told) had gathered in the mosque to await permission to enter, as was the custom. Chief Judge Husam al-Din Ghuri had been among them. He was deep in prayer when Hagg Ali the Stuart—the waiter, that is—crept up to the door of the mosque and took a good look at him. Hagg Ali disappeared and then came back with one of the kitchen help in tow. Pointing at the judge, he said, "That's him!"

"That's who?" asked the kitchen help.

"The one who ruined my life and put me through hell!"

"That's Chief Judge Husam al-Din Ghuri," said the kitchen help, "and you're the Sultan's steward. What he got to do with you?"

"He's a lousy bastard, that's what," said the steward. "That's why I hate him!"

"What did he do to you?"

"A while back, I asked him to mediate a dispute I was having with my wife. He took her side—that bitch!—and he made me look bad."

"I see. So what do we do now?"

"This is my chance," said the steward. "I'm going to beat some respect into him and get him back for what he did to me. You with me?"

"Right or wrong!" said the help.

The two then vanished for a good while, during which the Chief Judge prepared to catch up with his colleagues, who had already started up to the Citadel. The moment he set foot outside the door of the mosque, the kitchen help and a crowd of chef's apprentices and general riffraff, armed with forks, spoons, knives, pot lids, ladles, and tureens, not mention the sticks and clubs, set upon him. The only thing that saved him from the furious assault was his collapse into the arms of his attackers, which kept them from getting a clear shot at him. But they did manage to pull his turban down around his neck and set it on fire and rip up his clothing. Then they began beating him with shoes, shouting, "You're with Qawsun, you infidel, you sinner!"

As Ibn Taghribirdi finished recounting the event, a great guffaw burst forth from Naguib Mahfouz and exploded as delightfully as a canister of laughing gas. All the while, Abdel Rahman al-Sharqawi was smacking his lips and slapping his palms together like a sagacious peasant still in command of all his faculties. For his part, Husayn Fawzi was looking around furtively and fluttering about like a malignant butterfly. Summoning one of the boys from the mob, he began whispering in his ear but then gave him a nasty pinch. When the Citadel itself shuddered, I couldn't tell whether it was because of what had happened, or because of Naguib Mahfouz's booming laugh, which you can hear from one end of Cairo to the other. Meanwhile, Judge Husam al-Din Ghuri was still pleading with his attackers, "Muslims!" he was calling. "How could you let this happen to one of your judges?"

All of a sudden, a standard-bearer with his crew of Mamluks were upon us, lashing out at the rabble and the kitchen help. Fighting their way through the mob, they rescued the Chief Judge, who by then was looking like a limp rag. Aydughmish had sent for some of the Grooms, who found the judge and carried him off to his house in an enormous stretcher. The Mamluks, meanwhile, set about dragging away the rioters. Those they arrested they handed over to Aydughmish, who ordered them beaten on the spot, which they were, with such severity that everyone present prayed they would die and escape their misery.

Tired of watching the rioters being thrashed, I went out to get a breath of air uncontaminated by the smell of blood. But the rabble and the common people who lived outside the Citadel were still boiling up like the Nile at its most turbulent. Carried along by the flood tide, I found myself in front of the Chief Judge's house in Salihiya. The Grooms had brought him there immediately, only to find that the mob had descended on the place and stripped it to the walls, even ripping out the doors and windows. By some miracle, they had overlooked the inhabitants—his wife and children—who fled to the neighbors' house. In fact, some of the attackers helped carry them there, then returned to join the sack and pillage. Aydughmish, who must have realized that something like this was going to happen, sent along a troop of soldiers and idlers who managed to stop the mob from doing further damage.

Having carried out their mission and seen to it that the doctor had arrived, the Grooms left some of the soldiers on guard and headed for a waiting wagon. When I introduced myself, they greeted me and invited me to join them. After they got out, they ordered the driver to take me to the Citadel, which he did. Now that the driver knew how important I was, I thought about taking advantage of him and asking him to give me a ride to the storehouse, if only so I could catch up on what was happening there. But I was afraid that Khazaal would force me to stay, thereby depriving me of the luxuries that had finally fallen to my lot by virtue of my talent for buffoonery. So I told the driver to let me out. Rummaging through my pockets for some coins to give him, I found nothing except some odds and ends. A refugee's pocket never holds very much, I told myself—at least, nothing that anyone wants, gratuity-wise.

After climbing up to the Citadel, I strode into the Sultan's quarters with everyone looking on in envy. Pushing the door open, I realized that I hadn't prepared a suitable entrance. After a moment of thought, I went through the door backwards making noises like a train. Then I spun around in circles, snapping my fingers merrily. At the end of one of my turns I dropped into a chair—except that there was no chair and I hit the ground like a ton of bricks. I jumped up, shouting and grabbing at my aching head, only to see that the room was empty. I peered into all the corners, thinking that they might have hidden there to trick me, but there was no one there. Crestfallen, I went out into the anteroom and asked someone I had seen on my way in where the Sultan was. He told me that he had gone out on parade.

"Why didn't you tell me, you dimwit?"

"And why should I?" With that he scuttled away. I set off running and caught up with the procession at the base of the Citadel. My watch read Thursday, 13 Shawwal, in the same old year of 742. Running after the procession, which had already started, I realized that the wagon had brought me by a different route. The Sultan was standing with his retinue, but when I got closer I found him sitting down, with the judges, the chief judges, the Caliph, the Grooms, the Cohort, and the rest of the Mamluks and hangers-on having formed another procession.

By the time I came in, the Sultan had finished giving robes of honor to every last one of the emirs, and was giving a gift of ten thousand dinars to Green Garbanzo; and everything he had brought with him from Syria—that is, four thousand dinars and a hundred thousand silver dirhams—to Qutlubugha. He then summoned the vizier, Nigm al-Din, and ordered the Falconer and his associate put in charge of falconry and the conduct of state. That was the only announcement that people seemed unhappy about, to judge by their expressions. Evidently, the Sultan had given control of state affairs to the most despicable characters he could find. But great powers, I told myself, always needed despicable men to safeguard them as they went about doing their despicable deeds.

I expected the Sultan to resent the disapproval provoked by his announcement, but he paid no attention to anyone and, putting his arm through mine, pulled me along with the retinue following behind. Though conscious of the great honor he had thereby conferred on me, I felt a sudden disgust at the sticky smoothness of his flesh, and tried my best to wriggle free of his arm in as genteel a manner as possible. I reached his sitting room first and saw him dismiss his entourage with a savage gesture of contempt. The entourage backed away and vanished.

The young men of Karak received us half-naked. Their slim, effeminate bodies disgusted me immeasurably. Were they the ones who had corrupted him, or had he corrupted them? All I knew was that each of the parties could outdo the other in debauchery and neither would cede to the other when it came to lunacy.

As soon as the Sultan sat down on the cushion stuffed with flamingo down, glasses, plates of snacks, and musical instruments made their appearance. It became clear that the men of Karak, in addition to their other talents, could play all of the usual instruments. Not everyone from Karak was necessarily like them—the city doubtless produced men of all kinds—but this faction, at least, was the product of a palace education.

No sooner had the Sultan settled in for a nice relaxing session when his chamberlain, the Falconer, came in and said that Green Garbanzo had arrived, as agreed. The Sultan looked as if he could recall no such appointment. He thought about receiving him in the other room, but then looked down and saw that most of his clothes were missing. The Karaki cupbearer made a gesture that meant "Tell this visitor of yours not to spoil our fun." Deciding to stay put, the Sultan fell back into his chair and ordered the Falconer to admit the man. The chamberlain went out, and a moment later Green Garbanzo entered the room. Examining him as he approached, I sensed that he was only pretending to approve of these proceedings and that his smile concealed a bitter resentment that would have welcomed the opportunity to lash out.

As if realizing all this, the Sultan refused to do him even the courtesy of looking at him. Coming right up to him, Green Garbanzo knelt, kissed the ground before him, then kissed his hand and foot. The Sultan ordered him to kiss his foot again.

"Already done, Master," said Green Garbanzo.

"You missed and kissed the foot of this nice young man from Karak instead. His foot happened to come between mine."

"You think it was a mistake, Master?" asked the nice man from Karak. "Get lost!" he said, poking Green Garbanzo in the shoulder.

The Sultan shook with laughter. "You should be happy," he said. "You got a kiss fit for a sultan!"

To my surprise, or lack of surprise, Green Garbanzo was playing along and laughing with the Karaki.

"To reward Green Garbanzo for his kindness to you," said the Sultan, "I confer upon him a robe of honor and confirm him as my viceroy in Egypt. Rise, Green Garbanzo, go forth, and do your duty!"

A grateful Green Garbanzo covered the Sultan's hands and feet with kisses, then hopped up and strode out like the newly appointed master of the universe. My watch said it was Saturday, 15 Shawwal.

The nice young man from Karak got up and put on a dancing sash, and the musicians launched into a voluptuous melody of marvelous sweetness. You couldn't tell if it was Turkish or Persian or Andalusian or Egyptian. Probably, it was a mixture of them all. Once it started, even the soberest of spectators would have found it impossible to resist. We started clapping out a rhythm for the nice young man from Karak and wriggling around in our seats, keeping time with our bottoms, shoulders, eyebrows, heads, and chests. For a long moment I lost all sense of myself. When the Karaki collapsed exhausted into his seat and the drinking resumed, I looked at my watch again and saw that it was Monday the 17th.

At that moment the Sultan sat up straight, pushed away another Karaki who had settled onto his lap, and clapped his hands, said, "Time to do a good deed!"

The Falconer came in. Telling him to sit, the Sultan said to him in the gloating tone of a man about to be avenged: "You know who that accursed Abdel Mu'min is, don't you?"

"He's the governor of Qus, damn him!" said the Falconer. "We've got him in prison."

"Is that all you know about him?" asked the Sultan.

"He's the damned villain who murdered my master and your brother, the late Sultan, when he was sent into exile in Qus."

"You surprise me," said the Sultan. "It's time to do the right thing in the sight of God and give him what he deserves."

"Whatever you command will be done."

"Find the worst carpenter in the Citadel," said the Sultan. "Tell him to bring us some big rough nasty nails, and if all he can find is the blunt kind, have him carve out points on the ends. Got it?"

"Yes, Master." The Falconer got up and left. The Sultan rose too, saying he was going to take a nap so he'd feel fresh for the evening. He put his hand on the shoulder of the nice young man, but another Karaki pushed him away. Pleasantly surprised to see another Karaki standing in front of him, the Sultan returned his pleading gaze with a smile and a nod of assent. Dodging around his fellows, the Karaki raced off to the bedroom. I gave the lot of them a look of loathing, which they ignored, and went out.

I walked down from the Citadel, through the square, and into the streets, letting my feet take me to the Mansuri Hospital. Evidently, I had let a mass of spectators, who were marching along in portentous silence, carry me along. When I arrived, I saw a sight no human being should have to watch. How could these people witness similar things every day without turning a hair?

The luckless Abdel Mu'min, former military governor of Qus, was brought forward under guard with his hands tied behind his back. The wooden scaffold that held the cross had been set up at the gate. Dressed in his prison clothes, he was handed over to the carpenter, who seized him by the shoulder like a plank of wood, measured him against the frame, then thrust him back to the soldiers. The carpenter loosened the scaffold and widened it a bit, tightening a joint here and chiseling a groove there. Then he pulled Abdel Mu'min over, got a good grip on him, and put him on the scaffold. The fit was perfect. Next he asked them to untie his arms. A soldier pulled each hand out to arm's length and laid it on one of the wooden posts and the carpenter pounded it into the groove. All the while, Abdel Mu'min was screaming from deep in his gut and pissing and shitting himself but the soldiers paid him only the attention it took to spit on him or slap him. Then the carpenter took out a nail so big that he needed a crowbar to hammer it home. With a single blow, he drove it through Abdel Mu'min's hand, then did the same with the other. He plunged a nail into one arm, then the other, then dropped and did the same to the balls of the feet, then rose and did the same to the groin. Straightening up, he began hammering the nails home. By now the body had turned into a shrieking mass of flesh that begged and pleaded, impossibly, for any kind of mercy. I marveled that a body that had suffered so much could still house a spirit capable of doing anything at all.

All at once, the camel was brought out and made to kneel before the crucified form. The soldiers came forward, picked up the cross, and strapped it onto the camel's hump. Commanded to rise, the camel rose and set off, with a great cavalcade of wretches following in its wake. I resolved to stick with the procession until the end. By the time it was over, it had circled back on itself again and again for six long days before the body finally gave up the ghost. All the while, Abdel Mu'min let a stream of words fall through the scaffold, amounting to a confession of all his crimes, including his attacking Nashw, the Sultan's Treasurer, and stabbing him to death after mistakenly taking his fallen turban for his severed head; as well as his killing of Mansur, the son of Nasir Muhammad, in Qus, by orders of Qawsun. At the end of the sixth day, the wooden post was tossed onto the aqueduct. Thinking that the incident was over, I was surprised to learn that he was also condemned to be beheaded. Left atop the aqueduct, his body was torn apart by rabid dogs.

17

A River to Water Shriveled Hearts

I WAS MORE DISGUSTED THAN I had ever been in my life. The image of the rabid dogs tearing at the corpse of Abdel Mu'min, governor of Qus, had stuck in my mind's eye and refused to budge. What surprised me the most were the dogs. I had always thought that ours were kind and long-suffering. They take a liking to newcomers: they'll protect a visitor and watch over him at night even when the only thanks they get is a blow of the shoe to the snout. But now it turned out that underneath it all they were seething with rage. Egypt, I suddenly felt, was a mix of two temperaments: ferocity on the part of the rulers and kindness on the part of the ruled. The emirs, I reminded myself, treated each other brutally even when they were friends. In a manner unbefitting a respectable Mamluk of the Sultan, I spat loudly onto the street.

My path had taken me to the palace district. I found myself in front of the mansion of Bashtak, who had reportedly been killed in Alexandria. Looking up, I wondered aloud what fate had in store for the building. "It's called Bashtak Palace, man," said a passerby, giving me a nudge. I turned to see who it was and found myself in the middle of a moment right out of the fourteenth century of the hijra. It lasted only an instant, but it was long enough to see Ibrahim Shami the actor hurrying back to his place in Khurunfish and a group of my colleagues going into a nearby restaurant famous for trotters. Before I could catch up with the moment and ride it back up to the age I was born and raised in, it was gone. I had hardly taken another step when there in front of me was Khazaal, coming out of the storehouse, which a fourteenth-century-hijri moment ago had been the Mosque of Husayn. I stood rooted to the spot. Since becoming a high and mighty Sultan's Mamluk, I had stopped bringing news back to the storehouse and paying visits to the Emir.

Bashtak's mansion was awash in sorrows, as if some vital prop of the universe had collapsed. His lovely wife, the daughter of Sultan Muhammad and the sister of the merry Sultan Ahmad, was looking down from the highest balcony in the house, her white face glowing through the dark archway. Her Turkish blood gave her face a pinkish cast without overwhelming the Tatar features she had inherited from her mother, the daughter of the Tatar king Uzbek Khan. I felt an enormous pity for her as she gazed into the distance, seeking her fallen throne. Her husband had been killed in an Alexandrian prison. He had owned estates worth two hundred thousand dinars a year and his master Sultan Muhammad had once granted him a gift of a million dirhams in a single day. Every day without fail, fifty sheep and horses were slaughtered to feed his family and guests. According to what my friend Ibn Taghribirdi had told me the day he introduced us, Bashtak was so standoffish that he would speak only through an interpreter. He had built a mosque by the Sycamore Road aqueduct and a bathhouse in the market of Izzi. Even in the fourteenth century of the hijra, the minaret of his mosque was still the tallest and most splendid in the city. (Oddly enough, the inhabitants of that century called it the Mosque of Mustafa Pasha Fadil because the Pasha's mother, Princess Ulfat Hanim Kadin, ordered it restored as it was next to her son's palace, which became part of a school called the Khedival Madrasa.) I remember Bashtak as a slender, handsome man, and the minaret seemed to take after him. He was so close to the Sultan that the latter referred to him simply as "the Emir." He commanded seventeen honor guards of drummers drummeries—more than Qawsun. Even though Qawsun had died in the same round of fighting, Bashtak inspired a special kind of bereavement. So much was clear from the face of his wife, the Sultan's daughter, as she withdrew behind the lattice.

As a gentle, invisible hand slid the panel to close the window, a curtain was pulled aside inside my head and I could see the future. There again was the Mosque of Husayn, now some distance away. There was Azhar Street, al-Azhar itself, and the narrow street that runs alongside it. A crowd of citizens were leaping about and brandishing pocketknives, slashing at each other's faces and stabbing and hacking at any part of each other they could reach. I could see that a bloodbath like it took place here almost every day between factions whose identities were impossible to pin down. There was no way to know which faction the fruit vendors, coffeeshop waiters, sheet-metal workers, barbers, and vagrants, not to mention the fugitives from all of the above, might have belonged to, though it was certain that they belonged to more than one. A constabulary they called "the police" came along, leaping and maneuvering in its turn before disappearing briefly indoors. When the officers reappeared, they had arrested certain passersby for purchasing narcotics. As they marched the suspects toward their Honda van, they left the drug dealer standing in front of a line of addicts, selling them poisonous words before selling them a poisonous high. "Unbelievable!" I said, gesturing as if to wash my hands of the lot of them.

At that moment a painful jab jolted me back to the past. Groaning, I looked around and saw Khazaal walking along beside me and getting ready to jab me again as we made our way toward the Fatima Nabawiya quarter. Despite the pain, I managed to say, "Emir, you know I can't handle that heavy-handed horseplay of yours." To distract him, I asked him whether he knew why I had been distracted a moment ago.

"I was homesick for my own time," I explained, "and I got to see a glimpse of it."

"I don't need to see your time," he said with a dismissive gesture. "This one's enough for me. You'd need ten lives to begin figuring out how to deal with it. Anyway, that's some nerve you've got, walking next to me and complaining about my 'heavy-handed horseplay.' What a rude and disrespectful way to behave!"

Laughing nervously, I apologized, saying I could never be rude to him. "You're my emir and sovereign, and if I spoke out of turn, forgive me! I didn't mean to."

"Or maybe," he said belligerently, "now that you're a Sultan's Mamluk, you think you can look down on me. If that's what you think, you're crazy, and short-sighted too, for two reasons. First, I'm the one who gave you to the Sultan in the first place. Second, that Sultan of yours is practically one of *my* Mamluks!"

Realizing he was right, I straightened up respectfully as we walked along. Having been a pickle-seller for a long time, I've come around to selling sweets: that is, I drank enough brine to cure myself of being a sourpuss, and now I'm a total sweetie. Rather than believe anyone or anything, I put absolute trust in reality. When that drug-dealing gangster of a café owner curses everyone and says he'll screw over his rivals and his enemies, I buy it. When an embezzler robs millions of people blind and still lives like an emperor, I buy it. When my mother says she can't afford to fill a prescription even though her children are taking joyrides at a summer resort, I buy it. When my little boy says, "Buy me a plane with a gun on it," I buy it. I buy all that, so why shouldn't I believe Khazaal?

"Of course, Emir," I said. "I respect how important you are."

With a hostility that seemed uncalled-for, he went on. "If you don't already know it, you should realize that the only real power in Egypt is naked force, and naked force obeys no rules at all. Force is opposed to logic—or maybe it just has a logic of its own. If you're strong, you rule, even if you're dressed like a servant. Power here is a matter of gold and slaves. Plunder some gold and buy yourself some Mamluks, and you'll be a sultan—and what a sultan! Me, though, I became a sultan my own way: by leading the people who can't afford slaves. If they don't own slaves, they can *be* slaves. And who can buy them without paying for them? Me. All I have to do is manipulate them and take revenge on the people who mistreat them. To do that, I let them take it out on each other—including their own families. If I want to kill a man, I have his son do the job for me: all I have to do is drum it into his head that his father is his mortal enemy. So don't make any mistake about who you're dealing with, Ibn Shalaby! Get too big for your britches, and I'll boot you out of history altogether."

Realizing he was right, I marched alongside him without so much as raising my head or looking around. As we continued down the street, the fourteenth century of the hijra would pop silently into view for a moment here or a moment there until Khazaal interrupted by asking if I had learned anything about the Sultan's favorites or whether I had become a royal Mamluk who no longer cared about collecting information.

"I swear, Emir," I replied, "that merry Sultan Ahmad is a spectacle all by himself. He's his own theater and his own entertainment."

"Well, then, you should know . . ." He paused as if he wanted to keep me in suspense. Then he went on, "Here's something to cheer you up. You know the Polo Master, right?"

"And who doesn't?" I replied. "Especially if you live in the storehouse!"

"The Sultan has made him governor of Hama instead of Tuquzdamur, so good riddance to him for standing against us! The Sultan also made Baybars governor of Safad, replacing Aslam. He made Aysunqur governor of Gaza, and Qutlubugha governor of Damascus. Aydughmish is now governor of Aleppo and Qumari, the Master of the Hunt, is now

Master Equerry in place of Aydughmish. Ahmad the Beverage Master is the new Master of the Hunt, and Aqbugha is governor of Hims. Aydughmish has already left for Aleppo and Qutlubugha's left too, along with the rest of the Syrian troops. The Sultan's viceroy and all the emirs saw them off at a big banquet. Didn't you attend it?"

"Strange!" I said. "This is the first I've heard of any of this." Then I caught myself. "A man should be more concerned about his family and friends than he is about the doings of the high and mighty."

As if overlooking the tedious implications of my remark, Khazaal asked if I would like to see the new viceroy, Green Garbanzo, in his new sultanic splendor. I said I would.

"Follow me!"

I went along meekly as he continued his account. "As I'm sure you know, he's started mobilizing the lower orders."

"I didn't know," I said, "but I'm not surprised."

"Why not?"

"He seems to meet all the usual requirements: bold, ambitious, brave, no care for anyone but himself, seeking glory at any price, the people and his conscience be damned."

We were walking past the Viceroy's audience hall when Khazaal jabbed me with an elbow. "Look!"

I looked. Dozens of people were waiting in weary silence or chasing after any emir who happened to pass by. All were carrying gifts of various kinds. One of the Viceroy's Mamluks blocked our way, but Khazaal told him that he was on his way in to see the Viceroy and wanted to be announced. There was a flurry of whispers, as always when Egyptians find themselves in such a situation.

"He thinks he can walk right in!"

"What if he knew I'd been here for four days?"

"Listen, you! You could bring a petition with the Sultan's stamp on it and he wouldn't listen—he'd just make an example of you."

"The Sultan's not even taking complaints any more."

"I pity the fool who thinks Green Garbanzo would ever intercede for him."

Khazaal took all this in without blinking. The Mamluk who had gone in to see the Viceroy now reappeared. "This way, sir," he said. Khazaal pulled me in after him as the waiting crowd looked on in amazement.

Green Garbanzo, the Sultan's Viceroy in Cairo, rose to his feet in an unwonted display of deference. The man I saw kneel to kiss the Sultan's foot, not to mention the extra Karaki foot that had interposed itself, and who had proven himself an old hand at putting a good face on things and toughing them out if necessary, couldn't quite pull off the trick of standing there as if he were a sultan. Of all the feelings out there, self-respect is the one that tells you the most about who a person is. Anyone who has self-respect would never kneel, no matter what the reason. By deferring to him, the Viceroy was making Khazaal look like the real ruler. Taking the cue, Khazaal took a seat and crossed his legs in the arrogant manner of a sultan, leaving Tashtamur to test out various different positions as if looking for the one appropriate to the company and the situation.

Tashtamur had hardly settled into his seat and ordered some refreshments for us when the door opened and one of the emirs came in. The Viceroy ignored him. When the emir came forward and greeted him, the Viceroy made a surprisingly rude gesture that ended up looking like a salute. The emir tried to whisper something into his ear, but the Viceroy gave him a sharp sideways glance that conveyed the message that he—the emir—had overstepped his boundaries. Concealing his embarrassment with a broad grin, the emir tried again. The Viceroy complied only symbolically, with a stagy inclination of the head, and the embarrassed emir said that he would come back later to convey his message. On the way out, he even saluted us. After he had gone, the Viceroy clapped to summon the chamberlain and showered him with abuse for admitting one of "them"—meaning the emirs—making them sound like criminals. The chamberlain looked as if he had something he wanted to say but was unsure whether he should say anything with us present. Tashtamur urged him to speak up. Smiling feebly, the chamberlain asked whether the emir had said anything to the Viceroy. "No, nothing," replied the latter. "What's going on?"

When the chamberlain hesitated, the Viceroy shouted at him, commanding him to speak. Stumbling over the words, the chamberlain explained that one Nasir al-Din, known as Roof Rat, had used his acquaintance with the young men of Karak to have himself appointed prayer leader; he was now leading the Sultan through the five daily prayers. He had also got himself appointed Inspector of the Sayyida Zaynab Mosque, replacing Taqi al-Din Qastillani, the preacher at the Mosque of Amr and the Laborers' Mosque. To top it all off, the Sultan had given him a robe of honor.

Hearing this, Tashtamur the Cupbearer, also known as Green Garbanzo, leapt up as if stabbed through the heart. "Without telling me? The Sultan did all that without telling me? How could he? Listen, you: get me ten hefty deputies and send them to Roof Rat. Tell them to strip off his robe of honor and hand him over to the commander Ibrahim ibn Sabir."

The chamberlain bowed and left. Time passed, during which Tashtamur called in various persons and conferred with them in whispers some distance away. Finally he came back. As soon as he sat down, the chamberlain announced the arrival of the commander Ibrahim ibn Sabir in person. Ibrahim came in, made a reverent bow, and reported that everything was under control. He had raided the hall where Nasir al-Din held audiences in his capacity as prayer leader and stripped off the robe of honor.

"Nice," said the Viceroy happily.

The commander added that they had beaten Roof Rat to a pulp.

"Beautiful," said the Viceroy, biting his fingers in malicious delight. Ibrahim added that they had demanded a hundred thousand dirhams from Roof Rat, but even after beating him they could only find forty thousand, so they took it and let him go, warning him never to go up to the Citadel again.

"Well done!" cried the Viceroy, and dismissed him with a flick of the wrist.

I decided that I didn't much like Green Garbanzo. I felt depressed: how could anyone put up with Khazaal and Tashtamur at the same time? Leaning over to Khazaal, I whispered that I had an urgent appointment with the Sultan. He gestured at me as if to say, "Good riddance!" I said good-bye to him and Tashtamur and rushed out, heading directly for the Sultan's room.

As soon as he spotted me, the Sultan pushed away a mischievous little Karaki and called out, "Where the hell have you been all day?" I told him the truth and he nodded, then ordered me to take over for the cupbearer. So I began pouring wine for him, keeping him entertained, and adding some pep and zip to the party. Despite my efforts, though, he seemed no happier than before. Surprised, I asked him, "Chief, what's wrong? You don't look so hot."

"That's for sure," he said. Clapping, he summoned Falconer the chamberlain and asked him apprehensively where the Mamluk commander Anbar and Emir Aqsunqur were. The chamberlain replied that he had sent urgent messengers after them. Grabbing a glass and gulping it down, he left. A moment later, Anbar and Aqsunqur came in, bowed, kissed the ground between the Sultan's feet, and at his command took a seat. He asked them whether the chamberlain had told them what was expected of them.

"Yes," said Anbar, "and everything's ready to go."

"There's something else," said the Sultan. "I want you to call out Bashtak's and Qawsun's Mamluks. Bring them down and let each of them have an estate."

"Does my master the Sultan intend to have them join his Mamluks?" asked Anbar.

"That's right. And the other thing, the one my chamberlain told you about, should proceed as ordered." They inclined their heads in compliance and the Sultan dismissed them with an old-school sultan's gesture.

The party went on and on. I had nearly run through my stock of vulgar jokes and anecdotes from my student days on everything under the sun when the chamberlain came in to announce that it was time. The Sultan rose, and we did too. We followed him out to the hall where the dining carpet was spread. I could tell that some kind of shindig was planned, and that the Sultan was preoccupied with thoughts of the guests who were doubtless already on their way.

We took our seats on the carpet next to the Sultan and the emirs made their entrances one by one. The Sultan was smiling in a way that seemed ill-natured and vengeful to me. I leaned over. "What's going on, chief?" I whispered in his ear. "You're smiling."

His smile grew wider. Never taking his eyes off the procession of emirs, he said, "Watch carefully."

I looked, but noticed nothing in particular. I mentioned this to the Sultan, who replied that he was amused by the simple-minded system that Green Garbanzo had set up during his term as viceroy. He had forbidden the emirs to bring their Mamluks into the palace and spread a carpet leading from the entrance into the building, as Sultan Ibn Qalawun had done at the beginning of his reign.

"What's so funny about that, Mr. Sultan, sir?"

He replied that Green Garbanzo was going to be hoisted on his own petard.

"How's that?"

"You'll see."

A moment later, Green Garbanzo came in with his two sons. He greeted the Sultan, who returned the greeting while giving him a look of barely concealed hostility. Then everyone turned to look at someone I couldn't see at first. Eventually I found him: a strongly built man whose sudden appearance had caused a flurry of glances I couldn't interpret. I recognized him: it was Kishli, the Grand Armorer, one of the Sultan's Mamluks. He began circling around the guests and the fuss died down. The Sultan came forward and began eating. Everyone followed suit, throwing themselves at the food in a manner quite astonishing, until the platters on the carpet had been picked clean. Then we stood at the edge of the carpet waiting for the signal to come forward and wash our hands. I was watching Kishli, when all at once he vanished.

Looking around for him, I was surprised to see a startled Tashtamur leap up as two powerful arms closed around his shoulders from behind. We stood stock-still and dumbstruck as Kishli overpowered Tashtamur and wrestled him into irons. A group of Mamluks came forward, took Tashtamur's sword, and threw ropes around him as if he were a sack. After doing the same to his sons, they hauled the three of them out of the room. The merry Sultan applauded enthusiastically and laughed a low-class sort of laugh. Tittering, the young men from Karak laughed too. Then the Sultan invited us to wash our hands, saying that we'd also be washing the place clean of that filthy Tashtamur, who had gone altogether too far.

One by one we stepped up and washed our hands using the pitchers and basins, of which there was a vast number, all made of gold, and attended by junior Mamluks. As we sat down again right away to address ourselves to dessert, Emir Mas'ud the chamberlain approached the Sultan, kissed the ground before him, and reported that he and a party of Sultan's Mamluks had gone down to Tashtamur's house, surrounded it, seized his Mamluks, and imprisoned them. The Sultan was delighted. The young men of Karak laughed and began hitting on Emir Mas'ud, who took it all in good spirits, even if sparks flashed in his eyes when one young man made an obscene remark and pinched him on the rear.

Next, the Sultan asked Emir Altunbugha, Emir Asunbugha, and Emir Salah to take fifteen or so of the commanders and a thousand of the Sultan's cavalry and go arrest Qutlubugha. The Emirs left immediately to carry out the order. The Sultan leaned over and whispered to me that he hoped they would succeed and that Aqsunqur would manage to help them.

Finally, the Sultan rose to signal the end of the party. Taking me by the hand, he pulled me away and, arm in arm, we left the palace, heading for a place I knew only vaguely as the royal cattle pens. I was surprised to see him go there, but then I remembered that the merry Sultan knew no limits.

"Everything's ready, master," said the emir who served as livestock manager.

"Great!" said the Sultan happily. "Here's hoping it was a good haul."

"It's not bad," said the manager.

He bid us enter and we did. Before us were vast numbers of sheep and cattle: four thousand of the one and four hundred of the other, to be exact.

"Are these my father's?" asked the Sultan.

"Plus Qawsun's," came the reply. "We put them all together."

"Get everything ready to move to Karak!"

"The boys'll carry them," said the manager. "Everything's ready to go."

We took a walk through the pens and the yards. There we saw birds of every description, as well as horses, mules, donkeys, giraffes, and lions.

"Is all this going to Karak?" I asked.

"Every last feather," replied the Sultan.

"But how?"

"We've got porters and water-sellers who can carry them on their heads," said the livestock manager.

"All the way to Karak?"

"To the ends of the earth if they have to," he said.

"Well, thanks for the info, Emir," I said.

Then the Sultan took me with him to the munitions room. As we stood before the door, I wondered what it was he was planning to do with his munitions.

18

Swim in the Sea of Love . . . and
Drink from the Wells of Greed

I HAD THOUGHT THAT THE munitions store that we were standing in front of was filled with ammunition, but when the caretaker came and unlocked it I could see that it was full of gold and silver.

"What a fine set of munitions!" I said.

"Is that everything my father collected during his reign?" asked the merry Sultan, in a transport of delight.

Said the caretaker, consoling him with tongue in cheek, "Your father, God rest his soul, was a generous man who couldn't resist good works. That's why he left only the little you see here: six hundred thousand dinars in silver and gold, and that chest full of gemstones."

"Wrap it all up in one bundle," said the Sultan, "and send it out immediately."

"Right away, master," said the caretaker.

Whistling and snapping his fingers, the Sultan turned away, leaving me gaping stupidly at his display of high spirits.

We crossed a broad hall that led to his private audience chamber by a door which, to my surprise, I had never noticed before, despite my having attended him in that room dozens of times. The young men from Karak were playing backgammon and making a racket in one of the adjoining rooms. Coming in right behind us was the Falconer, the chamberlain, who had yet to settle into a seat when the Sultan turned around and said, "You've got a job to finish tonight."

"Awaiting orders, master."

"I've been keeping track of my father's slave women," said the merry Sultan Ahmad, "and I know what each of them has been up to."

As if envious of the Sultan's skill, the Falconer replied, "But how, master? I've worn myself out spying on them and I've put the whole apparatus to work, but I've hardly learned a thing."

Handing him a slip of paper, the Sultan said, "Here are their names. Call each of them in one by one, and tell each one that I'm coming to see her tonight."

With a mischievous look in his deep-set eyes, the Falconer replied, "You're spending the night with all of them? If my master had said he was seeing one of them, I would know he was joking. But all of them? That's rich!"

Deliberately ignoring the mischievous look, the merry Sultan said, "That's what you're going to say to them. You're not responsible for whether it happens or not."

The Falconer stared into the merry Sultan's eyes as if searching there for something mysterious and obscure. The Sultan assumed an expression of diffident amusement.

As if seeking a pretext to prolong his visit, the Falconer read the paper again. "But Master, this list has only some of the women," he said. "The number of women in my master's household is enormous."

"I know, but those are the ones I want," said the Sultan. "They're the best endowed."

At that the Falconer shot him a nasty look that said, "Aha! I see what you're after, you rascal!" He turned and went out.

The young men of Karak came in, rolling a low table topped with bottles and glasses. The cupbearer assumed his usual position, pouring and serving the Sultan, who gulped down what was offered in a sort of adolescent funk, with expressions of misery flickering across his features. One of the young men poked at him affectionately. Another tousled his hair. A third said something, but he didn't like it. Me, I told all the Sultan Gazzar and Husayn Far and Hamada Sultan jokes I knew, in a rapid-fire barrage that provoked not a single laugh; and I realized that I had been right not to laugh at those jokes back when I first heard them in the fourteenth century after the hijra.

I don't know how much time passed before the Sultan stirred, scowled at us, and ordered us out. But as I got up to follow the young men out, the Sultan stopped me and asked me to wait. I sat down and he said, "Are you interested in women?"

"Not at all, master," I answered.

"Are you an ascetic," he asked, "or impotent?"

"Probably both, Master."

"In that case," he said, "You're just the man I need."

I shuddered at the thought of being left alone with the slaves of the great sultan. "What am I supposed to do?"

"I'll tell you," he said, "but only after you answer this question. Can a woman make you feel sorry for her? I mean, do you feel sympathy for women?"

"Sometimes," I said.

"You know that Eve was the reason that Adam was driven out of Paradise, right?"

"Yes," I said, "and she's still the reason I get driven up the wall."

"In that case," he said, "you'll have no trouble if you do what I tell you."

"Do you want me to cut their heads off and get rid of them for you?"

"I'm not *that* angry at them," he replied.

Here the Falconer came in and announced that the women had arrived, suspecting nothing. None had seen any of the others, and each of them thought that the Sultan had asked only for her.

"Send one of them in!" said the Sultan merrily.

The chamberlain went out. I was still trying to guess what it was the Sultan was after when a slender woman whose beauty testified to God's good work entered the room. How, I wondered, had such a blossoming, delicate, perfumed creature gotten along with a potbellied sultan like her late master? She had arrayed herself in her most splendid attire and put on every ornament she owned. As I sat there heaping fervent blessings on the Prophet and the Creator, his Majesty was carefully inspecting her hands, chest, and feet. Pointing to a cushion, he commanded her to sit beside him. After she did, he kept peering at her, trying to make it look as if he was glancing at her jewelry only by accident. Then he clapped his hands to summon the chamberlain and told him to take her into the bedchamber. Bewildered, the slave looked at your humble servant. But the Falconer beckoned for her to get up and she did. Pulling her after him, he disappeared. Turning to me, the Sultan said, "So you know what to do?"

Trembling, I said, "No, we hadn't agreed on what it was."

"Take off all her jewelry, piece by piece," said the merry Sultan. "And don't forget the anklets."

"Then what?" I said indignantly.

"Then you leave her where she is and bring me the jewelry."

"All right," I said, forming a plan of my own, "but it might take a while."

"You're not to waste time with her," he said suspiciously. "Just stay as long as you need to get the jewels off."

"But that's going to require a lot of clever planning and dexterity."

"Dexterity isn't allowed either," he said, wagging a threatening finger at me.

"Sorry to say so, master," I replied, "but those are my conditions for taking on this assignment."

"Then have a seat."

Calling in one of the young men from Karak, he ordered him to go into the bedchamber and strip the slave of all her jewelry.

"What if she's got gold in her clothes?"

"Take the clothes off too, and bring them."

Without further discussion, the Karaki went off to do as he was told. A short while later, he came back carrying at least three pounds of gold and gemstones, along with a gold-threaded dress slung over his shoulder. Some of the jewelry was spattered with blood, and we realized that the Karaki had stripped it forcibly off her wrists, ears, feet, and chest, with her resisting him all the way. The Sultan congratulated him on his bravery and asked about the slave. He replied that he had sent her down a secret stairway that led to a corridor that led outside.

Again the Sultan summoned the Falconer and ordered him to bring the next slave. When she came in, the Sultan looked her over carefully but saw no ornaments of any kind. Pouting, he recoiled in distaste, even though she was one of the most splendid-looking women I had ever seen. Looking at her furiously, he asked, "Where's your jewelry, woman? What I mean is: how can you appear before the Sultan without putting on all the jewelry you own?"

"Long live my master!" said the woman, sounding as if she were desperately hoping to win him over. "I have no jewelry. I've been poor and unlucky all my life. But I feel that fate has finally smiled on me. I was given as a gift to the late Sultan, and I was waiting for him to come around to me but he passed away before my turn came. I never had the chance to enjoy his favor, so I never acquired any jewelry."

So warmly and earnestly and happily did she make this speech that it stung my heart to hear it, but the Sultan only looked revolted. When she finished, he waved her away, saying, "Fine, go back to your room, then, and we'll send for you another night."

She blushed and then turned deathly pale. "What our master means," I said consolingly, "is that he's very sorry for what you've gone through, and he's postponing your meeting until he feels better."

She didn't believe me. Crestfallen, she turned to go, hoping that the earth would swallow her first.

Smacking his palms together in frustration, the Sultan said, "How did that happen? Either the information I got about her was wrong, or she knew what was coming and she tricked me."

He clapped his hands and the Falconer brought the third woman in. There was nothing obviously beautiful about her, but she was loaded down with as many trinkets as a jeweler's display case. That level of adornment meant that the former sultan must have been happy with her. "How," I wondered aloud, "did someone like you enjoy so much favor when the Sultan had more beautiful women at his disposal?"

"My master," she said meaningfully, "knew that inner beauty is deeper and more enduring than outer beauty, the former being a matter of essence and the latter only of form."

That shut me up good and proper.

The Sultan gestured with his chin for the Falconer to take her into the bedroom. The young man of Karak trotted after her like a pet dog. Some time later, he reappeared, looking the worse for wear, but carrying the gold ornaments.

And so it went for hours and hours. We witnessed one robbery after another, and the Sultan grew happier and happier as the pile of loot next to him grew higher and higher. Then he called for a drink. The cupbearer came in and began pouring again. The Sultan sat in worrisome silence. Feeling sorry for him, I went over to him, leaned over, and asked him in a whisper what was wrong.

Absently, he replied, "Nothing, Ibn Shalaby. I'm just thinking."

"No, chief," I said. "There's something on your mind. What is it?"

"Those emirs," he said. "Devils! Sons of slave-drivers!"

"What did they do?"

"They're trying to trick me," he said, repressing his anger.

"How's that?" I asked.

"The wars that Qutlubugha Fakhri is fighting are all the proof I need."

"Don't let it get to you," I said. "The emirs have always been like that."

The Sultan twisted around in his seat and drank twice. He would drink once as soon as the cup was filled and then again to finish off what was left, even if it was only a single sip. Then he would wipe his lips and toss the cup away. With practiced dexterity, the cupbearer would snatch it up and refill it. As for myself, the perennial hunger that lay deep inside me had me picking at the plates of snacks that were sitting on trays scattered around the room, even though I wasn't hungry or thirsty. The snacks must have had the same intoxicating effect on me that wine does on people who've eaten, as I found myself saying to the Sultan, "Listen, chief! You want to know my advice? Two wrongs don't make a right, so kill 'em with kindness!"

The Sultan laughed so hard he fell backward in his seat. "You sit with sultans and the best you can do is cite the wisdom of the rabble in the street? That's all well and good if you're hungry and weak, but you're sitting with the fat cats now! Anyway, don't worry: I'll forgive them. Not based on that lame philosophy of yours, but for reasons of my own."

He clapped to summon the Falconer and told him to order the Stuart to start roasting geese, one for each emir. "Around noon tomorrow," he said, "send each emir his goose!"

"Right away, sir," said the Chamberlain. Then he turned back. "But it's nearly noon now, master. You stayed up all through the night and into the next day without realizing it."

"I had no idea!" I said. "I don't know if the night always passes so quickly here at the Citadel or whether this was a one-time thing. But it really is hard to tell night from day around here."

"Save the philosophy," said the Sultan. "Nighttime is whenever we decide to stay up."

"But should we really stay up so late all the time?"

"Why not?" he asked. "What else is there to do?"

"Is it passion that keeps you sleepless?"

"It's my passion for passion," he said. "What I love most is love itself. When I love, I love madly. What is the world but a sea of passions? Let the waves break over you, and so many meetings and intimacies become possible. If you have children, teach them to swim in the sea of passion. If you teach them anything else, then you're a wretched parent, with children who'll be miserable. Do you know why I agreed to take you on as a Sultan's Mamluk? In a word, so I could watch you—to see for myself that there really are people out there so backward that they still concern themselves with philosophies and values and glorious achievements and matters of historic importance and all kinds of meaningless delusions! Look behind you at the Pyramids. They're like corpses practically screaming at you to live your life as you want to live it, and with passion. Don't talk to me about noblesse oblige and the hopes of the people. I come from a line of sultans and I've watched their every move and studied everything they've done. My father Nasir brought me professors and teachers and tutors and trainers and attendants by the dozen from every corner of the earth. They gave me books and ink and pens and paper; they laid before me everything they had experienced in the different places they came from; they revealed their dreams, their joys, and their sorrows, not to mention their vices and depravities, which turned out to be a good deal more numerous than their virtues. In fact, it was their vices, not their virtues, which gained them entry to the palaces of sultans and gave them the means to entertain themselves and their families. The late great Sultan believed that enlightenment and progress come from overseas. But the only thing we've gotten from abroad is obscenity. You'll find that half the sultans were raised by common wretches who used their vices and depravities to disguise themselves as extraordinary people and clever tutors.

Every sultan's childhood is marked by exposure to all sorts of depravity. Fortunately, though, depravity can easily become a virtue—the kind of virtue that carries us to the top!"

Staggered by this diabolical philosophy, I gaped stupidly at the merry Sultan and, without thinking, produced a flattering reply. "If that's really how your father and grandfather thought about things, your family wouldn't still be in power."

Chuckling at my naiveté, the Sultan told me I was wrong to think so. "I'm telling you how all sultans think, dimwit! Of course, not all sultans are alike; some are better at disguising it than others. Take me: I come from a line of rulers exceptionally good at hiding behind masks that can't be ripped off, even with gunpowder. 'Defend the country,' we say, or the caliphate, or religion, or agriculture, or prosperity—even though the only ones prospering are the rulers themselves—or morality, or whatever."

He burst out laughing. Recovering, he went on, "Now if you take a good look at me, you'll see that my mask is the toughest to dislodge, maybe because it isn't even a mask. I defend passion and the freedom to love. Every being has the right to live as it wishes, in comfort and joy. As to how they should manage—that's not my problem. Not at all! I'm a theorist and an advocate, but I'm not responsible for achieving something that all the sultans in the world put together could never achieve. Do you really believe that a single ruler, no matter how much power he has at his disposal, can be responsible for an entire people? In reality, he's barely able to look after his own family. And my case is even worse: I'm the sultan, but I still need other people to help me make the most of my prosperity."

I noticed that the Falconer was still standing there and, like me, regarding the Sultan in astonishment, though what struck me more was the malice in his eyes. Stepping forward, he said, "Well now, Master, you've kept on ruling straight through noontime, but you haven't told me what we're going to do about the geese."

"Send each emir a roast goose as soon as possible, along with a message from me—any message at all, even 'Many Happy Returns.' But it has to be done now, and all at once, so that come lunchtime there's a goose on every emir's table."

"Yes, master," said the Falconer, and departed.

"Are you doing this for charity?" I asked.

"No, you dimwit," he said. "It's bait. I've invited the emirs to come here before, but half of them sent excuses and the rest never came. I was planning to grab them all last night, but Gawuli was late showing up for duty."

"Do you suppose that the goose will really bring them in?" I asked.

"I'm certain of it," he said. "There's no more powerful royal summons than receiving a goose. Each of the emirs will think that he was the only one to get one, and he'll feel obliged to come in and say a word or two of thanks, if only out of politeness. The emirs all act as if they were raised in a barn, but they still look at me with distaste. Why? Because, the way they see it, I've ripped away the veil of propriety they've kept over their faces, even when it gets in their way, like when they're alone with their wives. It's become an inseparable part of their moldering selves, and even they find it bothersome. That's why they resent me for not wearing it! I know them and I know exactly how to deal with them. The first thing you learn as a sultan is to grab up as much stuff as you can and part with it when you have to. Some of us have learned to hide our greed and some of us haven't, but we've all been good sultans."

"Are you going to arrest all the emirs, master?"

"Of course!" he said. "Each one will come, bloated with roast goose, and sit beside me. Without realizing it, he'll be in my power. I can't let Fakhri get away without making them pay!"

At that moment the Falconer came in to announce the arrival of Yaka Khudari. In an agony of apprehension, the Sultan shot up in his seat. "He must have news of Fakhri," he said. "I know he was the only one who would follow him as far as Arish and Gaza. Bring him in!"

The Falconer disappeared and Yaka Khudari made his entrance, kissed the ground before him, kissed his feet, rose with theatrical aplomb, and announced that Qutlubugha Fakhri had been arrested. In a transport of joy, the Sultan invited him to sit and offered him some wine. Then the Falconer came in again to announce the arrival of several emirs who had come to pay their respects to the Sultan. The Sultan told him to receive them as rudely as possible and then send them away with orders to present themselves again the next day. As the chamberlain was leaving, the Sultan ordered him to have Fakhri sent to Karak. As the chamberlain once again prepared to leave, the Sultan stopped him again, this time telling him to send Green Garbanzo out on a litter—a sort of contraption used for sitting on the back of an animal—guarded by a troop of Sultan's Mamluks. The Falconer turned to go, then stopped on his own initiative as if expecting further orders. When none came, he departed. The Sultan whispered in my ear, "I've changed my mind about the emirs. Now that I've got Qutlubugha, I'll leave them be."

As the night wore on, everyone grew tired and listless. Yaka took his leave and the Sultan went off to his bedroom. I sat up playing backgammon with the young men of Karak. Though I'm no good at backgammon, I beat them all one after the other, but only because they were giving only half their attention to the game; the other half was directed toward the Sultan's bedroom in case he should call for one of them. They had a system where the loser would give up his turn with the Sultan. I refused to abide by that tradition and suggested instead that the winner should slap the loser. If he beat him again, he could punch him; and if he beat him a third time, he could pound away at him until he was too tired to hit him any more. I worked off my pent-up anger by knocking one to the ground and smacking another upside the head, until I had tired myself out and felt much better. They got tired of the game too, but they weren't sleepy. I thought this might be a good chance to ask them about Karak, the town that the Sultan was so passionately fond of. Each of them described a different part of the town, but I got the sense that none of them knew anything about it. "How, for God's sake," I asked them, "could you not know anything about your own town?"

"Who said it was our town?" answered one.

"We were born there, that's all," said a second.

"Our families came from elsewhere," explained a third.

Surprised, I thought of playing by new rules that would let me shoot them. They were on the verge of agreeing when the Sultan came back in half-dressed and they all stood to attention. He ordered them to pack their things and be prepared to leave. He called me over and put an arm over my shoulders, saying he was going out to meet the emirs. The young men disappeared.

At the conclave of the emirs, we were welcomed with an enthusiasm that smelled of roast goose. The Sultan greeted everyone and announced the capture of Fakhri to general acclamation. He paid his respects to the Caliph, who was there too, told him that he had appointed him supervisor of the Sayyida Zaynab shrine in place of Ibn Qastillani, and asked him to accompany him to Karak.

"Karak?" cried all the emirs. "Again?"

"And again, and again!" said the Sultan. Exchanging glances, the emirs fell silent.

"I've ordered the Inspector of the Army and Judge Ala al-Din the Secretary to come with me as well."

There was no comment from the emirs. The Sultan added that he had summoned eight of his Mamluks and invested them with robes of honor at the treasury gate; given a robe of honor to Aqsunqur and appointed him Deputy in Absence; given a robe of honor to Adlani and made him judge of the frontier; and given a robe to Zayd al-Din al-Bustuli, appointing

246

him Chief Judge of the Hanafi rite in Egypt instead of Husam al-Din Ghuri. Then he signaled that it was time to depart.

From the Citadel came a great stately procession as heavily laden as Noah's Ark. Accompanied by the emirs, the Sultan rode down Citadel Mount. I was given a royal horse and rode down with them. Under heavy guard, we proceeded through the city and out to Victory Gate. There the Sultan stopped and the emirs dismounted. One by one in order of rank, they kissed his hand and backed away. Then he dismounted and was given a bundle of clothes. When he opened it, I could see that it was a complete, loose-fitting Bedouin costume, including a turban with two trailing cloths to wrap around his face. The young men of Karak assumed the duty of fitting the Sultan into his disguise. When he was dressed, he signaled for the emirs to depart, which they did, except for Qumari, Maliktamur, Abu Bakr, Umar ibn Arghun the Deputy, some of the Sultan's Mamluks, the young men of Karak, and two slaves.

I was the last to leave. I went up to him in his Bedouin dress and we embraced. There were tears on his cheek and on mine too. I stood watching the cavalcade as it grew smaller and then disappeared amid thick clouds of dust.

19

Crying When It's Time to Laugh:
A Genuine Egyptian Talent

THERE'S NO DOUBT ABOUT IT: Egyptians weep easily. When saying goodbye, especially, they'll cry you a river, even when the person leaving is a debauched louse like the merry Sultan Ahmad ibn Qalawun. What I had really wanted to say to him by way of a farewell was, "Good riddance, and may God never bring you this way again, or debase the Land of Egypt with anyone like you!" Instead of saying that, though, I embraced him; and even worse, I cried. Was I really sad to see him go? Or was it the instinct for flattery, so deeply ingrained in the poor and miserable Sons of Shalaby? The fact of the matter is that we Sons of Shalaby of the Egyptian branch laugh and distract ourselves with jokes even as the boot-heels of our oppressors grind us down. Then, when the bad times are over, we weep, as if our love for good company were stronger than the need for revenge. Our servile ancestors used to say, "Put up with a bad neighbor and wait for some calamity to carry him off, or for him to leave on his own." Throughout the ages, the historical reality of life here has done its best to apply this dictum as literally and unfailingly as possible. All our bad neighbors, whether sultans, emperors, emirs, or invaders, have been dispatched by fate, which uses them to destroy each other. We ourselves, and others too, may suspect that we abandon the field altogether and leave Fate to fight our opponents for us. In reality, though, we help Fate along as best we can. If you ask me how, I would have to admit that I have no idea. But there are ways and means—knowledge of which is either secret or unconscious—that we Egyptians can employ, without realizing that we're employing them, to leave our enemies to the tender mercies of History. What it comes down to, simply put, is leaving them to their own devices: not helping them or encouraging them in any real sense, but giving the impression of doing so. No matter how implacable the foe, when he sees that no one is resisting him, he becomes despotic and tyrannical, and hauls himself up to a place so high that he inevitably comes crashing down. Now if you ask how it is that we of all people on earth should have acquired this habit, the Pickle-and-Sweet-Seller would answer in all frankness that we have never had any interest in ruling anyone. There are, certainly, people who struggle against the government, but they aren't common people like us: they're emirs and contenders for the throne. While the contenders contend against each other for as long as it pleases God to let them, we keep away, as if the outcome were none of our business—as indeed it isn't. But just let anyone try to snatch the bread from our mouths: when that happens, we fear no one, no matter how many medals and ribbons he might be wearing.

The pointless tears in my eyes had me seeing double. Then everything in front of me began to acquire a gloomy hue. The shining splendor faded away, to be replaced by a sticky, stuffy, musty-smelling rust. Our steps slowed and silence fell. Suddenly I found myself standing on my own feet, when a moment before I had been sitting astride a thoroughbred royal steed. Before me, too, had been a procession of emirs assembled at the Victory Gate outside Cairo to bid farewell to Sultan Ahmad, who was leaving for Karak. Now it was gone, utterly gone, but the place where they had been was still there.

I tried to hold on tightly to the place and ride it up to a conscious moment. The portal of the Victory Gate still stood, rusted but unbowed, though all trace of life had vanished; instead there was only the spirit of History. The courtyard looked like a dragon with the gate as its mouth. To my right was a handcart stacked with crates of yellow dates and illuminated by a kerosene lamp. A thickly mustached Upper Egyptian was sitting cross-legged and smoking a water pipe. His son, who was standing beside him, had removed the pipe's clay bowl and was filling it with molasses-flavored tobacco. The man's wife was putting two of her children to sleep while playing with the other three. A donkey was champing at a feedbag looped around his head. The air reeked of unwashed bodies, straw, mildew, dates, sweat, and whatever was in the warehouses that belonged to the property-owners on Mu'izz Street. Seeing me standing there in a daze, the date-seller said, "That's the Victory Gate, Mr. Tourist."

Laughing, I told him that the tourists knew what it was; but I, being an Egyptian, probably didn't. Then, peering through the portal, which was arched and ornamented like a monumental fountain, I saw a road that seemed from a distance to be running through open fields. I looked for any sign of Sultan Ahmad's cavalcade, which had passed through only a moment before, but saw only cars shooting past like missiles.

I walked through the gate to the street and, as old historical maps would have it, passed out of Cairo altogether. I swear to you by God in Heaven that I felt a pang of fear, as if I were fleeing the city in secret, or as if it had spat me out. Beside me was the lofty city wall, topped with cornices and embrasures. With its majestic height, it seemed to confront visitors from the ends of the earth with a demand to stop and show proper respect, lest they be hunted down by hidden eyes like those of falcons. As I walked alongside it, I felt as if I were huddling against it for safety. When I stepped slightly away from it into the torrent of Binhawi Street, though I knew that the Bighala quarter was on my right and the wall on my left, I still felt as if what lay to the right was blank space and what lay to the left was safety. I turned back, now seized with the vague apprehension that the gate with its wooden lock would soon be shut. That, at any rate, is the feeling I had as I approached the Conquest Gate, which stood only a few meters from the Victory Gate. If you go out, it seemed to say, you may not be able to get back in; but if you do make it in, you'll be perfectly safe. Turning left, I went in.

The gate was fortified with massive walls on either side and decorated with elaborate patterns. With both hands, I took hold of the projections on the wall and saw that the iron door set into the gate had been pushed back flush with the wall and then had sunk into the ground. Time, I realized, had grown old and feeble, and carried me back to the fourteenth century of the hijra, where I was born and where I had lived. But even a doddering Time could not cast its hateful shadow over structures built in a young and vigorous age.

Meanwhile, I was still thinking about the merry Sultan Ahmad ibn Qalawun. I remembered that, a short time ago, I had wished that his distant era would slide off me and let me rise back up to my own time. But now that I had, I felt disgusted, empty, bereaved, and depressed. A voice in my head explained that anyone who had seen Cairo at her peak of splendor could hardly bear to see her like this.

Turning left, I saw a tower that I used to see standing outside the walls and which I imagined was part of old Cairo. It was one of two enormous, beautiful minarets attached to a mosque bordered on one side by the Conquest Gate and extending for a great distance beyond. The two minarets faced each other across the expanse. In front of the building was a courtyard off the street, big enough to hold three thousand worshippers. The door of the mosque itself looked like the door of an enchanted cavern leading to some pure and eternal moment. I knew this was the Mosque of Hakim, or the Anwar, the Luminous Mosque, founded by the Caliph Aziz and completed by his son Hakim, and called "Luminous" in analogy to al-Azhar, the "Radiant" mosque. According to my friend Stanley Lane-Poole, it was built in order to pull the rug out from under al-Azhar, which had become a strong-hold of Sunni Islam and a center for the dissemination of its creed, and to place it—the rug, that is—under the Luminous Mosque, which was to serve as a new center of learning for Shi'a of the Fatimid sect.

I stood rooted to the spot, watching as work progressed on the building. The people doing the work were nothing like the usual sort of Egyptian laborers, nor were they Western-ers. They wore clean white shirts and pants and white caps, and braided their beards. I was surprised at how odd they looked, and even more surprised at how clean they were, not to mention their working together on the sort of job nor-mally undertaken only by people strong and tough enough to handle it. Working in pairs, they were carrying floppy bas-kets full of bricks, dirt, or rocks back and forth, and they had set up scaffolds along the walls. The Luminous Mosque was coming back to life. From reading the newspapers, I knew that the workers were Pakistanis who volunteered to restore the mosque at their own expense. To be exact, they belonged to a sect called the Bohra, which was creedally rooted in one of the branches of Shi'a Islam, though God alone knows best. They included engineers, physicians, workers, teachers, professors, and mystics, but all of them wore the same cloth-ing, evinced the same magnanimous spirit, and exuded the same vital energy.

A little way off stood a pleasant-looking young man holding a satchel. He seemed not to mind that I was there uninvited. I returned his friendly glance. Like me, he was watching the workers. I wanted to convey to him how much I admired their devotion to their creed and their earnestness in carrying out its teachings. I approached the young man and greeted him, saying, "Salam alaykum."

"And peace upon you, and the mercy of God, and his bless-ings," he replied, in a foreign accent, but with all the sounds pronounced accurately. There is something winning in the sound of Arabic pronounced by foreigners who, in trying to get their tongues around it, find themselves slipping into its fluid, expressive rhythms. Shaking his hand, I introduced myself, "Ibn Shalaby, at your service."

He nodded.

"The Hanafi and Egyptian," I added.

He cocked his head as if expecting more.

"The seller of pickles and sweets," I said.

He looked baffled and his face went blank. Realizing that he didn't know Arabic, I asked him how many languages he knew. Counting off on his fingers, he listed Urdu, English, and Latin. I asked him if he could read the Quran.

"The *Holy* Quran, if you please," he said.

"As you like," I said. Using only gestures, he conveyed that he could read some of the verses. As we were speaking, many of the Pakistanis walked by and, with marvelously gentle courtesy, nodded at me in greeting. The young man's eyes brimmed with questions and a friendly desire to communicate as clearly as possible. I marveled at how it was possible to communicate and at the same time not communicate at all. This, I thought, was the age of wonders. But then I corrected myself: Egyptian history in its entirety was an endless series of wonders. That was why, on the level of conscious awareness, the various ages seem disjointed. What remains is the spinal column, the Mamluk system, which lies hidden like a bone under the flesh. Every time the cleaver of History cuts it asunder, it grows back, and eventually becomes the actual nervous system.

Suddenly the appearance of the Pakistanis and of the street itself changed completely. Everything was new and clean, and the mosque shone with splendor. Coming toward the building from the street was a crowd of more than three thousand men. "What is this, a demonstration?" I asked.

"It's the Caliph Aziz," said an attendant who stood waiting to receive the procession. "He's here to lead the first

Friday prayer now that the mosque's finished. Make way, or go in and worship!"

I looked and saw Aziz mounted on a steed. Next to him was another steed, on top of which was a small boy. I recognized him as Mansur, who would one day be named Hakim. The Caliph's parasol cast a shade over him alone. Looking at my watch, I saw that it was Friday, the fourth of Ramadan, 381. As soon as the Caliph reached the door of the mosque, he dismounted, removed his shoes, and handed them to one of the attendants. His son Mansur did the same. Following in their wake, the crowd poured in. Within moments, the outer courtyard was jammed with thousands of worshippers. Smelling of cleanliness, they reverently took their seats. I could pick up the sound of the Caliph's voice as he delivered the sermon. I began looking around for a place where I could hear better, but for every step I took forward, the ever-growing crowd pushed me back. Then everything went black.

When I opened my eyes, I found myself in a different sort of crowd. It was sparser: a few dozen men wearing turbans, fezzes, and costly gowns. I could pick out Yaqub ibn Killis, vizier to the Caliph Hakim. He was contemplating the mosque, which had expanded and grown several additions. The doors were now hung with specially made curtains of Dabiqi fabric. From the ceiling hung four silver chandeliers and numerous lamps, and the floor was covered with specially made mats. The pulpit had been set up and furnished. I pushed my way through the groups of spectators, who looked as if they were trying to guess the cost of the redecoration. The vizier said it had cost five thousand dinars. I looked at my watch: it was Friday night, the sixth of Ramadan, 403.

All of a sudden, something happened to electrify the crowd. A man had appeared, blue-eyed, sharp-featured, and slender. If not for the Fatimid regalia studded with gold, pearls, and rubies, I would have thought he was a movie star. But his appearance, and the fear he and his party struck in the hearts of the spectators, left no doubt that he was the Caliph Hakim. Except for the sound of his footfalls on the flagstones, the street was silent. Commoners would approach him, kiss his hand, and hand him folded slips of paper, which he would put into his sleeve and walk on. Led by the vizier, the men waiting in the mosque came forward to receive him. The Caliph said that he had given permission to those who spent the night at al-Azhar to come here. Then he disappeared inside the mosque. People carrying books began coming out, telling each other that they were heading for Azhar to catch such-and-such a lesson, while others were coming in, telling those they met that they were coming from Azhar to Anwar. People from both groups would stop for a long moment to take in the new setup: the Conquest Gate was now on the outside, and the mosque, which had been on the outside, was now on the inside. When I turned around to join the spectators, I was surprised to see an artist on a tall ladder holding a bag full of fine pens and brushes. Whirling around, I saw that the people and the clothes had all changed. On the buttress adjoining the Conquest Gate, the artist was writing:

BUILT IN THE YEAR 430 DURING THE REIGN OF MUSTANSIR AND THE VIZIERATE OF THE COMMANDER IN CHIEF

My watch read the same year. I stepped a few paces back, then went into the mosque to explore it from the inside. Noticing an ornamented wall fountain filled with Nile water, I asked the bystanders who had built it. They told me it was Commander Abdallah ibn Ali ibn Shukr. When I stepped back to take a good look at it, it began to contract and acquire a layer of dust. Workers came toward it with axes and then set about demolishing it.

"Who told you to do that?" I shouted.

"The Chief Judge, Tag al-Din ibn Shukr."

"But why?"

"To make room for more worshippers," they said.

"No," someone chimed in, "it's because it's so beautiful that it distracts people who are trying to pray."

"No," said another, "it's to complete the design of the main courtyard."

The number of people defending the workers was about the same as the number of those trying to stop them, and I was afraid that the situation might deteriorate. When I went out, the clothes people were wearing had changed again. There were fewer things for sale in the shops along the street, and the shops themselves looked different. The mosque boasted an addition, which had an odd appearance, including little churches with steeples that did not suit the Luminous Mosque at all. The bystanders looked peeved. I stopped and exclaimed, "What a travesty! True, it's a travesty that suits Egypt to a T, but what is it?"

One of the bystanders said, "The Caliph Zahir, son of the Caliph Hakim, started it but never finished it."

"Fine, but who put the churches in?"

"Zahir," came the reply, "but it was the will of God."

"How's that?" I asked.

"Some Frankish captives were imprisoned there. They built the churches."

I slapped my palms together and laughed bitterly. "So they put them here and let them do whatever they want, and then they just leave everything the way it is?" Then I said to myself, "Clearly, the reconciliation of opposites has been a part of Egyptian reality for a long time." I walked around and around the addition that had imposed itself on that unique monument.

All at once everything changed again. Soldiers in Ayyubid uniforms, and a crowd led by men carrying axes and shovels, were attacking the addition and pulling it to the ground. I went up to the soldiers and asked who the men were.

"They fight for Saladin," came the reply.

"Now there's a man of principle!" I said.

"He's not easy to fool," they said, "and he doesn't let things slide."

"That's for sure," I said. "So he's going to put up a new addition instead of this one?"

"No, he's building a stable."

No sooner had they finished speaking than their time began to slip deeper and deeper into the past. Troops of horsemen and baggage trains were riding into the courtyard. I looked around for a shop where I could sit on a wooden bench and recover from the sudden fatigue I was feeling. But then the earth began to shake like the escalator at the Omar Effendi department store of the fourteenth century after the hijra. I tried to hold on, but the earth started to pull me forward. Everything was swaying and dipping, and thunderbolts lashed at the skies and the buildings and the people. I realized that all of Egypt, including Cairo, was being hit with an earthquake. Everything was shuddering and rattling, and the walls and ceilings were popping and crackling. The earth seemed to be carrying us along as it spun out of orbit. It felt as if the sky had collapsed onto the earth. People came running out of their houses shrieking and howling, the women unveiled. The streets were swarming but no one could find a safe place to stand because of the falling walls, the caved-in ceilings, and the collapsing minarets. The Nile rose as never before, flinging moored boats as far as an arrow could fly, and then leaving them stranded on dry land. That's what Maqrizi told me in so many words as he emerged from the panicked crowd. Men, women, and children gathered in the desert outside Cairo, and spent the night in tents on the riverbank. The city emptied out. No house was left undamaged: all had tilted or crumbled or collapsed. In the mosques, people prayed and called upon God to save them. I looked at my watch and saw that the date was Thursday, 13 Dhu al-Hijja, AH 702.

After the earth had calmed herself, I made my way cautiously into the Anwar Mosque. The tops of the minarets and the roof and walls had been damaged, and many of the buttresses had fallen. We spent Thursday and Friday in front of the mosque beseeching God until the emir Rukn al-Din Baybars Jashankir, along with his judges and commanders, arrived and ordered that the damage be repaired and the buttresses restored. He said that he had set aside several endowments in Giza, Upper Egypt, and Alexandria to benefit the mosque. He also announced the establishment of regular lectures in jurisprudence according to the four Sunni schools of law, as well as a class in Hadith, each with an instructor and numerous students. He gave the position in Shafii law to Ibn Jama'ah, that in Hanafi law to Sarugi, that in Maliki law to Ibn Makhluf, that in Hanbali law to Agwani, and the position in Hadith to Harithi. He also named Athir al-Din to teach grammar, Shantufi to teach variant readings of the Quran, Qinawi to impart the other sciences, and Ibn al-Khashshab to perform regular recitations of Hadith works. He announced the founding of a substantial library as well as the appointment of teachers of Quranic recitation, readers to chant the Quran in continuous alternation, and a tutor to teach the divine scripture to Muslim orphans. Finally, he ordered the digging of cisterns in the courtyard, to be filled with Nile water for the fountains, and left open to the people on Fridays.

I resolved to stay and see what would happen. But as the laborers set to work on the restoration, a wave of panic ran through the mosque. From the minaret on the side nearest the Victory Gate came a cry of horror. I ran out, climbed the scaffolding, and saw something truly surprising. Inside the structure of the building, the workers had found a box. The foreman took it out and opened it. Inside it he found a human hand and forearm wrapped in cotton. The palm of the hand, which seemed freshly amputated, bore some lines of writing no one could identify. I heard the workers whispering that it was the sort of thing one should avoid asking too many questions about. I don't know whether they put the hand back where they found it or took it away and buried it.

The thing is, I was distracted by another incident. A big piece of stonework fell from one of the walls and was found to contain what looked like a secret inscription:

That thing whose name I here conceal
But solve this riddle to reveal:
A square whose root, if symbolized,
Gives one letter on both sides;
And in the middle of the square,
The very letter you saw there.
Say the first and fourth part of the same,
And call the stone its real name.

But no one could make sense of the lines or guess the name of the precious stone.

My watch now read 761. I saw Mamluk soldiers storming the elegant mansion that stood across the street from the mosque. People said it belonged to Muhammad Hirmas, who was responsible for the restoration. On Wednesday, 29 Dhu al-Qi'da of the aforementioned year, I saw the soldiers drag him and his son outside and thrash them senseless with switches and batons. Then others appeared and pulled down the house.

"What happened to him?" I asked, meaning, "What crime did the man commit?"

"He embezzled funds from the endowment," I was told, "and made himself rich."

"So people have been cooking the books forever," I said bitterly. No one replied, but I was so taken with the manner of punishment that I couldn't resist commenting that it was right to show people like him no mercy at all. One of the soldiers remarked that Hirmas and his son would soon be appearing at the oddest trial in the world. Then all of them were gone, leaving the street empty except for a few passersby and me. I sat down on a wooden bench that had come out of the house in one piece since it was only a wooden bench. I sat watching the Anwar Mosque as the merciless ages piled upon it one after another, heaping on layers of rust and dust. I saw the little fountain for ablutions become a warehouse with an additional story on top and a vendor sitting before it. I walked up to the vendor and asked his name.

"Ibn Karsun Marahili, seller of produce," he told me.

I asked him how he had taken over the fountain.

"I'm building another one, and a colleague of mine is restoring the minaret above the gate next to the pulpit."

I walked off, picking my way through the heaps of soil and piles of stones, so exhausted that some of the bystanders had to help me along. No sooner had I emerged from the ruins than I saw the Pakistanis going about their work again, with enviable earnestness and diligence.

Utterly disgusted, I continued walking down Mu'izz Street, asking myself how many great and historic buildings still stood in Cairo waiting for someone to rescue them from the ravages of time and the cruel indifference of their builders' descendants. Or were they waiting for foreigners to come and restore them? I spat onto a street full of *nouveau riche* traders, Honda mini-trucks, pickups, and handcarts. From the Mercedes-Benzes stepped potbellied, graceless men wearing American clothes and Persol sunglasses, illiterate, but deft enough when it came to calculating profits.

Leaving the citrus-fruit market behind me, I headed for Gamaliya, with its cafés and hashish dens. On a sudden impulse, I sat down at one of the cafés. I watched the patrons smoking their hashish with systematic precision. I also watched policemen and detective inspectors hauling away shamefaced suspects accused of buying and selling chunks of hashish. I jumped up and continued my walk as far as Judge House Alley, where I ran smack into Emir Khazaal. He was chasing a woman wrapped in black. "Where the hell have you been?" he shouted.

"I was saying goodbye to Sultan Ahmad."

"Come on, then," he said, taking me by the arm and pulling me back into the age of Sultan Ahmad ibn Qalawun.

20

Night at the Citadel . . . and
the Citadel by Night

TIME STICKS TO THE EDGES of human memory like honey, or germs, or glue, or an infection. There are times when memory cannot easily be disentangled from the stickiness, and times when it searches for the stickiness but cannot find it. Here I am walking beside Emir Khazaal, commander of the prison at the Storehouse of Banners, and the de facto head of state. As we make our way through the sidestreets and alleys, he sees the storehouse and I see the Mosque of Husayn. He's reclaiming his territory and I'm reclaiming mine. If the storehouse is Khazaal's province, taking his orders and spreading corruption in the Land of Egypt at his behest and for his benefit, then the Mosque of Husayn ibn Ali, built on the site of the storehouse and sanctified by the head of the Prophet's grandson, is mine. No matter how I look or how I feel or how little money I have, the shrine always welcomes me with open arms. If I drive into the square and get stuck or lost, hundreds of people help me find my way without even getting up from their seats. More than one springs to my rescue: "Back it up, back it up. . . . More!" And a little boy, all at once infused with the spirit of a wizened expert, tells me with enormous kindness, "Turn it all the way, sir. No, to the right. . . . That's it! Leave her there, and trust in God!" So it is that getting stuck turns into a popular demonstration like nothing anywhere else in the world. I can park anywhere, plunge into the square, sit at any sidewalk café, and talk with whoever is sitting there as if we were old friends meeting after a long absence.

I saw all that, I saw the crowds on Azhar Street, but with the walls of the storehouse standing in the middle of the shrine. A few landmarks had changed and some buildings had disappeared entirely in the interval between the two times, leaving narrow alleys and emergent streets that tripped me up and pulled me bodily away from Khazaal, who was striding through his own time with no difficulty at all. To be honest, I was tired, and I was hoping that one time or the other would pull its sticky fingers off the walls of my memory. But then the buildings built between the Emir's time and mine, the ones that were forcing us apart, would disappear behind me, and the structures that had been torn down would rise up and I'd find myself walking beside him again. Thinking I was near the shrine—so sure, indeed, that I took off my shoes and put them under my arm—I followed a faint light into the building. Khazaal burst into earth-shattering laughter. Recovering from the shock, I realized that, thinking I was heading for the south colonnade of the mosque, I had trampled some storehousers who were sitting or lying on the ground in a place where there was no colonnade at all. I apologized to the people I had stepped on, "Pardon me, gentlemen! I thought I was at the Mosque of Husayn."

Recognizing me, they asked, "Poor fellow! What's wrong with you?"

I said that I had always thought that a person carries his environment with him wherever he goes, but I had never realized that he also carries his time around with him to the same—if not a greater—extent.

With all the cunning of a savage philosopher, Khazaal said, "Everyone blames people for the effects of a poor environment. Should we start blaming them for the effects of a poor time, too?"

"Certainly, Emir," I said. "True, I can't judge whether environment is the result of time or whether it's the other way around. But I have no doubt that time is the one at fault when it's a noxious, defeated time full of bats and bloodsuckers. Anyway," I continued, "I don't think a person should be blamed for growing up in a poor environment, since he usually isn't responsible for it, or for his time either."

Meanwhile, Khazaal had lifted me off the ground, carried me into his enclosure, and tossed me into a chair. Sitting opposite me, he said, "What did you learn from your experience with Sultan Ahmad ibn Qalawun?"

"I swear to you, Prince, that I couldn't tell you right now. Maybe I learned a lot without realizing it, and when the time comes I'll figure it out."

"Have you heard the latest about that Sultan of yours?"

"Since I saw him off at the Victory Gate and watched him ride off to Karak, I haven't heard a thing. Anyway, that was only a few moments ago."

"What do you mean, a few moments? You went missing from our time for quite a few days. We looked for you in the Citadel and everywhere else, and finally we realized that you must have fallen into the well of time."

"I must have snuck out for a few days to visit my wife and children while I was attending the opening of Anwar Mosque."

"Visiting your wife and children," said Khazaal, "is something you should be sure you did, not something you can't quite remember."

"You'll be surprised," I said, "when I tell you that I seem to be married and I seem to have children. All I know for sure is that I have a big family to support."

"Getting married seems the right thing to do in your time."

"So don't hold it against me," I said, "or *your* time will be fair game for every Egyptian who's ever lived."

"How can you *not* know the latest news?" he asked harshly, as if resolved to rebuke me in return. "You *must* be getting constant updates. Otherwise, you'd never make it at what you've gotten yourself into."

"Take it easy, Emir," I said. "One way or the other I should be able to tell you something new."

"Go ahead!" he said, as eagerly as a man craving a glass of wine.

"Were you aware," I said, "that the merry Sultan Ahmad turned on Qutlubugha Fakhri, set the lower orders on him, and let them humiliate him? And that they mocked his womenfolk, and let the young men of Karak take all their property, even their clothes, and treated them terribly? Did you know that Qutlubugha and Green Garbanzo are now in prison at the Citadel of Karak? And that the Sultan has given himself over to debauchery and shut himself away from everyone besides the Karakis?"

He laughed mockingly. "Is that all you know about what's going on abroad? Tell me, then: do you know what's been happening in the Land of Egypt since the Sultan left?"

"All I know," I recited, "is that the senior emirs are in a tizzy; and Aqsunqur, the Deputy in Absence of the Land of Egypt, confiscated the property of Green Garbanzo and Qutlubugha and sent it all to the Sultan in Karak; and Aqsunqur is afraid to ride out on public procession days ever since he learned that a group of Mamluks whose master he'd arrested were conspiring with some of the emirs to attack him. He stayed scared until they gathered at his place and swore allegiance to him. But then on 5 Muharram, 743, they wrote to the Sultan saying that the situation had deteriorated in his absence. Aqsunqur had violated his agreements with the Arabs of Upper Egypt and provoked dissent, making the roads unsafe and conditions parlous. They sent their message with Emir Tuqtamur Salahi, a Sultanic Mamluk who had been viceroy in Hims. By God's grace, I, the Seller of Pickles and Sweets, was able to see the Sultan's reply as brought back by Tuqtamur to the Land of Egypt. What the Sultan said was: 'I like where I am, and whenever I want, I'll come back.' Tuqtamur also made a statement in which he clarified that the Sultan had been unable to meet with him and had sent someone to collect the letter and return a reply."

Khazaal had only to glance at the others who were sitting around us and they erupted in laughter over the musty antiquity of the information I had reported. Gesturing to one of the tattooed cannibals, he said derisively, "Tell His Highness"—meaning me—"the latest news you've heard."

"The most recent reports," said the tattooed cannibal, "are that the Sultan yesterday killed Green Garbanzo and Qutlubugha Fakhri."

"But," I said, trying to save face, "what are the details? In fifteenth-century Cairo, any student at journalism school knows that a report isn't complete until all the details are in place."

"Journalism, shurnalism," said Khazaal. "We've got our own school right here. If you want details, we've got an eyewitness just arrived from Karak astride a fleet steed. Come here, boy!"

The "boy" turned out to be a man of elegant and respectable appearance, seemingly of good birth, yet for some reason unoffended by Khazaal's vulgar form of address. He was introduced as a Mamluk of the late Sultan, exiled to Karak to serve the princes there, and on that account much resented by Sultan Ahmad. He had managed to escape in the confusion that surrounded the scene he had witnessed. Now a fugitive, he had naturally sought refuge at the storehouse from the Sultan's soldiers and police. The storehouse had granted his request and placed him under its protection. Starting tomorrow, he was free to wander anywhere in the land of Egypt, and no power on earth, not even the Sultan himself, would dare raise a finger to punish or harass him.

"Anyway," said Khazaal, "tell us, bro, what you saw with your own two eyes in Karak."

Looking not at all put out, the Sultan's Mamluk straightened up and said: "I was in prison in the Karak Citadel when the gate was opened and the two emirs, Green Garbanzo and Fakhri, were thrown in with me. By the time one or two meals had been served, I realized that the Sultan was planning to starve them to death. I used to give them a crust of my own bread at mealtimes. But after two days and nights of starvation, they broke out of their fetters, and ripped out the door with that amazing strength of theirs. It was as dark outside the prison as inside. They found the guard sleeping and took his sword away, but he woke up and shouted for the others, who arrested the two emirs and informed the Sultan. He happened to be out hunting, but as soon as he got the message he hurried back in his Bedouin costume and stood waiting at the moat. When they were put in front of him, covered in cuts and bruises, they didn't kiss the earth as usual. Instead, they looked defiant and insolent. The Sultan looked them up and down and up again, with contempt. Then he asked, 'What have you done? Talk, you two!' Garbanzo flew into a rage and started cursing back at him, but the Sultan was unruffled. All he said was, 'Yusuf'—meaning the guard—'off with their heads!' Then he turned away. Yusuf turned away too, and stepped back a little, drawing his sword, then spun around like a ballet dancer. Both heads flew into the air, followed by jets of blood that drenched the earth and spattered the Sultan's face, and my face, and everyone's face. I took off running. Thanks to the blood all over me, no one recognized me. I found myself near the stable, so I broke in, took a horse I knew, grabbed whatever else I could, and rode straight here without stopping."

"How," I asked calmly, "did you know about the storehouse if you were in prison in Karak?"

"Is there anyone in the region who doesn't know about the storehouse?" he asked with a smile.

With a flamboyant gesture, I jumped up and looked at my watch as if I were running late for an urgent meeting.

"Where to?" said Khazaal.

"To the Citadel, of course. I need to be there to report on what I was doing while I've been gone. Otherwise they'll think I snuck off with the Sultan back to Karak."

"When will I see you?"

"I'll be in touch as soon as I can."

"Off you go, then."

I bowed and sprinted off to the Citadel.

The first thing I did was drop in on Aqsunqur, the Deputy in Absence of the land of Egypt. I assumed he would pay little attention to me, but there he was, welcoming me warmly, asking me how I was, and if I was still in touch with the Sultan. I told him I was fine, and that although I did enjoy the merry Sultan's favor, I no longer had any way to contact him, since the only people he really trusted were the pages from Karak. He asked me if I needed anything from him. I thanked him and told him that, on the contrary, I had come to place myself at his disposal. He thanked me in his turn and assured me that I should consider him my friend, just as the Sultan had been.

"Will you give me as much freedom as he did?" I asked.

"Even more," he replied. "We're all at your service, Ibn Shalaby."

"That's great," I said. "Now I can relax!"

In the meantime, lunch had arrived. I took my place like a Sultan's Mamluk trained to serve his master, and dug in. When we finished, we had a few glasses of arrack and nibbled at a plate of faludhaj—pudding to you.

Then Aqsunqur jumped up and straightened his clothes. So I did the same.

"I don't suppose you'd mind coming with me?" he asked.

"Where to?"

"Emirs' meeting," he said. "We're gathering in the Citadel to decide what to do about the Sultan: keep him or depose him."

"Sounds important," I said. "I suppose I'd better come."

So I followed him to the meeting of the emirs.

Seeing them sitting and talking in all their splendor, I was actually moved. In fact, I was so bedazzled by their great numbers and vast wealth that I didn't notice how the discussion started or how it proceeded. In short, I had assumed the role of observer, though without seeing anything, and realized that people like me had no business being put in positions of responsibility or serving as ambassadors to advanced foreign nations. Our years of want and our unfamiliarity with life in prosperous societies leave us unprepared to play any role except that of observer. Anyhow, I came to my senses in time to hear them talk about Abul Fida Ismail, son of the late Sultan Nasir. One of the emirs was saying that during his exile in Qus, Abul Fida would fast on Tuesdays and Thursdays.

"He spent his time praying and reading the Quran," said another.

"He kept clear of the sort of trouble young men usually get themselves into," said yet another.

"Of all Sultan Nasir's sons," said Aqsunqur, "he really has the best heart."

"With God's blessing!" they said as one.

"Shall we make him sultan?" asked Aqsunqur.

They hesitated, each apparently waiting for someone else to call out an answer. In the end, though, they all spoke up, "Let it be so. We'll make him sultan!"

Aqsunqur jumped up to summon Abul Fida. When they returned, the emirs rose and bowed to him. He made a slight, nominal bow, but even then the blood rushed to his face. He sat and they followed suit. One of the emirs had summoned the soldiery, which was now waiting outside the Citadel. Aqsunqur took it upon himself to inform Abul Fida that the emirs had unanimously agreed to appoint him sultan. Abul Fida thanked them and they rose again. Then they put him in front and let him lead them to the throne room. There he sat on the throne and they sat around him. They swore allegiance in loud voices. From outside came the sound of the troops swearing the oath as well. Then Abul Fida rose and swore to harm no one and never to arrest an emir without cause. And so it was concluded. Asked to give himself a title, he said that he chose to be called Salih, "the Good." He was the sixteenth Turkish king, and the fourth son of Muhammad ibn Qalawun, to rule the Land of Egypt, after the deposing of his brother and by acclamation of the emirs. My watch read Thursday, 22 Muharram, 743.

Some of the emirs left to take part in the procession. The rest departed one by one, leaving only Aqsunqur and your humble servant. When I asked permission to go, the new Sultan said, "You're practically a member of the family. Stay here with us!" So I stayed in my seat. I watched him order a general amnesty in Alexandria, in Upper Egypt, and in Lower Egypt, excepting only those prisoners guilty of capital crimes. Aqsunqur seconded these proceedings. Then the Sultan asked him, "What do you think of my stepfather?"

"You mean Emir Argun Ala'i?"

"Do I have another stepfather?"

"A good man, no question about it," said Aqsunqur with a smile.

"I've appointed him head of the nawba," said Sultan Salih.

"Very wise!"

I said, "What, if I may ask, is the head of the nawba?"

Aqsunqur said, "It's the title of the officer who conveys the Sultan's or the master's orders to his Mamluks, 'head' here meaning 'fellow at the top.'"

"Thanks for the clarification!"

Sultan Salih continued, "I also appoint him head of council, and chief administrator, and my legal guardian."

"Very good," said Aqsunqur.

"What about you?" asked the Sultan. "What do you think of yourself?"

"A good man, no question about it," said Aqsunqur as if talking about someone else.

"Then you shall keep your job as Sultan's Viceroy in the Land of Egypt."

Aqsunqur bowed in gratitude. The Sultan continued, "Write to the emirs and deputies in Syria to let them know that they still have their positions. Tomorrow we'll send Emir Tuqtamur out with robes of honor for them. And have Aydughmish move up to deputy in Damascus. Replace him in Aleppo with Tuquzdamur, and replace Tuquzdamur in Hama with Sunqur Gawuli."

"Well done," said Aqsunqur, nodding.

The Sultan continued, "Now bring me Emir Qublay and Emir Baydara."

Aqsunqur leapt up, disappeared briefly, and reported that the two emirs were on their way. The Sultan called for paper and a pen and told me to write.

"What should I write, master?" I asked.

"A letter to my brother Ahmad."

"What should I say?"

"Greet him and tell him that when the emirs learned of his lack of interest in governing Egypt and his love for Karak and Shobak, they appointed Abul Fida in his stead as sultan. And tell him, Mr. Pickle-Seller, to send the royal parasol and the golden bird."

"Right away, master."

I had hardly finished writing what he had told me to write and read it back to him than the Emirs Qublay and Baydara came in and kissed the ground before him.

"Qublay," said Sultan Salih, "take this letter to Karak and deliver it to my brother, the former Sultan Ahmad."

Qublay bowed in assent, took the letter, rolled it into a cylinder, and wrapped it in a piece of silk.

"And you, Baydara," said the Sultan. "Take a detachment of grooms to bring the Sultan's horses back from Karak."

Baydara bowed in assent.

When it was time for everyone to leave, the Sultan asked me to stay, telling Aqsunqur that he needed me for something. I must have looked uneasy because Aqsunqur smiled knowingly, giving me to understand that Sultan Salih was not like Sultan Ahmad and did not demand the same sort of services.

After Aqsunqur left me alone with the Sultan, he sat up in his seat, forgetting that he was the ruler and I was a Mamluk. "So," he began.

"So," I said.

"Tell me about Ahmad."

"How can I tell you about your own brother?"

"My father sent him to Karak with his mother as soon as he was born," said the Sultan. "He grew up there, and we only saw each other in passing. I want to hear all about him from someone like you, who lived with him up close and got a real sense of his character. There's a lot of rumors going around, and I'm hoping you can clear them up."

"With pleasure, Master," I said, and began telling him about Ahmad, careful not to go into too much detail about his moral conduct, and generally doing my best to give the new sultan the sense that I could be trusted and that I wasn't the sort to start abusing a ruler the minute he's deposed. That's the sort of thing my mother always warned me about. Evidently, though, I was so careful that I made the former ruler look a lot better than he really was. Salih grimaced and said, "I can see that you didn't know him all that well. But no matter."

At that point the session had been going on for some days. When I looked at my watch, I saw that it was Saturday, the first of Safar, of the aforementioned year. The chamberlain came in and whispered in the Sultan's ear. Looking pleasantly surprised, he said, "Have them come in."

In marched a group of dignitaries, among them Qumari, Master of the Hunt; Ibn Arghun, the deputy; Maliktamur Higazi; the Caliph Hakim; the head Mamluk, the eunuch Anbar Saharti; and the Sultan's Mamluks. They greeted Sultan Salih and sat down. I realized that they had left Sultan Ahmad and come from Gaza. Everyone sat for a long time listening to each other's tales of the deposed Ahmad, with each storyteller hamming it up and reducing me and the Sultan to gales of laughter. In honor of the unexpected visit, the Sultan kindly invited everyone to have lunch. Afterward, we carried our storytelling session long into the night. When I next looked at my watch, it read Tuesday, the 25th of the month.

The chamberlain came in again and whispered something to the Sultan, who grinned broadly and almost jumped for joy. "Bring them in," he said.

The newcomers were Judge Ala al-Din Fadl Allah the secretary and Gamal al-Kufat, inspector of the army. The latter explained that he had escaped from Karak after learning that Sultan Ahmad was planning to kill them for fear they might go to Egypt and report what a dissipated life he was living. To escape, he said, he had bribed the Sultan's attendant Yusuf.

By now all the emirs had heard the news and joined the gathering. Amid the rejoicing, the Sultan gave them all robes of honor and confirmed them in their positions.

When the party finally broke up, the Sultan informed me that I should consider his home my own and that I was free to do as I liked. I thanked him and set off wandering through the Citadel as if I owned the place, making it clear to everyone that I was a counselor and confidant to Sultan Salih.

One day, as I was wandering along the ramparts and whistling a tune, a messenger arrived wanting to see the Sultan. I asked where Salih was, but no one could tell me for certain. So I took the messenger aside and asked him why he had come. He said that he was there on behalf of Shatt, the prince of the Bedouin, to inform the Sultan that Ahmad and some of his young men from Karak had decided to come to Egypt and kill him. I set off looking again and almost knocked on the Sultan's bedroom door, but was turned away by attendants who said, first, that he was on a secret mission; later that he was asleep; and finally that he was out hunting. So I informed the emirs of what Shatt's messenger had said. After a lot of whispering, they agreed to dispatch troops to attack Ahmad in Karak.

On the morning of Thursday, the third of Rabi' II, the detachment of troops, led by Emir Baydara, headed off to Karak, while I continued to try and figure out where the Sultan had so suddenly disappeared to. I learned to avoid the eyes of certain emirs, who seemed likely to ask me where he was.

One day, as I was walking through the colonnades of the Citadel, I heard shouting and shrieking from the quarters of Khund Urdu, the mother of Kuchuk, formerly Sultan Ashraf. I burst into the house and found several of her slave women coming out unveiled, with bloodied faces, black eyes, and bruises, as if they had just been in some raging battle. With all the effrontery of a eunuch, I marched into the room and found the mother of Sultan Salih holding tight to the mother of Sultan Ashraf, the better to kick her and butt her with her head. With some difficulty, I pulled them apart, with Salih's mother saying, "Leave me alone! Let me kill her!"

"What's wrong, mistress?" I asked.

"Confiscate her property!" she screamed.

"Fine, we'll confiscate her property! But why?"

"This fiend," she said, "cast a spell on my son, Sultan Salih!"

"How can that be?" I asked. "Cast a spell on him how?"

"He's had a nosebleed for days now," she said.

"Where is he?"

"In bed," she replied. "No one's allowed to see him."

I took off running and burst into the Sultan's bedroom. I found him shaking. Touching his head, I realized he had a cold. I prescribed a medicine, which they brought immediately. He drank it down and his nose stopped bleeding. His mother launched into a round of ululation and ordered that the city be decorated. Then she accompanied me to the shrine of Sayyida Nafisa, where we offered an oil lamp made of twenty-three pounds of gold.

21

A Low-Fidelity Abul Fida

NOTHING IN THE MEDICAL BOOKS could explain to the Sultan's mother why he had a nosebleed. Of course, the doctors continued to visit Sultan Salih, or Abul Fida, and spent good long hours with him without divulging anything about his condition to his subjects. But his mother had her own opinions and she was unlikely to give them up without a struggle. In her view, there was no point in examining him to find out what was wrong with him. Instead, the answer lay in books of spells and hexes. Sorcerers and magicians, it turned out, came in different kinds: just as some were good only for exorcisms at popular festivals, others had a clientele that included royalty.

The Sultan's mother had still not gotten over the fulfillment of her lifelong dream: that her son should inherit the throne with no effort on her part. How then could she let this good fortune slip away? She had to protect her son using every means at her disposal. Though she had always felt that he was blessed, she was also, in her heart of hearts, afraid for him. His name was Abul Fida, which means "one who offers up a sacrifice." She remembered that her husband, Sultan Nasir, chose the name to express his genuine sense of membership in "the tribe of Heaven," that is, the line of Arab prophets, with names like Ibrahim, Ismail, Muhammad, and Ahmad, or those of the Prophet's descendants. She felt that her husband, his father, and his grandfather had triumphed in their campaigns only because they had undertaken them for the sake of Islam, the religion of

God Almighty, who, when He blessed them with sovereignty over the lands of the Muslims and the cradle of all faiths, had doubtless been testing them and their good intentions.

She still remembered, on the day her son was born, how Sultan Nasir's face had lit up. "He's an offering to God," he said. "Let his name be Abul Fida Ismail." To be sure, his father had no intention of sacrificing him to anyone or anything. The name was merely a gesture, a way of telling God that they were willing to make sacrifices for His sake. That night she had giggled and teased the Sultan, "Are you trying to fool God, master?" He had laughed too, and in a slightly muddled manner tried to explain that God knows what is in men's hearts and doesn't mind when the strongest and cleverest of His creatures indulges in mischief at His expense. "Aren't we His children?" he asked. "Don't we smile when one of our children tells a white lie? God has blessed us with so much. God," he prayed, "let this son of yours be a sacrifice to redeem Islam and the lands of Islam."

At that, her heart pounded and the earth seemed to drop away beneath her feet. She knew that the Sultan had said what he had said to save himself, or to prove his good faith, as one does when swearing recklessly to divorce one's wife. Even so, she felt as if the heavens had opened at that moment to receive her husband's prayer and show him that such things should not be falsely wished for, as if to say, "You lied and said you wanted to make a sacrifice. Now make one!" And though it was true that she, like her husband, had come to have absolute faith in God and His prophets, she still didn't know whether she would be willing to sacrifice her son to any cause. This was a problem she had yet to consider.

Meanwhile, she was making me dizzy with her forays into the streets of Cairo and the Citadel. Escorted by slave women and eunuchs, she would take me to mysterious places full of learned scholars and illustrious divines who owned codices and manuscipts whose very appearance was enough to intimidate you into believing anything. The scholars never tired of opening their books whenever a question of any kind was asked, then they would read, sometimes to themselves and sometimes out loud, and pause to explain what they had read. What was really remarkable was that their learning wasn't so far off from what we call psychology. To tell you the truth, I actually enjoyed lollygagging around with the Sultan's mother: the world of magic is by definition an enchanting one, and magic—as I learned—is a real art form. The master sorcerers I met through the Sultan's mother were nothing like the con men, hucksters, and scam artists who exist in every age and make their living at the expense of a profession whose reputation had been built by genuinely competent practitioners. Rather, they excelled at using precise techniques to expose the workings of the human soul and bind up its wounds. By virtue of long experience and deep immersion in spiritual matters, a sorcerer could distinguish any ailment and determine the cause. "Have you ever experienced such-and-such?" he would ask his patient. "Do you do this or that? Have you ever noticed such-and-such?" Every time, the answer would be yes. The sorcerer would then lay down a course of treatment. It consisted of movements, or changes in habit, or wise words to illuminate the darkness in the sufferer's heart.

Eventually I told the Sultan's mother that there were no sorcerers left to see, especially since her son's health was hardly as bad as she imagined. He was simply feeling indisposed. In my day and age, I told her, people would come down with something called the flu and curl up in bed sneezing and coughing for days without going to a doctor or anyone else. But she was unpersuaded. Instead she would ask my opinion of some bizarre conjecture. If I hesitated before answering, she would fly off the handle: "Aren't you the Sultan's adviser? That means you have to answer me *right away*!" She might tell me, for example, that one or another sorcerer seemed to have a real affection for the Sultan, and ask whether his diagnosis was therefore more likely to be right; or say that one or another healer had seemed unenthusiastic and had mocked something I had said, and ask whether he wasn't in the pay of Khund, mother of the former Sultan Kuchuk, and was working to undermine Abul Fida's health. "Isn't that right, Pickle-and-Sweet Man?"

When, on one occasion, I said that such a thing was unlikely, she gave me look that practically accused me, too, of working against the health of the Sultan, forcing me to play along with her suspicions up to a point and then go back and set matters right after everyone had calmed down. She acted as if she had come around to my point of view, but of course she was only indulging me, just as I had been indulging her. So, as soon as we got back to the Citadel and entered the Sultan's bedroom, I threw myself on his bed, sat beside him, and entertained him so as to take his mind off his painful bloody nose.

We were still sitting there when Ayaz the Cupbearer came in to announce the sudden death of Aydughmish, the Sultan's deputy in Damascus. The Sultan summoned his viceroy Aqsunqur and told him to transfer Tuquzdamur from Aleppo to Damascus, Altunbugha from Hama to Aleppo, and Yalbugha to Hama. During the same audience the Sultan conferred the estates of the late Qumari upon Arghun and wrote to the deputy in Gaza and Safad telling him to lend assistance to Baydara in his siege of Ahmad in Karak. Then from Shatt, the prince of the Arabs, came wonderful news. He had taken his army to Karak and defeated Ahmad's forces, sending them fleeing back to their citadel. Ahmad had then given in and asked for time to write to the Sultan and ask him to send someone to take possession of the fortress of Karak. Great rejoicing erupted in the citadel in Cairo. I slipped away from the Sultan's bedside, claiming that I was going to have a word with the people who were making so much noise. I stood outside and let the Sultan hear me pretend to bawl them out. Then I disappeared into the crowd of soldiers and commoners at the base of the Citadel. In the meantime, though, everyone had stopped celebrating and begun glumly cursing Karak and the people of Karak and the sons of sultans for their treachery. I asked what had happened and they said that the former Sultan Ahmad had tricked Shatt's troops into giving him a respite and then gone right back to the fight. By the time Sultan Salih heard the report of his "defeat," Ahmad was in the field all over again. No one wanted to break the bad news to the Sultan for fear that the shock might be too much for him. I shouted that they were wrong and the Sultan needed to be told. In the end I promised to pass the news on as gently as possible. I ran back, certain that I would succeed in my task.

Back at his bedside, I cheered him up a bit and then let him have the news direct to the ear, all in one go. For a long moment he sat there, letting it sink in. Then he leapt to his feet. Appalled, I shouted at him, "Don't you dare go out like that, old man! Are you crazy? Get back in bed and under that blanket or I'll call your mother!"

Paying no attention, he shouted back, "Come with me!"

My heart sank. Was he telling me to come and fight? "Go with you where?" I asked.

"To a place near here where I can recover."

"What place is that?"

"Siryaqus," he said.

"Okay," I thought, "I can handle that." Siryaqus is an old town near Shibin al-Qanatir in the directorate of Qalyubiya, on the east side of the Ismailiya canal eighteen kilometers outside Cairo. My watch read Wednesday, the fourth of Ragab, 743. The Sultan had finished putting on a lighter version of his royal raiment and was waiting for me to change into some of the new clothes he had given me. Then we went out.

Of the emirs who knew in advance about the trip, most came along and a few stayed behind. Walking in front with the Sultan, I made the acquaintance of his brother, Emir Ramadan, a young, pleasant-featured young man who felt like a new classmate I might have met during my adventure-loving teen-age years. The Sultan had given him command of a thousand troops. When he introduced us, we took an immediate liking to each other. Then Ramadan put a hand on my shoulder and, looking around cautiously, whispered that he was very happy to have met me and would like a few moments of my time.

"Gladly," I told him. With a touch, he signaled for me to wait until his brother had moved away, but I told him I had to ride with the Sultan. "I'll ask him to excuse you," he said.

"Fine," I told him.

Ramadan went up to his brother and said, "May I have your permission to keep the Pickle-and-Sweet Man with me for a bit?"

"But I need him with me," faltered the Sultan.

"Just for a few minutes," said Ramadan. "There's something I need to ask him about."

"What you want to know," said the Sultan cannily, "he can't help you with: girls and love letters and that sort of thing."

I laughed and said that the Sultan was right. Ramadan laughed too and said that he would only keep me for a few minutes.

"Fine," said the Sultan. "I'll ride on and you catch up."

He rode off with the emirs and soldiers following him according to the usual protocol. Ramadan, I noticed, was making a point of trailing behind the group, and some of the emirs were doing the same. He gestured to the emirs, who had stayed behind out of courtesy, and they rejoined the Sultan's caval-cade, leaving him in the middle of a big knot of Mamluks. I suddenly got a feeling like the one I used to have when I worked as a journalist: I imagined that Ramadan was about to perform some impressive feat so that I would write about him in the newspapers. Instead, though, he called me over and introduced me to the Mamluks, saying with apparent pride that I was his brother's adviser, Mr. Pickle-and-Sweet Man in the flesh. The Mamluks welcomed me with a shout that rattled me and made windows open and heads pop out up and down the Citadel. Then Ramadan took my arm and led me some distance away.

"Mr. Pickle-Man," he said, "I've heard you're a wise man, as wise as the Egyptian people itself. And for that reason, you've got good judgment and a sound mind. And for the same reason, too, you've got a good heart and wouldn't hurt a fly."

"What are you getting at, Ramadan?"

"My brother Abul Fida, Sultan Salih, is a sick man, as you can see; plus he's unreliable, and poorly educated too."

Taken aback, I nearly exclaimed that that was no way to talk about his brother and sovereign. But then I decided to make light of the sitation. "God grant him health," I said with a smile, "and grant us guidance."

"Well, let *me* guide you," said Ramadan boldly.

"What do you mean?"

"Join me, and you'll be doing the right thing for the people and the country!"

Knowing I'd been placed in a no-win situation, I started thinking about how to escape. "What is it you want me to do?"

"I want to be sultan," he said.

"How?"

"It's all been arranged, God willing," he replied. "I've made plans with some of the Mamluks and emirs and soon it'll be time to put the plan in motion. So ride with us and don't run off."

Seeing my horse in front of me, I mounted, and so did Ramadan, leaving his Mamluks to conclude that he had won me over to their side. He rode out two paces in front of me and the Mamluks came along behind. Then we swerved off the path that the Sultan's retinue had taken. When we reached Ethiop's Pool, I saw a vast number of men mounted on horses and mules. Behind them was the town of Prophet's Relic framed against the Nile, as well as the Monastery of Mud, the orchards of Basatin, and the ford of Maadi, where I live. I told myself that it would be an easy matter to escape: all I had to do was move a bit to the right and I'd be inside my house, which is on the line between Maadi and Basatin. But then, to my surprise, the horses and mules suddenly began moving, then, slowing their pace, turned toward the Citadel. Ramadan was shouting to his men to bring their horses back to the right road.

Within moments, it was clear that Aqsunqur the High Equerry had learned of the plot from some Bedouin he had sent to keep an eye on Ramadan. After circling around the Citadel, he had come with several hundred armed men and lain in wait for the mounts. And so there we were, Ramadan and I, being pulled along like camels toward the Sultan's stable; and there were the troops collecting weapons from Ramadan's men. When we reached the stables, we dismounted and let the horses enter. Then the soldiers led us into the Citadel, and there was the Sultan sitting and waiting for us. I knew by instinct that he had received the news and raced back to the Citadel. No sooner did I approach his chamber than Ramadan disappeared, leaving me to go in and face Aqsunqur, the senior emirs, and the Sultan.

As soon as he saw me, the Sultan said, "So this is how you treat me, after I trusted you, you pickle-and-sweet seller, you?"

"You've got the wrong guy, old man, I swear!"

"We'll let it go," he said, then asked me to sit, making it clear that he knew that I had been an innocent bystander.

The night had grown deeper and darker. Everyone was downcast, and the only smiles I saw were sarcastic. Finally, the Sultan turned to Argun and said, "Argun, arrest all my siblings. Yes, all of them: old, young, male, or female. And while you're at it, arrest my mother, too!"

Argun leapt up to carry out the order, but I broke in with a shout, raising my hand like Sayyid Khalifa, an old fellow from my village: "Hey wait! Hold on there, will ya? Whaddaya mean, arrest your mother? Hang on! Whatever happened, she's still your *mother*, who carried you for nine months and nursed you and put up with all your problems and suffered with you when you were sick just now, what with the magicians and the fortune-tellers!"

The Sultan glowered and his eyes bulged out. "That's why I have to arrest her!" he shouted.

"Don't take this the wrong way, but you'd be making a mistake."

"Argun!" shouted the Sultan grimly. "Arrest the Pickle-and-Sweet Man too!"

I sat down in a panic. "No need for that! I take it back! I have no manners at all! Argun, old pal, go arrest anyone you want! Bye now!"

Argun looked helplessly at the Sultan, who waved him away. "Fine, we'll let it go this time. Go, Pickle-Man, and help him do his arresting."

I jumped up full of enthusiasm. "Right away, master. That bunch really deserves to get arrested. Even the lady your mother! That's right, the whole lot of them deserves to be arrested and put in jail for life."

I went out with Arghun and an escort of armed soldiers. At Ramadan's quarters, we stood back and sent some of the Mamluks and servants to find him. They returned with black looks that made it all too clear that he had cursed them and refused to come along.

"Drag him here by force!" yelled Argun.

No sooner had he finished speaking than Ramadan's mother stuck her head out the window and in a booming voice heaped a series of hair-raising curses on him. He cursed her right back, though with some restraint. But then she replied to his reply, and the two of them began a good long round of shouting and cursing. When Argun had had enough, he sent additional Mamluks and servants to bring Ramadan out even if they had to drag him out by the collar or the neck. But then Ramadan himself suddenly appeared, accompanied by twenty of his own Mamluks, who were carrying drawn swords. He called out to someone and asked where the Viceroy was.

Hearing that he was with the Sultan and the other emirs, Ramadan made his way toward the gate of the Citadel, his companions' swords still drawn. Mounting the emirs' horses, he and his retinue rode to the horse market under the Citadel, but found none of the emirs there. So they turned toward the Victory Dome, with me following behind to see what he would do next. Argun guessed that he was going to see the Sultan on his own initiative, and allowed that it was within his rights to do so. But to my surprise Ramadan passed the Victory Dome, left the Citadel, and stopped there with Emir Yaka Khudari. A crowd of people gathered around them.

I ran back to the Citadel to find the exhausted Sultan being carried out by four men. The Viceroy, the High Equerry, Qumari, and several others rode off, while the senior emirs stayed with the Sultan and I went down to the base of the Citadel. Hearing the drummers rap out the call to arms, I was appalled. "It was children who started this fight," I thought. "How did we grown-ups get mixed up in it? He's a stubborn kid who won't listen to reason. God help us!"

The sergeants went down to assemble their troops, just as they did before any campaign. The Viceroy led his troops out armed to the teeth, and I—in my advisory capacity—went with them as far as the Victory Dome. The Viceroy led us up to Ramadan, who, we were surprised to see, had gathered a big crowd of Husayni troops, Mamluks belonging to Yaka, and men of the lower orders. The Viceroy clearly found the sight distressing, as it meant that a battle was inevitable.

"What does the Pickle-and-Sweet Man have to say?" he asked.

"It's all up to you, sir," I replied, like any no-account adviser in any government office.

"Go back to the Sultan," he said, "and inform him of this development."

I returned under heavy guard to the Sultan at the base of the Citadel and informed him of the development. He was so disturbed that he recovered his health and, despite having collapsed shortly before, jumped to his feet and tried to mount his horse. The emirs rose too, congratulated him on his recovery, kissed the ground before him, and reassured him that Ramadan posed no problem at all. They kept at it until he sat down again. I went back to the Viceroy to inform him of the Sultan's wish to engage in some canny negotiation.

"You take care of it, then," came the response.

So I went off to talk to Ramadan on behalf of the Sultan. I told him that he was playing with fire and that he'd be the cause of a battle that would have the streets running with blood, but none of it did any good. I returned and informed the Viceroy, who sent me back to promise that he could trust us not to harm him if he surrendered. I kept at it, like Henry Kissinger with his famous shuttle diplomacy between Egypt and Israel. But Ramadan paid no attention to anything I said. At last I went back to the Viceroy empty-handed.

"Then we have to attack him," he said. "God, bear witness! I did my best to talk to him first."

Then he struck the battle drum, which was normally the immediate precursor to a ferocious assault. But when the lower orders heard the sound, they instantly went weak in the knees and scattered in all directions, leaving only Ramadan, Yaka Khudari, and a handful of Mamluks. Sensing imminent defeat, Ramadan and company bolted. The soldiers set off in pursuit, firing arrows as they went.

After the rebels were captured, the Sultan ordered Ramadan and his other siblings kept under guard and their Mamluks put in prison. Then he rose to dine and then to go to bed. I followed him, expecting that he would send me away with the excuse that he was tired and needed to sleep. Instead, though, he sat up and asked me to stay, saying that for the first time in his life, he felt that the world was not a happy place at all, and that everything in it—having grown, as it did, from impure soil—had no meaning or justification or even any real existence at all.

"No offence, old man," I said, "but aggression runs in your family. What I mean is, your brothers are quick to attack each other."

"That's what being sultan is about."

"That's what the *obsession* with being sultan is about."

He said that his father Nasir had followed the practice of *his* father Mansur, who married more than one wife, and other rulers had made the most of their harems, spawning endless numbers of children; but in none of these cases did the children fight the way he and his brothers had: that is, for no good reason. Why not? he wondered. Brothers had fought for power in every time and clime, but not to the same degree of treachery and murder and bloodshed.

"Well," I said, "brothers and uncles everywhere have always fought over the throne. But the battles ended with the victory of one group over another. In other words, it was always groups against groups. Each group had a ruler, and each ruler would foster someone's aspirations—his group's, or the country's. Now the battles *you* fight, sons of Qalawun, are all about individuals fighting individuals, and the winner is the one who outwits his brother and pays off the army. Do you want to know why that is, master?"

"Tell me."

"No reason except that you're Mamluk slaves. Your grandfather, who belonged to Nigm al-Din Ayyub, wrested the throne from him, and passed that power-grabbing streak on to his own sons."

Sultan Abul Fida Salih was glowering at me, looking as if he were about to order my arrest. The only thing that saved me was the arrival of a message from Yalbugha announcing that the former Sultan Ahmad had been captured.

22

Black Slave Women and Blue Eyes

AFTER THE MESSENGER HAD LEFT, the Sultan Salih leaned over to me and said, "Don't believe what you hear. They deliver these reports to me because they think they'll make me feel better."

I asked him if he thought his brother Ahmad was invincible. He answered that Ahmad was not so much powerful as wealthy, having plundered the treasury and carried the spoils off to Karak. He added that the task now was to wear him down until his reserves were depleted and he was forced to surrender. In that case, he might receive a sultanic amnesty.

"What's a sultanic amnesty, old man?"

"It's when you—if you're a sultan—put your enemy in fetters and throw him in prison, and then pardon him."

"Sounds like a good deal!"

The Sultan stretched out his legs, which were red and skinny as a goat's, and flecked with red, black, and gray hairs. He was a steady, thoughtful sort, as I had heard, and as I had confimed for me by Maqrizi, who had written two books on the kings of Egypt. The Sultan was indeed slow to do harm, quick to do good, gentle, kind, and affectionate, as well as good-looking, fair-skinned, and sallow, with a mole on his cheek. He had funded courses of study at the Qubba Mansuriya, the school founded by his grandfather Qalawun. He had also renewed the appointments of the caretakers of the Prophet's shrine in Medina and undertaken several projects in Mecca, such as the Hospice of the Lote Tree, where there is an inscription bearing his name. He was twenty years old at that moment when, sitting together, we heard the news that work on "the Marvel," which he had commissioned as his private audience room in the Citadel, was finished. He was transported with delight.

"Lucky you, Pickle-and-Sweet Man!" he said. "You get to open the Marvel with us. It's a good thing, too: if the news hadn't come just now, you would have been in serious trouble."

"First of all," I said, "why is called the Marvel?"

"Because when you see it, you marvel at it. That's how I wanted it to be, and that's how it turned out."

"And why were you planning to hurt me?"

"Because you're a pickle-and-sweet man with no manners," he said. "You're honest and to the point, but you're doomed to a miserable existence because you don't know how to flatter people and suck up to them. That'll be it: trouble and strife throughout your life, and a bad relationship with your children, too, no doubt. But, so long as honesty counts for something, and frankness retains any value in society, you'll be remembered. God, at least, will be on your side; and someone, I imagine, will take the trouble of putting up with you."

To be honest, I liked the little speech the Sultan had made. I even felt embarrassed at the compliment he had paid me. I was reconfirmed, too, in my impression that he had a kind heart and a fine mind. From the scholars and sages I had met, I had learned that kindheartedness was the product of broadmindedness, and that when the two traits are present in the same person, he becomes receptive to all sorts of people, even to complex cases like us; for his kind heart and open mind allow him to grasp the essence of a person's character.

I had just finished explaining this to him when someone came in to announce that Yaka Khudari had been dealt with once and for all.

Now the Sultan turned out to be a snake in the grass, as the saying goes. Just when we thought he was an innocent, serious-minded lad, he began to reveal himself as someone who'd been around the block a time or two.

Early the next morning, after preparations had been made for an excursion, I noticed unaccustomed activity near the Sultan's bedroom door. Among the white slaves were black slave women of extraordinary beauty, with bright, bronzed faces like statues finely chiseled out of fragrant sandalwood. All the slaves were chattering excitedly and displaying flamboyant affection for each other, even if their jealous glances told a different tale. From out of her chamber came the Sultan's mother, dressed in colored silk and, like all the women, wearing a Birghali cap—that is, a pointed hat made of horse leather lined with wolfskin and studded with gemstones and pearls. I had put my clothes on, and had come to wake the Sultan and place myself at his service. When I found that an entire crowd of slaves had come to wake him too, I pushed my way through to his door and knocked.

"Who's that knocking?" he asked.

"It's me, old man." I said.

"I'm on my way, Ibn Shalaby."

I could tell from his tone that he was very busy doing something, so I said, "Okay, I'll wait for you downstairs."

"Go on," he said. "I'm right behind you."

I raced down to the foot of the Citadel. Saladin Square looked different. It had been decorated in different bright colors—precisely the colors of the clothes and gems the slave women were wearing. Some of the women were scattered here and there like flowers. I knew that they had houses outside the Citadel, which they would visit at prearranged times. But then I saw something I didn't know about. Respectable-looking men of the upper class were stopping some of the women, kissing their hands, and giving them closed parcels. I asked a harfush who was standing beside me watching, "Are those wedding gifts?"

He laughed. "All those parcels are bribes, shocking to say!"

"Bribes? For slave women?"

"Bribes and a story, too."

"What do you mean?" I asked.

"Everyone who has a complaint," he said, "writes it up and puts it in the parcel, along with some money so she'll do her best to intervene on his behalf."

"Are the slave women really that popular?"

"I guess you're not from around here," he laughed. "The slave women run the whole show."

"What do you think of the Sultan?" I asked him.

"He's a good guy. His only fault is that he loves black slaves more than he loves the throne, the country, or anything else."

"We can't win, can we?" I said. "His brother loved young men from Karak and now he loves black slave women. Oh well, it's all good."

Noticing that the procession was nearly ready to leave, I raced over and found the Sultan standing waiting for me.

"Sorry, old man," I said.

"And just where the heck were you?" he shouted.

"Taking a pee," I said.

"Where?"

"Right here, against the wall of an old house."

He raised his eyebrows in surprise and said angrily, "So you leave the Citadel to go pee in the street? You really are a low-class pickle-seller."

"Sorry, old man."

I dimwittedly took my place at his side and he curled his lip in distaste. Then the procession started, with a number of favored Mamluks taking the lead. Behind them came four of the senior emirs, surrounded by soldiers bristling with swords and daggers. Each emir was flanked by horsemen. Then a black woman I had never seen before came forward. When she came opposite the Sultan, they both smiled lustfully and I could almost hear his heart beating. This, I realized, was his favorite. I was surprised to see nothing in her outward appearance to explain his attachment to her, unless it was the traces of a nearly vanished beauty. Even so, there was something unnatural in her face, and some obscure instinct told me that she was no ordinary person. Self-assured, nimble, and cheerful, she mounted the hackney, and did it well. Directly behind her, a group of men carrying lutes, violins, pipes, drums, tambourines, and guitars mounted in turn. Behind them, also on hackneys, came the mother of the Sultan and two hundred ladies in colored silk dresses and tall caps studded with pearls and gems, with eunuchs marching before them. Next, surrounded by so many servants, eunuchs, and Mamluks as to be almost invisible, came the Sultan. Then it was my turn to follow along behind him.

Turning around, I could see a group of women riding Arabian horses with silk trappings and playing with a ball, which they were merrily tossing back and forth with practiced skill. My horse, meanwhile, had realized I was a novice, and was ignoring me and dragging its feet. That was fine with me, since I hoped that he would carry me back to the cluster of women at the end of the procession, where I could catch some of those appetizing scents. But the damned creature suddenly pulled itself together and picked up the pace.

I realized that someone had prodded it along, and there he was: a big fellow who seemed to be a person of consequence, riding along beside me. Taking the initiative, he said, "Good morning, Sweet-Seller!"

"Who are you?" I said, looking him in the eye.

"Abu Anbar," he said. "Don't you recognize me?"

"I haven't had the pleasure."

"Your humble servant Anbar Saharti," he said. "I'm the Sultan's lala."

"Nice to meet you," I said. "But what's a lala?"

"It's a Persian word that means 'head tutor.'"

"Ahah!" I exclaimed. "Now I know what Lala Market is named after!"

"What?"

"Nothing, nothing. So *you're* the lala!"

"What do you mean by that?"

"I've heard a lot of good things about you."

"Such as?"

"Hats off to you," I whispered in a friendly tone. "You're the senior palace servant and the power behind the throne. It's thanks to you that the attendants and eunuchs have so much power."

Anbar smiled wickedly and said between clenched teeth: "Look here, Pickle-and-Sweet Man. Rule by servants is nothing new. It's been going on for years in the Land of Egypt. Wasn't Mansur, the Sultan's grandfather, the slave of Nigm al-Din Ayyub? Everywhere you look, it's servants. The throne of Egypt never asks about your origins or your plans for the people. All it wants to know is: do you have the power to keep the throne forever? We're slaves and eunuchs, it's true; and yes, we do have some influence. But what right do *you* have to say anything about it? So enough about that. Tell me what else you've heard about me."

"All good things, of course," I said. Then I recited, "You collect hawks and falcons and ride out to the sultans' hunting ground, where the falconers release birds and then send the birds of prey to hunt them down, by way of royal diversion. That hunting ground, by the way, is now a cemetery called Ghafir." I continued, "You ride to the hunt in embroidered silk gowns and gem-studded gloves. And you have your own private corps of attendants and Mamluks at your disposal."

Anbar looked as if he were about to get angry, but he choked it back, exclaiming, "Are you a spy, or just a gossip?"

"Sorry! That was a stupid trick, is all. But I do have some advice for you. As you may have noticed, the senior emirs are beginning to find you tiresome."

He glowered aand sputtered.

"You've bought up a lot of properties, Anbar, and done a lot of trading, all by virtue of being tutor to the Sultan.

You've set up your own ball-playing field. You've told people you can take care of their requests. People come to you now for help, and the only way to get an estate or a job is through the harem."

Anbar growled and shook his head. "They're jealous, and they say things you wouldn't believe. Don't pay them any mind."

Preoccupied as we were with the conversation, we let the horses pick up the pace. They carried us out of the procession and we turned to ride alongside it. Suddenly we found ourselves next to the black woman who had caught my eye and exchanged smiles with the Sultan. Anbar slowed his horse and gestured for me to do the same. As I did so, the lady passed ahead of us again.

"Who's that?" I asked.

"It's Harmony."

"What?"

"That's her name," he said. "Harmony. She's a lutenist."

"Amazing! And the Sultan's in love with her?"

"To the point of raving lunacy."

"As a concubine or a lutenist?"

"I can't say. Both, perhaps. Either way, he lavishes favors beyond reckoning upon her. And he's surrounded himself with entertainers, especially musicians, to keep her happy."

"So he's an artist, then," I said.

"But when he sits down to listen to Harmony and her troupe," said Anbar, "he gets so wrapped up in the music that he wouldn't budge even if the whole land of Egypt caught fire."

"So *that's* his problem!"

"Did you know she's the mother of his son?"

"No way! Really?"

"You should have seen the celebration he gave in her honor."

"How nice!"

After that I kept quiet until we reached the Pyramids. We riders left our horses and strolled about in the great outdoors for a bit, then reassembled in a spacious seating area screened off with embroidered silk. Perched on blankets, the Sultan presided over the gathering. Next to him was Harmony, and around them his favorite concubines. His mother was busy preparing the food. When she invited us to eat, the dining carpet was spread on the ground, laden with fried and roasted fowl and every other tasty morsel you can think of. We dug in. The Sultan was tearing strips of meat off the birds and hand-feeding them to Harmony, who was doing the same for him. When we were sated, the carpet was swiftly removed and the cups and bottles brought out. The musicians began taking out their instruments and tuning them up. I kept my eye on the Sultan. His face was suffused with pleasure, and the pallor in his cheeks was replaced by a vivid crimson.

Then the music started. At first the whole troupe played together, and then each instrument played in turn with minimal accompaniment. After that, the vocalist cleared his throat and began to sing poems in classical Arabic to melodies that sounded like a Turkish overture. When he finished his section, another singer took over, then another, until Harmony was good and warmed up. She played a solo on the lute so thrilling that it could make a child's hair turn white. I thought the Sultan was going to evaporate altogether. I had every intention of sitting in front of Harmony until the end of time. But the Sultan must have noticed, and in a fit of jealousy whispered in my ear, "I have a mission for you. Are you ready?"

"I'm at your service, of course; but when?"

"Now!"

"Might the Sultan put off his request for a bit?"

"Are you serious?"

"You're the boss," I said. "What do you need, old man?"

His Majesty sat up, took me aside, and told me that Aqsunqur the Viceroy was up to something fishy and needed to be kept under surveillance until it was decided what to do with him. Starting immediately, I, the Pickle-and-Sweet Man, was to mingle with him and figure out what was going on.

If there's one thing that makes me ill, it's spying on people, in whatever form, even if it's in the public interest. That's why I decided only to pretend to obey the Sultan's orders. I was also casting about for excuses to stick around until Harmony had finished her performance. At that moment one of the eunuchs came up and whispered loudly to the Sultan that Emir Baydara, Aqsunqur's brother-in-law, and Emir Faraja the chamberlain, his brother Ulaja, and Altunbugha, the junior secretary had been arrested as per the Sultan's orders. The eunuch did not notice that I had overheard, while the Sultan must have thought that the music would drown out the whispering. He told the eunuch to put off arresting the others on the list until further notice. The eunuch departed and the Sultan poked me with his elbow and ordered me to get up immediately and begin my assignment, then come back to him at the Pyramids campground, where he would be for the next two days and nights. In short, he said, the plan was for me to go as his representative to ask about the Viceroy's health. Unwillingly, I got up and asked for a mount and some servants. My request was granted instantly, and just as instantly I set off to the house of Aqsunqur the Viceroy.

I arrived to find him eating lunch. He rose to greet me, but I reminded him that it was customary for eaters to continue eating instead of shaking hands with guests. He went back to his meal and I sat beside him and answered his questions about my health, the Sultan's health, and how things were in general. There was a knock on the door and he invited the caller to enter. He was a man of standing, with a written petition in his hand. Aqsunqur shook food off his hand, unrolled the paper, and asked for a pen. Poised to sign, he looked at the petitioner and said, "Ahem . . . What do you need? I mean, what's in the petition?"

"Let me read it for you, my lord," said the man, embarrassed.

"No need. Just tell me."

"God save you, my lord! My wife's given birth to triplets, but I'm a poor man and need help."

Aqsunqur made a mark on the paper and said, "Let a parcel of agricultural land in the Giza region, estimated area ten feddans, be granted to petitioner, three feddans to each child and one to the father. The relevant authority shall undertake to prepare and transfer said parcel in such-wise as it becomes his property in perpetuity. Right. Good luck, man."

Taking his paper, the man went out smiling. But there was something about the smile that made me think he had been lying.

No sooner had he left than there came another knock on the door and another visitor was admitted. He greeted us and Aqsunqur asked him what he wanted. Repressing enormous anger, he said, "My lord, I'm the owner of a big estate in Imbaba. I inherited it from my forefathers and added to to it with my own hard work and brought it up to a hundred feddans, including a farm and a mansion."

"Welcome," said Aqsunqur. "What can I do for you?"

"I want my property."

"Where is it?"

"A man came to you when I was away on a trip and asked you to give it to him as a gift and you did. When I came back I found out what happened, and I found the man in possession of the property."

"So what can you do about it?" said Aqsunqur. "Some poor fellow got your property. But if you pick another one, we'll give it to you."

"If that's how it is, then all I can do is pick an estate of three hundred feddans with a farm and mansion. True, it's bigger than mine, but I know you're a generous man. Here's my petition, with a description of the estate I've chosen."

He gave the document to Aqsunqur, who made a mark on it, saying, "We hereby command the transfer of the aforementioned estate."

The man left. Aqsunqur wiped his hands on a napkin in his lap. From beyond the door came a great shouting. Then there was a knock on the door. A man came in weeping and tearing at his clothes in grief.

"Stop blubbering like a woman," said Aqsunqur. "Sit down and tell me your problem and we'll solve it, God willing."

"I own the estate you gave to the man who was here a minute ago," said the newcomer. "I got up off my sickbed and dragged myself here to save my property. My lord, that man threatened me and said he would do this to get back at me, and now he's gone and done it!"

Aqsunqur patted him kindly on the back. "Damn the fellow! But we've given him the estate, and that's that. So pick another one you like and we'll let you have it."

"There's no estate like it in the country," sobbed the man.

"So how much would you sell it for?"

"You'd buy it, my lord?" asked the man in surprise.

"Why not?" said Aqsunqur. "How much do you want for it?"

The man mentioned a large sum. Aqsunqur took out a paper and marked it, saying, "Pay to bearer sum requested as price of estate."

The man took the paper and left. Then one of the Mamluks came in and said that a women had died in a distant quarter leaving her children orphaned and destitute. "Bring them here to live with us, enroll her children in our school, and give them all the money they need, at our expense."

By then I was flabbergasted. I told him that even if he was doing what he was doing out of kindness and charitable feeling, it still needed to be checked over. He glared at me and said, "Pickle-Man, what do you mean?"

"How do you know that these people aren't inventing these problems to make a killing? I mean, it seems stupid to believe them, sorry to say."

"What do you have against people making a living?" he asked angrily.

"It's not a living," I said. "It's plunder and pillage!"

"It's none of your business," he said, even more angrily.

I decided to button my lip. I also decided to submit a frank report mentioning my disapproval of such irresponsible conduct.

Suddenly, three tough-looking men came in dressed as paupers, with petitions in their hands. When Aqsunqur turned his back, one of them pounced on him from behind and pinned his arms. Another pulled a rope out of his shirt and began tying his wrists, and a third stood brandishing a dagger. Looking out, I saw a huge number of eunuchs armed with swords and daggers ready to pounce at the slightest show of resistance. A hog-tied Aqsunqur was dragged out, put on the back of a horse, and hauled away by the Sultan's guards.

Mounting my horse, I rode back toward the Sultan's camp at the Pyramids. Someone caught up with me and asked if I was happy with how things had turned out, and I said I was. The fellow said that the Sultan had ordered the arrest only moments before, when he learned that Aqsunqur was in cahoots with the former Sultan Ahmad and was receiving messages from him. Argun had insisted on arresting him and the Sultan had agreed.

"That's the charge they always come up with, may God spare us," I thought to myself, and rode off without turning aside for anyone or anything. I reached the Pyramids camp-site but found no trace of the Sultan. I was told that he had returned to the Citadel on urgent business.

Hurrying back, I ran up to the audience room, where I found the Sultan sitting on the couch with a man—one I thought I'd seen before—standing in front of him. Looking more closely, I recognized the man as the Polo Master, that righteous fellow who had gone head to head with the storehouse and been forced to leave the quarter altogether and move to a house he owned in Abbasiya. I realized that the Sultan was investing him as viceroy in place of the aforementioned Aqsunqur.

The Polo Master was standing there looking abashed and saying, "Master, I'm honored by your confidence in me. But I beg to ask certain favors in return for accepting the position of viceroy."

"Speak up, then," said the Sultan. "What are your conditions?"

"The storehouse, master," said the Polo Master. "It's become the worst spot in the country. It's like a festering boil!"

"What do you propose?"

"To demolish it and banish everyone in it."

"Your request is granted, emir," said the Sultan. "But it's a big job. How are you going to handle it?"

"With your permission, I'll make arrangements with the military governor and see if we can't come up with something."

"Godspeed," said the Sultan.

The Polo Master bowed, said goodbye, and kissed the Sultan's hand in gratitude. He looked enormously happy and relieved. I felt a delicious thrill of fear.

23

War Declared against the
Storehouse of Banners

I NOTICED THAT THE POLO Master, Emir, Pilgrim, and Viceroy of Egypt, was giving me looks that verged on the hostile. If not for his residual respect for the Sultan, he would doubtless have been more forthright in expressing his contempt for my meager person. Once he had kissed the Sultan's hand and sat down, he reined the hostility in a little, even though he was clearly still asking himself where he had seen me before. I was just as clearly hoping that he wouldn't remember that it was at the Storehouse of Banners. I could tell that he was annoyed at my free and easy manner with the ruler and found it hard to accept that I was being treated as a fellow human being. Though I knew the Polo Master was a righteous man, I hated him anyway. How, I wondered, could one hate a righteous man? I answered my own question: the more curdled and spiteful a person's heart is, the more he hates others. Take me, for example: I'm curdled and spiteful because I'm allergic to the respect people have for men they consider virtuous, especially men like the Polo Master who think that peace and quiet boil down to religious behavior. He wouldn't mind having foreigners come and settle in Egypt and do whatever they want so long as they didn't drink wine. Even if they drank and he knew about it, he might still not care, so long as they did it discreetly.

The Polo Master was not simply an emir, nor even one of the senior emirs. In fact, he represented a whole class of emirs: the ones who had no interest in becoming sultan and thereby spared themselves any dangerous surprises. I knew that real authority in Egypt belonged to the dirham and the dinar, which allowed them to overcome every obstacle. I had no doubt that from the day God created them, and even before the Prophet of Islam brought his message to the world, Egyptians had always believed that God was One and had no partner, which made theocracy the method par excellence for winning their loyalty. When I looked at the Polo Master, I saw, beneath his even temper and the bright intelligence that shone in his eyes, a greedy need to devour life and a darkness that combined innocence and malice.

The Sultan, who was still only twenty years old, was sitting and staring off into space. For the first time he truly did look emaciated and feeble. Straightening up and smiling pleasantly, the Polo Master said, "With the Sultan's permission, I would like to bring up some conditions I had forgotten to mention."

The Sultan, his voice as faint as a cry from a bottom of a well, told him to say whatever was on his mind. But I didn't like the way the Polo Master was taking advantage of him, and I especially didn't like the way he had begun a conversation even though it was clear that the ruler was nearly prostrate with exhaustion. Deciding to intervene, I said that the Sultan had tired himself out negotiating with all the emirs who had been offered the post of viceroy but had failed to come to terms. The Polo Master turned on me in a fury. Smiling to myself, I added that the Sultan "had been forced" to offer him the job because none of the others would have it. I went on elaborating the story, presenting it as a plea on behalf of the Sultan, until the Polo Master looked positively clammy, but he would not be dissuaded. "My conditions," he said, "include a commitment from the Sultan not to make any decisions unless I advise him to, and a prohibition on wine, and full enforcement of God's Law, and no objections to anything I do."

The Sultan nodded and said, "Your conditions are granted."

The Polo Master was prepared to move into the viceroy's palace immediately but then realized that if he did so he would lose prestige. The next morning, accordingly, he was officially invested during the communal prayer by a delegation sent down from the Citadel. My watch read Friday, the twelfth of Muharram, 744. I stood alongside him as we performed our prayers. When I finished, I looked behind me, past the row of emirs and high officials, and saw that some of the Armenians and Franks who lived in the Storehouse of Banners had joined the worshippers. I wondered why they had been allowed into the Citadel mosque. As people began hurrying out, some of the rows in front and behind began to break up, and I found myself standing next to one of the Armenians from the storehouse. "I came here to find you," he whispered in my ear. "Emir Khazaal wants to see you right away."

"What about those others?" I asked, trembling.

"They're here for other reasons," he said, "probably to find other people. The important thing is that none of us knows why the others are here—or even that they're here in the first place."

I leaned over and whispered to him to give my best to Emir Khazaal and to tell him that I was in a somewhat awkward position and, in the interests of the storehouse, needed to stay close to the Polo Master, at least for the moment. The Armenian replied that meeting Khazaal would be no trouble at all. I told him that going to the storehouse would be a risky business for me.

"But why would you go there?" he asked. "Emir Khazaal is waiting for you right here, in the last row!"

I was stunned. How had Khazaal been allowed to enter a restricted mosque? And how could they not have recognized so striking a figure?

Seeing that the Polo Master was busy with the end of the Friday prayer and the reading of additional verses from the Quran, I snuck away and ran back to the last row of worshippers. I noticed a raised hand that seemed to be praying and pointing to me at the same time. It belonged to an old man with a long, thick beard. When I went up to find out who he was, I realized from the ruddiness of his complexion and the look in his eye that it was Khazaal. My limbs atremble, I sat down next to him and whispered, "How did you get in?"

"I disguised myself as a respectable old man, obviously."

"Why?" I asked. "What are you here for?"

"To ask you to prove your loyalty to your country—by which I mean the storehouse."

Ignoring the reference to my loyalty, I asked him what he wanted.

"We need to know the Polo Master's plans over the next few days," he said. "We know he's plotting revenge against us. Some of the boys came up with a plan to assassinate him, but I ordered them to squelch it. I've decided to kill him off in a different way."

"What way is that?" I stammered.

"No business of yours."

"As a first-class citizen of the storehouse," I said, "and as someone who's going to be fighting the same enemy, I have a right to know."

"We're going to strike him with the same weapon he used against us," said Khazaal. "He's got something against wine, so we're going to let wine defend itself. We'll have everyone, high officials and citizens alike, thinking that he's a boozer like us, who drinks, gets drunk, and passes out. And that's not all. We'll have them think that he's the main source for every brand of wine that comes into the lands of the Arabs. We'll have irrefutable proof of all this. If that doesn't strike him a fatal blow, then we'll finish him off once and for all!"

To tell you the truth, I was feeling a little frightened. If Khazaal could do this to the Sultan's Viceroy for the Land of Egypt, what might he do to a man like me? So I decided to keep my objections to myself and told him that I would give him the information he wanted in the next few hours.

I stood up and turned around to see the Polo Master still kneeling, with his hands placed reverently over his face, as if God himself were speaking to him at that moment. He was clearly a believer, one whose faith was unassailable. Islamic civilization was an extraordinary thing: no matter how stony the soil, it would scratch away with bloodied fingernails until it planted the seed of faith in worldly hearts. These people, famous for their pride, their arrogance, and their coarseness, had invaded our country and taken it over, and in doing so had learned of God's message to His creation. We Egyptian Arabs had served as their firm, broad stepping-stones to Heaven. But the seed of faith, like any other seed, needs healthy soil, good care, and proper watering, which the hearts of conquerors can hardly provide. Thus it was that only a few sprouts grew up in the full light of the sun and drank in its radiance. Yet the seed of faith might find one mortal heart and, having barely begun to grow, might sprout a bough in a second heart, blossom in a third, and bear magnificent fruit in a fourth. The seed had sprouted in the heart of the Polo Master and the tree that grew there exuded the fragrance of faith. On the outside, though, his left hand was destroying what his right hand had built. He fought with unflinching determination, but against something of secondary importance. If he had struggled as fiercely against the root and source of our affliction, then things might have been different for him, for us, and for Egypt. He was, moreover, trying to defeat the forces of evil by diving down from the surface, which results either in floundering about in the spray or sinking to the bottom and drowning.

The Polo Master kept stealing quick glances at me. In his eyes I read only suspicion of me and arrogant satisfaction with himself. He may have been prostrating himself humbly before God, but he radiated hatred for me and everyone standing in the rows behind him. He was prostrating himself not out of humble worshipfulness but out of a desire to lift himself up.

He and God were friends: how could he stoop so low as to befriend mere mortals, like the ones in the back rows?

As I stood there like the transparent barrier between the first and second-class seats on the crowded, sticky, vile, nasty Cairo buses of the fifteenth century after the hijra, I was truly at a loss to know which side to join. I asked myself straight out: should I put myself at the service of the storehouse and spring the trap on the Polo Master? Or should I put myself at the service of the Polo Master and spring the trap on the storehouse, thereby preventing unrest and bloodshed? To be honest, I could have played either role but not both at the same time, even though many of my fellow Sons of Shalaby would have been perfectly capable of the latter. Many of us live as nobly as prophets, but just as many have all the integrity of double agents. In my capacity as a seller of pickles and sweets and a writer, I think of my true self as being manifest in my attachment to causes I can be proud of. A shrill voice in my head screamed at me in no uncertain terms: "Side with the storehouse, you moron! It may be unprincipled, but that's the only thing that will protect you against an excess of principle. It's thanks to the storehouse that you rose through the ranks and became a Sultan's Mamluk who sits with high officials and prays shoulder to shoulder with the Viceroy. Even if it offers asylum to thieves and bandits, it also offered asylum to many downtrodden, powerless wretches who would otherwise have been devoured by the wolves. It's a good thing that we have such a powerful counterweight to Mamluk tyranny."

At the same time, another voice, this one even more impassioned, rose from deep inside me, shouting: "Shame on you, man! The storehousers are lowlifes with no sense of right and wrong, and the storehouse is an infected, suppurating, maggot-infested wound. You can help purge it from society! Help build a mosque! Help build a house of prayer!" The last bit came from my memories of those fellows who go around with boxes collecting donations in the fifteenth century after the hijra.

Driving those images from my mind, I responded to the second voice, which was saying that the storehousers were not only rabble, but rabble who had declared open season on the land of Egypt, my ancestral homeland, and laid it waste; no matter what they did for me, they would always be my real enemies. Sputtering, I replied that both sides were my enemy: "Both of them are happy to beat me with shoes and would gladly shoot me, too, if they could. Both of them think they have the right to humiliate me, enslave me, mortgage my future, and sell me in return for a night of pleasure. As long as both of them are in power, and can hurt me if I disagree with them, then I'll be a good Egyptian and will steer clear of them both. I'll tell them whatever they want to hear, but I won't take sides. Instead, I'll just wait for them to knock each other out. I hate and despise both of them, and have no interest in helping either one."

Then a third voice, in the warm, plangent tones of an old-time singer, rang out above the others: "Listen, Pickle-and-Sweet Man, it's wrong for you to throw yourself in with the crowd. If you do, then you're thumbing your nose to Islamic civilization itself. Doesn't it call on you to stand up for justice and enlightenment?"

"So who do I stand up for?" I asked, carried away by the music. "Neither side is worth it!"

"Remember what Tariq ibn Ziyad said when he found himself in the same position," said the warm, stirring voice. "He had the enemy before him and the sea behind. If he wanted to save himself and his regiment, he had to choose one or the other. He decided to follow the principle that he believed in. You have to do the same thing. Even if there's no principle involved, let there be one in yourself. Of your two enemies, one represents Egypt and acts in its name. Stand with Egypt, even if that means standing next to a crude, hard-hearted interloper and usurper. You aren't defending him, but your country. Stick to that principle and spare yourself an eternity of torment. One evil principle is better than two.

As you love God, Pickle-and-Sweet Man, don't help bring *two* forces of evil to power in this country."

Stirred by this peroration, I found myself rising up to join the Polo Master. I felt an unaccountable exultation. As we left the mosque together, we passed Khazaal, and I shot him a look of vituperative contempt.

I had lunch, and later dinner, at the Polo Master's table, among his closest friends, including the prayer leader of the mosque he had built for himself in Husayniya. All night, the only thing we talked about was the sinful storehousers who had flooded the streets with wine and made a public spectacle of themselves. I felt myself getting steamed up. How odd that I should be so repelled by the mere mention of things I had seen with my own eyes without turning a hair! Like a person neck-deep in mud, I supposed, I had stopped feeling dirty. If outhouse cleaners were to stop and think about what they were doing, they would feel nauseous forever. In the same way, I had lost all sense of how strange the storehouse's way of life really was. No sooner had I stepped away from it, though, and resumed my place among the clean-living people of Egypt, than I began to feel repulsed by it. Now, sitting in the Polo Master's guest hall, I felt an aversion that ran bone-deep.

I also felt compelled to warn him of the plot being hatched against him. Now that I had taken sides, I was obliged, as a matter of principle, to be as honest with him as possible, and warn him of the danger so that he could take steps to protect himself. When he excused himself for a moment, I started to follow him out in the hope of catching him alone and sharing my apprehensions with him. But no sooner did I say, "Could I have a word with you?" and take a few steps into the foyer than I found myself surrounded by a knot of soldiers dressed in civilian clothes, ready to pounce on me and search me. It was then that I realized that the Polo Master didn't trust me, and wouldn't ever trust me, no matter how close he allowed me to get. Miserable tears sprang to my eyes, but I concealed the pang with a wan smile and told him I would catch up with him when he came back.

I resumed my seat feeling wretched. Wave after wave of resentment came crashing over my head. My head would go under, and I would decide not to say anything and let him fall into the trap. Then I would go tumbling into a trough and I would decide to get up immediately and rejoin the storehouse. Then a third wave would hurl me back up and I would realize that I was psychologically paralyzed and no longer had the power to take any position at all. From that moment on I was no longer present in the assembly. The waves of resentment continued to pound at me until, in the last watch of the night, the Polo Master leaned over to me and, with some gentleness, apologized for the way his "boys" had treated me. He had, after all, chosen them for their toughness. The he asked, "What did you want to say to me?"

His smile was oily and I sensed that his apology, with all its feigned courtesy, was insincere; what he wanted was to trick me into revealing what I knew. I decided to get back at him by not telling him the truth. But I also decided not to help bring him down. "It's nothing," I said, and in response to his insistent questions, eventually told him that I wanted him to do me a favor connected with my career as a Sultan's Mamluk. He nodded derisively and went back to the others; I lapsed into the depression that always lies in wait for me. When everyone got up to leave, I said I was going back to the Citadel to sleep. He knew better than to insist that I stay, lest I imagine that he was keeping me prisoner. Cleverly, though, he called his troopers over, ordered them to apologize to me and to make up for their rudeness by escorting me to the Citadel. I was furious enough to pop: now he expected me to thank him for this new humiliation! Repressing my anger, I did not thank him, but only said goodbye. As soon as my feet hit the street, I took off running, leaving the guards behind as if they had nothing to do with me. When I reached the Citadel, I gave them a quick wave and then plunged into bed, ready for some bad dreams.

On Saturday morning, I was roused by an urgent summons from the Viceroy. I washed up and went out to find the same troop of soldiers waiting for me. I realized that they had stayed where they were all night. They welcomed me with a smirk and said they had been assigned to escort me to the Viceroy's. I thanked them and asked them teasingly whether they had gone back to Husayniya or stayed awake guarding me all night. With astounding effrontery, they insisted that they had never seen me before. Their tone and their bearing conveyed a sense of arrogance, malice, and self-importance that made it impossible to like them.

When I reached the viceregal hall, I found the Polo Master sitting in the seat once occupied by his predecessor, Tashtamur, the Green Garbanzo. I greeted him and placed myself at his disposal. He told me to stay close, as he would need my advice on a matter of imminent importance. I thanked him for his great faith in me and went back to feeling miserable.

There was a knock on the door, which opened to admit and the military governor of Cairo. He paid his respects and waited until the Polo Master asked him to sit down.

"Your job depends on routing the storehouse," said the Polo Master in a dangerously resolute tone. "What are you planning to do about that?"

Sitting up straight in his seat, the military governor assumed a fierce expression that frightened me. "What storehouse, my lord?" he said. "I thought my job depended on driving out our Frankish foes."

"Are you prepared to go to war with the storehouse?"

"War?"

"Absolutely," said the Polo Master. "The place is occupied by thousands of armed criminals who have no scruples about killing and shedding blood."

"I know who they are," said the governor.

"So why have you ignored them so long and given them a chance to build up their strength?"

"Listen, my lord Viceroy," said the governor. "Nothing in Egypt maintains itself by itself. Anything that exists goes on existing because people in high places profit from it. Do you need me to spell it out for you? Inside the storehouse is a man who's made himself into a ruling emir and built a state of his own. Until very recently, he was sending monthly salaries to a huge number of officials. Our government has been nothing but a shadow government that exists to protect the real one, which is the Storehouse of Banners."

I glared at him with as much contempt as I could manage. I knew quite well that he himself had received—and was still receiving—monthly payments drawn on the spoils piled up in the storehouse.

"All I care about now," said the Polo Master, "is whether you're ready to fight."

"Certainly," replied the governor. "I've known for a while that you were opposed to the storehouse. As soon as I found out that you'd been appointed viceroy, I started preparing for this fight. So, yes, I'm ready."

"Good luck, then," said the Polo Master. "All the wine there has to be destroyed and everyone living there has to be tossed out."

"Don't worry. You'll be hearing some good news shortly."

"Go, then, and trust in God!"

The governor looked over at me as he rose to go. "Let me take Mr. Pickle-and Sweet-Seller. I might need him to answer some questions for me."

With a gesture, the Polo Master ordered me to go and do as I was told. I got up and turned to the governor, who bowed, said goodbye, and went out with me on his heels. As we passed through the viceregal hall, I saw that he was morose and uncomfortable, and I wondered why. Then we got to Citadel Square, which was was crowded with emirs and tattooed cannibals from the storehouse. Grinning, one of the emirs rushed over to us and threw his arms around the governor, greeting him and asking him how he'd been, and leaving no doubt that the two had been friends for ages. Watching the scene, I was delighted to see the miserable governor doing his best to pretend that he had no idea who the other man was. The emir, as spontaneously as could be, was explaining that he had gone looking for him once at the office, several times at home, and several more times at places he named using only gestures. All the while, the governor, trying to keep his face stretched tight as a drum and the smile off his lips, was saying in a cracked voice, "I'm sorry, do I know you?"

At that, the storehouse emir shot him a look that almost felled him. But the governor, bold as brass, replied that he didn't recognize him, and walked away. Recalling my presence, and seeing that I had witnessed the whole shameful scene, shouted at me apropos of nothing, "What the hell is going on?"

"Ask yourself," I taunted him.

"Watch your mouth!" he shouted.

"Listen," I shouted back. "I'm the Sultan's press secretary. You know what that means? Well, I have nothing to say to you, either. Goodbye!"

I stomped off in a huff, leaving him glad to see me go.

I turned off toward Palace Square and climbed up to the roof of one of the palaces—no longer luminous, alas—and stood there until morning, watching the storehousers pour barrel after barrel of wine into the streets. I also saw people of every description emerge from out of nowhere, plunge into the rivers of wine, cross the road, and make way for dozens of soldiers armed with swords, daggers, and axes. On the other side, an island of storehouse rabble launched grayish projectiles that thrashed and wriggled and dropped on the soldiers' faces, making them jerk in alarm and drop their weapons. It wasn't long before I realized that the projectiles were live rats, collected—God knows how—in vast quantities, then kept hidden somehow in laps and pockets and hidden baskets.

24

A Morning Draped in the Robe of God

IT WAS A DAY TO be remembered. People were fighting one another with a savagery that was impossible to explain. If you had been standing with me and looking down from the roof, you would not have been able to tell which side was which. Except for the soldiers in their uniforms, everyone was dressed in more or less the same way. The storehousers had adopted Egyptian clothes, while many Egyptians—first the wealthy, then the semi-wealthy, and then the hoping-to-be-wealthy—had taken to imitating the clothes that the storehousers had brought with them when they entered the country. The result was an endlessly captivating carnival of Egypto-Indo-Perso-Arabo-Byzantine-Andalusian garb. As if possessed by demons, the people inside the clothes were going at it with clubs, swords, knives, chunks of stone, and rats and cats that had been set on fire. This scene, too, was captivating, in the sense that the fighters might have been the sort of rampant bacteria that begin by eating each other and end up consuming themselves. The most touching thing was to see the ruffians and the harafish joining in with gusto, as if they were parties to the conflict with every reason in the world to be there.

Turning around, I saw that the roof had filled up with spectators. I didn't know if they were residents or neighbors or passersby but I didn't want to ask. A ruffian dressed in the style of a prosperous merchant asked why they were attacking people in their houses. "What do they want from them?" he asked suspiciously.

"Ask both sides why they're attacking us," responded a harfush wearing little more than a wise expression. "What do they want from *us*?"

Next to us, a woman shrieked, slapped at her face, and trilled in distress. "Oh, this is terrible! Terrible!" Looking closely, we could see jets of blood spattering against all the gratings and mashrabiya windows along the street. An imperious voice rang out: "The Sultan's representative says, 'Tear down the Storehouse! Tear it down!' Who's with me? Muslims! Defenders of the Law! Pull down that den of wine-drinkers and crush the sinners! The Polo Master is offering a reward to anyone who kills one of them or catches him with wine!"

I recognized the voice of the crier, who sounded a lot like the Sultan himself. Many other voices picked up the cry, repeating it with variations. I recognized the voices of the common people, of scholars, merchants, officers, and men who wore the Sultan's robes of honor. I saw men emerging from the storehouse carrying limp and battered corpses, as well as casks of wine. They poured the wine out, flooding the streets in all directions. The wine was mixed with dirt, blood, and animal droppings, but the nasty mixture had its takers: men of all ages were coming out with pots and pans and covertly scooping up what they could.

Then a great crowd armed with pickaxes, shovels, and cutting tools made their way directly to the storehouse and began to demolish it. I knew that there were other incidents, invisible to me, taking place in the streets behind the building. I ran downstairs. The dress that marked me as a Mamluk of the Sultan provoked glances of deference or feigned respect. As in my Cairo of the fifteenth century AH, when a little rain or a burst sewer pipe can turn the streets into a sea for human microorganisms to swim through, the torrent of wine made it impossible for people to walk. Even so, the harafish in all their motley dress were smiling as they rolled up their pants and performed acrobatically impossible tricks to get around the puddles and the mud, all the while making fun of themselves, mocking their lot, and jeering at everything in existence. The earth was feeling no pain, said one. It didn't even mind being stepped on, said another. "The fun should last until dawn," said a third, "and that's a long way off. It might not come at all!"

"It's already here," said a fourth. "It started when we began knocking down the storehouse and pouring out the wine."

"True," said a fifth, "but we don't recognize dawn as observed by the government."

"We don't recognize it because it's cracked," said another.

"So the dawn's cracked too?" called another from the end of the street. "I thought we were the only ones who were cracked."

"Wise-cracked, maybe," said another from atop a little hill he had managed to reach.

"Or just a wiseass," retorted another through an open window.

Thus did the Egyptians chew up the tragedy and spit it out as if nothing had happened.

I can catch the smell of a place and recognize it even if it looks different than it used to. I am an Egyptian, after all; and aren't Egyptians, of all the people in the world, the most geographical of creatures? I'm an Egyptian citizen of the highest degree and there's no one who feels his citizenship more than I do. I'm a citizen who, like a dog, is trapped where he lives because dogs, as a species, are incapable of breaking down the imaginary separation between time and space and thus remain prisoners of whatever time they happen to be in. The Sons of Shalaby, including me, have an extraordinary talent for canonizing and commemorating time. The memorials we raise are made of the very stuff of time, composed of many elements, of which the first is man. I caught the scent of Umm al-Ghulam—the mosque that contains the tomb of Umm al-Ghulam, right behind the Mosque of Husayn. It's a time as a much as a place, and the smell of it in my nostrils was bodied forth in all the times we walked past it or around it in the Cairo of the fifteenth century AH. At the moment I began to clamber over the debris of the storehouse, I recognized that Umm al-Ghulam would one day be built over that spot. Oddly, too, I could smell other ages I had never visited or seen or heard of before. In Egypt, the sages of yore used to say that a place with history was a place that, when you left, you felt a need to come back again and again.

At Kiman al-Darrasa, which I recognized once I got closer to it, I saw a group of people milling around, surrounded by a troop of heavily armed soldiers. They had evidently escaped the storehouse by the skin of their teeth just before it was leveled. As I raced toward them, I could hear them whistling and roaring, which alarmed me because they were pointing at me. In a babble of voices, they were saying—or so I understood—that I was one of them and that I needed to join them if I wanted to retain my right to live in Cairo. The soldiers looked me over carefully and hesitated a bit before signaling that I was free to join my kinsfolk. I thanked them with a smile and told them sheepishly that I was a Mamluk and the property of Sultan Abul Fida Ismail as well as press secretary to the Polo Master. They asked me what a press secretary was.

"It's when a returned pilgrim or a religious authority or a capitalist chooses a person with experience in journalism to accompany him everywhere as a way of appearing more impressive."

They appeared not to have understood a word of what I said, but they did seem more respectful of me. I then looked over the captives. A vague, nameless fear took hold of me and my knees went weak. Most of the survivors were cannibals and emirs, and I expected to see Khazaal among them, but there was no sign of him. I looked more closely. One of the figures facing me had assumed a posture of authority vis-à-vis the other captives. His face, like all their faces, was covered with a layer of dirt that obscured his features, though I should still have been able to recognize him. I excused myself, taking leave of the soldiers with the grace and politesse expected of a respectable sultan's Mamluk. When I stepped closer to the captives, the figure who looked like a leader came forward and greeted me with the harsh accusation that I was the one responsible for what had happened to them.

"Did Khazaal make it?" I asked.

"He did."

"Where is he, then? Why isn't he here now to represent you?"

"He's representing us before a higher authority," the man said.

"What do you mean?"

"He's speaking with the Polo Master himself!"

"Good for him!" I said. "How did he manage that?"

"That's how are things now," he replied. Then, to allay any doubts I might have about Khazaal's reach, he added, "If the Polo Master won't help, then the Sultan will!"

"How on earth?"

"Our Emir can meet the Sultan—or two Sultans—any-time he wants!"

The fellow was raising his voice a tad more than necessary, and I realized—with my hard-wired storehouse instincts—that he was not so much talking to me as to the soldiers, in order to intimidate them into treating the captives more gen-tly. It was equally clear to me that Khazaal was still using them as a bargaining chip and leading them to believe he was more powerful than he really was. Then, without preamble, the man asked me what I had done to help, accusing me of becoming a Mamluk and forgetting my old friends, and threatening that if I didn't extend a helping hand they would toss me from Heaven and back into Hell. Smiling to hide my anger and my fear, I played the *grand seigneur*: I nodded sagely, thanked him for his kindness, and promised to do what I could.

When I turned back to the soldiers, I saw the Viceroy's vanguard: a pony carrying a conceited-looking figure, followed by two horses, then three, then four, then a number of toughs walking on foot. After all of that came the Polo Master's cavalcade. I felt it was proper for me to hurry over and receive him so I did. He gave me his fingertips to shake and asked, "What's the pickle-and-sweet man doing here?"

"Just checking into a few things that I may be able to advise on later," I replied.

"Well done," he said. Then he stopped and gazed at the captives with the vindictive air of a man avenged. The other members of his retinue had caught up and were now all around him, exchanging opinions on what to do with the captives.

"We've given them what they deserve," said the Polo Master. "We've poured out their wine and destroyed their power, and as far as I can see the only ones left are these few here who couldn't make trouble if they tried. No, no, I've done what I've always dreamed of doing to these sinners and infidels. But I stand by my promise to reward you for bringing to me anyone you catch drinking or carrying wine."

The storehouser who had taken Khazaal's position of authority assumed the tragic pose of the humiliated, and refused to meet my eyes for fear of the implied question: "Where's Khazaal, then?"

At that moment, a voice rose from the retinue. "My lord, what do we do with them?" it pleaded. "They're our responsibility now. Aren't they foreigners? Didn't the Prophet, peace and blessings be upon him, command us to care for strangers? Here we honor foreigners for the sake of the Prophet. So what does my lord the Viceroy command us to do with these poor wretches who no longer have a roof over their heads?"

The Polo Master was forced to grope for a reply. During the pause, the storehouser who had assumed a position of authority shot a glance at me as if to say: "See? That's Khazaal speaking! He was too important to appear in person in a place like this, but now here he is, as apparent as you please."

"If the Polo Master takes that tone," I was thinking to myself, "that is, if he lets the prisoners stay in Cairo and treats them as fellow citizens even though they're the last few enemies he has left, then Khazaal really will have made a difference."

I watched the Polo Master as he took in Khazaal's plea for leniency, complete with aphorisms on the sweetness of mercy, the reward that awaits those who have the right and the power to punish but choose instead to forgive, and the high standing in Heaven of those who show forbearance, not to mention the fact that the offenders had learned their lesson and wouldn't forget it. The Polo Master thought for a while and then spoke. "Settle them in a valley with no comfort or friendship. Find them a narrow alley somewhere near the Citadel, so we can keep an eye on them and crack down on them if they're tempted to try anything like this again."

One of his officials, perhaps the one responsible for endowed properties, cried out in protest. "We don't have the space to give away land to this rabble!"

With enviable finesse, the Polo Master said, "You're right. In fact, we shouldn't be giving this sort of people shelter in our neighborhoods at all. But my master Sultan Nasir gave them permission to abide in the land of Egypt, and my conscience does not permit me to flout his wishes after his death. So I'll consider him sufficient authority for what I'm about to do. Now then: pick out the ones with the best character and the best education and take them, and toss the rest into Kiman al-Darrasa!" The official called out an order to the man behind him. "Take the riffraff to that ruin of a house near Sayyida Zaynab! And look for a house at the Citadel for the highborn ones." Then the Polo Master turned to the people and cried, "Anyone who wants to claim land where the storehouse was is free to do so. Anyone who wants to build a house or a mill may do so without asking me again."

A member of his retinue gestured for the chamberlain to bring the captives and follow him. Drawing himself up, the chamberlain shouted some orders that I couldn't make out. Within minutes, though, the troops had arranged themselves in formation and begun pushing the captives before them like a herd of sheep. But then the Polo Master called out to him to wait. The chamberlain stopped in his tracks and asked what was wrong.

"Take that one with you, too," said the Polo Master, pointing at me with loathing.

I looked at him angrily. "How can you do that, Master?" I shouted. "How?"

"Aren't you a storehouser?"

I was so disgusted with his treachery that I nearly spat in his face. "But Master, you know I'm the Sultan's press secretary. What I am, in essence, is a Mamluk with the rank of consultant. Do you mean to insult me and insult the Sultan as well?"

With matchless effrontery, he replied, "All I know is that you're a storehouser. Your being a Mamluk of the Sultan isn't my problem. Anyway, I refuse to recognize you as a Mamluk just because you entered the Sultan's service somewhere along the way."

"All that hard work wasted!" I cried out, slapping my palms together in frustration. "Down the drain!"

"What do you mean by that?" asked the Polo Master.

"I performed some extraordinary services for the Sultan. I created good publicity for him even though he didn't deserve it. I wrote epistles glorifying him and giving him credit for historic achievements in the arts and sciences, none of which were real. And now I'm supposed to go home empty-handed?"

"Did the Sultan ask you do any of that," asked the Polo Master, "or did you volunteer to do it all by yourself?"

"I volunteered, of course, but . . . but . . . the thought of compensation was in the back of my mind, certainly; or at least the thought of gaining some standing. I wanted to be a Sultan's Mamluk—and mind you, I've got the qualifications. I just recently got the degrees and everything."

"I don't think you've done too badly for yourself," said the Polo Master. "You had your moment of glory, and you raked in some unearned cash from parties eager to avoid the Sultan's wrath by winning over his subordinates. And whatever qualifications you claim to have, you acquired on the strength of your relationship with the Sultan. It's time to quit while you're ahead. Go back to the storehouse: you two deserve each other."

"Why don't we ask the Sultan to be the judge of that?" I called out in panic. "This is an important decision and you shouldn't make it all by yourself!"

"I'm the only one giving orders here," he thundered. "I've been promised that, when it comes to the storehouse, whatever I say goes. And that includes you."

"Let's go to the Sultan anyway," he said. "I insist!"

"You insist?" he laughed. "Chamberlain! Drag him out of here!"

I started to say something else but the chamberlain yanked me over and tossed me roughly into the herd of captives. The frightening feeling that I had just had a stake driven through me leapt from my guts up into my brain.

Overwhelmed by despair, I marched off with the other captives. But then I remembered that I had something that they didn't: I had Time, the time that for them was still the future, where I had lived and walked. My fear gave way before the comforting thought that nothing had actually happened. It was as if the Polo Master's revolution had never been, because it was based on the superficial notion that one man could rise up and purge the country of wine-sellers and pork-eaters, and the bloodshed would suffice to teach the libertines never to make wine again. Thus, an inner voice said, everything would soon be back the way it had always been.

As we crossed the Citadel and looked down at the shrine of Sayyida Nafisa, the crowd of people walking around me began to fade. All around me a great clamor arose. I found myself bumping into people and apologizing as they shouted at me. I bumped into more people, and they started to shove. Gasping, my head spinning, I stood still for a moment.

When I opened my eyes, I was standing at the Citadel Square bus stop, with the number 72 bus from Liberation Square to Basatin pulling up in front of me. I hurried over and climbed aboard. The hands of my watch had stopped at Friday, the twelfth of Muharram 744. Knowing that I could get off at Basitin and walk, as I usually did, to the outskirts of Maadi, where I live, I pushed my way through the crowd of riders. Then someone asked me for the time. I looked at my watch and saw that the day and date had moved: it was now Friday, the fifth of Safar, AH 1500: 1 January, AD 2077.

Notes

Abdel Fattah Barudi: Egyptian poetic and dramatic critic, d. 1996.

Abdel Rahman al-Sharqawi: Journalist, poet, novelist, and biographer (1920–87).

Adid: The last Fatimid caliph (r. 1160–71).

Baha al-Din Qaraqush: Saladin's viceroy in Egypt (d. 1200 or 1201), famous for his appearance in the proverbial expression "rule by Qaraqush," meaning arbitrary government.

Dar al-Ratli: Apparently the area around the watercourse called al-Ratli, named after a maker of weights (artal). Maqrizi describes it as a place of popular revelry.

Grooms: Originally the Mamluks of the *ujaq* (modern Turkish *ocak*), the "fireplace" or "hearth," sometimes explained as those responsible for the Sultan's horses, but here described as a kind of police force.

al-Hakim: Sixth Fatimid caliph, r. 996–1021, famous for his cruelty and bizarre behavior.

Ibn Abdel Zahir: State secretary and historian (d. 1292) active under the Mamluk sultans of Egypt.

Ibn Taghribirdi (d. 1470) is the author of a history entitled *al-Nujum al-zahira fi muluk Misr wa-l-Qahira* (The Flowing Stars, on the Kings of Egypt and Cairo). His long Turkic name sounds funny in Arabic, and Ibn Shalaby draws attention to it by inventing nicknames (Ibn Taghri and Ibn Birdi) for him.

Ibn Tuwayr: Fatimid official (d. 1220) and author of *Nuzhat al-muqlatayn fi akhbar al-dawlatayn* (A Journey for the Eyes: A History of the Two Dynasties).

Ibrahim Mansur: Literary mentor, political activist, and fixture of Cairo's café scene (1935–2004).

Ismail: In Muslim tradition, Ismail (Ishmael) is the son whom Abraham intended to offer as a sacrifice to God.

Maqrizi: Maqrizi (1364–1442) was a Cairene preacher, mosque administrator, Hadith-scholar, and historian. His *Topography* (*Khitat*) describes the monuments of Fustat, Cairo, and Alexandria, and provides a wealth of detail on Egyptian history.

Muhammad Barakat: A journalist and colleague of the author at the Egyptian Radio and Television Journal.

Muhammad Qandil (1929–2004): Egyptian singer and film actor popular in the 1950s and 1960s.

al-Mustansir: Eighth Fatimid caliph, r. 1036–94. Under his rule (1067–72) Egypt suffered from political chaos and a prolonged famine.

Naguib Mahfouz: Novelist (1911–2006) and the 1988 Nobel laureate for literature.

"Runaway Mamluk": The Runaway Mamluk and his horse leapt off the Citadel to escape the massacre of the Mamluks carried out by Muhammad Ali in 1811.

Shaykh Shaarawi: Egyptian religious scholar and television personality, d. 1998.

Tariq ibn Ziyad: Commander of the Muslim armies that invaded the Iberian peninsula in 711.

Umar ibn al-Khattab: A Companion of the Prophet and, according to Sunni Muslims, the second caliph (AD 634–644). He is traditionally disparaged by Shi'a Muslims, who regard him as having usurped an office that belonged properly to the Prophet's cousin and son-in-law, Ali ibn Abi Talib.

Wali al-Dawla Abul Farag Ibn Khatir, brother-in-law of Nashw: Nashw was Sharaf al-Din ibn Fadl Allah, an official known for his extortionate policies.

Date Concordances

Dates in the original are given according to the Islamic calendar, which begins with the Prophet Muhammad's emigration *(hijra)* from Mecca to Medina in AH *(anno hegirae)* 1 / AD 622. Ibn Shalaby's native time is the end of the fourteenth and beginning of the fifteenth centuries AH: that is, the late 1970s and early 1980s AD.

AH	AD
1 Ramadan, 358	19 July, 969
7 Ramadan, 362	June 11, 973
Ramadan, 380	Late November / early December, 990
Friday, 4 Ramadan, 381	14 November, 991 (actually a Saturday)
11 Safar, 401	24 September, 1010
Safar, 401	mid-September to mid-October, 1010
Friday, 6 Ramadan, 403	21 March, 1013 (actually a Saturday)
Monday, 5 Muharram, 440	20 June, 1048
501	1107 or 1108
512	1118 or 1119
524	1130
Ashura (10 Muharram), 567	13 September, 1171
13 Rabi' II, 567	14 December, 1171

AH	AD
Tuesday, 23 Shawwal, 698	24 July, 1299
Thursday, 13 Dhu al-Hijja, 702	29 July, 1303 (actually a Monday)
727	1326 or 1327
741	1340 or 1341
Saturday, 16 Rabi‘ I, 742	30 August, 1341 (actually a Thursday)
Monday, 18 Rabi‘ II, 742	1 October, 1341
Saturday, 26 Jumada II, 742	7 December, 1341 (actually a Friday)
Tuesday, 29 Ragab, 742	8 January, 1342
Wednesday, 7 Sha‘ban, 742	16 January, 1342
Thursday, 7 Ramadan, 742	14 February, 1342
Thursday, 13 Shawwal, 742	22 March, 1342 (actually a Friday)
5 Muharram, 743	10 July, 1342
Thursday, 22 Muharram, 743	27 June, 1342
Saturday, 1 Safar, 743	6 July, 1342
Wednesday, 4 Ragab, 743	3 December, 1342 (actually a Tuesday)
Friday, 12 Muharram, 744	6 June, 1343
Ramadan, 761	mid-July to mid-August, 1360
Wednesday, 29 Dhu al-Qi‘da, 761	October 11, 1360
792	1390
1 Muharram, 1400	21 November, 1979